Hooflandia

by Heide Goody and Iain Grant

Pigeon Park Press

Published by Pigeon Park Press
www.pigeonparkpress.com

PART ONE –
DREAMS OF HOOFLANDIA

CHAPTER ONE

Four-hundred-and-something Chester Road.

Boldmere.

Sutton Coldfield.

The house was built something like a hundred years ago, back in a time when people were shorter but ceilings were inexplicably higher. Three storeys tall and deeper than it was wide, it had probably been home to the family of a factory manager, a minor civil servant or a small-time professional. They might even have had a maid or a cook. It had been that kind of house.

In leaner, post-war times, it was divided into self-contained flats. As the barriers between social classes blurred, the divided house became home to a variety of factory folk, council servants, professionals of varying dubiousness and even a maid or cook or two – all living cheek by jowl.

Then, in the early twenty-first century, for some very convoluted reasons, it became the home of a man, a woman, the devil and an angel and there was a period of stability (in the same way that the Cold War was a period of stability). This did not last long.

Most recently, after a series of calamitous incidents involving (but not limited to) a psychotic capuchin monkey, a fire-breathing ferret and an apocalypse-obsessed landlord, the house had been virtually destroyed and rebuilt and was now the home and property of only three occupants. The man and the devil lived in the first-floor flats. The woman lived on the second floor with her dog, Twinkle. The angel was in prison, but the ground-floor flat he had once occupied was neither empty nor unused...

Jeremy Clovenhoof and Nerys Thomas stood outside the door to flat 1b, waiting for Ben Kitchen.

For the third time in as many minutes, Clovenhoof tested the padlocks on the door.

Nerys tutted.

"It never hurts to check," he said.

Clovenhoof had a key to one padlock. Nerys and Ben had keys to the other two. They had all chosen high-security locks. The jargon came back to him: *ball-locking, hardened shackles, reversible dimples*. He shuddered with anticipation and shouted up the stairs.

"Come on, Kitchen! We're waiting!"

"Someone's eager," said Nerys.

"You have to admit it's spiced things up no end," he said. "The three of us living in this place... Things get stale." He waggled his eyebrows lewdly.

"Patience," said Nerys, taking her padlock key out of her cleavage.

"What's keeping him?" tsked Clovenhoof. "Doesn't he know I'm a busy man."

"No, you're not. You have no job. You're not even a man. Let's just be thankful he doesn't know you're... you know." She mimed a pair of horns.

"Well, he should know this is the highlight of my week. I went out to buy essentials and everything."

Clovenhoof took the giant tub of petroleum jelly out of his bag.

"Whoa, what's that for?" said Ben, coming down the stairs.

"It's the only way to do some of those trickier manoeuvres," said Clovenhoof.

Nerys glanced toward Ben. "You were the one complaining about chafing last time."

Clovenhoof fished a key out of his underpants. Ben removed a folding leather key wallet from his pocket.

"Ready?" said Nerys. She and Clovenhoof unlocked their padlocks.

Ben hesitated.

"What are you waiting for?" said Nerys.

Ben licked his lips. "Do you ever wonder what people think?"

"All the time," said Clovenhoof. "Usually they're thinking 'who is that smoking hot devil of a chap staring at me?'"

"I mean about this," said Ben, waving his hands at the door. "It's a bit weird, isn't it?"

"We're all consenting adults," said Nerys.

"Sure," said Ben, sounding anything but. And he put his key in the lock.

CHAPTER TWO

The Old Place.
Hell.
Downstairs.
Hell had come into being at the very moment its first resident attempted a rebellion against the Almighty. It had been a bold military move on Satan's part, a full one-third of the angels had been on his side, but he had failed to take into account that the Almighty had that whole omnipotence thing going on. It was a short war.

There was no time in Hell but, nonetheless, for a long time it was used as a dumping ground for those who did not match up to Heaven's standards. The human equivalent of bruised fruit, bent cucumbers and rotten apples were barred entry to the posh supermarket of the afterlife and sent to Hell to be punished for being variously bruised, bent and rotten. Its first resident, Satan, found his role transmogrifying from prisoner to governor. He didn't enjoy either role, so the change went almost unnoticed.

Most recently, after a series of calamitous incidents involving (but not limited to) an attempted coup in Heaven, a management reshuffle, a heat malfunction and a Hell-wide flood, the abode of the damned was now ruled by a disgraced saint and undergoing a major architectural refurbishment programme.

Rutspud stared down at the latest addition to Hell's landscape, one he had more than a hand in creating. Rutspud was proud of his contributions to the Infernal Innovations Programme. For a minor demon, working in Hell's R&D department was a dream job, one he'd secured based on a combination of luck, intelligence and being a seriously sneaky bastard. His boss, Belphegor, Lord of Sloth and the original inventor demon, had a solid grounding in engineering principles and a Byzantine supply chain network that could secure any source material that they needed. With Belphegor's political clout and Rutspud's gift for ideas (many of them shamelessly plundered from the internet), they had produced initiative after initiative that enriched Hell's torments immensely.

Before them lay their latest creation.

"The Pit of Big Cats with Assault Rifles," said Rutspud. "It needs a snappier name."

"Names do not matter," countered Belphegor. "It's the results that matter."

It was an old argument between them and one they both enjoyed. The technical challenges of creating this had been interesting, but not insurmountable. They had discovered that although big cats lacked opposable thumbs, their razor-sharp hunter's minds and generally high levels of misanthropy made them enthusiastic employees. As soon as R&D had developed aiming and firing mechanisms that could be operated with a paw, the Hellish cats turned out to be crack shots.

"I still don't see why hunting is suddenly so sinful," said Belphegor. "The Other Lot have got a bloody patron saint of hunting, Hubertus. Ever met him?"

Rutspud shook his head.

"A man in love with himself if ever there was one. The Celestial crowd shoved him sideways into some filing department just to get him out of the way."

"It's not hunting itself we're punishing. It's this 'canned hunt' nonsense," said Rutspud.

Belphegor pressed a button on the arm of his steam-driven wheelchair and a pair of opera glasses on a stick popped up. Belphegor peered through them.

"Let's give it a final test, eh? Line up the target."

Rutspud whistled and waved down into the pit where a demon cowered at the edge of an otherwise empty floor. "Boffjock! Get in position!"

"There's been a lot of interest in canned hunts on social media," Rutspud said to Belphegor. "Rich arsewipes going into fake wilderness to shoot a sick or elderly lion. It creates a lot of outrage. You know how humans are about cats." Rutspud shuddered. Even the thought of the furry critters was enough to creep him out. "Someone shoots a cat. Boo-hoo, everyone cries. It was too weak and pathetic to defend itself? How terrible! The shooter was some rich bloke, probably an American? He deserves the full fury of Hell!"

Boffjock was shuffling reluctantly into position, taking the smallest steps that he could manage and still be moving.

"You know, the scale of Hell's punishments isn't determined by internet likes," said Belphegor. "This place isn't a popularity contest."

Rutspud gave him an appalled look. "Of course, it is. The Other Lot are all trying to crawl into the Almighty's good books. And us... well, it's better to reign in Hell and all that. Move it, Boffjock!"

Unable to delay any longer, the target demon took his mark. Belphegor nodded and turned to the lion that was strapped into the firing harness. "Fire away, Mr Wiffles."

The lion pedalled his back paws to swivel his gun mount, turning the entire platform to line the gun barrel up with the target. He adjusted the angle of the rifle, sighted the target and used his right paw to press the trigger.

Boffjock's head exploded in a delightfully visceral display. Mr Wiffles made a noise like a sneeze, the closest thing to a laugh that was available to a big cat.

"I think we can call that a success," said Belphegor, tossing a strip of flesh to Mr Wiffles. "Now let's get our inaugural victim in there. Did we go for Hemingway in the end?"

"No. Despite the fact that 'Papa' is clearly not suffering in the Pit of Angry Feminist Sharks, we've selected a new arrival. He should be here by now. We've put up the welcome bunting, even got some party poppers." Rutspud twanged the bunting then added a festoon of Boffjock's intestines to enhance the festive feel.

Belphegor pulled up a tablet device and scrolled. "Lord Claymore Ferret. Pre-fate check-in had him due to die four hours ago. And he was put on the fast track for processing. We don't get many lords these days, do we?"

"No," said Rutspud. "They've kind of fallen out of fashion on earth."

"Really? Why's that? You're our resident earth expert."

Rutspud pondered. His experience of life on earth was limited to a tiny Welsh island inhabited solely by half a dozen monks and about ten billion sea birds. Belphegor sometimes failed to appreciate that most of what happened on earth didn't happen there.

"Couldn't say. I'll be happy as long as he gets here before any demons walk off with our party poppers and use them as eyes."

"Why would they do that?"

"Because they're eyes," said Rutspud. He squeezed a couple to illustrate his point and they exploded wetly, gushing translucent gloop into the air. "Is it possible," he pondered, "that Lord Claymore Ferret, his lordship, Lordy McLordface or whatever we call him has been given a last-minute reprieve?"

"You're worrying," said Belphegor. "The man's a grade one sinner. As well as his hunting activities, he was a slum landlord, an arms dealer and when his drilling company poisoned an entire township in central Africa, he sent every bereaved family a 'buy one get one free' voucher for his Slice O'Beef burger bar franchise. You eaten earth burgers, Rutspud?"

"No, there were no Slice O'Beef burger bars on Bardsey Island," said Rutspud.

"There aren't any in central Africa either," Belphegor noted.

"The monks of Bardsey were forced to eat whatever Brother Manfred cooked. We're testing his pickled onion and melon ball starter in the Pit of Michelin-Starred Chefs Who Tell You You're Eating Their Food Wrong."

"Shankrule!" Belphegor called to an approaching demon. Shankrule's body was covered in human faces. As the demon in charge of logistics, he claimed that it gave him the ability to organise multiple things at a time. Rutspud suspected that he just liked picking his noses.

"We're expecting a celebrity guest," said Belphegor. "Has Lord Claymore Ferret been held up?"

"He's not coming," said one of Shankrule's faces and several more made noises of general agreement.

"But we've dug a whole new pit. Bring him here immediately."

"No," said Shankrule. "I mean he's not coming. At all. We've had today's intake and he's not there."

"Not there?" said Rutspud.

"You'll just have to put someone else in your new pit," said Shankrule.

"Like who?"

Shankrule shrugged and looked at the vengeance-ready animals in the pit. "What about some vegans who secretly eat bacon? Always good for a laugh."

Belphegor revved his wheelchair and moved back and forth a few times in frustration. "Hardly the poetic irony we were going for with this pit." The ancient demon sighed, lifted a cheek and farted thoughtfully. "Very well, bring us some of those then."

"When we get some, I'll have them sent here," said Shankrule.

"Just pull some out of the line at the gates."

"We haven't got any in the line," said one of the faces on his shoulder.

"What he said," said Shankrule's face (the one in the traditional face-spot on the front of his head).

"Nearly two hundred thousand people die on earth every day. It's not unreasonable to assume we get a fifty-fifty split. We've got to have several hundred vegans, real or otherwise, in that lot. You telling me we don't have a few bacon-snafflers among them?"

Shankrule bowed obsequiously. "You are welcome to go to the gates and have a look, my lord."

Belphegor stabbed a pre-set on his wheelchair's navigation system and sat back while the steam-powered chariot ploughed a path towards the gates of Hell. Rutspud had a little difficulty following. Belphegor had a very simple attitude to navigation; if the shortest distance between two points in Hell was a straight line then a lord of Hell had every right to follow that line. Cushioned by a complicated pneumatic suspension riding above its all-terrain wheels, and most importantly, featuring a cow-catcher on the front, Belphegor's vehicle surged ahead of Rutspud as he scrambled through the broken remains of walls, pits and damned souls.

"So," Belphegor called back to him, "what kind of animal is a melon anyway?"

"It's a fruit. They scoop out balls of its flesh. No animals are involved," said Rutspud.

"Sounds horrific," said Belphegor. He flicked through files on his tablet, merrily ignorant of the chaos he left in his wake. "We've missed out on a number of big ticket inmates recently."

"Yes?" said Rutspud.

"The roller coaster in the Pit of Indigestion for that guy whose theme park concessions put addictive substances into the food. Never used." He flicked again. "Same with the Pit of Savage Chinchillas for the fashion designer who found that it was cheaper to use real fur and pretend that it was faux fur."

"Odd," said Rutspud, tripping and cartwheeling over a smashed Centre of Torturing Excellence and the dozen damned underneath it.

"Odd!" huffed Belphegor. "Those chinchillas were promised some quality entertainment. Nothing worse than a savage *and* bored chinchilla."

They were near to the gate now. Hell's basic geography had mostly stayed true to the original designs: huge cavernous spaces, jagged stalactites and stalagmites, a suffusing red glow of fires near and distant, the promise that however bad this spot here was there was somewhere worse just around the corner. However, the gates of Hell had been updated in recent times. The gate itself had been replaced by a giant concrete arch on which were etched the words:

Abandon all hope, ye who enter here

And then in smaller letters:

No alcohol beyond this point
This is a designated no-smoking area
Please turn off your mobile phone

As the damned moved through the arch, they passed beneath a series of thrumming air nozzles. Part of the delousing process, Rutspud assumed.

The entrance was divided with retractable tape into queuing lanes that formed a zig-zagging labyrinth. Some of the lanes ended at dead ends. Some merged with others to create points of angry congestion. At the centre, there was a beautiful recursive lane (based on Escher-geometry) where the person you were queuing behind was yourself. Ultimately, the lanes let out at a long row of security booths. They were staffed by several dozen former members of the UK Border Agency, so naturally, only one of the booths was open.

Rutspud was astounded to see that the total queue to get into Hell amounted to less than a hundred people (plus a very angry man in the recursive queue who was about to pick a fight with himself).

"There's no backlog," said Rutspud.

"Not just no backlog, no people," said Belphegor.

Rutspud went up to the one open booth and tapped gently on the glass. One of the damned gazed down at him, her eyes betraying nothing but her desire to see right inside him and understand his innermost secrets.

"I wonder if you could check a couple of names please?" he asked her. "There are some recently deceased that we seem to be missing." She continued to stare at him with that disconcerting look. "Um, perhaps you need the names?" he added.

"Harrumph, seen this before," said Belphegor and, bringing a walking stick over his shoulder, battered violently on the glass of the booth. The woman's eyes sprang open, revealing that the previous gaze had been somehow painted onto her eyelids. Rutspud marvelled at the technique. He was a past master at efficient loafing, but this was new to him.

"Check these names against your list please!" ordered Belphegor. "Claymore Ferret, Hank Schlaeber-Foster and Futon Le-Phew."

The woman turned to the interior of her cabin, glanced through some paperwork and pressed buttons on an unseen machine.

"No," she replied through the intercom.

"No what?" said Belphegor.

"No, they're not on the list."

"But they're dead."

"Are they? That's nice."

"And they should be here."

The woman looked at her paperwork again. "They're not on the list."

Belphegor was disconcerted. "This is not normal, Rutspud, me lad. The queues should be much longer."

"We're just really efficient out our job," said the woman. "They come to us, processed and – wallop – they're through."

"I've been waiting here for three weeks," said the damned man at the head of the queue.

"Shut it, mush!" snarled the woman. "You want me to set Cerberus on you again?"

"Ah, there's a thought," said Belphegor and trundled off.

"What's a thought?" said Rutspud, following.

Down at the very entrance to Hell, straining against a thick chain embedded in the rock was the three-headed hellhound Cerberus. Rutspud kept his distance. Cerberus bared all of his available fangs and growled. Drool spattered on the shredded remains of what might have been Cerberus's bed, might have been his last meal.

"You think the dog ate them?" said Rutspud.

"No, you fool. He's going to help us track them. Cerberus, devourer of the dead. He can sniff them out wherever they hide. You're going to find that nasty Claymore Ferret for us, aren't you?"

One of the heads barked in eager agreement. Another was already sniffing at the ground. The third, Rutspud could swear, was eyeing him up as a pre-hunt snack.

"Unchain him then," said Belphegor.

"Me?" said Rutspud, tremulously.

"I can't do all the work round here, can I now?"

Rutspud gathered his courage – there wasn't much of it to gather so it didn't take long – and sidled round the hook tethering Cerberus to the rock. Three heads tracked him but didn't attack.

Rutspud swallowed hard as he reached for the chain.

"There, there. Good doggies. Uncle Rutspud's going to unleash you. That's right. Good boy. I mean, boys. See? Off comes the hook and now we're going to goooooooo...."

"That's it!" yelled Belphegor after him as the hellhound bounded off, dragging Rutspud behind. "Follow that trail! Don't let go, Rutspud. I'm right behind you!"

Bounced off walls and floors, the world around Rutspud was a blur, a painful blur at that. However, he could see that they were heading out of Hell, away from the gate.

"Is he heading towards Limbo?" called Belphegor, intrigued.

Rutspud would have answered but he was physically occupied with holding onto the chain and mentally occupied by the mystery of what damned souls might be doing out in Limbo. There was nothing there but, well, nothing and at some ineffably distant point, the Celestial City.

CHAPTER THREE

The Celestial City.
Heaven.
Upstairs.
The Celestial City came into being in the very moment of creation. The Celestial City, free from the bonds of time, gravity, physics and all manner of inconvenient real-world stuff, was eternal and unchanging. As such, it had no history. But that didn't mean things didn't happen there...

Joan of Arc frowned at the sight before her. There was plenty in Heaven to make one frown if one thought about it. The Almighty was omnipresent – He was everywhere – and yet He had a throne on which He sat. Similarly, worship in the Celestial City was to be directed to the Almighty but, given that the Celestial City was where the Almighty resided, trying to pray in the right direction was like watching a compass at the magnetic north pole. And yet there was the Great Hall of Worship with rows of marble pews as far as the eye could see, all facing undeniably towards the Almighty.

It was at these pews that Joan was frowning. They had been home to buttocks of all creeds and nations but she'd never before seen towels placed upon them. These were not normal towels either. They were huge gaudy things, emblazoned with the *Manchester United* logo, cartoon characters and national flags. It was very strange...

They were also putting something of a dent in the gleaming white majesty of the place and, without a moment's thought, Joan was gathering them up.

"Oi! Oi. What's your game then?" came a shrill voice.

Joan looked up. The woman had a look of extreme surprise, mostly caused by her eyebrows, drawn on with pencil, several inches above where a normal human would keep them.

"I was tidying up," said Joan.

"Ooh no missy, you don't go moving a person's towel. No, that's against everything that's right and proper, that is. We have the right to bagsy a spot with our towels, everyone knows that."

Joan was about to question her but heard the sound of harp playing that signalled one of the showier angels making an entrance. She looked up to see Eltiel, bathed in holy light, although this light looked a little unnecessarily 'disco'. Joan's relatively-recently-deceased friend, Evelyn, always referred to him as 'Eltiel John' but Joan didn't get the joke. When you'd been dead for nearly six hundred years, a lot of jokes went straight over your head.

"Joan," said Eltiel, his hands clasped together in prayer, "St Francis of Assisi would like your help in the Blessed Animal Sanctuary."

"I'll be there in a minute. I need to ask this –"

"It is most urgent. He was keen for me to make that point in the strongest terms possible," he intoned solemnly, with some extra mystical reverb for emphasis.

"Fine. I'll be there in a jiffy," said Joan. Joan turned to the woman while Eltiel performed a complicated spotlit routine above her. "What is this thing, 'bagsy'?" she asked.

"It's bagsy." The woman dragged a Disney Princess towel out from the pile over Joan's arm and placed it back on a pew seat. "Let's say I have reserved a spot then, if we're going to get all stuck-up about it."

Joan looked at the woman and then looked around at the Great Hall of Worship.

"The Hall is infinite in size. Why would you feel the need to reserve a spot?"

The woman gave Joan a look that was part confusion, part pity but mostly contempt. "How else can we be sure we get the best spot?"

"Best spot?" said Joan and was about to point out that this was Heaven and that every spot was the best spot when Eltiel gave a meaningful cough and she accepted she probably needed to be somewhere else.

Joan ran through the Celestial City, dodging and weaving through the strolling crowds of the blessed dead, although crowds tended to part naturally for someone sprinting in gleaming plate armour. Despite her urgency, something made her stop. Amongst all the gentle souls and good people of the city, the man winking at passers-by at the entrance to the Blessed Animal Sanctuary stuck out like a slug in a salad.

Joan was happy that the blessed dead came in all shapes and sizes, and knew that it was useless to judge people based on their appearance, but this man just didn't look as though his heart was pure. Was it the creepy nudges that he kept giving people as they approached? Was it that she'd heard him call every single woman who walked by *darlin'*? No, she decided, it was the sign he held in his hands that said *Gin and Whores, this way.*

"What are you doing?" she asked.

"Sellin' gin and whores, darlin'," he said. "How'd you like to get something naughty inside you, eh? Or you could have a gin!" He laughed raucously at his own joke. Joan stared at him stonily. "Well, yes all right," he coughed. "Move along, will you darlin', you're putting the punters off."

"But what are you doing?" she insisted.

"Which bit don't you understand, is it the gin or is it the whores? I ain't got time to be doing the birds and the bees wiv you, luv."

She frowned. She was getting a serious frown work-out today. "Sex and alcohol are not forbidden in Heaven."

"No, they are not, luv."

"But you are selling them."

"Yes."

"And thereby turning something fine and appropriate into something..."

"Ah you got me darlin'! It's all about the inappropriate, ain't it? What's the fun of doing something if no one's gonna object. I'm all about sorting people out with their favourite bit of inappropriateness and them sorting me out with some ready cash in exchange."

21

"There's no money in Heaven," said Joan.

"Shows what you know, darlin'. I got a big fat wad in my trousers that'll –" He stopped. Joan's blade was an involuntary muscle jerk away from cutting his throat. He swallowed, his bravado gone. "I meant this, nothing mucky," he said, drawing a fat bundle of paper from his pocket.

Joan put her sword away and snatched the notes from his hand. She gave them a cursory but furious glance.

"Who's this meant to be?" she said, tapping the illustration.

"It's the baby Jesus, ain't it? He's on the five dollar note."

"He's got his thumbs up!"

"That's right. He's saying, 'good on yer, mate. You've got five dollars. Why not earn yourself ten dollars? It's got me mum on it.'"

There was a cough from on high. Eltiel hovered above her.

"Are you following me everywhere?" she snapped and ran into the Blessed Animal Sanctuary which she was given to understand was much like modern day zoos on earth except the monkeys in the celestial version didn't debase themselves in public or fling filth at passers-by.

St Francis of Assisi stood before the lion enclosure looking even more flushed than usual. He had his hands on his hips, facing off with a man who had a large rifle hooked over his arm and a small group of cronies behind him.

"How goes it?" said Joan, seeing that things weren't going all that well.

"Thank goodness you're here, Joan," said Francis. "This dweadful man wants to take one of the lions."

"Why would you want to take a lion?" asked Joan, eyeing the rifle.

"Just borrow it for a bit," said the man. "Spot of big game hunting would go down a treat. Stay and watch if you want to see an expert in action."

"There will be no shooting of lions here. Or shooting of anything else," she added firmly. "Put the gun away."

"Cecil finds it tewwibly upsetting," said Francis, looking all dewy-eyed at the male lion hunched mournfully in the corner of the enclosure.

"I think you'll find, missy, that I have a right to shoot what I want. I've very much enjoyed the bird shooting here, but I need something smart for my new digs. Lion's head'll be just the jobbie."

"Fine," said Joan. "You want a lion's head on your wall. We'll put one there."

"As long I get to bag the beast."

"You mean kill it?"

"Chwist pweserve us."

"Claymore Ferret doesn't hang another man's trophy on his wall," said the man. "That's worse than taking sloppy seconds with a Milanese whore. Of course I want to kill it."

"I cannot believe," said Joan, "that I need to explain why you're not allowed to kill something – and I can't emphasise this last bit enough – *in Heaven*."

"The theological conundwum of what death-after-death might even be like is staggewing," said Francis.

The man gave a knowing laugh.

"You see, little miss here doesn't get it. She may wear the shiny armour but underneath it all she's a girl. Doesn't know a man's got needs. To stalk, to take, to feel the life go from a body beneath him. You, my good man, you understand. And I know what you're after." He pulled out a wad of paper notes that looked awfully familiar to Joan. "I always got what I wanted in life, and if this is Heaven, then *obviously* I should get what I want now. That's the point of Heaven."

"It's really not," said Joan but the man ignored her.

He pulled away a half inch pile of notes and tucked it in the top of Francis's robe. "A little something for your conscience. There's a good chap."

Francis looked at the cash in disgust. "Bwibewy?"

"Bribery is a dirty word. But if you're worried about that, forgiveness is only a click away."

"You're wasting your time, Claymore," said a skinny woman in impossibly high heels. "They're simple proles. They don't know how it works. You can't expect the lower classes to understand."

"You might have hit the nail on the head, Cynthia," said Claymore. He tipped an imaginary hat at her and spoke in a theatrical aside to nobody in particular. "Third mistress, definitely the one with the brains, although that's not what I normally look for in a mistress! Ha!"

"There are no 'proles' in Heaven," said Joan wearily. "There is no class. There is no property. There is no money. No one kills anyone else. No one has power over others. Everything is free and we're all equal."

"My God," said the skinny woman. "She's a bloody commie."

"French one at that," said Claymore, amused. "Money is power, and power is everything, *mon cherie*."

"Not. Here," snarled Joan.

"Even here," he said. "They say money is the new God, don't they?"

Joan, sickened, turned to Francis. "Get the lion out of the enclosure."

"Knew you'd see sense," grinned Claymore, slapping Joan's bottom playfully. "You're a good girl. And feisty too. Bloody arousing watching you and Cynthia having a little ding-dong. How do you feel about a little ménage à trois, as you Frenchies say?"

Joan whirled, drawing her sword for the second time that day. This time, she didn't even care if she took his throat out or his entire head. She was willing to put the notion of death-after-death to the test.

"The lion is coming with us for safekeeping. You have no right to behave this way. You certainly have no right to touch me like that."

"Christ," said the man, excited rather than afraid. "You have fire, baby. With spunk like that, I'm surprised the French lost so many wars."

"Not the ones I fought in," she said.

"Good grief!" shouted Venerable Pope Pius XII, climbing up onto his chair as Joan of Arc, Francis of Assisi and Cecil the lion entered the committee chambers. "Francis, you go too far! We put up with the wolf of Gubbio for far too long, but you've crossed the line now!"

In the Celestial City, everyone was equal (apart from the Almighty) and no one (apart from the Almighty) had power over anyone else. But that didn't mean the city lacked government. The

24

committee chambers housed the decision-making department of the Celestial City, the ministerial cabinet without whose decisions the city would fall apart. Probably fall apart. Well, maybe struggle a little. Or not. Probably not. Joan had long ago formed the opinion that the Heavenly committee primarily existed to give certain self-important busybodies something to do and keep them out of harm's way. Nothing she had seen since provided any evidence to the contrary.

There was a small snort of laughter from the corner.

"Who's laughing?" said Pius, casting glances at the lion.

The Archangel Gabriel, St Thomas Aquinas, Joan and Francis all looked down the table to where Mother Teresa sat, scribing the minutes of their meetings. Her quill scratched across the parchment.

"Crossed the lion," she tittered very quietly.

"If that creature can sit down without harassing any former pontiffs and there are no further interruptions," said Gabriel sternly, as Pius cautiously got down from his chair, "we should return to item one on the agenda."

"No," said Joan, sitting down with a clatter of armour. "I need to talk to you about an urgent matter. Some very upsetting behaviour. People trying to claim ownership of seats in the Great Hall of Worship. Some new currency going round."

"Gabriel's on the fifty dollar note," said Thomas Aquinas, snapping a note tight as he held it up.

"Where did you get that?" said Francis.

"Payment," said the rotund theologian, patting a small pile in front of him. "I've been asked to do some private sermons. Exclusive events. Charity gigs."

"You're taking payment?" said Joan.

"It's the woot of evil," said Francis despairingly.

Thomas gave him a patronising look. "Giving us quotes from the current lord of Hell? Really?"

"And it's the *love* of money that's the root of all evil," said Pius. "So many people get that wrong."

"Oh, they love money all right," said Joan. "And they love lording it over others."

"And shooting!" blurted Francis. "They weally, weally love shooting animals."

"Among other things," Gabriel sniffed. Trying to keep his chin up, he turned so that the new arrivals could see the tattered mess that was his wings. "Item one on the agenda."

"Claymore Ferret was the man's name," said Joan. "Says shooting animals is sport."

"It didn't feel like sport," said Gabriel, pulling his wings around to inspect the damage. "And I'm not an animal."

"Although he did keep calling you his feathered friend," pointed out St Thomas.

Gabriel curled his arm protectively around his right wing, as he attempted to straighten some of the feathers.

"I told you," said Joan. "We've got a problem."

There was a jangly burst of harp and in a blaze of pink and silver light, Eltiel appeared.

"I'm going to put up a do not disturb sign in future," tutted Gabriel.

"And a 'no animals' sign," added Pius.

"The strangest thing," said Eltiel.

"You've not been shot as well?" asked Gabriel.

"There are demons at the gate."

Joan was on her feet. "An invasion?"

"Not unless Hell thinks they can take the Celestial City with two demons, a wheelchair and a dog."

"A doggy?" said Francis.

"A horrible fiend with three heads and shreds of flesh hanging from the fangs of at least two of them. It's tried to bite anyone who gets near."

"There are no howwible dogs," said Francis. "It's pwobably just tewwitowial behaviour."

"Yes, that's all vewwy well. I mean very well," said Pius. "But what do they want, these demons?"

Eltiel descended in cascades of rainbow glitter. "The strangest thing. They want to know if we have any recently deceased souls here in Heaven who don't belong."

CHAPTER FOUR

Ben removed the third padlock and with a bit of jostling for first place, the three of them entered the space that had once been flat 1b.

"Daddy's home!" said Clovenhoof as he took in the view.

A table stood in the centre of the room. And the table had a board game at its centre. Other game boards sprouted off on every side. Duct tape joined cut-up strips and pieces, and model bridge supports (supplied by Ben) held them up between tables.

How many tables were in play now? Clovenhoof wasn't sure if a hostess trolley counted as a table, so he called it six.

Each of the three players had their home zone, where they kept their cash, tokens, spells and special cards. This was the reason for the high level of security. Each of them had a mound of closely-guarded treasure and worried constantly that the others might cheat and mess with their stuff or tinker with the playing pieces to change the course of The Game.

Clovenhoof ran his hands over his banker's cash pile, assuring himself that all was well. He slipped five bundles of extra cash from his sleeve and added them to his pile, knowing that Ben and Nerys were counting their own money and were unlikely to notice. He'd invested in a ream of coloured paper and had printed enough currency to enable the most profligate of playing styles.

"Initiating start-up routine," intoned Nerys. "Counting the playing pieces."

"Five blue?" said Ben, reading from an over-stuffed lever-arch folder. "Chicken, train and three bottle tops."

"Check," said Nerys.

"Four green? Cowboy, owl, baguette and Jeremy's tissue."

"Check."

"Three purple comedy grape people?"

"Check."

Clovenhoof knew that the pre-game checks were critical to prevent cheating but he zoned out as he checked the date on the newspaper that was wedged solidly under the first game board. Four months they'd been playing The Game.

They called it The Game because no one could pronounce *Qizi-o'yin Vaqti*.

It had started as some much-needed tidying out of the cupboard in flat 1b. After the refurb, they realised that flat 1b might actually make them some money if they could rent it out to another tenant. Unfortunately, that meant emptying it first. Whose stuff was in the cupboard? Nobody knew. There were dozens of board games. The one with the most interesting box turned out to be some sort of property trading game. Clovenhoof's first guess of *Guess how many of these plastic shapes I can stuff up my arse?* was very quickly quashed. The name and the instructions were all written in something that they initially guessed to be Turkish, but which, after extensive research, Ben declared to be Uzbek, although he wasn't confident on that point.

"Hey Kitchen, *kutok bosh!*" said Clovenhoof.

"That is *not* part of the start-up routine Jeremy," frowned Ben, "and if you put as much energy into translating the rules as you did into learning the swear words of Uzbek, we might have finished The Game months ago."

They all paused, aghast at the idea.

"I like to think that my creativity shaped what it is today," said Clovenhoof. "A bit like when Nerys threw in all the extra game pieces, and the Lego and the contents of that sewing box or whatever it was."

"I think you give Nerys too much credit for basically being drunk and dropping things," said Ben.

"Play nice, boys," said Nerys. "We've got the most important part of the start-up routine to do now."

"No, wait! We haven't signed the non-liability waivers!" said Ben.

Nerys pushed a piece of paper at both of them. Ben read the whole thing.

"It's the same as last week's Ben, come on, just sign it!" said Nerys, exasperated.

"No, it's got the normal stuff about if one of us gets murdered it's a crime of passion because of The Game, but you've added something new at the bottom. Nobody is allowed to use demonic powers. What on earth is that for?"

Nerys glanced quickly at Clovenhoof. "Just in case. Covering all bases, you know?"

"And we're all happy that Lennox at the Boldmere Oak continues to be our arbitration service?" said Ben. "He has the final word and we trust his judgement."

Nerys huffed with impatience. "As I was saying. Most important part –"

"Oh wait!" said Ben, heaving a giant wad of pages out of the way in the rules folder. "I re-translated subsection 5 of part IV of the rules. I'm pretty sure it's right this time. It goes like this: *When we want to bake a transaction correctly, the player to the right must capitulate without despair.*"

Nerys stared at Ben. "What on earth does that mean?"

Ben nodded and thought for a few long moments. "I think it's one of those things that will become obvious when we get to it. It's all about context."

"So we get Lennox to decide," said Nerys with a roll of her eyes. "He is the expert on context."

"Reminds me, Nerys. That was a nice try with the dictionary," said Clovenhoof airily.

"Eh?" said Ben, confused.

"Nerys gave Lennox a new dictionary. A thoughtful gift, if it wasn't for the edits she'd applied. Lennox showed it to me. If you look up key terms like *beneficiary* it tells you that it must always be a woman."

Nerys scowled at Clovenhoof. "Do you want to do this or not?" she said, holding aloft a cocktail measure. I have everyone's lucky glass here. Or bucket in Jeremy's case. I will fill to the agreed lines. Toilet break times are the usual, limited to three minutes away from play."

"Fill 'em up, Nerys!" whooped Clovenhoof.

Nerys passed the drinks around, grinning giddily. "I read my horoscope today. It said that I would achieve global domination.

I'm paraphrasing slightly, but that was the gist of it. Watch out, boys."

"Well if that was true, then you'd be sharing the world with a twelfth of the population," said Ben. "I wonder what mine said?"

"I can pretty well guess," said Nerys. "It would say that you'll mostly be wallowing in rules and trying to crush your housemates' dreams."

"Oh, that reminds me, I need to update the Risk board. You do the weather, Nerys."

Nerys consulted a weather app on her phone. She went over to the wall and removed a cardboard cut-out of a blazing sun from a hook. She replaced it with a sun that was partially obscured by cloud. "There we are. Tell me Ben, how did crushing my dreams remind you of the weather and the Risk board?"

"I read the news before we came in. I'm just not sure whether world domination's going to be possible today with so many smaller territories vying for independence. I'm going to split Cornwall away from the rest of England on the Risk board. We've got an increased nuclear threat over North Korea as well, so pass me a marshmallow, will you Jeremy?"

Clovenhoof plucked a marshmallow from the bag, passed it over and then changed his mind at the last minute, popping it into his mouth instead. "Uh ook, orl beh-ah!" he said, his mouth full.

Ben sighed. "We need to reflect the actual state of the world. I *said* we should use mushrooms rather than marshmallows, at least they wouldn't get eaten so often."

Once Ben had positioned another marshmallow, they all sat up straight in their chairs, ready to commence play.

Clovenhoof had always derided Ben's wargaming hobby – it was a cornerstone of their relationship. Watching nerdsome beta-males taking on the roles of savage and masterful military leaders, pretending that their little battalions of lead miniatures were representations of real might, was a pathetic and obvious parading of their personal and emotional shortcomings. They might as well walk around carrying signs saying, 'I am a waste of food and oxygen with a tiny penis.' And yet... and yet, with his collection of property cards in front of him – Highbury Hall, the BT Tower, the Alexander Stadium – backed up by his pretend wealth and his various action cards – including a Get Out of Jail, Escape the Traffic Jam, several artfully forged Volcano cards and even an STD Clinic Gives You The All-Clear – Clovenhoof felt a warming sense of ownership and pride. This was his realm, his kingdom, his own little Hooflandia. He'd even started composing a little national anthem and hummed it to himself now.

"Ben to start," said Nerys.

"I get an extra dice, remember?" said Ben. "Because I own a fitness gym."

He popped the dice into a cup, put his hand over the top and shook, muttering a soft incantation of *throw a seven*.

They all gasped as he threw the dice and Nerys squealed in anticipation. The dice settled.

"Seven!" shouted Clovenhoof. "He shoots, he scores! It's a seven! What does that mean then?"

They all leaned over to watch Ben move his counter, which was an egg cup with the face of a clown on it. They had renamed all the property squares on the board with local landmarks. Villa Park, the Custard Factory and Lickey Hills were a bit more meaningful to them than *Kukelras Bidzu, Shayakh Babur* and *Suzani-oi-Suzani*.

"Birmingham City Football Club," said Ben. "That means I can –"

"No, you can't!" shouted Nerys, and slammed a small plastic traffic cone onto the board. "I am the traffic controller and I am going to have to insist that you move to –"

"No, you're not," said Ben.

"What? Of course, I am. It's listed in my roles manifest."

"You're not wearing your hat."

Nerys went to reply but the words died on her lips as she felt the top of her head and found that it was, indeed, hatless. "Arse," she said. Well I can fix that. Hold on." She went to the back of the room and returned with a full-sized traffic cone. She put it on her head. "Hah! Behold Birmingham City Council's newest recruit. It's Wizard Nerys, the sexy traffic controller, and she is putting a traffic blocking spell on you, so there!" Chardonnay slopped from her glass as she swigged triumphantly at the same time as she held a card aloft.

Clovenhoof looked at the board. "She's got you mate, you'll need to park somewhere else."

"No! I don't think so. I'm going to complain to the council about those cones."

"I *am* the council, puny mortal!" shouted Nerys. "You can take your complaint up with my colleagues, Mr Up and Mr Yours!"

Clovenhoof picked up the rules folder and flicked through. "No, it's a thing, Nerys. Here's what we're supposed to do. You and I phone a number of our choosing and then Ben must make his complaint to them. If he can keep them on the line for two minutes without laughing, stalling or repeating himself then his complaint is upheld."

Clovenhoof whipped out his phone and brought up his favourites. Nerys leaned over and whispered in his ear.

"Oh, I'm way ahead of you," he said. He put it onto loudspeaker and placed it in front of Ben as the call connected.

"Candy here, what's your name, caller?" came a throaty voice.

"Hello Candy, it's Ben, and I'm calling to report a problem."

"Has it made you angry, honey?" Candy asked.

"Well yes, a little bit," said Ben.

"I can help you with that. Tell me about it while I slip off my panties and bend over. I need you to tell me how angry you are and how much I need to be punished."

"Right, well – wait, what did you say?" He covered the phone and mouthed *"This a sex line again, isn't it?"* Clovenhoof and Nerys made mocking *dur* noises and pointed at the phone. "Well, actually I'm angry about someone who illegally applied a cone."

"Ooh honey, I can picture you there now, you must be *so* mad. Give a little swivel along with me. I spank, you swivel: how does that sound? Slip it further in. You'll thank me later. Did I tell you I'm using a leather whip? I can change to a paddle if you want me to, but I like the noise it makes on my flesh."

There was a loud *thwack* from the phone.

"No, please! You don't need to hurt yourself!" said Ben in horror.

"Oh, but I've been a *very* naughty girl. How's that cone feeling, honey? Lube it up and slip it in a little more. You can take it."

"The cone isn't giving me that sort of problem," said Ben, contorting uncomfortably, as though his prudish embarrassment was melting his spine. "It's just, um, in my way."

"Oh sweetie! *Thwack.* Argh! See how bad I feel? You didn't tell me I was at a party! Your friend with the cone can't wait for you to take its place."

"I don't even know what that means," he whimpered.

"Come on, show off what you've got," said Candy. "Take that cock in your –"

Ben ended the call, threw the phone down and shook himself off in disgust.

"I'm going to have to disinfect that phone before I use it again," he said as his friends offered him entirely unsympathetic laughter and finger-pointing.

"The cone remains in place," said Nerys, and set them off again.

"Yes, yes. Well it's the next square for me then," huffed Ben. "The Fort shopping centre. I think I'll buy it."

"Oh good," said Clovenhoof, "I always enjoy this part. First of all, let's see your stamp duty."

Ben peeled a second class stamp from a book under the edge of the board and stuck it onto his forehead.

"Looking good Ben," said Nerys. "Right, it's credit score time!"

Clovenhoof pulled the giant-sized tub of Vaseline from his bag. "Are you feeling lucky, Ben?"

"We don't want any friction!" called Nerys gleefully.

Clovenhoof scooped up a huge handful of lubricant and winked at Ben. Then he knelt on the floor and applied a thick layer to the Twister mat.

Ben stepped resolutely forward. "Right, tell me what the colours are worth," he said.

Nerys and Clovenhoof used the spinner to determine the highest scoring colours and Nerys set an egg timer.

"Go Ben! Remember blues are high this round!"

Ben launched himself at the slippery mat. Clovenhoof and Nerys stomped and clapped as he struggled for purchase. It looked for a moment as if he might secure a decent score but then his foot skated away and he landed heavily on his bottom.

"Come on! You can recover that!" screeched Nerys.

Clovenhoof had a sudden flashback to the Pit of Greasy Nuns back in the Old Place, but he shook his head. No point dwelling on nostalgia. He was sure that Hell was getting on fine without him. They'd probably even forgotten who he was by now.

CHAPTER FIVE

"This is Satan's fault," said Gabriel. "It has his stink all over it."

"Maybe," said Joan, unconvinced.

The committee room door opened noisily and the demon lord Belphegor trundled in. The minor demon, Rutspud followed close behind. Joan had met them both before. On occasions when Heaven had been required to step in, to steer Hell away from trouble and put it back on course, Joan had been there. Belphegor, one of the true powers in Hell, was usually there, busily trying to fix the current catastrophe. And Rutspud turned up surprisingly frequently, very near the epicentre of the troubles but always just a couple of steps to the side and just outside the blast radius of actual guilt.

Angels and saints visiting Hell was commonplace, but invitations were never reciprocated. Pius failed to conceal a shudder of horror as Belphegor wheeled into a gap at the table beside him.

As the door swung shut, Joan could hear St Francis outside.

"Ah, who's a good doggy, eh? You are. You are. Cecil, come say hello to Cerbewus. Play nicely you two..."

Gabriel spoke to the new arrivals in the tones of one who really wasn't happy with the situation but, by the Almighty, was going to be dashed civil about it.

"Please, my friends. Sit. Sit."

Rutspud looked at the cushioned chair and then, uncomfortably, at Belphegor. Belphegor gave him some stern and silent eyebrow waggling and nostril hair flaring. Rutspud leaned over to his superior and whispered.

"But it's so.... fluffy."

Belphegor flipped a switch. A nozzle rose from his chair arm, angled round and blasted the offending cushion with blue fire. Rutspud plonked himself happily onto the burning ruin.

"Are we all comfortable now?" said Gabriel.

"They're not meant to be comfortable," said Thomas Aquinas. "The fallen angels carry with them their own darksome atmosphere and wherever they are they endure the pains of Hell."

"It's all right, tubs," said Rutspud. "I'm not fallen."

"Hellish, born and bred," said Joan, giving a nod of greeting to the two of them.

"Well, not born," said Belphegor. "Not bred."

"Hell-made," said Rutspud. "I think I've got a manufacturer's mark stamped on me somewhere."

"It seems," said Gabriel, "that Heaven and Hell have found opposite ends of a shared problem."

"We have not established that we have any kind of problem at all," argued Thomas.

"My shredded wings would beg to differ," said the archangel and placed a handful of feathery remnants on the table.

"I don't know what problems you've got up here," said Belphegor, "but we have a list of missing souls and we have reason to believe that you're harbouring some of them."

He typed on a keyboard. A screen descended from the committee room ceiling and with a finger swipe, it came to life with scrolling lists of names, dates and profile images.

"Sorcery!" declared Pius in alarm.

"Bluetooth," said Belphegor. "See you guys get the nice hardware. But you should really look at your security settings. 'GodIsLove' isn't much of a password."

Joan watched the screen. There was the 'gin and whores' man. There was the 'towel bagsy' woman. And there...

"Claymore Ferret," she said.

"You've seen him?" said Rutspud.

"I don't think we have to tell you who we have and haven't seen," said Thomas.

"I don't understand what game you're playing in the Celestial City," said Belphegor, "but if you're harbouring fugitives from Hell then we must politely insist that –"

"Why would we harbour fugitives from Hell?" said Pius disdainfully.

"I couldn't say," replied Belphegor coolly. "Maybe you've been bribed."

Thomas Aquinas attempted to slide his recently acquired pile of cash out of sight.

"Charity gigs," he mumbled, guiltily.

"You have some very bad people hiding out in Heaven," said Belphegor. "Don't you?"

"And you have money," added Rutspud. "Since when did the Celestial City need a currency?"

"Heaven can neither confirm nor deny that we have any problems at all," said Thomas stiffly.

"I think it's fairly obvious that we do," said Joan.

Eltiel had ushered a silver-winged angel into the committee room and they were now crouched together behind Gabriel's chair having a low-voiced discussion over his ravaged wings.

"Can you mend them?"

"Mend them? I'm a miracle-worker but even I have limits. I don't think I've brought enough thread."

"So, it's doable?"

"Doable. All things are doable but the question is whether they're worth doing. Sometimes it's just better to give up and move on."

"What?" hissed Gabriel, looking back whilst trying to maintain a presidential demeanour for the visiting demons.

The tailor-angel, popped up and put a hand on Gabriel's shoulder. "If you had to choose – *had* to choose – between flight and looking fabulous, which would you go for?"

"I have to choose?"

"*If* you had to choose."

Gabriel gave him a look both stern and terrified. The tailor-angel pouted, dipped down from sight and continued to work.

Belphegor reached into the chair behind him and produced a handheld device, a chunky plastic box. It was covered in little lights and had two wing-like sensors on the side.

"What is that thing?" said Pius.

"Basic sin detection equipment," explained the inventor demon. "It goes all Christmassy in the presence of sin. I'm sure any wrongdoers or general wrongdoing will immediately stand out in your gleaming and virtuous city like a turd on a wedding cake."

"Turd," smirked Mother Teresa as she scribed.

"It will only light up because you're here," said Thomas, unconvinced.

"No, guv," said Rutspud. "Demons can't be sinful. To sin you have to choose to do bad. We started out on the bad side. It's just who we are."

"Devils incapable of sin?" said Thomas. "Poppycock."

"We all know one devil who was quite clearly capable of sinning," said Gabriel.

CHAPTER SIX

Clovenhoof watched as Ben tried to wipe away the worst of the Vaseline with a towel. Ben had passed his credit check, and Clovenhoof's ribs hurt from laughing.

"At least I can build something now," said Ben, surveying the game board.

"Don't be so sure about that," said Nerys. "It appears that you're in an area of outstanding natural beauty."

"I've seen the Fort shopping centre, it's about as natural as David Dickinson's tan," said Clovenhoof.

"I've got a card that says it is an area of outstanding natural beauty," said Nerys, raising her hand to reveal it.

Ben gave her a triumphant smile. "Well, then it's lucky that I have a fast-pass building permit, isn't it?" He held up his own card.

Nerys scowled and they both placed their special cards on the discard pile. "You need a quote for your building work then. I'll get Twinkle."

Twinkle was Nerys's miniature Yorkshire terrier. Clovenhoof was fairly sure that this dog was not the original one. In fact, now he came to think about it, he was certain that the current Twinkle was a shape-shifting, genetically modified hellhound that Nerys had adopted after it was liberated from the lab where it was created. It was adorable and obedient for its owner but was demonically aggressive towards the rest of the world. But didn't that description apply to all tiny terriers? It was hardly evidence of malign forces at work.

"Twinkle, you're on," crooned Nerys as she plucked him from his basket.

Tiny Twinkle fitted comfortably into the large hamster ball. The ball could roll to any of the numbers that formed the outer boundary of its miniature arena. Nerys held Twinkle up before popping him into the ball, and whispered loudly into his ear.

"Now remember your training. This is *not* Mummy's turn so you need to head to the left. *Head to the left!* A nice high quote for silly Ben. Do Mummy proud."

She shut Twinkle in the ball and placed it on the starting spot.

"Spin it!" shouted Clovenhoof.

"You can't spin it, you'll make him puke," said Nerys. "It's animal cruelty."

"Oh, I think we've already established we're willing to do animal cruelty," said Ben guiltily.

Nerys gave the ball a small twist.

"You've twisted it towards the high numbers," cried Ben.

Clovenhoof raised his hands and walked towards Twinkle. "Let me help," he said and flipped the hamster ball upside down on the spot.

Twinkle staggered upright and lurched to the right.

"No! No!" said Nerys. "Go left Twinkle. Left! Remember left is Dinky Granules and right is Wholesome Milky Nutrition Compound. Think Twinkle, think!"

Twinkle rolled the ball further to the right.

"A hundred quid?" whooped Ben with delight. "I will take that quote."

"Gah!" Nerys rolled her eyes. "You got lucky there. Blindfold, Jeremy. It's building time!"

Clovenhoof blindfolded Ben and handed him the bucket of Lego. He knew that Ben practised his blind Lego-building skills every day, so he threw in a bar of soap, a small black pudding and a mousetrap. At a look from Nerys he pulled the mousetrap out.

"Spoilsport," he mouthed. "Thirty seconds to build something, Kitchen, starting..."

The doorbell rang.

Clovenhoof looked to Nerys. Nery looked at Clovenhoof. Ben peeked out from under his blindfold.

"There's somebody at the door," said Ben, in the arch tones of a bad actor.

"On games night," said Nerys with equal playfulness.

"What a coincidence," said Clovenhoof with deliberate woodenness.

Visitors had become a recent staple of games night. Involving other people added an extra frisson. A few weeks before, Ben had introduced a group of angry tenants. They staged a sit-in and bore placards, protesting about Nerys's extortionate rent increases. They eventually uncovered that these people knew Ben through LARPing, which (Clovenhoof later discovered) wasn't anywhere near as kinky as it first sounded. But it had set a precedent. Murder mystery actors, strip-o-grams, and even unwitting Deliveroo drivers had since been used to add a bit of am-dram *je ne sais quoi* to the evenings.

"Get building, Kitchen. I'll go," said Clovenhoof and with a hoofy hop, skip and a jump was at the front door which he opened to find a slender woman dressed in a business suit. Clovenhoof grinned at her.

"Jeremy Clovenhoof?" she asked.

"The one and only! And who awaits his pleasure?" he asked with an exaggerated bow.

"My name is Narinda Shah. I work for Her Majesty's Revenue and Customs office. I have written to you numerous times, Jeremy."

"Mmmm," he looked her up and down approvingly. "Love the naughty accountant outfit."

"I'm sorry?"

"I don't know whether to show you my undisclosed assets or ask for some double entry action."

"Are you trying to be vulgar, Jeremy?"

"Thought I was doing better than trying," he said, a little dispirited. "But please, come in. Don't want the others to miss out on this whole performance."

He ushered her into the flat. Ben and Nerys looked up with interest.

"Oh," she said, taking in the runaway mental illness that was their game-playing area. "This is very... interesting. What are you doing?"

"Mostly lying, cheating, stealing each other's money. It's like a home from home for a 'tax inspector'," said Clovenhoof, marking the air quotes as he kicked the door shut.

The impact of the door closing made the board wobble and Ben's new building toppled over. Clovenhoof was impressed to see that the roof had been formed from a bar of soap, but possibly that was what had made it top-heavy.

"Oh, dear," said Nerys with gleeful malice. "You've got to forfeit the building now."

"No way! It's not my fault that Jeremy slammed the door like that. Wasn't there something in the rules that if we can't find someone to sue for damages," he looked darkly at Clovenhoof, "then we can declare it to be a ruin and charge admission. I'll do that, but I'm really not happy about it."

"Hmmm, a ruined shopping mall," mused Nerys "Sounds like quite the tourist draw! We got rid of the ruins clause a month ago. It was a change that you introduced, saying it was more likely to be bad foundations," said Nerys. She turned to Narinda. "Anyway, who's our guest?"

Clovenhoof gave a big grin, like a bad TV host.

"This is Narinda Shah, everyone. She's from 'Revenue and Customs'."

"No need for the air quotes," said Narinda. "I am from Revenue and Customs."

"Sorry." She 'is' from Revenue and Customs."

"You did it again."

"Sorry. 'She' is from Revenue and Customs."

"That doesn't even make sense."

"And which of us are you here for?" asked Nerys.

"I really do want to talk to Jeremy here," said Narinda. "But it is a private and confidential matter so I'm sure you'll understand..."

"Well it's my turn now, so you'll just have to wait," said Nerys. "Pull up a pew, Narinda." She took a huge swig from her wine glass and rubbed her hands together. "Right, well I'm not going to roll the dice for my next move. I have here a chartered flight card." She held the card aloft and made sure that everyone got a good look. "This girl's headed straight to the Mailbox!"

"Oh dear. It could be that a natural disaster might have to change those plans for you Nerys," said Clovenhoof. "A volcanic ash cloud has stopped all flights." Clovenhoof gave a quick waggle of his volcanic ash card, but leapt up to do the fun part. He wheeled over the trolley that contained their papier mâché volcano with vinyl streamers running down the sides. "Been dying to try this out!" he said.

"Yes," said Ben doubtfully. "A volcano in Birmingham. I'm still not sure how we decided it was remotely authentic but please don't light it, Jeremy."

"It's ages since we had a fire," said Clovenhoof sulkily. "And they're only indoor fireworks inside it."

"Indoor fireworks does not just mean fireworks you've brought indoors."

"Stands to reason," said Clovenhoof

"Right, flight's cancelled," said Nerys. "Change of plans." She rolled a standard movement dice. "Aston Hall."

"That's one of my properties!" said Clovenhoof. "It's an expensive stop, Nerys, you're looking at ten thousand pounds rent."

Nerys made a huffing noise as she checked her cash reserves. "Well I can't pay."

"Forfeit!" said Ben and Clovenhoof together. Ben did a fingertip drumroll on the table edge.

"Fine," said Nerys and started to pull off her top.

"No," said Clovenhoof, standing. "Not the strip forfeit again."

Clovenhoof looked down. As he'd jumped up, he'd dislodged the extra volcanic ash cloud cards that he'd wedged up his sleeve. They all now formed an untidy pile on the floor. Even Narinda, who wasn't fully up to speed with The Game looked at him questioningly.

"Well, I expect you're all waiting for me to explain the perfectly good reason why I had a few spares," he started.

"You cheated!" said Ben, flushed with outrage.

"It's forfeits for you now, scumbucket!" crowed Nerys.

"Perhaps we could just pull away from this for a few minutes and have a little chat, Jeremy..." said Narinda.

Nerys wagged a finger in threat. "Don't you bloody dare. He's been caught red-handed and you're not getting your man out of it."

"She's not mine," said Clovenhoof, jerking a thumb at Narinda. "And anyway it's your turn, and *you* need to do the forfeit."

"But you knocked over my building," said Ben. "You need to do the forfeit."

"That's history. Stop clinging to the past, man."

"You stuck cards up your sleeve. That's the issue here," said Nerys.

"Oh, you too harping on about the past! Someone knocked over a building. Someone had some extra cards. Maybe it was you, maybe it was me. It's all lost in the mists of time. Who knows?"

"So, the rent I owe you is ancient history too. If that's the way you want to play it."

"Don't try to wiggle out of paying your debts. It's unseemly. Could ruin friendships."

"And with that in mind," said Narinda, "if I could just chat with Jeremy for a few minutes. Important though this all is..."

"Is no one listening to me?" said Ben.

"Don't think so," said Nerys.

"I was constructing a lovely little building."

"It fell over. End of."

"He slammed the door!"

"It wasn't deliberate."

"He was out of the room when it wasn't one of the allotted toilet breaks!"

"I went to answer the door!"

"And whose fault was that? Who hired this woman, huh?"

"It wasn't me!" said Nerys.

"Trying to hide it now?" said Clovenhoof.

"I can assure you that no one hired me to do anything," said Narinda.

The three of them glared at one another with poorly contained fury.

"Lennox!" growled Ben.

"Lennox!" replied Nerys with passionate righteousness.

"Lennox," said Clovenhoof darkly.

As one, they stood.

"Can someone explain to me what's going on?" said Narinda.

"In the beginning," said Clovenhoof cheerfully, "the Almighty created the world and his first big mistake, in my opinion, was the –"

Nerys punched him in the arm and smiled at Narinda.

"We're off to the pub. Ms Shah. You look like you could do with a drink. Ben, put some clothes on."

Ben put fingertips to his jelly-smeared chest. "But I'm still sticky and unpleasant."

"All the more reason to cover it up."

CHAPTER SEVEN

Rutspud watched as Belphegor flipped a toggle on the sin detector and it began to hum. The wing-like sensor rods on the side rose into position.

"As we know," said Belphegor, "sin is formed from discrete particles of spiritual matter than come into existence in the presence of wrongdoing."

"Sin, I've always thought," said Thomas Aquinas in the drawn-out tones of one about to begin a much-loved lecture, "is essentially the absence of good. The Almighty can create only good things so evil things must simply represent an absence, a turning away."

"Yes, what a lovely notion," butted in Belphegor. "Utterly wrong but lovely. Sin is real. It is real and measurable. It has its own scent, doesn't it, Rutspud?"

"Certainly does."

"It spontaneously comes into existence in the presence of wrongdoing and sticks to the sinful. The unpleasantness of sin clings to them all and is detectable no matter how one tries to cover it up," said Belphegor. "Acts of confession, contrition and the granting of indulgences causes this sin to diminish or dissipate. When a person is absolved of their sins, they are both metaphorically and literally washed clean. It is the presence of sin, or indeed lack of it, that determines who goes Down and who goes Up. Have a shufti, Rutspud."

Belphegor passed the detector to his underling. Rutspud jumped down from his still-smouldering chair and began to scan the room. He watched the wing sensors and the light-up dials as he waved it over walls, floors, furnishings and occupants. He noted with absolute delight how the good folk seated at the table each stiffened slightly as he neared. He chuckled inwardly; everyone had something to hide.

"The normal order of things is that those with sin still clinging to them after such purgatorial services they're entitled to come to us in Hell," said Belphegor.

"The place must be a filthy sea of the stuff," said Pius with a sneer that was delight and disgust in equal measure.

"No. Invisible or not, we can't have it sloshing around, clogging things up. The dead are not sinners. They have sinned in life but now they have faced judgement and sin no more. Before his departure, Satan was the great attractor. Sins would fly from the damned to him."

"And then what happened to the sin?" said Gabriel.

"Nothing. Well, back in the day he liked to do a bit of walking the earth and tempting the faithful, which basically entailed flinging clods of sin at people and seeing what would stick. But otherwise it just stayed with him. He was evil personified, made flesh. He became more and more sinful until..."

"Until what?" said Joan.

"Until you fired him and sent his sinful carcass to earth where I'm sure he's been spreading it around with joyful abandon. Meanwhile, in Hell, we've just had to adapt and find other ways to scrape the sin from new arrivals."

Rutspud recalled the air nozzles arranged around the concrete gateway into Hell. Sin extractors then, he thought.

"*We* have a thorough control of our sin situation," said Belphegor. "The sinful come to us and become the eternally damned. This recent problem, I suspect, is all due to sloppy screening on your part. Rutspud. Readings?"

Rutspud looked up.

"Nothing, boss."

"Nothing?"

He waved the detector about. "Nothing."

Thomas Aquinas giggled in embarrassed relief. "Well, of course there's nothing. This is the Celestial City after all."

"What about that pile of money?" said Belphegor. "There's always some residual sin clinging to –"

"Nothing, boss. Not even a picopeccadillo."

The peccadillo was the basic unit of minor sin. In one peccadillo there were one thousand millipeccadillos, or indeed a trillion picopeccadillos. Going up, there were a thousand peccadillos in a peccado, a major sin. A thousand major sins made a kilopeccado. A million made a megapeccado.

Hell had been able to create much more refined and balanced torture since establishing a standard system of measurement. Sin was still sin, and it was still correct to say that two wrongs didn't make a right but at least you could measure which one was biggest with some accuracy.

"And yet there are, you say, evil people in Heaven?" mused Belphegor.

"We didn't say evil as such," said Joan.

"Just not *our* sort of people," said Pius.

"*Our* people don't shoot at archangels," said Gabriel.

"You're fifteen minutes from fabulous, dear," said a voice from behind Gabriel's chair.

"Well, you'd best hope that someone somewhere has made a mistake," said Belphegor, "otherwise you're stuck with these characters."

"Surely, we just need them to slip up," said Pius, "catch them doing wrong –"

Gabriel coughed loudly and emphatically.

"Twelve minutes to fabulous," said the tailor-angel. "Beauty takes time."

"Catch them doing wrong and then what?" said Belphegor. "Just as with the damned in Hell they've already passed through judgement. You can't judge them again. You can't punish them."

"Actually, I might have an idea about that," said Rutspud.

"I still say it's Satan's fault," said Gabriel.

Belphegor chuckled grimly. "You know that old joke then."

"What old joke?"

"Knowing that his end was near, Stalin wrote two letters to his would-be successor, Khrushchev, telling him to open them, one at a time, when things got bad and the wolves were at his door. In Soviet Russia that didn't take long to come around. Khrushchev opened the first letter from Stalin. It read, 'Blame everything on me.'"

"Oh. I see. Very funny."

"Of course, the next crisis wasn't very far away and Khrushchev soon opened the second letter."

"What did it say?" asked the archangel.

"Just three simple words," said Belphegor. "'Write two letters.'"

CHAPTER EIGHT

On the way out of the house, Narinda pointed at the table where they sorted their post.

"Do you not open your mail?" she asked.

"Oh, I have a system," said Clovenhoof. "If it looks like a parcel, I open it straight away. If it looks like a hand-written letter, I try to guess the horoscope sign and favourite sexual position of the person who's written it. If it looks dull, I throw it to the back. Sometimes I have a look and see who it's addressed to, but that's if I'm feeling really organised."

"If I may," she said, scooping up a dozen of the topmost letters and bringing them along as they stepped out onto the pavement. "Here, look."

She passed Clovenhoof a brown envelope.

"From us, at HMRC. If you'd opened it, you'd know that you owe close to a million pounds in income tax."

"Taking the cosplayer to the pub," said Nerys. "And she's staying in character. This one's gold. Where did you find her, Ben?"

Ben cradled the rules folder in his arms and flipped back and forth, marking the relevant parts by slotting in pieces of paper.

"Not one of mine," he said.

"There is also a footnote to the letter that says a squashed squirrel cannot be submitted as a tax return," said Narinda.

"That's a good forgery," observed Clovenhoof, looking over her shoulder. He had come to appreciate a decent fake document since they had been playing The Game.

"I am confused how you were able to make so much money from a cat cremation service," said Narinda, conversationally. "I looked at one of your adverts, and to make the amount of money that you have, you would need to have cremated at least fifteen million cats in the last tax year. As I understand it, there are only around nine million cats in the whole of the United Kingdom, and at least some of them are still alive. Look, here is your most recent tax demand."

They trailed down the road. While Nerys argued loudly that the scale of cheating should be considered and have a suitably weighted punishment, Clovenhoof spent the time securing the spare volcano cards back up his sleeve and ignoring Narinda and her boring questions about net and gross income.

"Oh, it's some special promotion night tonight," said Nerys as they arrived outside. "*Sanatogen and Sangria. Spanish themed evening for the over sixties.* The place will be chocka!"

They entered warily, not wanting to be trampled by over-stimulated oldies. Lennox stood at the bar overlooking a completely empty pub.

"Where are all the pensioners?" asked Clovenhoof.

"Alan Titchmarsh signing in the town," said Lennox gloomily. "That celebrity gardener's like old-lady catnip. And I went to an effort – little wicker donkeys, romantic tea light candles on the tables."

"Never mind. Means you get an easy night of it."

"And no takings. Keeping a pub financially afloat isn't easy."

"Reckon it'd be a piece of piss," said Clovenhoof. "Even thought about making you an offer on this place."

"Half a million pounds. If you've got it, mate..."

He certainly has not," said Narinda.

"Anyway, Lennox my man, it means that you're free to help us. We have a situation that needs resolving, just as soon as we all have a drink in our hands."

Lennox was already on the case and moments later Clovenhoof sipped on a delicious Lambrini, while Ben had a cider and black, Nerys had a large chardonnay and Narinda had a glass of tap water.

"Water?" said Clovenhoof.

"I'm driving," said Narinda. "This was meant to be a flying visit on the way home."

"But we're in a pub."

"I don't have to drink just because we're in a pub."

"I think you do. It's the law or something." He shook his head, bewildered. "I didn't even know pubs did water."

"So, the things you need to know, Lennox," said Nerys. "First, Jeremy was caught red-handed with a load of fake cards up his sleeve. The ones that let him cancel flights with a volcano ash cloud."

"You will need to study paragraphs four and five on this page," said Ben, pointing at the folder.

Lennox put on his reading glasses.

"Next thing you need to know is that Jeremy knocked over Ben's building by slamming the door when he came in the room," said Nerys.

"Act of God," said Lennox, without looking up.

"Good one!" chortled Clovenhoof.

"Don't let's forget that Nerys owes me money, and wasn't able to pay," said Clovenhoof.

Narinda nudged him in the ribs. She had another letter. This was one out of a white envelope with a jolly cartoon pound sign logo.

"*You* owe money. You have a loan against the house, one you haven't paid in several months. You owe nine thousand pounds there. I assume you're aware of this. And then this one." Narinda pulled out another prop letter. "Here's one – no, one of one, two, three... well, several letters from a debt collection agency."

"Yeah, yeah," said Clovenhoof.

"So, did Nerys do a strip forfeit?" asked Lennox. "That's her usual."

"How can it count?" asked Ben. "We've all seen Nerys naked too many times now for it to be a worthwhile forfeit."

"Yeah, but you haven't changed the rules to reflect that," said Lennox, pushing his glasses up his nose with a finger.

"It is a mystery to me why it appears that you are struggling financially and yet you clearly have undisclosed millions somewhere," said Narinda.

Clovenhoof wasn't yet sure what Narinda's role in The Game was. He wished she'd get to the point. Or start her strip if that was her plan, he wasn't fussed either way.

Nerys thumped the bar in front of Lennox. "I think we're overlooking Ben's forfeit."

"My forfeit?" said Ben.

"You made a building with bad foundations, if it was so easy for Jeremy to knock over. You should still pay a forfeit."

"Says what rule?"

"Well, if you stopped hogging the rules book, maybe I'd find it."

Narinda held up a letter for Clovenhoof to see.

"And this. Your house is being repossessed, Jeremy. Are you aware?"

"Okay, drama college. You've played your part. The adults are drinking now. You can knock off the act."

To make his point, he plucked the letter from her fingers and did the only thing that seemed sensible. He held it over one of the table candles and set it alight.

"You can't solve your problems by setting fire to them," said Narinda angrily.

"She's very good," said Ben.

"So, didn't you hire her?" said Nerys.

"No, did you?"

"No."

A strange sound made them all look towards the door. "Oh Twinkle!" said Nerys. "I forgot to take you out of the hamster ball! Bad mommy!"

The ball had something trapped in the opening. It was a vinyl streamer which pulled taut behind it, dragging the trolley with the model volcano. The whole procession made its way to the bar as Twinkle sought out Nerys.

"Come on my beautiful baby, let's get you out of there." As Nerys bent down to retrieve Twinkle, the flames of the burning letter reached Clovenhoof's fingertips.

"Ow!"

Ben saw where the burning paper fell.

"Duck and cover!" he shouted.

The top of the volcano began to sparkle gaily.

"Oh, not as bad as I thought," said Ben, uncurling himself from a protective ball. "Quite pretty really."

Nerys hugged Twinkle apologetically. "Yeah, but wouldn't it be just like Jeremy to start with nice sparklers and then –"

Her words were lost in the blast.

As closing time drew near, two humans, one devil and a Yorkshire terrier sat in a corner booth. Three of them had sooty scorch marks on their faces. The fourth was slightly singed around the edge. Three of them sat in stunned silence. The fourth was lapping at a bowl of pale ale. The stunned silence was a mixture of fireworks-induced deafness, the discovery that the taxwoman (who had stormed out in apoplectic and soot-streaked fury some hours before) was indeed a real taxwoman, and the discovery that one of them had, yet again, put their home at risk.

Ben sipped at his sixth cider and black of the evening and winced once more at the pink burn mark on his lip.

"It doesn't make sense."

"I know," said Clovenhoof. "The Catherine Wheel didn't go off."

"You have secured a personal loan against our house for several thousand pounds. Bailiffs are coming round to repossess everything you own and potentially evict us. And yet – and yet! – simultaneously, Her Majesty's Revenue and Customs think you are a multi-millionaire and owe them hundreds of thousands in unpaid tax. I mean, how do you do it, Jeremy?"

Clovenhoof gave him a winning smile. "You've just got to reach for the stars, hold onto your dreams and believe in yourself."

"It's literally the worst of both worlds! How are we going to find the money to pay off your loan and foot that massive tax bill?"

"We don't have to," said Nerys.

Ben turned to look at her.

"Our only concern is our home," she said coolly. "It's in joint names. Leaving aside the legality of him getting a loan against it, if we can pay off the debt-collectors, then the house is safe."

"See?" said Clovenhoof brightly. "I knew there'd be an easy solution. And the tax bill thingy, Nerys? What about that?"

"That's your problem. Do you like prison food?"

Clovenhoof was not impressed. Ben seemed to be nothing but impressed.

"Wow."

"What a cold-hearted cow," said Clovenhoof. "Can you believe her, Ben?"

"I can," he said without hesitation.

He leaned across the table to her.

"So, we rustle up the money together, settle the debt and then get Jeremy to sign his share of the house over to us."

"Exactly," she said. "Now I've got some cash stashed in the flat. The last of a little bonus for shifting so many properties last year."

"Okay," nodded Ben. "And I've got my fifty pee collection."

Nerys was sceptical. "We're going to need a lot of fifty pence pieces to make – what was it? – nine thousand pounds."

"These are rare and collectable fifty pees. I check every coin that comes through the shop and put any rare ones aside. I've got more than a dozen stamped with Mrs Tiggy Winkle on the reverse. They're worth a quid or two. I've got some 2009 Kew Gardens ones that are worth at least fifty quid each. And a stack of London Olympics swimming ones and they're going for over seven hundred on eBay."

"Seven hundred pounds?"

"Each."

"Ah," said Clovenhoof, dropping that single syllable into the conversation like a concrete block on a train track.

"Ah?" said Ben.

"Ah."

"What the fuck is 'Ah'?" said Nerys, her voice rising in pre-emptive anger.

Clovenhoof took a fortifying gulp of Lambrini. "Yeah, Ben, you know when I said I borrowed some change to buy the petroleum jelly..."

"There were nearly a hundred coins in that collection. You can't tell me you bought fifty quids' worth of Vaseline."

"And some lottery scratch cards."

"You are an absolute bastard, Jeremy Clovenhoof," seethed Ben.

"And that money you've got stashed in your flat, Nerys..." said Clovenhoof.

"Yes?" she said warily.

"Which you keep in the bedside drawer underneath all your lady toys."

Nerys was shaking her head, fuming silently.

"Well, you know how you said that the toy money we've been using in The Game recently looks *almost as good as* real money?"

"You didn't! That's my money."

"Almost as good as your money."

"I'm going to kill you."

"Hey. At least I replaced it with something."

Nerys smashed her wine glass on the edge of the table, leaving a jagged stem in her hand.

"Woah," said Clovenhoof. "I can see you're upset but there's no point crying over spilt Chardonnay. Let's just talk about this like adults."

There was fire in Nerys's eyes. "Hold him down, Ben. I'm going to rip his throat out."

Clovenhoof rapidly emptied the contents of his pockets on the table. "Look! Scratch cards! Maybe there's a fortune waiting for us here."

"Can you sodding believe him?" said Nerys but reached for a scratch card anyway.

"You know, we could be the answer to each other's problems," said Clovenhoof.

"I think the evidence points to the exact opposite being true," said Ben.

"Nah, hear me out," said Clovenhoof, signalling Lennox to get another round in. "You need cash. I need to get Little Miss Tax Compliance off my back. I'm the one with the business smarts. You two are people people."

"*I'm* a people person," said Nerys.

"I know people," said Ben.

"You're a miniature wargamer," she said. "Those are not real people."

"Talk to the Shah woman. I'll get your cash," said Clovenhoof. "You scratch my back and I'll scratch yours. Speaking of which..." He looked at the foil boxes on the scratch card in his hand. "Um, do either of you have a coin?"

CHAPTER NINE

The party of demons, angels and blessed dead walking through the Celestial City towards the Heavenly Moral Records Centre drew an understandable number of gasps and looks from the general populace. Thomas Aquinas's reassurances that it was only 'a pair of foul creatures from the Bottomless Pit' were surprisingly ineffective.

As they walked, Joan inspected one of the heavenly bank notes she still carried. The intricacy of the note's design was beguiling. All those finely executed swirls of green ink encouraged one to think of it as a thing of value and meaning, a thing to be respected, loved and accumulated. Joan hated it. But she couldn't put it away.

"Do you have money in Hell?" she said.

"What would we spend it on?" said Rutspud, pointing the sin detector in different directions as he walked.

Joan spotted a familiar sight ahead.

"Scan him."

"Who?"

"Him."

"Which one?"

"The one with the sign that says 'Gin and Whores'."

"Ah. Okay."

Rutspud ran up to the man and waved his detector wand.

"Oi, oi, mate," said the Gin and Whores man. "How's tricks? Don't see many of your type around here."

"I'm a demon," said Rutspud, concentrating on the device readings.

"I think you'll find you're a discerning customer, mate. Perchance I can interest you in some gin or whores?"

"Whores..." said Rutspud. "Remind me?"

"Priceless. You a young man of the world and not knowing what whores is. The ones I can interest you in are the sweetest bit of totty in this corner of the afterlife. Women? Girls?"

"He's asking if you'd like to have sexual congress with women," explained Joan. "In exchange for money, of course."

"Oh, I see," said Rutspud, clearly giving some thought. "It's really not my thing but..." He looked at the man. "How much are you willing to pay me?"

The man was mentally thrown and momentarily speechless. Rutspud showed the detector readouts to Joan. They meant nothing to her.

"He's clean," said Rutspud.

"Clean?"

"Sinless."

Joan's opinion of Hell's technology took a nosedive. "He just tried to sell you sexual favours. Prostitution. Fornication."

"And it scores zilch," said the diminutive demon.

"That's just strange," said Joan.

"Says the woman expecting to find sinners in the Celestial City."

The pair of them hurried to catch up with Gabriel, Thomas and Belphegor who had reached the steps of the Moral Records Centre.

"We will find the truth here," said Gabriel. "We keep meticulous records on every individual in creation. Every sin, every virtuous act."

Belphegor's wheelchair gave a smoke-spewing roar of acceleration and powered up the steps to the door.

"That's a lot of sins to record," he said.

"They are a busy department indeed," said Gabriel, holding the door open for them all to enter.

The space inside was bigger than the building outside could possibly accommodate. Beneath a circular glass dome that let in the golden light of Heaven's glory, vast rows of shelves filled a hall larger than any cathedral on earth. Next to Joan, Rutspud put his head back to take in the towering wooden shelves of scrolls and tomes and only stopped when he got a crick in his neck. Angel workers fluttered between shelves, their arms weighed heavily with manuscripts.

"The recording angels," said Gabriel. "Recording the good and the bad and submitting souls to psychostasia."

Two flying angels approached an industrial-sized set of brass scales hanging from the ceiling by an anchor chain. The angels each deposited their loads in opposing scales and a metal needle the size of a church spire, wobbled left then right.

"And another soul is granted entrance to the Celestial City," said Gabriel happily, "after some minor purgatorial cleansing. A little scrub up."

"Yes, yes, lovely," said Belphegor. "All delightfully metaphorical and symbolic. I was expecting something a little more precise."

"The devils are all about the details," said Thomas, critically.

"We are fond of actual facts, yes," said Belphegor.

"Then you'll be delighted to discover that one of our brightest and best is helping us make a transition to the digital age," said Gabriel.

A bearded saint dressed in huntsman's garb and a red felt hat bounded out from between the shelves with an almighty and very self-satisfied "Booyah!" of greeting.

"May I introduce St Hubertus," said Gabriel.

The huntsman gave the archangel a slap on the back that sent his halo spinning.

"The jägermeister is in the house!" grinned Hubertus. "High fives for all!"

The man then did a quick circuit of the group, giving each individual a hearty high-five, apart from Thomas Aquinas who refused and got a playful cheek slap instead. Belphegor held out his hand but was given special treatment. Hubertus gave the demon lord's stomach a speedy and impertinent mini-massage.

"Belly-Belly-Belphegor. How's it hanging, dude?" He turned to the others. "This guy. This guy! We go way back."

"Sadly," said Belphegor.

"Worked on some crossover projects together. This demon works hard but he plays hard too. Huh? Huh? Am I right?"

"I've genuinely no idea what he's talking about," said Belphegor dourly and Hubertus apparently found this uproariously funny. He even held his stomach with both hands as he laughed which, in Joan's experience, was something no real person actually did.

"Hubertus..." began Gabriel but was cut off by another halo-dislodging backslap.

"You've come to see sin central, right?" said the ever-cheerful saint. "The inner sanctum through which every dirty little deed passes? Right? Yeah!"

A deer with a glowing crucifix between its antlers had appeared behind Hubertus.

"Hirsch-baby," said Hubertus, "get a round of drinks in for our guests."

The deer bleated questioningly.

"A round of shots for starters," said Hubertus. "Then let's see where the mood takes us."

The deer galloped off.

Grinning, Hubertus waved everyone towards a set of descending stairs. "Come into my lair, *meine Gäste*."

As the group followed, Rutspud sidled up to Joan.

"Okay, I've got some questions about that guy," he said. "Starting with 'what?' and moving onto 'seriously, what?'"

"Hubertus is one of various patron saints of hunting," she explained.

"I got that."

"Hirsch. That's the holy deer that turned him to the faith. Hirsch gets around a bit. Does a lot of good work."

"Fair enough. And he's in charge of this place because...?"

"He's also patron saint of accountants and mathematicians."

"Right. But the wonderful but probably quite-soon-to-be very irritating frat boy attitude? That's...?"

"Yes, well, that's a recent thing," said Joan. "An alcoholic drink manufacturer decided to use some of Hubertus's iconography on its bottles."

"A party drink, yeah?"

"That is the odd thing," Joan conceded. "It's a digestif, made from herbs and spices. The kind of thing working class German grandads would have to settle their stomach. And then bizarrely, overnight, every party hound and student boozer is downing them like they're the hippest thing in creation."

"A bit of saintly intercession?" suggested Rutspud, nodding towards the strutting saint.

"Maybe," said Joan. "There's no other rational explanation."

They had descended into a modern office space. Computer screens dominated the walls. As lights automatically came on, Hubertus tapped a touch screen.

"Voice ident required," said a mellifluous computer voice.

"Jägerbomb!" growled the saint raucously.

"Ident accepted."

A broad translucent screen came to life in front of Hubertus. He slipped his hand into something a bit like a glove or more like the skeleton a dead glove would leave behind if gloves had skeletons. He bunched his fingers and flung them out and a universe of data exploded across a score of screens in fire reds, goblin greens and neon blues.

"Magic," said Joan.

"Augmented reality gear," said Rutspud. "And I thought Hell had all the best tech. Actually, some of this looks like Hell technology..."

Graphs and records flew about the room like educated disco lights.

"You have questions, dear guests," said Hubertus. "And I have all the answers. This" – he pointed at a wavering red line on a chart – "is the current sin level. As measured at the point of judgement. Currently registering at seven point two megapeccados per second. This is the relative sin index value."

"And what's that?" asked Gabriel.

"How much each sin is worth."

"The value of sins may go down as well as up," said Belphegor.

"Surely, a sin is a sin," said Thomas.

"Really, Tommo?" said Hubertus. "You sure? Is stealing fruit a big sin or a little one?"

Thomas blustered. "Well, really, it's all about context and the, er..."

"A sin is a sin, you said."

"It's a little one. A little sin."

"And yet..." Hubertus flung his hand out and a graphical representation of humanity's early history appeared overhead. "When Adam and Eve took from the Tree of Knowledge, the value of sin went off the chart. The good folk of earth are still catching residual fallout from that even to this day."

"In virtuous times, each sin weighs more heavily," nodded Joan, understanding. "But in sinful times, everyone is given a bit more grace."

"Simple market forces," said Hubertus. "So, specifics? You're itching to tap into my expertise."

"Our... counterparts from Hell," said Gabriel, "are under the impression –"

"Very much an impression," added Thomas.

"– that we've got some individuals in the Celestial City who should have gone down instead of up."

"But certainly not due to any error on our part," said Thomas.

Belphegor had his tablet screen out and with a tap and a swish, the images and details of the suspiciously unvirtuous joined the data on the big screens. Lines of connection of all the colours of the spectrum, created a web between individuals and moments in recent earth history.

"Who slept with who and borrowed from where," said Hubertus. "And who partied the hardest. Ha!"

"So, they're sinners?" said Joan hopefully.

Hubertus gave her a reproachful look and the tiniest hint of a playful come-on. "There is such a thing as forgiveness, Joan." With a wrist twist, the data span and became a landscape of projection lines and possibilities. "Some were indeed Hell-bound but throw in some extenuating circumstances and a couple of Christmas Carol changes of heart..." He brought the data back to the original line graph. "They're all squeaky clean and exactly where they should be."

The profile pictures of the unlikely but apparently virtuous slid across the screen into a tidy pile of data windows, stacked away, dismissed as irrelevant.

"That line," said Rutspud. "The amount of sin. It is going down. So, we are definitely seeing a drop off of people coming into Hell?"

"The level of sin fluctuates naturally," said Hubertus.

"Fluctuates naturally," echoed Thomas.

"It goes up in summer when passions rise. It decreases in cold periods."

"Cyclical," said Thomas.

"Hell's gates are rammed in August," agreed Rutspud. "So you can show this decline is temporary by extending the range of the data."

"Sure," said Hubertus and drew his glove round to the left, zooming out. "Hmmm." He pulled out further. "Hmmm." A third zoom. "Oh. This doesn't look good, does it?"

Hubertus's worried reverie was momentarily broken by the arrival of a deer with a silver tray laden with shot glasses wedged in its horns. Without taking his eyes from the screens, Hubertus reached over, took a glass and necked the liqueur. He then repeated this nine further times.

"Nope," he coughed. "Not made it any better."

To Joan's eyes, the story of the graph was very clear. After an initial explosion of sin at the beginning of time the line meandered like an unhurried snake across the course of human history only to take a sharp but unmistakeable dive off a cliff at some point in the last few months.

"Sin's going down," she said.

"It's cyclical," insisted Thomas Aquinas.

"That cycle's got a flat," said Rutspud. "What's happened?"

"Look," said Thomas, "we've just emerged from a period of high sin. A lot of wars in sandy countries. A lot of drugs. Sin is falling."

"Did *everyone* just stop taking drugs?" said Rutspud.

"And then you've got some things that are only just being reclassified from sinful to not. There's a lot of buggery in there that's not being counted anymore. Could it be that?"

"Are you trying to argue that there hasn't been a decrease in sin?" said Joan, astounded. "Look at the data."

"Yes," wheedled the fat saint, "but how reliable is that data? When did accurate records really start?"

"Why are you so keen to sweep this problem under the rug?" said Rutspud.

"Laziness," said Belphegor, who was Lord of Sloth among other things so probably knew what he was talking about.

"I might ask *you*," said Thomas, "why you're so keen for there to be a problem? What have you got to gain?"

"What is there to be gained?" said Rutspud.

"That is the question. I sense a conspiracy."

"I sense an idiot."

"Come, come, friends," said Gabriel. "It's certain something is a bit awry."

"There's a lot of absolution flags on these people," mused Herbertus slightly drunkenly. "We ought to cross-reference with the prayer assessment people."

"Clearly," continued Gabriel, "something has happened in the recent past to cause this."

"I can tell you one thing that has happened," said Belphegor.

"What?"

"You lot banished Satan to earth along with every crumb of sin that was clinging to him. And I imagine he's not spent the meantime doing good deeds in the community."

CHAPTER TEN

The newspaper man at the door passed Clovenhoof a copy of the Sutton Observer from his hi-vis shoulder bag.

"That'll be thirty quid please," said Clovenhoof.

"Pardon?" said the newspaper man.

"Thirty quid. It goes up to sixty quid if you take more than seven days to pay."

"What are you talking about?"

Clovenhoof tapped the sign beside the front door to four-hundred-and-something Chester Road.

"Last night, I was trying to think of ways to make money. And I thought, how do we make money from each other in The Game?"

"The Game?" said the newspaper man, taking off his glasses to read the tiny font on the sign.

"Yes. Its proper name is utterly unpronounceable. You travel round this square board landing on properties, buying them up and then charging the other players rent if they land on them. They really should do an English language version. It's surprising that they haven't."

"'By stopping here, you are entering a contract to pay for parking slash residency slash ground rental services,'" read the newspaper man.

"Yes," said Clovenhoof. "It's like those private car parks. As long as there's a sign up, I can charge you anything. Apparently."

"But I'm not parking here," said the newspaper man. "My conscience is clear. Even if it wasn't, I've got a phone app that sorts it out for me."

"You're stationary. You're here. I think it's fairly clear cut, mate. Thirty quid."

"Piss off."

"Tell you what, as the first customer of the day, let's call it a tenner, eh?"

The newspaper man stormed off, his hi-vis bag swinging angrily behind him.

Clovenhoof put the newspaper on the side table and then took his box of equipment out onto the pavement. He marked off a long stretch of pavement outside the house with yellow spray paint and filled it with a cross hatch of lines. He then placed his prepared signs against the garden walls at either end of the section.

PAVEMENT TOLL-ZONE. £5 EACH WAY
You are on CCTV. Face-recognition is in effect.

He then chained the honesty cash box to the gatepost of the house and, with a little scrambling and grunting, wedged his CCTV camera into the lintel above the front door. It wasn't actually a CCTV camera – it was a chunky shampoo bottle that he'd painted white with Tippex – but it looked authentic enough.

He was very pleased with himself and, as a reward, took himself down to the Boldmere high street to have a slap-up Full English breakfast and to peruse the Births, Deaths and Marriages section at the back of the newspaper.

Afterwards, he sauntered down to the little hardware store and then the charity shop to make some essential purchases before dropping into Ben's shop, *Books 'n' Bobs*. Ben was at the counter with a customer, a book between them. Normally, at the prospect of actually selling a book, Ben would be beaming with delight, but Clovenhoof could clearly see that Ben was uncomfortable.

"Have you read this?" the woman asked. She was tiny and clutched a tartan shopping trolley. These women only came out during the day, menacing the ankles of Boldmere. Clovenhoof had often wondered whether he should buy one of those trolleys and perhaps enhance it with spinning knives on the axles, maybe even reupholster it in leopard skin or something equally tasteful.

"No," said Ben. "I haven't."

"I need to know if it's properly hardcore," said the woman. "I don't want it if it's just soppy."

"Hardcore?" said Ben, glancing at the cover. "Let's see. *Beating Around the Bush*. The cover art makes me think that it might be a little bit, um racy, yes. A lot of leather there. What did you have in mind, when you say hardcore?"

"The usual. A bit of S&M, some girl on girl action, three in a bed maybe, raunchy actions with knobs on."

"Yeees," said Ben slowly. "All the trimmings, yes."

"And knobs," she said. "I want proper throbbing cocks, not just bulging manhoods. Surely it's not too much to ask?"

"Of course. Why don't you take a seat and have a flick through before you buy?" said Ben faintly, waving the woman across to an armchair.

"My kind of gal," observed Clovenhoof as the woman pulled out her reading glasses and settled into the chair. "So, you worked out how to get the tax office off my case?"

"Nerys says she has a plan. Apparently, I am an integral part. No idea what it is but she's dropping by later." Ben looked down at Clovenhoof's purchases. "And these? Integral to your moneymaking plans?"

Clovenhoof considered the wheelbarrow and spade he'd bought.

"Gonna make me a minor fortune."

"And the black top hat?"

"To add a bit of dignity to proceedings."

"You and dignity aren't exactly well acquainted, Jeremy."

Clovenhoof blew a raspberry. "Just because I'm a bold and dominant figure of a man, unafraid to cross social boundaries."

"I like a dominant man," came a quavering voice from over his shoulder. The old woman was out of her chair, looking him up and down. "No, I think I'll give it a miss," she said, inexplicably disappointed with what she saw.

"Hey, it's not the state of the bodywork you should be looking at but what's under the bonnet," he said. "I'm a seasoned gigolo. And I specialise in the over seventies."

She slapped down some money onto the counter.

"I'm bringing this back if it's not got throbbing cocks in it," she told Ben.

"I've got a throbbing cock," Clovenhoof called after her as she left with her book and trolley. "Call Jeremy for all your gigoloing needs." She didn't even look round. "Can you believe that?" he said to Ben.

"I know. I'm sure little old ladies didn't use to be so vulgar," said Ben. "The world has become a cruder place."

"We do our best," said Clovenhoof.

Nerys entered the shop, hands full, looking over her shoulder. "Jeez, that blind bat nearly had me with her shopping trolley. Was she looking for the opticians?"

"No, she was looking for a little excitement in her life," said Clovenhoof. "I could go after her. Do you reckon she's got false teeth? I've always wondered how that –"

"Seriously, no!" said Ben. "Just take your barrow and go get us some cash."

"What's the barrow for?" said Nerys.

"The body, of course," said Clovenhoof. He unfolded his morning newspaper. He'd circled a number of likely candidates. "Best be off. And what have you got there?"

Nerys held up the electrical device. It looked like a cross between a deep fat fryer and a foot spa. "Hot wax."

Ben was shaking his head.

"Waxing yourself's got to be painful. I'm surprised that women put themselves through it."

"Yeah, about that," said Nerys, giving him a very meaningful look.

Clovenhoof cross-referenced the notices page of the newspaper with his Google search and the satnav on his phone, wheeled his barrow up the right driveway and knocked on the door. At the last moment, he remembered the top hat and slapped it on his head.

A youngish woman in a black pant suit answered the door. "Yes?"

"Pick up for Mr Douglas Cook," said Clovenhoof.

The woman looked at the wheelbarrow, tried to process Clovenhoof's words and gave up.

"Wh-what?"

"Mr Douglas Cook. He still here?"

The woman came onto the step, drew the door to a little behind her and lowered her voice.

"Douglas - my father-in-law – he's dead."

"Yes."

"The funeral's today."

"That's right." Clovenhoof checked the notice he'd circled in the paper. "At eleven. I thought I'd get here early."

"Early?" She still didn't get it. "Who are you?"

"Jeremy Clovenhoof." He tipped his hat. "Semi-professional funeral services."

"You're from the funeral directors."

"I'm from *a* funeral directors," he said. "Past tense. It burned down. A funny story. I was only sixty, maybe seventy percent responsible. Who did you go with for the funeral?"

"Manpreet Singh Funerals."

"Ah, Manpreet set up by himself after the fire, did he? Excellent. Great chap. Real sense of customer service. Charges a pretty penny too though I should think."

The woman didn't look like any of this was sinking in. Her face was going all wobbly. Clovenhoof wasn't a great reader of human emotion and couldn't decide if she was going to burst into tears or punch him in the face. People had done both in the past, sometimes simultaneously.

"Are you familiar with the term funeral gazumping?" he said.

"What? No."

"That's because I just invented it. Now, I reckon Manpreet will have charged you around four grand for the kind of funeral service your old pop-in-law deserved. But, for the knock down price of three hundred knicker, I can have him in a hole before lunchtime and get in the first round at the wake. What do you say?"

The face-wobbliness continued. The woman was keeping it all in for the time being but Clovenhoof estimated that it would all come pouring out at high pressure very, very soon. Best close the deal.

"I've got a plot lined up, I've got the tools. All we need to do is slap the old man in the barrow and scarper before Manpreet's lot get here. You don't want to see a funeral service turf war. It's not a pretty sight."

At that point the woman hit him. First with her hands, then with a flowerpot and then with Clovenhoof's own spade. She hit him so hard it snapped the spade in two. This was a bit of a disappointment and Clovenhoof had to nip back to the hardware store to buy a new one before trying the next house on his list.

CHAPTER ELEVEN

Many individuals failed to realise how big a deal prayer was. With billions of faithful individuals on earth, many of them offering up dozens of prayers, spoken and unspoken, every day, the volume of messages, pleas and queries to the great hereafter was massive. The Celestial City contained an entire district devoted to prayer handling. There was the General Devotion Centre, the Intercessionary Plea Hub, the Non-Specific Prayer Assessment Unit, the Supplications and Applications Decision Force and a dozen other buildings, filled with call handlers, assessment committees and teams devoted to either granting or ignoring the prayers of the living. And, because this was a place of work, the district also buzzed with the coffee stands, lunch halls, restaurants and other little outlets that any workforce required during their downtime. That workforce, by tradition, was made up of minor angels and deleted saints who had no other function in the afterlife.

The Forgiveness Archives (motto, 'Ask, and you shall receive') was a long, low building staffed entirely by Saint Ursula and the eleven thousand virgin handmaidens who were martyred alongside her in third century Cologne. The Church on earth had decreed that, historically speaking, none of them had ever existed which Joan guessed was one of the reasons why every single one of the women there had a sour and miserable look on her face. The fact that St Ursula and an uncertain number of her companions were put to death by bow and arrow and here was the hunter Hubertus riding into their lobby on a stag probably had something to do with it too.

The investigative party of saints, angels and demons followed Hubertus in. At the counter, the patron saint of hunting vaulted from the back of his deer, landed drunkenly on the floor and overcompensated in his recovery, throwing in some jazz hands to mask his idiocy.

He peered at the badge pinned to the woman's tunic.

"Handmaiden four-four-oh-six. What a lovely name! I'm –"

"We know who you are," she said curtly. "What do you want? We're very busy."

Joan looked at the hundreds of virginal clerks wheeling trolleys of paperwork between shelves and filing cabinets. None of them appeared to be in any kind of hurry.

"We've got some absolution flags in the Moral Records Centre that we'd like to cross reference."

"Details," said the virgin.

Hubertus pulled out a glass tablet device, swiped it and a hologram of informational representation appeared in the air above it. It spun like nightclub lights.

It took Joan a moment to realise that Hubertus instinctively gave the display a little background beat, a throaty "boots 'n' cats 'n' boots 'n' cats" soundtrack. Next to her, Rutspud threw in an accompanying "um-cha, um-cha, um-cha" and some rhythmic footwork.

"Stop that," said the virgin.

Hubertus stopped. He pointed at a number of white call-out boxes in his data. "These. There's quite a lot of them.

The virgin assistant began to copy down numbers and called out to one of her colleagues to help.

Joan turned to Rutspud. "You said you had an idea about how we could deal with our... less virtuous guests."

"I did," said Rutspud. "It's quite clever, even if I do say so myself."

"Yes?"

"I was thinking that you don't want these people in the City."

"I didn't say that."

"But you don't. You want them out of the picture. You want rid of them."

"I think we should always be willing to welcome people with open arms and hearts filled –"

"Okay, drop the lovey-dovey crap, Joan. I know what you're obliged to say but you want them gone. You want to exclude them."

Joan bit down on the words that came too naturally and found what she really wanted to say.

"Yes," she admitted.

"And these are people who want to live the lives of sickening excess the rich and powerful enjoy back on earth."

"Yes."

"Well, that's good news," said Rutspud. "You see, the rich and powerful like anything that's 'exclusive'."

Joan frowned. It was a frown of near-comprehension, the wonder at seeing a jigsaw puzzle half done.

"Explain."

Rutspud rubbed his hands together. "I'll just need some paper, something to write with and access to a photocopier."

Belphegor had sidled up to listen in, although it was hardly sidling given that he was driving a chugging piston-powered wheelchair.

"I've got a photocopier in here somewhere." He pulled out a lap tray from the arm and spun it round to reveal a glass scanning surface. "Used it make copies of demons' poker work for analysis. Ah, the number of damned arses I've had sat in this lap... so, what's the plan, Rutspud?"

"It's not very complicated but I will need some help. To work, it relies on the rich thinking they're going to get access to something available to no one else."

CHAPTER TWELVE

Clovenhoof had spent the entire day trying to gazump funerals with zero take-up. It wasn't a complete bust, because one angry widow had thrown a whole Edam cheese at him. He sat on the wall outside the crematorium, eating cheese and wondered why the bargain-hunters of Sutton Coldfield were so resistant to a last-minute change of plan when it could save them so much money.

"What have you been trying to do, Jeremy?"

He turned to see his old boss approaching. His benign face was distorted into a frown.

"Manpreet! Good to see you. Have some Edam. What sort of drugs have you been slipping your customers? There's brand loyalty and then there's blind devotion."

"Funeral gazumping?" said the usually chilled out undertaker. "It's a new low, even for you. Did you ever stop to wonder why you never hear of such a thing?"

"Because I am the first genius to come up with the idea?" ventured Clovenhoof.

"No, because it's ridiculous. Ethically, you couldn't really get any lower."

"Why thank you, my friend."

"Take funeral crashers," said Manpreet, clearly on a roll now. "I always thought they were the lowest form of life, but you..."

"Funeral crashing?"

"People who go to the funerals of people they don't know just to get free food and drink," said Manpreet. "Taking advantage of the recently bereaved –"

"– and that all-important English politeness," said Clovenhoof thoughtfully.

"Yes, it's despicable. Now back off. I don't want you bothering any more of my customers, understand?"

Clovenhoof nodded absently as Manpreet stalked off. His thoughts turned immediately to free food and booze and he pulled the newspaper back out to see where the next opportunity would be. Frustratingly, the notices didn't always include details of the after-party, but Clovenhoof prided himself on his lateral thinking skills. There was a service underway at the crematorium right now. Maybe funeral crashing was just a case of light speculative fishing.

He wandered back into the crematorium and slipped into the back row, knowing that an invite to 'join us for some light refreshments' would follow the main event.

He settled down for a spot of people watching. The assembled mourners were dressed in the manner of the wealthy upper classes, which meant that the men favoured ancient woollen suits with an acrid whiff of mothballs while the women formed two groups. Some were skinny and wore fashionable dresses with high heels and others wore more matronly garments with large chunky necklaces: definitely upper-class types or super-upper-middle-class types. And yet, his time working at the funeral parlour, Clovenhoof recognised a coffin that was so cheap it wasn't even in the standard brochure. It looked like a piece of flatpack furniture. Interesting.

A middle-aged long streak of piss of a man walked to the front as the vicar finished talking reedily about the Valley of the Shadow of Death. Clovenhoof had always assumed it was an ancient euphemism for a bum crack, especially with those outrageous 'rod and staff' references. He'd never got round to asking the Almighty about that; he made a note to do so one day.

"Well we all know the score for today, don't we, eh?" drawled the long streak of piss. "Old Claymore Ferret's bought the farm. Probably bought it for a knock down price and paid off the surveyors to lie in their report. And he's finally promoted yours truly to the position of senior Ferret. Watch out, ladies! Maldon's at the helm. Now, I'm pencilled in to talk about the many ways in which I loved and respected him, blah blah. Sounds all a bit touchy-feely to me. Don't think I ought to do that. A rum thing and no mistake. Might catch gay or something. No. The only way I can think to describe our relationship is to borrow a saying from the bumper sticker he had on his favourite safari jeep: 'How can I miss you if you won't go away?'."

There was a brief flurry of nervous laughter throughout the room. Clovenhoof wondered why more funeral services weren't this good.

The younger Ferret warmed to his theme. "So, unlike the cancer, he finally *has* gone away, and so far, I haven't missed him at all. But, as the bumper sticker on his second favourite safari jeep said 'I told my ex-wife I missed her. But I'll get her next time'." He laughed at his own joke and slapped the lectern. "Right, I think we can conclude our business here."

The vicar gave a brief nod of respect and walked back to the lectern.

"No," said Ferret. "I mean we don't need any more hymns or prayers or anything. Let's wrap things up, shall we? Press the button, pater, and then we'll go and soak up some booze to remember the old goat."

The vicar looked appalled, but he reached for the control panel on the wall anyway.

"Come on, chaps," said Ferret, waving his arm for the guests to join in. "Three! Two! One! Blast off!"

The vicar pressed a button and a curtain slid slowly toward the coffin.

"How bloody slow is that?" Ferret huffed impatiently. "No wonder we didn't win the space race." He went over to the control panel and stabbed at all the buttons. While the curtain hadn't got halfway round, the coffin slid backwards into an opening.

Ferret beamed at the congregation. "Right! Cars are outside. We're off for some light refreshments at a place called the Boldmere Oak. Last one there's a socialist."

Clovenhoof followed the small crowd out to where a row of limos was waiting. The first two were quickly filled with a chattering crowd, leaving a small group of couples. An elderly gent touched Clovenhoof's arm.

"You're one of the Westley-Burroughs lot, I'll wager?" he said.

"Yes?" tried Clovenhoof, not sure what he was agreeing to.

"I knew it. That ruddy complexion of yours is a dead giveaway. Come and ride with us and I'll tell you some tales about your Auntie Ray that'll make yer hair curl!"

Clovenhoof grinned and climbed into the limo.

When he walked into the Boldmere Oak, Lennox called over to him. "Oi. Closed for a private party this afternoon."

Clovenhoof walked to the bar. "Well as it happens, it's a private party that I'm invited to. What's on the menu, Lennox?" Clovenhoof searched his memory for examples of fine dining. "Pigs in blankets? Happy meals? Tell me there's going to be Crispy Pancakes?"

Lennox shook his head and whispered conspiratorially. "To be honest, the only reason I got this booking is that I advertise the cheapest rate of buffet food in the area on that local forum *suttonskinflints.net*. It's a round of cheese and pickle sandwiches and a small glass of cheap wine for you, my friend."

Clovenhoof was joined at the bar by an elderly woman with a playful smile. Her makeup was applied neatly, almost like a colour-by-numbers painting. Small circles of rouge on each cheek and crisp, pearly blue semi-circles above her eyes. Clovenhoof was reminded of a sex doll, a slightly deflated sex doll.

"By any chance, is that stuff on the tables the cheapest gut-rot that money can buy?" she asked Lennox.

Lennox opened his mouth to protest, but Clovenhoof held up a hand.

"Lennox is bound by client-patient confidentiality, but I can confirm that it is from his special collection. It turns up from time to time as a raffle prize. The wasps of Boldmere know it well, as everyone uses it in those little traps where the wasp is attracted to the faint, sickly smell of the alcohol before drowning in the toxic effluent. Actually, it might taste better when it's passed through the digestive system of a wasp. Did you ever think of that Lennox? Anyway, enjoy!"

"I'll have a G and T, thank you," said the woman to Lennox, who gave a small shrug and reached up for a glass.

"So, you're some sort of connoisseur then?" she asked Clovenhoof.

At that moment, Lennox returned with a gin and tonic in one hand and a full bottle of Lambrini in the other for Clovenhoof.

"Good God!" she said, staring at the Lambrini. "Surely there's something in the Geneva convention... They still sell that stuff?"

Clovenhoof smacked his lips. "A connoisseur indeed, madam. Nobody has a more refined appreciation of this delicious nectar than yours truly."

"How did you know Claymore Ferret?" she asked, once she had taken a sip of her drink.

"Fairly recently," said Clovenhoof, truthfully. "I didn't know him well, but I wanted to help send him off."

"Ah, yes," said the woman. "Can't blame you for that. I think a lot of people wanted to make sure he was definitely dead. Including his son, by the sound of that eulogy."

"Not a close friend of yours then?" hazarded Clovenhoof.

"We don't really move in the same circles," said the woman. "I'm Alice Calhoun by the way."

"What circles do you move in Alice?"

Alice Calhoun took a hefty swig from her drink and reflected for a moment. "Well, since my husband died, I don't even know if I have a circle, but let's just say that it's quite a few rungs down the ladder from Claymore Ferret. My sister Cynthia clawed her way up there when she was alive, but then she had the talons for it. She and Claymore were very well matched."

"Ah, your sister was Claymore Ferret's –"

"– bit of stuff yes. His, er, third I think. He managed to get onto number six before he died."

"Busy boy," said Clovenhoof appreciatively.

"He had a type," said Alice, with a significant nod across the room.

Clovenhoof looked over towards the buffet table where a small gaggle of high-heeled women hid behind sunglasses and yet made clear their disdain for the buffet, the surroundings and the company.

"Yes, I wonder what they all saw in the multi-millionaire Claymore Ferret," said Alice with a wry smile. "By all accounts, the man was an absolute pig. I mean all men have their little foibles. Take my Bill. He was a good man, kind and thoughtful, but he was terribly messy. Never could read a paper without spreading it all over the table and chairs. I was always picking towels and clothes up off the floor. And the smell! He had such a wind problem." She took another sip of her drink and stared into the glass. "I miss him so much."

"You miss his bad habits?" asked Clovenhoof.

"I do. I really do. Strange, isn't it?" said Alice.

"No, not at all strange," said Clovenhoof. "As a matter of fact, I have an established business model that caters exactly for needs like yours." It was true. It had been established for at least three seconds.

"Needs like mine?"

"Have you ever heard of gigoloafing?" asked Clovenhoof, confident of the answer, as he had just invented the word.

"No," said Alice.

"It's where you pay someone a very reasonable subscription for them to come round to your house to replicate the experience that you're missing. Give us a tenner now and I'll pop round later."

Alice Calhoun stood for a moment, her mouth open, aghast. Then she gave a small shrug and reached for her purse.

CHAPTER THIRTEEN

On a long table in a side office of the Forgiveness Archives, thousands of individual paper records were arranged in various piles and clumps. A team of virginal admin staff carried in more by the minute. The demon Rutspud had gone off with his photocopies and his brilliant plan which was probably just as well, thought Joan, as there was barely enough room for the people and paper currently in the room.

"Indulgence," said Joan, reading the heading of one.

"This pile," said Gabriel, taking it.

"Any confessions and penances, bring over here," said Thomas Aquinas. He glanced at the next one passed to him. "Absolution granted to Mickey Fletcher by Bishop Kenneth Iscansus for the act of procuring prostitutes and running a house of ill-repute."

"Iscansus," said Joan. "I've seen that name already."

She rifled through the pile already in front of her. "Here. two absolutions granted by Bishop Iscansus."

"I guess Mickey had a lot to confess to his bishop," said Thomas.

"Then so did Hank Schlaeber-Foster and Yukari Shima," said Belphegor. "Forgiven for their sins by Bishop Kenneth Iscansus."

"Bishop Iscansus," said Gabriel, finding an example near the top of his pile.

"Another three, four here," said Hubertus.

"Is this the link?" said Belphegor. "One priest has forgiven them all?"

"Wiped the slate clean for each and every one of them," said Joan.

"Individually," said the virgin bringing in the latest pile of records. "All individual acts of forgiveness and absolution."

"Including," said Gabriel, waving a sheet with righteous anger, "forgiveness for the gun-toting, angel-shooting Lord Claymore Ferret."

"He's been a busy man," said Joan.

"Indiscriminate," said Gabriel huffily. "Ferret, forgiven."

"Forgiven," repeated Belphegor in a dead tone. "And we'd built a pit in Hell especially for him. It was beautiful too."

"Well, you've found your answer," said Hubertus. "Closure. That's the important thing. Time for a celebratory round of drinks! Hirsh! Hirsch-baby, shots all round."

Gabriel stared at the sheet in front of him, the confirmation that Claymore Ferret, wing assailant, had as much right to be in Heaven as anyone else.

"No," he said softly. "This cannot stand. You!" A finger stabbed at a random virginal clerk. "I want to see the paperwork every act of absolution, forgiveness and ministerial pardon given by this over-eager Iscansus priest."

"What? All of them?" she said with an uncooperative pout of derision.

Gabriel's eyes blazed with the fires of creation. "ALL OF THEM!"

CHAPTER FOURTEEN

Clovenhoof strolled through Boldmere, his pockets filled with Lennox's unloved cheese and pickle sandwiches and a payment from his first gigoloafing client. As he passed Ben's bookshop he heard screams coming from inside. It was quality screaming as well. Clovenhoof wouldn't have broken his stride for the 'eek-a-mouse' level of scream, but this was sustained and heartfelt. He went inside and found Ben, attempting to escape into the cellar. He was naked apart from a pair of underpants and had wax strips applied all over his chest, legs and torso. Some were tucked into the top of his underpants, which was a very Ben look, Clovenhoof decided. Nerys held some of the removed strips in her left hand, while she was finding the corner of another with her right hand. Ben wriggled to escape, and when he saw Clovenhoof he mewled with relief.

"Jeremy, you have to stop her! She's gone mad!"

Nerys turned, one hand on her hip. "Ben's being a baby about this. He agreed to the plan and now he won't go through with it."

"I didn't agree to be waxed," wailed Ben. "I just said I'd talk to Narinda. She seems like a nice lady. I don't see why waxing is necessary."

"Yes you do, we've been through this. You need a makeover so you can properly turn her head."

"I don't want to turn her head! Have you forgotten that I am still technically married to your sister?"

"Jayne? Don't worry about her, I'm sure she'd understand that we're dealing with an emergency here. Now, We're just going to start with a little light manscaping and then we'll move on to the deportment and assertiveness lessons. Jeremy, your hands are free, google the best way to incapacitate someone will you?"

Ben made a break for it. He wriggled from Nerys's grip and dodged around Clovenhoof, using him as a shield. Clovenhoof turned towards Ben.

"Hm. Hold on a moment, Kitchen. You've given me some inspiration for my list." He pulled a piece of tattered cardboard from his pocket. "Pen?"

"On the counter. What list?" said Ben.

"In my quest for making money I have been listing my many talents. I'm just adding two more. One. Doing things that other people can't bring themselves to do. Two. Taking things too far."

Clovenhoof put the list back in his pocket and then grabbed a wax strip from Ben's shoulder, ripping it away with a flourish.

"Oww! Jeremy, I thought you had my back! Why would you do that to me?" Ben clutched his shoulder."

"Just helping make you into a smooth operator. Had you thought of oiling him up and taking pictures for a calendar, Nerys?" Clovenhoof asked.

"No," said Nerys, "but it might be worth a shot."

"Wait," said Ben, "What was the thing you said about always taking things too far?"

"Oh that?" said Clovenhoof. "Let me show you." He reached into the top of Ben's underpants with both hands and yanked all of the wax strips upwards at the same time. It made a satisfying tearing sound, which was musically enhanced by Ben's screams.

"Oh good," said Nerys, watching Ben faint to the floor. "No need to google. Job done."

The three of them walked back towards home. Ben wore knotted tea towels as a makeshift sarong after finding that his jeans chafed too badly against his newly-plucked skin. Clovenhoof especially enjoyed that the tea towels sported novelty designs, so Ben was wearing what amounted to a skirt featuring cartoon lobsters and cats drinking wine.

"Right Ben, this is a great opportunity for you to practise the alpha male swagger," said Nerys. "You're wearing an idiotic outfit, and the only way to deal with it is to *style it out*. Imagine you're David Beckham, launching a new fashion line."

"Nerys, I don't think you realise that every single part of that idea is utterly alien to me. Even if you said I should imagine I'm David Beckham selling books, it would be a struggle," said Ben.

"That's because you don't sell many books," Clovenhoof pointed out helpfully.

"Think about how you're walking," said Nerys, ignoring both of them. "What you're doing now is an embarrassed slouchy thing like an emo with low self-esteem. You should be doing an alpha strut. Stick out your chest and your chin."

"Like this?"

"Hm. Tuck your bum in. It's a bit funky chicken at the moment. Now, slow it all down, take your time, because the world is your oyster."

"But oysters –"

"No!" roared Nerys. "Not a word about your allergies! Take a look at Jeremy. It's not often that I would hold him up as a role model, but he has mastered the art of walking unselfconsciously. Look at that unconcerned, arrogant swagger."

"Why thank you," said Clovenhoof, adding a little jiggle and a pelvic thrust.

"Arse-scratching, farting, tackle-shuffling, you could even add the same sort of embellishments as Jeremy," urged Nerys.

"But why would I do that? Narinda is a nice lady. She doesn't want a drooling Neanderthal!"

"Ben, deep down, all women want a bit of drooling Neanderthal. Remember, we're trying to appeal to the subconscious, lustful part of her brain."

Ben stalked unhappily down the road. It was very much like watching a freshly-damned soul who had been used for poker-shoving practice.

Outside their house, Clovenhoof checked his honesty box. It contained a small handful of loose change along with a fluff- and dog-hair-covered sweet.

"Thirteen pounds twenty. Someone's not paying their way," he grumbled.

Coming down the pavement towards them was a gaggle of youngsters, riding what appeared to be...

"Are those shopping trolleys?" said Nerys.

Clovenhoof stepped forward and held up his hand. "Spartacus Wilson. You know there's a toll on this part of the road, don't you?"

"What's up, paedo?" said the juvenile terror who seemed to have suddenly grown into a gangly pre-teen. "I don't see me moving, do you?"

"A parking fee then. What's all this?" said Clovenhoof, gesturing at Spartacus' novel transport.

Spartacus grinned with pride. He stood in a shopping trolley, and seven of his friends stood behind him, each at the helm of their own shopping trolley.

Clovenhoof recognised Kenzie Kelly, PJ McTigue, Jefri Rehemtulla and couple of the others. They had been members of the St Michael's cub scouts when Clovenhoof had helped out for a few months. All of them (Clovenhoof included) now had the proud distinction of being banned for life from all wings of the scouting movement. There was a herd of cows in Shropshire that still had traumatic flashbacks to a certain camping trip a few years back and would faint at the sight of a neckerchief and woggle.

Right now, Spartacus and chums looked like a raiding party of urban Vikings about to set sail for the grocery aisle in Tesco. "We've invented a new sport."

"What sort of sport?" asked Clovenhoof.

"Street polo," said Spartacus. "Our mom showed me polo in a celeb magazine."

"It's all posh boys wearing hats and daft clothes," sneered PJ McTigue.

"Bunch of bloody toffs," agreed Spartacus.

"That's why it's called polo," said Clovenhoof. "You have to be minted to play it." Spartacus gazed blankly at him. "*Mint*ed. It's a joke," said Clovenhoof.

"Are you sure?" said Spartacus. "Anyway, the sport's well due a makeover. First thing was the horses. These here are Boldmere Ponies. Adapted for the street."

Clovenhoof thought momentarily about the times that he'd struggled to make a supermarket trolley go where he wanted even when pushing it, never mind punting it along with what looked like a washing-line prop. "Aren't the wheels a little bit...what's the word?"

"Crap. Yeah. Kenzie found a load of skateboard wheels. He's pimped our rides. These Boldmere Ponies are customised."

Clovenhoof looked down. Clusters of skateboard wheels replaced the usual will-they-won't-they-turn-when-I-want rigid wheels. "They look good. Did Kenzie find some aerosol paint for the paint job as well? You talk a good game, Spartacus my man, but what are they like in action?" asked Clovenhoof.

"You're in luck old man," said Spartacus. "Watch and learn. We don't just play Street Polo, we do synchro too."

"Sin what?" asked Clovenhoof.

"Synchro," said Jefri Rehemtulla. "We do a synchronised display."

"Watch us and be amazed," said Kenzie.

Clovenhoof watched as the shopping trolleys swooped into formation. Each member of the team had a long pole (mostly clothesline props, but some fishing rods as well) and once they had formed a line, they linked together by bracing the poles horizontally across the group, leaving those at the side to punt and steer them down the road. They moved along in a box formed of two rows, four trolleys wide. Just as Clovenhoof was getting used to this spectacle, the four boys in the middle started a routine that was a bizarre combination of parkour, pogoing and Morris dancing. They jumped and stepped between each other's trolleys, balancing precariously on trolley handles and basket edges, with mid-air high fives.

"Ben, I take back everything I said about you looking ridiculous," said Nerys as the Boldmere Ponies finished their bizarre routine and zoomed away down the road. "Now the world has gone completely mad, I think tea towel sarongs are the new normal."

"I think we're all missing the key point here," said Clovenhoof, "which is that several people have now passed this point without paying." He cast around, anxious that no more freeloaders would make it past without putting something in his honesty box. "You! You over there!"

Clovenhoof walked over to the man who was sitting on the pavement, poking at a narrow grass verge with a trowel.

"That's Festering Ken," said Nerys. "He's harmless." Nerys tutted loudly and ushered Ben into the house.

"Ken, you need to pay the pavement tax for sitting there," Clovenhoof said.

Ken was clearly homeless. He had the grubby coat and shoes so worn and filthy it was impossible to say what kind of shoes they had once been or indeed if they had really ever been shoes at all. A lot of the homeless people Clovenhoof saw these days fit a certain mould. They had the beany hat and the scruffy beard and the sleeping bag and the little dog that sat on their lap while they begged with one hand and played Candy Crush with the other. But Ken was old school. His hat looked like he'd stolen it off a scarecrow. He had the beard of a department store Santa on the run for undisclosed sex offences. He didn't have a little dog or a mobile phone. He had fingerless gloves, newspaper for socks and a red nose that shone like a warning light to any medical professional who saw him. Nerys had told Clovenhoof that it was not politically correct to call homeless people tramps but the word suited Ken so well that Clovenhoof made an exception for him.

Right now, Ken had dug a shallow hole in the verge and had put his ear to it.

If you're going to be a while we can work out a daily rate," said Clovenhoof.

"How about half a pasty?" Ken started to move his hand towards his pocket.

"Half a pasty? Well that doesn't seem like enough, really." Clovenhoof looked more carefully at Ken and concluded that maybe it was all that he had.

"It goes a long way," rasped Ken. "Like loaves and fishes."

Clovenhoof straightened up. "No pasties for me. Have you got any actual money you can give me? We can work out a repayment – "

Ken cut him short with a loud "Shhh!" and a spray of spittle. He put his ear to the hole again.

"What is it?" said Clovenhoof.

"I'm listening."

"For what?"

"The little hoofy-woofies."

"The...?"

Ken sat upright suddenly and grabbed at Clovenhoof's trousers. "You ever seen the devil, man?" he asked with surprisingly clear diction.

"Every day," said Clovenhoof.

"And do you know where he lives?"

"I do."

Ken put a finger to his lips. The man's fingers were bloodied and marked with scratches, scrapes and more than a few trowel-inflicted cuts. He pointed at the earth.

"They say Hell is down there," whispered Ken. "But is it? Is it?" His milky eyes scanned Clovenhoof's face.

"Not in my experience," said Clovenhoof.

Festering Ken sniffed.

"Give us a quid, mate."

"Haven't got any money," lied Clovenhoof despite the clear evidence of the cash in his hand. "I've got a half-eaten hairy sweet if you fancy a suck."

"Give us a quid. I need it."

Clovenhoof sighed and, after looking round to make sure there were no witnesses, put a fiver in Ken's hand.

"You have to promise to spend it on booze and hobo hand jobs though," said Clovenhoof.

"Oh, you're a bad lad," said Ken and then, hunched over his new wealth, ran off down the street.

Clovenhoof went into his house and called out to Ben and Nerys. "Oi! You two. I didn't see you paying the pavement toll!"

CHAPTER FIFTEEN

When Rutspud returned to the Forgiveness Archives, a little out of breath from his exertions in the Celestial City and all but out of the photocopied sheets he'd taken with him, he found angels, demon and the blessed dead pondering over a table laden with documents. The papers were arranged in neat stacks, some several feet high, so that the overall effect was of an attempt to recreate the skyscraper cityscape of downtown Manhattan.

"Invites distributed. I've told them we'll meet them at the city gates within the hour," said Rutspud. "Tried to inject a sense of urgency in it all to get them motivated."

No one said anything. Gabriel was shaking his head. Thomas clutched at his lips pensively. Belphegor twirled an extra-long nose hair in thought.

"What?" said Rutspud.

Joan placed her hand lightly on the nearest pile.

"Guess how many acts of forgiveness Bishop Kenneth Iscansus has carried out in the past six months," she said.

"Oh, I know that one. Came up in the pub quiz last week."

"Four million, seven hundred and fifty-one thousand, nine hundred and six."

"You didn't even give me a chance to guess," he said and then thought about it. "That's a lot."

"That's eighteen absolutions a minute, day and night, for the last six months," said Joan.

"He's a busy boy."

"That's what I said."

"But here's the stranger part," said Belphegor. He held up two sheets. "On the second of April at eleven oh eight, he granted absolution to one Timothy Ng in Hong Kong. One minute later, he granted absolution to Anna Cauldfield in Pennsylvania, USA."

"They're nowhere near each other," said Rutspud. "Are they?"

"You're Hell's earth expert. You tell me."

"What does this mean?"

"It means something fishy is going on," said Gabriel, "and it demands further investigation."

"Good," said Rutspud firmly. "Nice to see someone taking action on this issue."

"We're going to send an investigative team to earth."

"Excellent."

"Putting our best people on the job," said Belphegor.

"As you should."

"Individuals who can blend in."

"Covert-like. Good."

"Those with the most experience of dealing with twenty-first century mortals," said Gabriel.

"Yes."

"Those who have been to earth quite recently."

Rutspud stopped.

Rutspud looked at Joan. Joan looked at Rutspud.

They looked at each other a long time because Rutspud truly couldn't find words to describe how he felt.

"Okay, okay," said St Hubertus, downing a shot and then leaning against his cervine drinking buddy-cum-barman. "I see where this is going. You need a hip party animal to go down, mix with the kids, mix things up and come up with the goods. In liquor there is truth. You want me to do it, fine. But I've got conditions."

"You certainly have," said Gabriel. "No, we don't want you, Hubertus."

"And you don't want me," said Rutspud, backing away, bumping into a chair and turning to apologise to the chair in his unhappy confusion. "I don't even like earth."

"You spend enough time there," said Belphegor.

"But Joan..."

"Led a successful mission to resolve a unresolvable prayer issue a few years back," said Gabriel.

"But Joan, she wouldn't want me as a partner. She's a saint, I'm a demon. It's..."

"Actually," said Joan with a shyly cheeky expression, "I put your name forward."

"But... what? ... why?... You!" He growled to clear his mouth. "Did I do something to offend you?"

She shrugged, armour plates sliding against each other. "It's like Belphegor says, the best people for the job."

Rutspud fumed. He fumed at the cosmos in general because that was a usually good place to start. He fumed at the teenage saint who had just dropped him in it. But, mostly, he fumed at himself. He had spent all of his existence maintaining a careful balance. Be clever but not too clever. Be useful but not too useful. Seize power in dribs and drabs but never too much. Build a protective wall around yourself but never put your head above the parapet.

Now here he was, capering along the battlements and some damned French girl had shot him in the face.

"I do this under duress," he said.

"Good," said Belphegor. "Hell prefers it that way. We wouldn't want you to actually enjoy yourself."

Rutspud gestured, still angry, at the mountains of papers on the table.

"And where is this Iscansus fellow then?"

"His absolutions are popping up all over the globe," said Gabriel.

"So, you don't know?"

"No, but Kenneth Iscansus was – technically still is – the bishop of the city of Birmingham. So, you could start there."

"Birmingham?"

"Yes. Have you heard of it?"

CHAPTER SIXTEEN

Clovenhoof stepped out of his flat wearing a shabby suit and did some practice lunges on the landing to see how much give there was in the crotch. Loud, angry voices came from Ben's flat. He could make out the sound of Nerys shouting bossily and Ben complaining bitterly. It was like a well-loved tune, where words weren't necessarily needed. He went to see what they were doing.

"Ah Jeremy, you can help with this. Alpha male training assertiveness module," said Nerys.

"It's games day," said Clovenhoof.

"Precisely," said Ben. "So, no time for any of this alpha crap. Um, what the hell are you wearing, Jeremy?"

Clovenhoof gave them a twirl. "An old man's suit."

"You been raiding the bargain bin at the charity shop again?" said Nerys.

"It's for my gigoloafing session tonight. I will be inhabiting the role of an old man and getting paid for it by a sweet old cougar called Alice."

"You smell like an old man," said Ben.

"Thank you. I've been working on that. Mostly by stuffing my pockets with leafy vegetables and pissing my pants."

"You piss your pants anyway," said Nerys.

"A lifetime of rehearsal is about to pay off. Now, to the games room!"

"Not yet," said Nerys. "Ben needs to get his alpha skills up to scratch."

"Games day!"

"And I've told Narinda to come over later to discuss financial matters with you – which is a little white lie – so Ben can start a-wooing her."

"I'm not ready for a-wooing," said Ben. "And I strongly doubt that Narinda wants any wooing of any sort."

"That's a defeatist attitude," said Nerys.

"We don't know if she has a boyfriend already. Maybe even a husband."

"She doesn't."

"You know?"

"Maybe."

"You been stalking her?"

"Is lightly googling someone stalking? Is making a few phone calls stalking? Is sitting outside someone's house with a camera and telephoto lens stalking?"

"It's the third one," said Clovenhoof.

"Definitely the third one," agreed Ben.

Nerys huffed. "Any successful seduction begins with thorough research. Trust me."

"Someone else's lifelong habits about to pay off," said Clovenhoof snidely.

Nerys scowled. "Well, 'old man,' if you're so keen to inhabit roles you can help with this next exercise."

"Yes?"

"We're going to roleplay being in a bar."

"We need alcohol then," said Clovenhoof. "To make it properly realistic." He sniffed a bottle that was on Ben's table, but it was the thinners that he used for his model painting. He gave it a tentative swig. Not bad.

"Right. The challenge is to be served first at the bar," said Nerys. "It's a well-known test of alpha male superiority, and the contest will have two rounds." Nerys held up two fingers for emphasis, and possibly, just because she could. "The first round is to see how loud you can be. I am both judge and bartender, and I will award points for attention-grabbing language, but most of all volume. As loud as you can. *Go!*"

Ben looked at Clovenhoof. He leaned on an imaginary bar and raised his voice slightly. "Can I please get served?" he asked Nerys.

Clovenhoof shook his head in pity. "Serve me now!" he bellowed ferociously. "I want a Lambrini and I want it right now!"

Ben shook his head. "I can't behave like that, it's appalling!" he cried.

"Nice touch of anger, Ben. Use it! Channel it!" urged Nerys.

"I want a drink and I don't want to have to make a fuss about it!" said Ben, more stridently.

"Good work," said Nerys. "Wait, where's Jeremy off to?"

Clovenhoof was back in Ben's flat in a minute and feeling pleased with himself. He lifted the loudhailer. "PUNY MORTALS, DO MY BIDDING! GET MY DRINK AND DO NOT WASTE ANY MORE OF MY TIME!"

Ben and Nerys covered their ears and looked pained. Clovenhoof put down the loudhailer.

"I win, yeah?"

Ben and Nerys looked at him, not responding, both tenderly probing their ears.

"I said, *I win*. Yes?" repeated Clovenhoof. He was clearly not getting through. He picked up the loudhailer again.

"Jesus fucking Christ Jeremy, don't you dare!" said Nerys. "You've made us both deaf."

It took several minutes before Clovenhoof got confirmation that he had, in fact, won. He didn't feel as though his victory came with the respect that it deserved, though.

"Right, round two is body language and positioning. Same challenge. You want to be served by the barman, played by me," said Nerys. "We're looking to be closest to the bar, which will be the table, here." She positioned herself behind Ben's table. "You get there by discreetly pushing and shoving as needed. The person who has their knees and elbows in front, up against the bar, when I complete the countdown is the winner. Three-two-one, *go!*"

"Ten!"

This seemed straightforward to Clovenhoof. He pressed himself against the table, braced against any efforts to dislodge him. Ben sidled up and tried to push him sideways with his hips, but Clovenhoof was going nowhere.

"Nine!"

Ben tried another tactic. He leaned across the table and twisted, using the whole of his upper body to push Clovenhoof backwards. Clovenhoof sank his teeth into Ben's shoulder.

"He bit me! He bloody bit me!" screeched Ben.

"Five!" said Nerys, ignoring him.

Ben used his legs now, levering with his feet and his knees. However, Clovenhoof's legs were not built in quite the same way as Ben's (although Ben failed to notice, as did everyone else). A quick backwards flick and a vicious hoof stomp later and Ben was sprawled on the floor, clutching his injured foot.

"Aargh, I think it's broken!" howled Ben.

"One! Jeremy wins again," said Nerys.

Clovenhoof performed a victory dance, which was tenuously based on the Haka that he'd seen on the telly the other day.

Ben rolled away, fear in his eyes. "Nerys, make him stop before he gets my other foot!"

"I'd be more worried about catching something off all the crap that's falling out of his pockets," said Nerys, withdrawing with a grimace.

They adjourned to the games room in the ground floor flat but not before Nerys had inspected Ben's foot, declared him to be a 'whinging softy' and then dressed him in his Narinda-seducing gear. Ben looked uncomfortable in the leather trousers and designer shirt, although Clovenhoof was warming to his old man suit. It had so many pockets! And not just your standard pockets but double-stitched reinforced pockets. He could keep enough change in his trouser pockets to run a small bank and the inside pockets of his jacket just cried out to be stuffed with 'man stuff': ticket stubs, handy-sized tools, stationery and all those little oddments that men seemed to accumulate. Clovenhoof found himself increasingly drawn to creating a snail sanctuary in one of them or perhaps opening the world's tiniest pencil stub museum.

"Ah, no Lambrini for me," said Clovenhoof as Nerys reached for the bottle of fizz.

"What?" she said, stunned.

"Got to get into character," he said and produced a bottle of Thunkerston's Super-Dark Stout. "Old Bill Calhoun liked a drop of stout." He broke off the bottle top on his horns and poured it out into a cocktail glass.

"Did old Bill like it in a Lambrini glass?" asked Nerys.

"Hey, I've got to pretend to be him, not actually become him," said Clovenhoof. He tipped his fingers in the stout and dabbed a bit on his neck. "Fragrant!"

Ben moved forward to roll the dice for his go. His trousers gave a mournful squeak as he did so. He did it again, with an exaggerated leg shuffle, to prove it was the trousers. Nerys rolled her eyes.

"Get on with it Ben, and do me a favour will you? Land on my Club of Exotic Delights, I need the cash."

"I didn't think it was that much to get into your club?" said Ben.

"No, I make most of the money from the compromising photos I get of you while you're in there," said Nerys. "It would be so much fun to do that while you're all dolled up for Narinda."

Ben tugged uncomfortably at the fitted shirt that Nerys had selected. The top buttons were undone and Clovenhoof observed that what Nerys had described as a *gleaming, bronzed Adonis* look was more akin to *chicken breasts – reduced for quick sale.*

Ben rolled the dice and Clovenhoof crowed with delight. "Saint Philips Cathedral. Get in!"

"Okay," said Ben. "We need to consult the new rules on religious buildings."

"New rules," said Nerys.

"Yes," said Ben, getting up and crossing to a row of filing cabinets Clovenhoof had never noticed before. "Properties that represent the headquarters of a significant religious group are subject to a new set of rules and playing –"

"Where did those filing cabinets come from?" said Nerys.

"I had them installed," said Ben. "We just had too many files."

He opened a file drawer filled with sheets and wallets, all neatly labelled with brightly coloured tabs. "Here we have the basic rules." He continued along the row of cabinets, pointing at drawers. "These are the rules for property purchase, surveying, conveyance, contracts and ownership clauses. These are the rules for various actions – legal and illegal – although the criminal justice system sub-rules are filed over there in the general law, policy and governance drawer. These are the rules regarding appeals, arbitration, conciliation and judgements. (I've given Lennox his own set.) The next two drawers are for *exceptions* to the rules: acts of God, force majeure and weird phenomena. Finally, we have a drawer for bits of the original rules book that we can't translate or are currently subject to edit wars on Wikipedia."

"Oh, my God, it's a monster," said Nerys.

Ben sat back down with a file clutched in his hand. He had an uncomfortable look on his face although Clovenhoof didn't know if that was because of the leather trousers or because no-one seemed particularly in awe of his rules overhaul. "So, subject to the new religion rules we have Saint Philip's Cathedral, Saint Chad's, the central Mosque and the Scientology headquarters."

"Ah, but is Scientology a religion or a cult?" asked Nerys.

"For the purpose of these rule changes it's a religion, although the debate might influence a future change in direction," said Ben. "If a player lands on one of these squares, then they must pay the rent to the player who owns the property. The rent will be based on the number of followers that the owner has."

"Followers?" said Nerys.

"The number of followers is calculated thus," said Ben. "We add up their Facebook friends and twitter followers. We subtract the number of twitter followees –"

"Is that a word?" asked Nerys.

"– followees and then we add on the number of people whose attention the owner can attract from the front doorstep during the course of ten minutes."

"Well, I suppose there's Festering Ken for one," said Nerys.

"I think he's gone wandering off to dig up devils or something elsewhere," said Clovenhoof.

"Yes," said Ben thoughtfully, "I wonder if we ought to add in a clause about followers being of sound mind?"

"No," said Nerys firmly.

"The player must then take a miracle card," said Ben, "and the quality of the miracle multiplied by the number of followers is the amount payable."

"Good. We can play now," said Nerys.

Ben shuffled uncomfortably and tugged at his tight trousers.

"How's Ben going to seduce Narinda when he's pulling a face like his nads are on fire?" asked Clovenhoof.

"They are on fire!" moaned Ben, "Waxing is inhumane and these leather trousers were a terrible idea. I hope you realise that I could get an infection!"

"You could always pull them down until she gets here, let the air circulate a bit," said Clovenhoof. "Soak your delicate parts in your cider and black for a bit of a cooling-down. I sometimes do."

Nerys and Ben turned to stare at him.

"What?" he said.

"I hope one of those miracle cards says 'Jeremy Clovenhoof decided not to be a complete knob today'," said Nerys. "It would be a rare and precious thing if it ever happened."

"I don't remember discussing these rules," said Nerys.

"We brainstormed them in the pub a few days ago," said Ben.

"But we were drunk," she argued.

"We all signed a non-sobriety waiver agreement, though."

"And were we drunk when we signed that?"

Ben sighed and re-read the new rules. "We need to calculate Jeremy's followers," he said. Nerys, can you check his Facebook and twitter?"

Nerys flicked through her phone and tapped into the calculator. "Total of Facebook friends, twitter followers, minus twitter followees is... forty thousand three hundred and seven."

Ben stared at her. "What?"

Nerys shrugged. "I have no idea either, but for some reason Jeremy is quite the social media star."

"Don't forget I get the chance to increase my followers from the front doorstep," said Clovenhoof.

"Is it worth it to make it forty thousand three hundred and eight with Festering Ken?" asked Ben.

"Yes, it is," said Clovenhoof, standing. He walked to the front doorstep and pulled out his phone. "Ten minutes, yeah?"

CHAPTER SEVENTEEN

Rutspud nudged Joan as they approached Heaven's gates. "See, it's worked like a charm."

There was a gathering of newly deceased near to the gates, all clutching their tickets pumped out by Belphegor's lap-top photocopier.

Claymore Ferret was holding court amongst his friends.

"It's time these people recognised that we're a breed apart. We need that exclusivity to make sure standards are upheld. Take my funeral for instance, they'll have had it by now. Only the cream of society invited. Roast swan for all the guests, you know? Not everyone can do that, but we Ferrets have been roasting swans for years. Special arrangement, you might say. String quartet, harp player and a hundred white doves released at the end of the service."

Joan rolled her eyes. "So what's the deal with your tickets, Rutspud? They all think they're going somewhere?"

"Yes, they are going somewhere," said the demon. "It's going to be... special."

"You're not going to just cart them off to Hell, are you?"

"Heaven forbid."

"Yes, it probably would. Gabriel and Eltiel are meeting us out in Limbo. Belphegor's gone to where?"

"Back to Hell. Says he needs to make preparations for our journey." Rutspud looked up at the teenager. "I still haven't forgiven you for that."

"Earth will be fun," she said.

"Don't make it worse by being optimistic," he grimaced. He waded in amongst the gathering. They looked at his gnarly demon body with disdain, which cheered him no end. "Right," he said, "can I make sure that you are all holders of these exclusive tickets? We can't allow just anyone along on the trip we're about to make."

He made a big show of checking everyone's ticket, to the accompaniment of much muttering, along the lines of *don't you know who I am?*

When he was satisfied, Rutspud addressed them again. "I'm sure you've noticed by now that Heaven contains everything you could possibly need, but its populace probably doesn't reflect the social structure that you're used to. What you'd really like is somewhere a little more *exclusive.*"

There were mumblings of agreement from the entire crowd.

"Follow me then," he said and led them through the massive gates that swung open before them. The Celestial City had twelve gates. The famous pearly gates where St Peter used to stand and tick the newly dead off a list, like a maître d' at a pretentious restaurant, were elsewhere; these gates had no regular traffic, opening only onto the creamy mists and dreamscape of unformed Limbo.

The ungrateful dead all followed Rutspud, clearly keen to see where he was taking them, but careful to maintain the louche swagger of those who might decide to go somewhere different at any moment.

Rutspud faltered as he saw something up ahead in the swirling mists of Limbo. He could hear faint sounds.

"Go get it! Good boy."

Rutspud glanced at Joan.

"I recognise that voice," she said.

"Cewbewus, to you! Good doggie, well caught!"

Ahead, Hell's three-headed guardian leapt and twisted in mid-air. His mighty jaws mashed together onto a frisbee, catching it and sending splinters of plastic in every direction. Against all the odds he landed back on his feet as Saint Francis reached inside his robes for a replacement frisbee.

"Go on Cecil, off you go!"

The lion stopped nuzzling Francis's legs and bounded over to catch the frisbee.

"Pass me my gun, Cynthia," said Claymore.

"There's no hunting in Limbo," said Joan, firmly.

"Go on," whispered Rutspud. "Let him take a pot shot at Cerberus. At least, let him try." Cerberus slobbered in anticipation from all three of his muzzles, but Francis whistled urgently.

"Cewbewus! Cecil! Come this way, quickly!"

The terrifying Hell hound and the elderly lion bounded away, and Rutspud led the group forward. The Celestial City, like Hell, was finite but out here in Limbo space and distance were as utterly meaningless as time. The geography here was essentially an infinite plain of cotton wool fluffiness, as featureless as the inside of a ping-pong ball. They had walked sufficiently far that the Celestial City was completely lost to sight. A soul could get utterly lost out here. A human soul at least; Rutspud could feel the rock solid tug of Hell in *that* direction and an opposing revulsion from the Celestial City in *that* direction and assumed that the angels felt something similar but entirely opposite.

Thinking of angels...

Gabriel and Eltiel stood on a short cloudy hillock of their own making up ahead.

"You got those images I described?" he called to them.

"We are competent, little demon," said Gabriel. "Remember your place."

Rutspud climbed the slope while Joan stayed to corral the vaguely-blessed dead.

"My place is a hop, skip and a jump over that way," Rutspud said to Gabriel, "and the sooner I get back there the better, your Archangelness."

Gabriel huffed dismissively and pushed up his robe sleeves. "Very well, we shall start with serene Palladian arches, sublimely symmetrical facades and pure, tranquil vistas."

"The photos," said Rutspud. "Did you not look at the photos?"

"Yes," said Gabriel, "but I feel we can do better."

"Better? Those photos I showed you of gated communities in Cheshire and luxury apartments in Shanghai? Purpose built holiday villages in Spain. Luxury compounds in Dubai."

"Yes, yes. All that but we can make it much more tasteful."

"No! the whole point is that it should drip with ostentatious wealth and excess," said Rutspud. "Think crystal-encrusted. Think gilded. Think made from rare and irreplaceable resources."

"Finery, yes."

"But with zero class or artistry," Rutspud emphasised. "Imagine you gave a six-year-old ten trillion quid to build a palace. That. But we also want swimming pools, hot tubs, saunas, the largest Nando's in the world –"

"Nando's?" said Gabriel.

"I do love me a cheeky Nando's," grinned Eltiel.

"And a casino. And a George and the Dragon pub with Sky Sports in every bar. And shops. Lots and lots of shops. And I want it so that the residents, whatever they want, whenever they want it, it will just appear."

"Then why do they need shops if they can wish for stuff and it will just appear?" asked Gabriel.

"They don't need them but they'll want them," said Rutspud. "Trust me. All of that but make it, you know, more."

Eltiel waggled his eyebrows. "You know that *more* is my speciality, right?"

Gabriel grimaced but rubbed his hands together and concentrated hard as he set about creating a glorious enclave for their guests. Eltiel showered the audience with glittering motes of heavenly light and made accompanying whizzbang sound effects as each new building popped into existence. When it looked as though Gabriel was almost finished, Eltiel walked around, casting a critical eye on each turret, pathway and wall. If he saw an unembellished surface he made sure that it was embellished. He went back round and added embellishments onto the embellishments. When the whole thing looked as if would give a Disney princess a migraine, he declared it ready.

Rutspud beckoned to the waiting crowd.

"Freshly minted, nobody else has set foot in here," announced Rutspud. "I think you'll find that it contains everything you could wish for. You're all welcome to move in here right now."

"Unsullied by the hoi polloi," he heard Cynthia whisper to Claymore Ferret. "It's got to be better."

"Well, cream rises to the top as always, darling," Claymore replied. "I knew we'd be treated properly once this lot caught on to who we are. We'll take this place, I think."

He addressed Gabriel. "So, listen, boy."

"Boy?"

"How can we be sure that we'll be protected from the proles who want a bit of what we've got, hmmm?"

Rutspud cut in before the archangel could launch into what would undoubtedly be a sermon. "We can make absolutely sure that your private residence remains undisturbed," he said, "We'll shut these gates, and only authorised members of Heaven's committee will be permitted to unlock them."

"See to it," said Claymore and they all trooped in happily, eager to claim their own place in their own private Heaven.

Joan looked at Rutspud. "So, your response to selfish ingrates throwing a hissy fit was to give them exactly what they wanted?"

"Exactly."

"Hardly very devilish," she said.

"Joan, the devil is in the details. The details."

She gave it some thought. "I knew I was right to choose you to go with me to earth."

Rutspud scowled. "Well, we're going to Hell before we go to earth."

"What for?"

"You think we're going on this mission unequipped?"

CHAPTER EIGHTEEN

Clovenhoof put a finger to his lips to try and stop the indignant bleating noises from Ben and Nerys. The call connected.

"We've got Jeremy from the West Midlands on the line," said the radio presenter. "Hi Jeremy."

"Hi Trish, Jeremy Clovenhoof here," he said. "You want my opinion on fracking, yeah?"

"I certainly do Jeremy. Tell us all what you think."

"Well I think that as long as it's between consenting adults then it's fine. People worry too much."

Clovenhoof didn't wait for a response, he killed the call and checked his watch. "Eight seconds to go." He looked up and down the road. Only Festering Ken was in sight. Clovenhoof put his fingers in his mouth and gave a piercing whistle. Ken looked up and Clovenhoof gave him a cheeky wave.

"So," he said, "you'll need to add together the listening figures for BBC West Midlands, BBC Coventry and Warwickshire and the internet radio station Angry Folks Moaning About Stuff."

"The rules did not say that you could use your phone!" said Nerys.

"Nor did they say that I couldn't," said Clovenhoof. "My church attendance figures are based on the total number of people's attention I can draw while stood on the doorstep. I'm on the doorstep. Attention has been drawn. Get totalling, Nerys."

A car pulled up outside the house.

"And add one to that total," said Clovenhoof.

Nerys segued from a string of fruity swear words into a warm greeting as Narinda got out of the car.

"You've all come to greet me," she said, mildly perplexed to see the three of them crowded on the doorstep.

Clovenhoof tapped the parking sign he'd put next to the door. "As much as I'd like to let you off because you've come here at my invitation, I know you're a stickler for rules, so I'm going to have to charge you thirty quid for –"

"Not now," said Nerys. "Narinda is our guest for the evening."

"I've come to put Jeremy's tax matters to bed," said Narinda. "I'm not stopping long."

"Of course," said Nerys smoothly. "Ben, why don't you get Narinda fixed up with a drink while Jeremy and I calculate these figures?"

Ben adopted the alpha male body language, as drilled into him by Nerys. He stood with his feet in a wide stance and his arms away from his sides, chin jutting out slightly.

"Are you all right, Ben?" said Narinda. "You look a little tense."

"We're all a little tense. I suspect I owe Jeremy a great deal of money." Ben waddled inside. Whether he was maintaining his alpha male stance or suffering the after-effects of waxing wasn't clear.

"Well," said Nerys, after tapping it all out on her phone, "I reckon your new follower total to be three hundred and seventy thousand three hundred and seven. Let's go and see what that means for Ben, shall we?"

As they entered the games room, Ben was performing a cocktail-mixing routine for Narinda. Clovenhoof stared. He'd watched the rehearsal of this, with Nerys shouting instructions and something here wasn't quite the same. Then he saw the kettle and realised that Ben was making a cup of tea. Narinda was equally transfixed, especially when Ben attempted to juggle sugar cubes.

"Ah, no sugar for me, thank you."

Ben dropped the sugar and turned his attention to the milk, shaking the bottle in the air to his left and to his right and then pouring a thin stream from a great height into Narinda's cup.

He used the teabag squeezers and a few pelvic thrusts to extract the teabag from the cup. He flipped the teabag onto his nose, put his hands on his hips and, after some strutting and shoulder-wiggling, ducked his head and deposited it into the bin.

"Thank you," said Narinda uncertainly as Ben handed her the cup. "And that routine was... did you perhaps lose a bet?" She scanned his new attire. "Several bets, perhaps?"

"He's about to lose something," said Jeremy, dropping into his seat and messily quaffing his glass of stout.

"Now, what's the update regarding your tax payments and your general financial position?" asked Narinda.

"Sorry, I think there's a more pressing matter to deal with," said Nerys.

"More pressing than the fact you're all about to be evicted from your home?" asked Narinda.

"For the next few minutes, yes. We need to see what Ben owes Jeremy for landing on his church."

"Cathedral!", said Clovenhoof.

"Surely a church is a free resting place?" said Narinda. "They don't take money off people in real life."

"Which does them no favours in the twenty-first century," said Clovenhoof.

"It's why they're selling some of them off to private buyers," said Ben. "There's a curry house in Tamworth in a church building."

"Maybe St Michael's should try selling curry instead of peddling horrible biscuits and lukewarm tea," said Nerys. "They might make enough money to make a proper nativity instead of wrapping dusters around the leftover power rangers from the jumble sale and hoping that people don't look too closely."

"I quite enjoyed the carrot that played baby Jesus last year," said Ben.

"It did get a little bit mouldy towards twelfth night though. Have you got the miracle cards, Ben?" asked Nerys.

"About the tax..." said Narinda.

Ben offered a stack of cards to Clovenhoof, who picked a card and held it up with a flourish. "A statue of the Virgin Mary in Saint Michael's graveyard is observed weeping. Visitors flock to see it from all over the world. Value one hundred thousand pounds. Cool, huh?"

Nerys gave a low whistle. "Hang on, let me check the number of zeroes. I make that thirty-seven billion pounds you need to cough up, Ben."

They all stared at each other.

"I wonder how much currency we actually have," said Ben.

"What, all together, with the extra that we've all added when people weren't looking?" asked Clovenhoof.

Ben nodded. "I don't think we have anywhere near that."

"Not to worry. Give me everything and I'll take an IOU for the rest," said Clovenhoof. "Or you could make part payment in grovelling recognition of my greatness as King of Hooflandia."

"Hooflandia?"

"My little empire," said Clovenhoof, gesturing to all he owned and wallowing for a moment in the prospect of having his own country. "I'm struggling with the words for my national anthem though. What rhymes with Hooflandia?"

"Please!" said Narinda, as loudly as a polite person could. "Are you all so wrapped up in this crazy game that you've forgotten you have some real-world problems to deal with? This here is a letter from a debt reclamation company. Bailiffs. They're coming any day now to repossess everything you own."

"But I'm about to strike it rich here," said Clovenhoof, casting his hands at the almost indecipherable expanse of The Game playing board.

"Strike it rich with real money?" said Narinda.

"Well, no."

"How much money do you actually have? Real, accessible and physical money."

Clovenhoof patted his pockets and frowned. "Well I thought I made some, and I don't remember spending it on anything enjoyable. Actually that normally means I've spent it on something enjoyable, but I'm not sure I've had time."

Narinda shook her head. "You need to do more. This is really urgent. What could you sell?"

Clovenhoof cast his eye over the board and a small idea blossomed in his mind. "Actually, there might be one or two things. Have you got a pen?"

He took Narinda's pen, jotted some notes on the back of his miracle card and pocketed the pen.

She held out her hand. "You're not selling my pen, Jeremy."

Clovenhoof grinned. "No, I have bigger plans in mind." He turned to Nerys. "I could set this up right now with a little help. Nerys, would you mind? I've got a couple of hours before my gigoloafing gig and I'm sure Ben and Narinda can manage without us for a few minutes."

Nerys gave an ostentatious wink. "Great idea. Be good, you two! Not too good though."

She followed him out and shut the door.

"Jeremy, you surprise me sometimes. Well played!" she said.

"What?" he said, leading the way to his flat, and more specifically his computer. "Oh the honey trap? Well it might work, I suppose, but I thought of something else. How do you feel about fraud?"

"I don't think I quite share your moral flexibility," she said thoughtfully.

"And that's why you fail," he said. "Who was it that said, 'When you sell a lie, you should sell the biggest lie possible?'"

"I don't know," she said, "but I suspect he wasn't a nice man."

CHAPTER NINETEEN

Joan of Arc was in Hell.

She wondered if it was any consolation to the Burgundian nobles who'd burned her at the stake that she was now, at least temporarily, in the place they'd hoped to send her. She supposed that any number of them might be down here somewhere and momentarily wondered if she should seek them out and say 'hi' and then dismissed the idea as probably unhelpful and potentially cruel.

The Infernal Innovation Centre overseen by Belphegor occupied several sub-basement levels beneath the ruins of the Fortress of Nameless Dread at the heart of Hell's capital, Pandemonium. Rutspud asked Joan if she could find her own way there as he apparently had some small farewells to make before their trip to earth. Fortunately, Hell had lots of helpful signs pointing out where things were. Unfortunately, it had even more unhelpful signs that declared useless nuggets such as *'If door does not open, please do not enter'*, *'Warning: No context for next five miles'* and *'The edges of this sign are sharp. You're welcome.'*

Eventually, after climbing down through the ruined fortress and passing through a foundry of belching furnaces and billowing smoke, Joan found herself before a cavern with the words Infernal Innovation Programme above the entrance. Rutspud was already there, waiting. He passed a paper bag to her.

"Hold this," he said and placed the sin detector he carried onto a little cradle gizmo by the door. A display flashed up.

Battery level 70%. Charging. Ejecting waste materials.

Pipes and pumps wheezed and hissed above the cradles.

"What's it doing?" she said.

"Getting rid of sin particles that it accumulates when taking a reading."

"And what happens to that sin?"

"Dunno," he replied. "Gets turned into something, I suppose. Jelly baby?"

She frowned. "The sin gets turned into...?"

Rutspud pointed at the bag he'd passed her. "Jelly babies. You want one?"

"Where did you get these?" she asked. The sweets, in a little white paper bag, looked like they'd been picked up from an old-fashioned corner shop. Joan suspected there weren't many of those in Hell.

"From a friend," he said. "I was saying goodbye. Come on, let's see what Belphegor has for us."

"But..." she said, pointing at the mysterious hissing pipes.

"Don't question Hell's proprietary tech," said Rutspud.

"Why?"

"It just spoils the mystery."

He beckoned her through to an open plan office where a strangely unsegregated workforce of demons and damned souls beavered away at draughtsmen's boards and holographic projection images.

"We're going to the creativity hub testing centre," said Rutspud, cutting through the busy design room. "A lot of the equipment Belphegor's sending us with will be experimental." He gave her a conspiratorial look. "Chances are, the reason we're being given it is because it is experimental and in need of a field test."

"Dangerous?" said Joan.

"Here's hoping," said Rutspud.

A damned soul in a black roll neck sweater approached Rutspud with a complex schematic in his hands.

"Mr Rutspud, sir, have you had a chance of speaking to Lord Belphegor about my suggestion?"

"Is this the 'extra circle' thing again?" said Rutspud tiredly.

"It's time Hell entered the digital age, sir, and –"

"Hell has entered the digital age, Steve. What you want for reasons known only to yourself is for Hell to go metric."

"Ten circles of Hell each divided into ten zones of high efficiency torment, sir."

"And what's this?" Rutspud poked at the schematic. "The Pit of Open Source Coders? The Pit of Microsoft Executives?" He sighed. "I'm not showing it to him, Steve. We don't need a tenth circle."

"You're just blinkered," the soul called after him as Rutspud walked on. "Hell needs an upgrade. They'll be queueing around the block to get in once it's installed."

Rutspud led the way through a bustling, spark-filled workshop. "That guy had better start pulling his weight," Rutspud said to Joan, holding the door for her. "Hell demands technological innovation and I don't think he's got what we need."

Joan looked critically at the machinery and gadgetry around them. "I am sure none of it is really needed."

"Oh, really?"

"What about the purity of honest labour? One of the glories of God's creation is that he made us all capable of so much, and yet I see that technology can encourage a certain indulgent sloth."

"Thank you," said Rutspud, emphatically. "It's nice to see our efforts recognised."

"I wasn't trying to be complimentary."

"Many of our proudest achievements encourage sloth, Joan. We worked hard to nudge forward the invention of the car. Then when people realised they were becoming fat and lazy we helped them invent exercise bikes. We realised at that point that circular, self-defeating technology was the way forward."

"Self-defeating technology?"

"We operate a television channel on earth as a testing ground for our new ideas, like labour-saving kitchen devices that cut vegetables into bizarre shapes *and* injure your fingers. And then there's a type of watch that winds itself when a human wears it. That's one of mine."

"But that actually sounds like a useful thing," said Joan.

"It *is* a useful thing, if you only have one," said Rutspud. "So we made them collectable, and now people need little cabinets to rock the watches they're not wearing."

"Oh," said Joan with a frown. "That's... that's stupid."

"Isn't it just?" Rutspud nodded happily. They passed through a pair of swing doors into an altogether quieter and more science-y looking space.

"Ah, Rutspud," said Belphegor. His wheelchair was slotted into an ergonomic workbench at the centre of a semi-circular rack of tools and supplies. "I'm just finishing work on an essential piece of your equipment."

He reversed out of the workbench and held up something the size and shape of a paperback book.

He was interrupted by a muffled monstrous roar from within a giant metal tank.

"Quiet, Boris!" Belphegor yelled. He handed the device to Rutspud. "Currency printer. Simple to operate. Feed in a sample of the local currency here," he pointed at a narrow, flat aperture, "and then you can print as many copies as you need."

"Useful," conceded Joan. "I guess we will need money on earth."

"This is a prototype," warned Belphegor, "so we haven't yet fitted it with a reset button. You will be equipped to reproduce one note only, but that shouldn't pose a problem."

"And what's this?" said Joan pressing a button on a not-dissimilar device on the end of the workbench.

"PERSONAL TORTURE SEQUENCE INITIATED. SCANNING..." The automated voice rang out from the small device.

"Ah," said Belphegor. "This should be interesting."

"VICTIM HAS 100% FUNCTIONALITY IN NERVE FUNCTION AND COGNITIVE RECOGNITION. SETTING PAIN DELIVERY TO MAXIMUM. INITIATING KNIFE FLAIL TO REMOVE FIRST LAYERS OF SKIN AND SUBCUTANEOUS –"

"It's going to what?" said Joan, backing away. As she moved, it did two things. A set of tiny rotors emerged from the top of the casing and it rose into the air, following her. From the sides, dozens of flexible arms tipped with scalpels wormed free and bristled in the air, giving the whole thing the appearance of a shiny flying gorgon's head.

"It's doing exactly what you'd expect if you requested a personal torture session," said Belphegor conversationally.

"I didn't request a personal torture session!"

"If you pressed the button then you did," said Belphegor.

"It's going to torture me?"

"Yes."

"And you think that's 'interesting'?"

"Absolutely. Not nice for you obviously. But definitely interesting."

Joan drew her broadsword. "Well I don't want to be tortured. Turn it off!" She brandished her weapon at the device, but it ducked and bobbed in the air, evading her swipes with its hummingbird manoeuvrability.

"We build a backdoor shutdown sequence into all of our devices," said Belphegor. "Can you remember what it is for this one, Rutspud?"

The device swooped forward and clattered along her gleaming breastplate, leaving scalpel sharp nicks in the metal as it sought out soft flesh.

"I didn't work on this one," said Rutspud, as Joan swung a wrench off a nearby workbench in the hope that it might be more effective at stopping the thing.

"It's on the tip of my tongue," said Belphegor thoughtfully. "Bagpipe sensibility. Bagpipe solitude."

Rutspud grabbed a manual from the bookshelf and flicked through. Knives clicked right in front of Joan's face, and nothing she could do would swat the thing away.

"Bagpipe sorcerer," said Rutspud.

The knives stopped and withdrew back inside the casing. The device steered back to the workbench and settled back into place.

"Sequence aborted."

Joan put down the wrench and glowered at Rutspud and Belphegor.

"What?" said Belphegor. "*You* were the one who pressed the button."

"I was merely curious," she said.

"And what did curiosity do to the cat?" said Belphegor. "Killed it."

"Effing murderlised," grinned Rutspud. "But it's probably best if you don't press any more buttons."

"Now, the key to your investigation on earth is identifying instances of priestly forgiveness," said Belphegor. "We've fast-tracked something that will help you to identify who is gaining absolution."

His wheelchair puttered over to another table and he picked up a wedge-shaped device.

"Obviously we needed to disguise this for you, so we consulted our film archive and we chose a Geiger counter. We believe they are fairly commonplace, so you shouldn't stand out. It clicks in the presence of absolution, and it's directional, so you will hear the clicking speed up when you approach the source."

Rutspud took the device. As well as the clicking, it featured a needle that twitched back and forth in an arc, on a background that went from green on the left to red on the right. "When you consulted the film archive, did you go to fiction or non-fiction?" he asked.

Belphegor looked at him blankly. "I don't dabble in the whys and wherefores, Rutspud. Obviously if you'd been here we'd have got you to do the research as our resident culture expert. Is there a problem?"

"No sir, not at all," said Rutspud, but Joan caught a look on his face that made her wonder whether Geiger counters were all that commonplace on earth.

"Last couple of items are over here," said Belphegor. "Up on the shelf, Rutspud. An invisibility cloak and a selection of fragmentation grenades."

"Invisibility cloak?" said Rutspud, impressed.

"Grenades?" said Joan, concerned.

"The cloak is fusion tech. The latest light-bending technology we stole from the Chinese but coupled with basic imp invisibility."

Rutspud fingered the entirely invisible material. "Imp skin. I thought it felt familiar."

"Do we really need grenades?" said Joan.

"There's a difference between need and want," said Rutspud, gleefully snagging a couple of extra grenades and slotting them onto the bandolier. "Wouldn't want to regret not taking them."

"Right, that's most of what you need," said Belphegor. "There's a couple of travel bags for you there."

Rutspud wrapped the grenades up in the cloak for easy carrying and stuffed them in a bag. Joan put the currency printer and absolution detector in a rucksack.

"What's all this other stuff?" she said.

"Standard field agent equipment," said Belphegor. "Phone. Tablet. Travel plugs. Inflatable pillow. Beach towel."

"The phone?" said Rutspud, waving the device at Belphegor.

"Uses the spiritual desire lines network."

"Fine," said Rutspud, although Joan had no idea what that meant.

There was another titanic roar from the vast metal tank.

"Shush, Boris!" said Belphegor. "They're going now."

"What is in there?" Joan asked Rutspud.

Rutspud shrugged. "Some sort of Armageddon doomsday project? We're always cooking something up down here."

"Come on, come on," said Belphegor. "In here, you two."

Belphegor herded the pair of them and their luggage into a small room with an iron door.

"Where do we go from here?" said Joan.

The door slammed behind them. Joan turned. There was a peculiar sucking sound around the edges of the door, as though the door was trying to seal itself perfectly by giving the frame an enormous slobbery snog.

"Well, that's an interesting metaphysical question," said Belphegor's voice from a tinny speaker in the top corner of the chamber. "Traditional symbolism would suggest the answer is 'up' but the spatial relationship between Hell and earth is complex at best."

Through a glass porthole, Joan saw Belphegor press buttons on a keypad.

"Whatever. The shunter will take you directly to earth," said Belphegor.

"I don't want to be shunted," said Joan.

"How do you know unless you've tried it?" said Rutspud casually.

"Nothing good ever happened involving the verb 'to shunt,'" said Joan.

"It's fine," said Rutspud. "This is proven technology, isn't it?" he asked Belphegor.

"We've used it several times," said Belphegor proudly, "with no loss of mass from any of the test objects."

"Test objects?"

Belphegor started to throw levers and set dials. "It will be very interesting to observe the results with both of you in there," he said. "Rutspud?"

"Yes?"

"In the archives. There's a film called The Fly."

"Ye-es?" said Rutspud warily.

"Fiction, right?"

"Yes, sir."

"Oh good," said Belphegor and pressed a large red button.

CHAPTER TWENTY

Nerys sat opposite Clovenhoof on the train into Birmingham. She carried the rolled-up banner he had hastily created.

"So, it's a crowdfunder you're doing," she said.

"In essence," he said, tapping away on her laptop.

"You know that lots of people have done 'pay off my debt' crowdfunders. They only work if you've got lots of friends or are very charismatic."

"I don't need to be either. I just need a good spiel."

Nerys looked back and forth to see if there were any passengers nearby.

"Listen. You're the devil. Can't you just magic up some cash?"

"What?" said Clovenhoof.

"Magic some up. Make some appear. Use your Satanic powers. Maybe give an evil laugh and in a puff of sulphur and brimstone make a great big pile of wonga materialise."

"You assume I want to," he said.

"You mean you can't," she said.

"I have learned that life is about setting oneself little goals and working to achieve them."

"So, you engineered yourself a massive personal debt and put our home at risk just in order to give you something to do?"

"Exactly," he beamed. "There."

He gave the laptop a final flourish of a tap just as the tannoy announced they were coming into New Street Station.

"You know, if you're the devil, you're a really crap devil."

"You trying to hurt my feelings, Nerys."

"Satan is meant to be like the great adversary, this mighty fallen angel. And you... you're stupid and petty and selfish and... you know what?"

"What?"

"You're not actually very evil. You're about as evil as a toddler on a sugar rush."

Clovenhoof tucked the laptop under his arm as he stood.

"I like to think I've matured since the bad old days."

"Gone to seed more like."

He looked at her down his nose. "I can still produce a puff of brimstone and sulphur if you like."

"No thank you," said Nerys, promptly standing up.

"Too late," he said and wafted a flavoursome bottom burp toward her with his free hand.

Nerys dashed to the exit, covering her face and coughing.

When the doors opened at the station, the stink rolled out before them. The noses of homeward bound commuters wrinkled in disgust and Nerys was compelled to declare, "It wasn't me. It really wasn't," but that just compounded her apparent guilt and made her sound crazy.

Clovenhoof was still laughing as they rode up the escalator.

"Shut up," said Nerys miserably.

"Oh, come on. That was hilarious. I've still got it in me."

She flashed him a furious look. "And I'll thank you to keep it there!" She repositioned the heavy banner in her arms. "So, what is this thing? And where are we going?"

"Picture, if you will, Birmingham as the board in a gigantic game."

"I can do that, funnily enough."

"And somewhere, someone has rolled the dice. Someone is hopscotching across the tiles. And they're going to land."

"Uh-huh. Clear as mud so far," she said.

"All we need to do is find a place to sell and some people in the mood to buy, people with more money and greed than sense."

"And you can find such people, can you?"

He grinned. "World's full of them, my dear. The world is full of them."

CHAPTER TWENTY-ONE

There was a flash of brilliant white and blood red.

Joan hoped it wasn't her blood.

She ducked and rolled. It was something she'd done many times before but it was never a comfortable experience when you were wearing a full suit of armour. The explosive power of whatever Belphegor's transport had done to her had triggered it as an instinctive response, but she was surprised to find herself tumbling down a small flight of steps carpeted in red.

The red was carpet. Good. Carpet was a good sign.

She stood and absorbed her surroundings. They had apparently emerged behind an altar. A woman who had been kneeling at a pew stood transfixed at Joan's sudden acrobatic display.

"We're in a church," said Joan.

"How long have you been behind there?" said the woman.

Joan considered this. "How willing are you to believe in the sudden manifestation of heavenly saints?"

The woman gave her a sceptical look.

"Um, we were hiding behind here all along," said Joan. White lies were quite acceptable if they calmed the nervous. "We were..."

"Fornicating," said Rutspud, clambering to his feet in a wobbly fashion. "We were fornicating."

The woman gave a little squeak of surprise.

"Where are we?" Joan asked.

"In the house of our Lord!" said the woman, disgusted.

"And more generally...?"

"This is St Philip's cathedral!"

"Birmingham?"

"Of course!" snapped the woman and taking up her handbag, stomped out, possibly to report the two of them.

Rutspud stretched, his bones audibly clicking.

"Why did you tell her we were fornicating?" said Joan.

"Firstly, because people automatically believe you," said the demon. "And, secondly, I understand that the Brits find sex so embarrassing, it kills off all future questions."

"Good to know," she said but her mind was already pondering the next question. "Why a church?"

"What?"

She put her hands on her hips and looked along the fluted columns and wooden upper galleries. "Why did we appear in a church?"

"Spiritual desire lines," said Rutspud.

"Pardon?"

"Prayers of the faithful create well-trodden but unofficial routes to the afterlife," said Rutspud. "Kinda like cow paths except with prayers instead of hoofs."

"Not sure I like you comparing the faithful to mindless herd animals."

"Seems pretty apt to me."

"But what has that got to do with Belphegor's shunting device?"

Rutspud's face twitched. "You know what. Absolutely nothing."

Belphegor's machine had worked, even if Joan did feel as though she'd been fired from a trebuchet. She followed Rutspud down the nave towards the exit. He held back at the doorway, a stricken look on his face.

"What's the matter?" she said.

"I can't do it," he said.

She looked out the door. The evening sun shone warmly on the grassy area around the cathedral and the tall office buildings, pubs and shop fronts beyond.

"It's fine," she said.

"Mmmm, no," said Rutspud. He was quaking. Joan could see that the usually uber-confident demon was shaking.

"You're not allergic to sunshine, are you?" she said.

"Demon. Not vampire," he tutted. "It's... it's too big."

She stepped out and looked up. "What is?"

128

"Everything! Up there. I can't see the roof." He gestured wildly with a skinny arm.

"The sky?" said Joan. "That's just what it looks like. I thought you'd been to earth before?"

"I did, but I really didn't go out much. Only at night anyway. It's not so bad when it's dark," said Rutspud, risking a quick peek up at the sky. "Satan's balls! They should put a lid on it."

"Heaven has a sky," she pointed on.

"No, it doesn't. That's just the Almighty messing about. My mate, Stephen, once told me how far away the sun actually is and…" He put a hand to his lips. "Makes me sick just thinking about it."

Joan took his arm. "Come on. You can do this. We need to go out there."

They took a few tentative steps along a path. It took them towards a road with tall buildings on the other side.

"So many people," breathed Rutspud. "I'm not used to seeing them all walking around like this. They're not even screaming."

"No," said Joan. "This is people being people. It's what they do while they're alive. In fact…" She stopped and looked round. "No one is screaming."

"That's what I said."

"But you're a demon. Those enormous eyes. The scaly ears."

"Flattering me to distract me from my fears, eh?"

"Why aren't they horrified? Screaming? Running?"

"Posting pictures on Instagram," added Rutspud. "Humans are stupid. They can only see what they want to see. Anything else they just blur out."

"Is that true?" asked Joan.

"Working hypothesis. Now, can we get a move on?" said Rutspud. "Let's have a look for the bishop guy who's in charge round here."

"And where will we find him?" She looked from building to building. "Not sure which of these might be the bishop's palace. That one looks sort of imposing. 'House of Fraser'. Is that it?"

Rutspud had squashed himself into a corner between the cathedral wall and one of the many pilasters around the outside. He crouched with his tablet on his knees.

"Come here," he said. "I need you."

"Yes?" said Joan.

"Stand there. Try and act like a wall."

"What?"

"And a ceiling too if you can."

She turned his back to him which was about as much of a wall and ceiling she was prepared to be and waited for him to finish googling on his computer.

Further along the cathedral wall, a thin crowd had gathered. A cloth banner on two poles said, 'INVEST IN A PIECE OF HISTORY. OWN THE FUTURE!' A woman who looked as if she wanted to be somewhere else (a brothel by the looks of her clothing) handed out leaflets to anyone who would take one and, somewhere in the crowd, a man with a megaphone was haranguing his potential customers, even the ones who had already stopped to listen.

"'But what good's a church?' I hear you cry. And I would say, first up, that it's not a church, it's a cathedral. Compact, almost pocket-sized but positioned slap-bang in the tastiest piece of real estate in Birmingham. Invest fifty pounds today and you will walk away with your own stamped, signed and watermarked certificate of sponsorship. Invest two hundred and you'll get a commemorative brick with your name on it. Invest five hundred and you will be included in the consultation group with voting powers at the point of privatisation."

"Are you saying that they're privatising the Church of England?" asked a loud man in an unnecessarily stuffy suit.

"They said they wouldn't privatise the railways," replied the megaphone salesman (who had a voice Joan thought vaguely familiar). "They said they wouldn't privatise the telephones or the gas or the electric. They said they wouldn't privatise the National Health Service."

"They haven't privatised the NHS," said the stuffy suit. "Um, have they?"

"Astute investors can see which way the wind is blowing. And they will want a piece of the action when it's ten quid admission price for a Sunday service and a grand for the big wedding dos. Check out our crowdfunder page for official details." The salesman clapped his hands. "Fifty quid sponsorship certificate to that man there. Come on, folks. Show us your green. You need to invest before the rest. Supplies *are* limited!"

"Got it," said Rutspud.

"Got it?" said Joan.

"Birmingham cathedral diocesan offices are on Colmore Row." He looked at a dot on a map on his screen. "Which is directly over there." He pointed.

Together they made their way across the bustling cathedral park and over a road crowded with red double-decker buses and bullish black taxi cabs. Rutspud hurried to stand underneath a protective coffee shop awning.

"Bardsey is nothing like this," he said. "So many people here. Is the rest of the world like this?"

Joan considered her scant knowledge of the modern world. "A lot of France is pretty much like this, only... nicer."

"Nicer how?" said Rutspud.

She gave a gallic shrug. "Well, it's in France for one thing. Where's this office?"

"Two doors down."

They moved on together, had a brief fight with a revolving door in front of an office building and found themselves at a reception desk. Rutspud had to stand on tiptoes to see over the top of it.

The man behind the desk treated them to a very white smile.

"Good afternoon, madam and... sir? How can Freddy help you today?"

"We would like to see the bishop," said Joan.

"The bishop?" said the receptionist.

"Bishop Iscansus," said Rutspud.

Freddy the receptionist's smile flickered, as though he'd considered telling Rutspud that he knew full well what the bishop's name was, and then immediately changed his mind.

He looked down at a diary.

"Do you have an appointment?"

"It is very important that we see him," said Joan.

"Too important for an appointment," said Rutspud.

Freddy gave a pained expression and an over-exaggerated sigh. "It's really, really important to make appointments. It's like trying to get a cut and blow from Toni and Guy. You can't just drop in and hope. It just ends in heartache and there's enough of that around. Chocolate truffle?"

He offered them a bowl from below the counter. Rutspud took one immediately.

"We don't want chocolate truffles," said Joan.

"They are delicious," said Freddy, "and you'd be doing me a favour. Freddy has somewhat overindulged of late. My stomach is like a mound of jelly. Wobble-wobble. You can poke it if you like. Have one. Go on."

Joan attempted to maintain her temper. She was a soldier. She was armed and armoured. She could take on an army on a good day. She had no intention of being defeated by a nice man with a bowl of chocolates.

"Please. We have something of great importance to discuss with him. We've come a very long way."

"And it is a lovely accent you have," said Freddy. "France?"

"Yes, yes, but we do need –"

"Freddy *loves* France. The fashion. The food. And Freddy cannot get by without a little bit of Edith in his life."

"Edith?"

"*Non, rien de rien,*" he began to sing in a passionate but strangled falsetto. "*Non, je ne regrette rien...*"

A woman in a severe suit came over to the reception.

"Anette Cleaver," she said, smoothly. "Perhaps I can help. Mr DeVere, you have other duties to attend to."

"Freddy was only trying to brighten the day," the receptionist muttered.

The woman, Anette, steered Joan and Rutspud a little distance away from the reception desk.

"I overheard you mention that you hoped to speak to His Lordship."

"We have something very important to discuss with him," said Joan.

"Perhaps I can help," suggested Anette.

"It has to be the bishop," said Rutspud.

Anette gave him an unpleasant look. "Then I really can't help you. His Lordship is not here at the moment. He is away on ecumenical business."

"Oh, he's been here, there and everywhere," said Rutspud. "We know."

"Then you'll understand that he has a very full calendar."

"So, do you know where he is now?" asked Joan.

"I'm not permitted to share that kind of information," said Anette, affronted. "I don't know how they do things in..." She looked Joan's armour up and down. "Wherever. But, here, you can't just wander in and demand to know where someone is."

"That was kind of our whole strategy," said Rutspud unhelpfully.

Joan wished he hadn't said that. Partly because it was sort of true.

"So, can we make an appointment?"

"The bishop's schedule is organised by the administration team. You will need to speak to one of them and I do believe they have all gone home for the day."

"We could come back tomorrow to speak to them then?" said Joan.

"I don't know about that," said Anette. "You will need to make an appointment."

"An appointment to make an appointment to speak to a man who is not here?" said Rutspud.

"Indeed. You have it exactly," said Anette, pleased. "Now, we are closing in a few minutes."

She gestured to the door, nodded curtly and left them in the cold and unhelpful reception area.

"That's it?" said Joan. "Defeated by bureaucracy. Our quest already over."

"Didn't even last long enough to be called a quest," said Rutspud.

"Suggestions?"

"Grenades?"

"Why? What will that achieve?"

"Shits and giggles?" he said with a shrug.

"No," she replied with a sigh. "Let's head out, see the sights and maybe something will occur to us."

"Maybe try the local cuisine," said Rutspud, fishing around in his bag and pulling out his jelly babies.

"This is Britain. They don't have a cuisine," said Joan.

Freddy the receptionist caught up with them at the door.

"There's no point in coming back tomorrow," he whispered secretively.

"Why?" said Rutspud. "Do we need an appointment to get an appointment to get an appointment?"

Freddy drew them behind a tall potted plant behind the door as though that would somehow conceal them from view. "The bishop's not here."

"We know."

"He's not been here for months. He's disappeared."

"As in... poof?"

"If only it was that simple. Now, what I hear – and you didn't hear this from Freddy – is that he stormed out of a financial accounts meeting months ago. Yelled something like, 'I didn't sign up for this!' and left."

"Oh, that's interesting," said Joan.

"And I mean months ago," said Freddy. "They took three weeks to report it to the Synod office and there's been no moves to get in a replacement."

"Are you sure?" said Rutspud.

Freddy looked down at Rutspud, knowingly. "Freddy works reception. Nothing gets by him. Eyes of the hawk. Ears of the wolf. Hips of the snake."

"So, even if we got an appointment..."

"There'd be no one to have the appointment with. The bishop is a missing person."

"Then we're truly sunk," said Joan.

"Are you two from out of town?" said Freddy.

"More than a little," said Rutspud.

Freddy delved into his jacket pocket and pulled out a wallet.

"We don't need your money," said Joan. "That's too kind."

"I was actually going to give you this," said Freddy, finger walking through the wallet until he pulled out a dog-eared card.

"They're all reasonable rates. I stayed with a couple when I first arrived.

"Christian guest houses," said Rutspud, reading the card.

"Somewhere to stay if you need it." He twitched as he closed his wallet and then reopened and passed Joan a five pound note. "A bus fare to where you're going and a Greggs pasty. Well, probably one or the other at today's prices."

"Thank you, Freddy," she said.

"Think nothing of it," he said. "And tell no one. Freddy gets into enough trouble as it is."

Rutspud rustled a bag at him.

"Jelly baby?"

"Why thank you," said Freddy with disproportionate enthusiasm.

He picked one out of the bag, dusted it down with his fingertips and regarded.

"Do you ever wonder if they're little boy babies or little girl babies?" he asked.

Joan resisted the automatic urge to give them an anatomical once over. "Does it matter?"

"Not at all," said Freddy. "Maybe they're neither one thing nor the other. Lucky things."

He popped the sweet in his mouth.

Rutspud and Joan stepped outside.

"What now?" said Joan.

"We track him down another way. Turn around."

Joan obediently rotated. Rutspud unzipped her backpack and furtled around inside. "Here."

He passed her the currency printer and held the absolution detector in his other hand. He waved it about speculatively.

"Shouldn't that thing be clicking?" said Joan. The device was producing no clicks, only a continuous high-pitched whine.

Rutspud smacked it a couple of times but that made no difference.

"Maybe the tall buildings are causing interference," he said but didn't sound particularly sure. "Let's explore and try to get some readings."

"You acclimatised to the sky now, yes?"

"Hell, no." He put his fingers in his mouth and produced a piercing whistle. "Taxi!"

CHAPTER TWENTY-TWO

Clovenhoof sat down in the armchair. It was a squashy thing, the springs gone completely in the middle of the seat.

"Right, Alice," he said, consulting his notes. "I'm here for two hours of paper reading, farting, general muttering and not offering any interesting conversation."

"Exactly," said the spritely senior. "Except my Bill wouldn't call it farting. He never swore. In fact, he'd be horrified if I pointed it out to him. If anything, he'd say 'pass wind.'"

"Gotcha," said Clovenhoof. "Bill Calhoun doesn't swear. And 'fart' is swearing, is it?"

"Yes."

"Shit?"

"Definitely."

"Crap?"

"Oh, yes."

"Crap is a swear word? Bugger?"

"Just about."

"Bloody."

Alice gave a wistful look. "Mmmm. Pretty much. Unless there's an American politician on the news or I put *Strictly* on the telly. Speaking of which..."

She picked up the remote control and switched the TV to the BBC dancing show.

"Bloody hell, woman, not this tripe," said Clovenhoof and rustled his Daily Express irritably.

"Spot on," she said and smiled. She had a surprisingly sexy smile for a septuagenarian. "Dinner's in fifteen minutes."

Alice went into the kitchen and Clovenhoof settled back and gufted merrily.

The smell of steak and kidney pie wafted from the kitchen. Clovenhoof sent farty harmonies into the air to compete and complement it.

"How was your day?" called Alice from the kitchen.

"I sold over two thousand pounds in sponsorship shares in St Philip's Cathedral," said Clovenhoof. "I don't know if any of them realised they don't actually own a share in it but simply get a bit of pretty paper to say that if I ever came to own the cathedral – which I won't – that they get a say in how it's run."

Alice was at his shoulder. "No, Bill wouldn't say that."

"Sorry, of course. What did Bill do for a living?"

"He was a manager at the Post Office sorting office."

"Ah. I should just chat some guff about letters and... a really big parcel or something?"

"Oh, no. I would ask Bill how his day was and he'd shut the conversation down in less than five words."

"Fine. Fine, I can do that."

"And, also, if you don't mind critical notes, your farts are too much like rotten eggs."

"Yes?"

"Bill's had more of a sprouty richness to them. Less sulphur, more decayed vegetation."

"Good. Critical notes are fine. There is only so much I can do right now without a change in diet but I'll do what I can."

"That's all I ask."

"Take two," said Alice and nipped back into the kitchen before calling out, "How was your day, love?"

"Same as always," said Clovenhoof gruffly.

"Perfect," said Alice softly.

A quarter of an hour later, Alice came through with two plates. "Dinner's on the table."

"Right," said Clovenhoof, noisily folding his paper to get up.

"Oh, Bill would refuse to come to the table. He'd want it on his knee in front of the telly."

"Even though it's *Strictly* on TV?"

"Yes. Bill would moan about *Strictly* but I always suspected he had a thing for Claudia Winkleman."

"She's the one with eye make-up like a panda."

"He used to say that too," smiled Alice. "I think to throw me off the scent."

"I'll have it here then," declared Clovenhoof.

Alice dug out a cushioned tray and presented Clovenhoof with a plate piled high with pie and mash and gravy.

"What did Bill die of in the end?" asked Clovenhoof.

"Heart attack. Salt?" said Alice with an encouraging gesture.

"Course I want salt, woman," said Clovenhoof, feeling his way into the character. He was tempted to try an accent but feared whatever he went for it would soon descend into grumpy Yorkshireman. He took the salt from her without thanks and sprinkled it liberally all over his dinner.

Clovenhoof attacked the deliciously fatty dinner with gusto. Alice took her smaller plate to the nearby table to eat. Clovenhoof made a special effort to confine his conversation to grunts and mutters and the occasional and random announcement that the dancers were rubbish and he had no idea who any of the so-called celebrities were.

Meanwhile Alice kept up a one-side conversation about her day and the doings of her family. She had two adult children and a significant gaggle of grandchildren and two sisters, the late Cynthia and another sister in Leamington Spa who she didn't talk to on account of an argument over offered lifts and missed texts that resulted in one of them being stuck in Coventry for far longer than was humanly acceptable. Clovenhoof made a special effort to ignore all of this because he knew it was what Alice wanted. However, during a long and convoluted monologue about her grandchildren's school woes, Clovenhoof felt the need to break character and interrupt.

"Some people do what?"

"Move house to get into the right school."

"There are right schools and wrong schools?" he said.

"I don't know," said Alice. "That's what Victoria says."

"So, Victoria's eldest, Alfie...?"

"Archie. He's in year six and he's going to secondary next year and Victoria wants to get him into St Michael's Secondary School on account of it being the best school for miles around. Church schools often are, don't you think?"

Clovenhoof didn't think but kept his thought to himself on that score.

"And some people will even temporarily rent a second house or flat near to the school they want their child to get into so they fall inside the catchment area or whatever formula the council use these days," said Alice.

"And they pay money for this?"

"Houses near good schools cost a lot whether you're renting or buying. People are willing to fork out a lot for –" She stopped. "Bill would have had words to say on this. Not many and not helpful."

Clovenhoof nodded, understanding. "It's ridiculous!" he hmphed. "In my day, everyone went to their local school. None of this choice malarkey. Ridiculous."

He stuffed a forkful of mash into his gob and mumbled something about the lacklustre pasa doble a former boyband member was attempting to perform on the television. As he did so, he silently tried to calculate how far his own house was from St Michael's Secondary. It wasn't far, not far at all.

Rutspud flung his arm out in a general north-westerly direction. "That way."

"That's back to Wylde Green," said the taxi driver. "Are you sure?"

Rutspud listened to the absolution detector intently. For the last two hours it had continued to produce a high frequency whine. Rutspud suspected – feared – that the whine did not alter meaningfully in whichever direction he swung it but Rutspud's ears were supernaturally sharp and he hazarded he could detect mild fluctuations as it moved.

"I think so," he said.

The taxi driver made a disagreeable noise. "You need to decide where you're going, mate. It's getting dark and I've got a fish supper waiting."

"Yeah, yeah," said Rutspud. He looked across at Joan, sat in the opposite corner of the passenger cab. "Any joy?"

She gave him a stern look. "Not since the last time you asked."

Joan had the currency printer in her hands. The five pound note the receptionist had given them was half-out of the feed slot and seemingly jammed. Each time she had pressed the button, the device had whirred, juddered and gone silent.

"I think Belphegor created it to process paper notes," said Rutspud. "These new plastic ones..."

"You said!" she said in a firm but controlled voice. "You've said that a dozen times now."

"Where to now?" said the driver as they reached another junction.

Rutspud waved the detector about but he could make no sense of its imperceptibly shifting warbles.

"Have you tried hitting it?" he said to Joan.

"I don't want to break it," she said.

"It's already broken, isn't it?"

"Where to?" said the driver, louder. There was a beep from a vehicle behind. The taxi driver made an expressive hand gesture.

"Give me a minute," said Rutspud.

Joan gave the box an angry thump with her gauntleted fist. It shrieked, juddered and then sucked in the five pound note and spat out a copy. It immediately followed this with a second and a third and did not seem inclined to stop any time soon.

"How many times did you press the button?" asked Rutspud.

There were car horn beeps from the rear, several of them now.

"I can't sit here!" moaned the driver and pulled round the corner and to the side of the road.

A small pile of five pound notes was accumulating on the floor. Rutspud gathered some of them up. Physically, they felt as authentic as the original but there was a crinkle in the copy image, a copy error from where the note had got jammed.

"Right!" huffed the driver. "Either you two give me a proper *final* destination or you get out here."

Joan was trying to catch the fivers as the machine spewed them out. Rutspud threw his bag at her and she dumped machine and notes into it, the machine still merrily printing away. Rutspud looked at the fare on the electronic meter above the windscreen. Well, at least they had enough money to cover that now.

Joan gave Rutspud a panicked look and held the neck of the bag tight.

"Fine," he said, defeated. He located the card of guest houses the receptionist at the church office had given him and passed it through the payment hatch. "Take us to the nearest place on that card."

The driver leaned back and peered long-sightedly at the card.

"That I can do," he said.

Within two minutes, the taxi had pulled up outside a tall house on a residential road. He put his handbrake on with a bad-tempered finality.

"Two hundred and eighteen pound sixty."

Joan counted out a bundle of bank notes from the maelstrom of money in the bag and passed them through to the driver. He gathered and sorted them and then inspected the top one.

"The queen on these," he said. "She looks kinda funny."

"Funny ha-ha or funny peculiar?" said Rutspud innocently.

The driver scratched at the note as though there was a crease that needed flattening out. "Kinda squinty, like she knows something we don't, like she's up to something."

"That's royalty for you," said Rutspud and followed Joan quickly out of the car.

The sky above was cloudy and the evening getting darker by the minute. With a little effort, Rutspud could pretend that above him was a really high and poorly lit ceiling. He still didn't like it though. Joan went up the path at the front of the house. A brass plate next to the frosted glass door read:

THE MISSION SOCIETY OF THE THROWN VOICE
SHELTER, SANCTUARY AND QUALITY BED & BREAKFAST

Joan rang the doorbell and reasserted her grip on the neck of the money-filled bag. Soon enough, a light came on. A woman in a lemon cardigan and a white clerical collar opened the door. There was a figure propped up in her arms. Rutspud did not consider himself an expert of humans. He understood human behaviour, but the rude mechanics and surface details were a bit of blur. He was prepared to believe that the thing in the woman's arms was a human child but sneakily suspected it wasn't. Its shiny face, massive swivelling eyes and shock of artificial hair were subtle clues. Also, there was the fact that the woman appeared to have her hand shoved up its bum.

"Hello?" said the puppet (although the woman's lips did move the slightest bit).

"Hello, is this the...?" Joan pointed stupidly at the sign.

The puppet's giant head rotated to look at the plaque.

"Yes, indeedy!" it said. "Looking for a place to stay? Come in! Come in!"

The woman backed down the hallway.

"Give your feet a good wipe and come sign in here!" instructed the puppet. "My name is Tommy Chuckles and this is Sister Anne. Say hello to Sister Anne!"

"Hello," said Joan. Rutspud gave her a wave and felt stupid for doing so.

Sister Anne gave them a shy smile and a nod.

"Now have you stayed with us before?" asked Tommy Chuckles.

"No," said Rutspud. "A man gave us a card and said we should come here."

"Word of mouth is the best recommendation. Now, we have dormitory beds for ten pounds a night or we have rooms from twenty-five pounds. You're not a couple, are you?"

"A couple of what?" asked Rutspud.

"No," said Joan firmly. "We're not. Separate room."

"Super-duper," said Tommy Chuckles. "And will you be paying with cash or card?"

"Cash. Definitely cash," said Joan.

"Very good."

Sister Anne took payment and went off to search for room keys. Tommy Chuckles went with her, naturally.

"This," said Rutspud, suspecting he didn't need to explain what 'this' he was referring to. "This isn't normal, is it?"

"I think holy houses and religious orders can often be places of refuge for people with social... idiosyncrasies," said Joan kindly.

"You mean nutters."

It made a certain sense. He was very familiar with the monks of Bardsey Island and they were, by turns, eccentric, reclusive, socially awkward and downright strange.

"This place will cater for all sorts," said Joan. "Whereas this perfectly delightful Sister Anne has a penchant for a ventriloquist's dummy maybe another member of this house has –"

"A dinosaur puppet," said Rutspud, deadpan.

A younger woman came down the hallway. The pink dinosaur on her arm waggled its cloth mouth.

"Hi, I'm Yazoo," it said in a sleepy melodic voice. "Tommy Chuckles says you might need a hand with your bags."

The demon and saint were momentarily dumbfounded.

"Er, no. We're fine, Yazoo," said Rutspud.

Sister Anne re-emerged from a side room with two keys, each on a heavy plastic fob.

"We saw you were both into your..." Joan mimed a little hand puppet. "Quite a coincidence to find two people with the same hobby."

"I thought you knew," said Tommy Chuckles as Sister Anne beckoned them on to the stairs. "All the sisters here have companions. It's a rule of our order."

"Is it?" said Rutspud, following.

Joan was confused. "Do we... In that, are guests required to have a puppet too?"

"No, silly," said Yazoo in his sing-song voice. "Only the sisters need companions to speak for them."

"Oh, why's that?"

Tommy Chuckles head turned a hundred and eight degrees to he could look back over Sister Anne's shoulder.

"Isn't it obvious? They've taken a vow of silence."

CHAPTER TWENTY-THREE

The doorbell rang. Clovenhoof skipped out of his flat to go answer it and bumped into Ben, locking up his own flat and heading out to work for the morning.

"And how are you this morning?" said Clovenhoof, with some very expressive brow-waggling.

"Er, yeah, fine," said Ben. "Apart from all the tossing and turning."

"I bet you were. Tossing and turning all night, the pair of you."

"The pair of us?" Ben frowned. "I spent the night with burning crotch rash from that barbaric waxing you inflicted on me."

"Didn't Narinda anoint it with soothing oils? I thought things were going well with you and Narinda."

"Oh, it was amazing," said Ben, his eyes lighting up in a way they so rarely did. "The things she showed me."

"That's more like it," said Clovenhoof. "Woman of the world, is she?"

"She's young but she's surprisingly knowledgeable."

Clovenhoof clapped his hands. "Give me details, Kitchen," he said, wondering what sordid little kinks and fetishes Narinda Shah had brought into Ben's life.

"Well..." said Ben.

"Yes?"

"For example, and it's just an example..."

"Yes?"

"If I use my flat to store merchandise or use it to do my paperwork..."

"Um, yes?"

"Then I can claim back some of my heating and lighting as tax deductible expenses."

Clovenhoof blinked.

"You and Narinda spent the evening discussing methods of tax evasion."

"Tax avoidance. Yes. All legal and above board."

"How tragically disappointing," said Clovenhoof.

"But useful. She's coming over again tomorrow to look at your finances too. Maybe she and I can actually work out what's going on with your money."

Nerys came up the stairs.

"There's a woman downstairs with an exquisite Kelly handbag. Hermès."

"Oh, I wasn't expecting Hermès," said Clovenhoof. "I'm waiting for a woman called Victoria."

"That's who it is," said Nerys.

"Why didn't you say?" said Clovenhoof and bounded down the stairs.

Joan rose.

The beds at the Society Mission for the Thrown Voice were definitely comfortable. Joan always perversely found herself preferring beds on earth to those in the Celestial City. Of course, everything in the Celestial City was perfect, the beds equally so, but while the beds of Heaven were naturally perfect, she knew that this earthly bed, any earthly bed, had only been made comfortable through the time and effort of designers and manufacturers and craftspeople and this made her appreciate it all the more.

After queuing for the bathroom behind two of the society sisters (Sister Marcus with her rag doll puppet Pepper and Sister Valerie with a fishy glove puppet called Bubbles), Joan went downstairs for breakfast and found Rutspud in the large kitchen-diner. Rutspud had a plate of toast in front of him but he was ignoring it and fiddling with the still-whining absolution detector.

"Sleep well?" she said, slipping into the bench opposite.

"Demons don't sleep," he said and poked at the back of the detector with a screwdriver. "And the bed was too soft. Give me a hard floor any day, preferably strewn with shards of volcanic glass. Did you sleep?"

"Divinely. The money making machine was still printing notes long after midnight. I had to put it in the bottom of a chest of drawers before I made my bag explode."

"Might be hard to explain away," agreed Rutspud.

Sister Anne came over and put a teapot, cup, saucer and miniature milk jug in front of Joan.

"Would you like toast and Marmite same as your friend here?" asked Tommy Chuckles.

"I'll just have a slice of his," said Joan. "I don't think he's hungry."

"Oh, you must eat up your toast and Marmite," said Tommy Chuckles, rolling his large wooden eyes. "Full of healthy, nutritious zinc."

"I'll bear that in mind," said Rutspud.

"Thank you, Tommy," said Joan. "And, er, thank you, Sister Anne."

When the sister and her dummy had gone off to continue preparing breakfasts, Rutspud picked up a piece of toast critically.

"You've got bread. Which is wheat flour mixed with water and stuff which then puffs up because a fungus inside it eats up the sugar content and inflates the bread with its farts."

"I don't think it's farts, as such...."

"And then – and then! – it's served with this gloop on it which is made by taking a tub of the same fungus and killing it off with salt poisoning or somesuch."

"I'm not familiar with this Marmite product," said Joan.

"It's fungus served with a topping of zombie fungus."

"But I'm sure it's delicious," said Joan and bit off a big corner.

The taste hit was sudden and unexpected. It was like an explosion of evil in her mouth. She coughed automatically but kept her lips politely sealed so she nearly ended up snorting toast and Marmite down her nose.

"How does it taste?" said Rutspud.

With shaking hands, Joan poured herself a cup of tea and used it to swill down the toast. She poured herself a second and drank that straight away before speaking.

"Visiting earth," she croaked, "is all about discovering new experiences."

She put the remains of the slice back on the plate.

The detector in Rutspud's hands gave a wild screech and then settled down to produce a continuous series of clicks, spaced just less than a second apart. Rutspud moved it round in an arc and the clicks changed in frequency.

"You fixed it," said Joan, delighted.

"It was never broken. That noise. That was just the device trying to click a gazillion times a second."

"What do you mean?"

"Belphegor had calibrated it to click every time there was a moment of ritual forgiveness in the local area and why not. Except, for some reason, this place is – and maybe all places are – buzzing with forgiveness."

"And you've just dialled down its sensitivity."

"Correct." He waved it about victoriously. "Which means we can go and track down the source of our current misery." He looked at the toast. "Unless you want to finish your breakfast first."

CHAPTER TWENTY-FOUR

Clovenhoof stood at his living room window and gestured to the road and the houses beyond.

"And you can probably see, just up that way, the spire of St Michael's church. That's how close we are."

Victoria Calhoun, daughter of Clovenhoof's gigoloafing client and anxious mother of young Archie, leaned on the windowsill and peered out.

"Oh, yes," she said. "Very close." She looked at the grime she now had on her fingertips and surreptitiously wiped them with a tissue taken for the glitzy handbag Nerys had eyed so covetously. "So, we'd definitely be in catchment if we lived here?" she asked.

"You certainly would," agreed Clovenhoof. "You put this address on the council application form and your little Archie will be a shoo-in at St Michael's Secondary."

"And you're only charging three hundred a month?" she said, casting an eye about the flat.

"Introductory rate for our pioneer customers."

She frowned quizzically.

"You're not the only people who want to rent somewhere near to their favourite school," he said.

"Oh. So how many flats do you have here?"

"There's the ground floor. There's the two on this floor and then you've got Nerys and her mad terrier in the floor above."

"And she's moving out, is she?"

"No. What?" He suddenly understood and laughed. "You've perhaps misunderstood me, Victoria. You need an address to put on the application. That's what I'm renting to you."

"Just the address? Not the actual property."

"We have to keep things above board," said Clovenhoof. He took a roll of wallpaper off the mantelpiece and rolled it out over the dining table. On the reverse, Clovenhoof had sketched out a scale plan of his flat and divided it up into squares. "I've done some rudimentary measurements of local kids and reckon you can get three children per square metre. Upright of course." He hovered over the plan with a pencil. There were half a dozen squares already filled in. "I could put your Archie in the back bedroom. He'd have it to himself for the time being."

"Does it matter where he goes?" said the confused mother.

"Doesn't bother me if it doesn't bother you," grinned Clovenhoof and scribbled the name Archie into the box. "Now, your mum told you I only work cash in hand."

"Yes," said Victoria, opening her handbag again. "I'm not sure what kind of relationship you have with my mother."

"A purely financial one," he reassured her. "I'm just stepping into the shoes of your dear departed daddy."

"Stepping into his shoes?"

"Yes. The man was enamoured of a patent leather brogue. Stylish in his own unique manner."

"So, there's nothing funny going on between you and mum?"

"We have a laugh but, no, I'm just being the new Mr Calhoun in her life and trying to fill that empty void inside her."

"Is that a euphemism?" she said.

"Tell me something that isn't," he replied. He held out his hand for the cash.

"I don't like just handing over money to people," she said, handing it to him anyway.

"But think of what you get for that money. You get a place at the local school. You get a proof of address if one is needed. You get a full 24-7 pretend residency service. I should be charging more really."

"Will you?" she asked.

"Not to you, valued customer," he said. "Cheap rates for those who get in at the ground floor, well, back bedroom."

As he ushered her down the stairs, the doorbell rang.

"Possibly another eager customer," he said.

He opened the door. A man with a bad haircut and a surly expression stood on the doorstep. Maybe he had the surly expression because he'd been given a bad haircut. Victoria Calhoun stepped past and Clovenhoof waved her off.

"Mr Clovenhoof?" said the surly man.

"Who's asking?" said Clovenhoof amiably.

"Robin Hood Debt Collection Services," said the man and tapped an ID badge clipped to his coat.

The ID badge identified him as Morten Morris. His ID picture also featured a different bad haircut and an identical surly expression which either meant surly was Morten's default expression or he had made the mistake of going to the same bad barber twice.

"In that case, no," said Clovenhoof.

"You won't be surprised to hear that a lot of people say that. I'm here to collect on an outstanding loan and am happy to take cash, cards or items of property of up to nine thousand pounds in value. So let's get to it, Mr Clovenhoof."

"Honestly, I'd love to help you, Morten, but you've been misled. There's no Clovenhoof living here. Obviously a made up name. Clovenhoof? Cloven-hoof? Some sort of joke."

Morten bent down and picked up the post that sat disregarded on the doormat.

"And yet here is a letter from the Sutton Railway Building Society addressed to a Mr J. Clovenhoof."

"I'd been meaning to report that," said Jeremy blithely. "Do you think it's just a mistake or some kind of identity theft thing? My name's Calhoun, Bill Calhoun."

"Really?" said Morten sceptically. "And would you have any form of identification to prove that?"

"Not on me but you can ask her," he said, pointing at Victoria who was not far down the road. "That's my step-daughter."

Morten stepped away from the door and cupped a hand to his mouth. "Oi! Darlin'! Is this man your dad?"

Victoria gave him a sharp look.

"He's not my real dad," she shouted back.

Morten pointed at Clovenhoof. "Mr Calhoun?"

Victoria gave a despairing but affirmative shrug and turned away.

"She's never quite accepted me," said Clovenhoof. He took the letters from Morten. "Do you think I should call the police about these?"

"We'll make our own enquiries, Mr Calhoun," said Morten. "And I may be coming back."

"Let us know when and I'll be sure to put the kettle on," said Clovenhoof and shut the door in his face.

Rutspud followed the clicks and ticks of the absolution detector. And Joan followed Rutspud.

She was a medieval girl at heart and, while no technophobe, she was happy to let someone else handle the gizmos. Electronic gadgetry held no allure for her. She could see what it had made the world.

Currently, it was making Rutspud very annoyed. He muttered obscenities and gave little squeals of frustration as the device led them on a meandering course through the suburbs of this grey modern metropolis. The one upside to the whole affair was that Rutspud's annoyance was distracting him completely from his agoraphobic fear of the wide-open skies.

"It's like it's coming from two places at once," he mumbled.

"Really?" said Joan, disinterested.

The device gave a flurry of clicks like a tap-dancing centipede. Rutspud whirled and dashed towards the nearby row of shops. Joan followed unhurriedly at a distance and waited in the shelter of an anaemic looking birch tree. Rutspud ran the detector over the short queue of people at a bus stop.

"Can I help you with something?" said a woman.

"Have you been forgiven recently," said Rutspud, looking at his readings rather than the woman.

"Pardon?"

"Bloody Jehovah's Witnesses," said a man in the queue.

"You're not Bishop Iscansus, are you?" Rutspud asked him.

"Am I what?" said the man.

As Joan watched this exchange, she became aware of a knocking against her feet. She looked down to find a filthy and wretched looking man in a poor excuse for a beard using a trowel to poke at the ground directly by her feet. Joan stepped aside and away.

"What are you doing?" she asked.

The man shushed her violently. "You'll scare them away. They don't wanna be caught."

"You're looking for something?" she whispered.

"Devils," said the man, placed his bulbous diseased nose to the ground and sniffed. "An' their tunnels."

"You can't do that here," she said. "We've already got one fool searching for something he can't find on this street and that's one too many as it is."

But the man was paying scant attention. He scraped at the soil at the base of the tree and listened. As he did so, he reached back and pulled a limp potato chip from his pocket and thrust it in his mouth. Without looking up, he reached back, pulled out another and offered it to Joan.

"Chip?"

"That's very kind, sir, but no," she said.

Rutspud stepped off the pavement and into the road, blithely ignoring the double decker bus that had to brake to avoid hitting him. He ignored the beeping horn and panned the device around.

"There's an echo," he called over to Joan. "It's like it's always coming from two places at once."

"Can you tell 'im to be quiet," said the filthy man. "What's he doin' anyway?"

"He's looking for someone," said Joan.

"Is the someone he's looking for radioactive?"

"He's a bishop actually."

"He don't look much like a bishop," said the filthy man.

"No, the man he's looking for is a bishop," said Joan.

"Uh. Anyone we know?"

"Bishop Kenneth Iscansus. Bishop of Birmingham."

The filthy man sat back on his haunches. "I'll not be able to hear them with the noise he's making."

"The devils," Joan said.

The man nodded. "Sometimes, I don't even think they're there. Uh'm sure I started doing it for a reason. Make some point. Grand philosophsi – oh, bugger, grand philososphical point." He reached into his other pocket and pulled out a stout plastic bottle from which the label had been ripped. "Helps me think," he told her before taking a swig. "You want some?"

"No, thank you."

"Okay but I asked. In case you're that sly bugger Jesus. Can't have you judging me later going, I was hungry an' I was thirty, was you there, was you there? I was here, Jesus," he said bitterly. "And I offered you a swig."

Rutspud was spiralling round back towards Joan. A thought occurred to her.

"I'm Joan," she said to the man.

"You look like a Joan," he replied. "S'good name."

"What's your name?"

He had to think about that for a moment. "Ken!" he declared loudly. "Dear me, forget my own trousers next. And I did once. Call me Festering Ken on account of this astonishing odour for which I will not apologise."

"Nice to meet you, Ken," she said. "What would you say if my friend and I offered to take you out for lunch?"

"Dunno, are you likely to?"

Joan smiled.

"You have nothing to smile about," fumed Rutspud, stomping over. "This device is just playing silly buggers –"

"Great game, great game," reminisced Festering Ken quietly.

"Rutspud, let me introduce you to Ken," said Joan. "Rutspud is currently scouring the streets for a missing bishop. Ken is looking for little devils in the dirt. I suspect you two could make each other very happy."

Rutspud gave Joan a look and pointed at the ragged man questioningly. Joan nodded.

CHAPTER TWENTY-FIVE

Clovenhoof strode with outwardly visible contentment towards the house of Alice, the widow Calhoun. He was experiencing something he had experienced a mere smattering of times in his long existence: job satisfaction. He was making cash for doing essentially very little and yet was providing a much-appreciated service to a delightful old bird. He got to wear shitty clothes, parade his bad habits and got a slap-up meal into the bargain. As such, he was starting to put in an extra special effort. He had combed his hair to match that of the late Bill Calhoun and had drunk four pints of artichoke and cabbage smoothie to hopefully tweak his farts to the right aromatic shade Alice was looking for.

As he crossed the main road, his phone rang. It had rung numerous times today, a slow but accelerating stream of calls to rent utterly fictitious flat space so that little darlings across the borough could get into the popular church school.

Clovenhoof put the phone to his ear. "Go for Clovenhoof."

"I'm sorry?" said a woman's voice.

"Are you? I wouldn't worry about it. No one else does."

"My name is Linda O'Brien."

"Nothing to be sorry about there."

"I'm calling about an application for St Michael's Secondary School."

"Then you've called the right number," said Clovenhoof, his chest swelling with pride and avarice. Mostly avarice. "Now, I've still got some spaces left, although some of them are in the bathroom and not the nice end either. Maybe you're not fussy."

"You've got what?" said Linda.

"Or I can do the broom cupboard in the kitchen. We've had a problem with mice in there. I say problem. I like to think of it as a feature."

"I'm sorry?"

"So you said."

"The application was made by a Ms Victoria Calhoun. Is it possible to talk to her?"

"Ah, Archie. Now, he's in the back bedroom."

"Is he not at school today?" asked Linda. "Is he unwell?"

Something should have clicked in Clovenhoof's brain but he didn't quite manage it. Something sort of 'clonked' instead. He stopped on the pavement and rewound the conversation.

"Who are you again?" he asked.

"Linda O'Brien. Admissions officer for St Michael's Secondary School."

"Ah, and you want to talk to Victoria…"

"About the application for Archie. I have some questions."

"Oh, I see," said Clovenhoof. "Yes, I'll get her for you. I'm Bill Calhoun. Her dad."

"So what was that thing about Clovenhoof?" said Linda.

"Clovenhoof? Don't know what you mean. But then again I do suffer from that… that Altimeter's Disease."

"Do you mean Alzheimer's, sir?"

"No, Altimeter's. I get light-headed when I go upstairs. Ah, here she is now." He cupped his hand over the speaker, closed his eyes for three seconds to hurriedly get into character and then spoke in which he considered his most convincing female voice.

"Oh, hellooo. Victoria Calhoun here. Sorry about my dad. He's quite mad but he's probably going to die soon so that's okay. Linda, was it?"

"Hello, Ms Calhoun," said Linda. "I'm calling about an application you submitted to attend St Michael's Secondary School."

Victoria had only come looking round the house an hour or so ago. Clearly a woman who didn't hang around.

"Why, I only submitted it this morning."

"The beauty of electronic applications," agreed Linda. "Now, the local authority makes the final allocations later in the year but, as a faith school, we have our own admissions criteria."

"Yes?"

"And I couldn't help but notice that the address you've given us is different to the one his primary school has on record."

"We moved. Recently."

"How very nice," said Linda. "Schools have to be mindful that some parents make fraudulent applications to get their children into a favoured school."

"You're not accusing me of fraud, are you?" said Clovenhoof. His best falsetto went up an octave in dismay.

"We do have to make certain checks. Church schools are increasingly popular. Which is funny really when you think about how church attendance figures are going down so much."

"Nerys says it's because of your horrible biscuits and crap tea."

"Oh, right," said Linda.

"But Ben said he really liked the carrot nativity last year."

"That's nice, I think. Is Ben your other son?"

"Yes, why not," said Clovenhoof.

Now, with young Archie off ill I take it you'll be at home with him for the rest of the day?" asked Linda.

"Um," said Clovenhoof.

"I have other visits to make, Ms Calhoun, but I'll come to your house shortly after three. Will that be okay?"

A decent excuse failed to materialise in Clovenhoof's brain. "More than okay, Mrs O'Brien."

"It's miss, actually."

"Saucy," said Clovenhoof and ended the call.

He stared at the ground for a moment. The admissions officer was coming round at three o'clock. Clovenhoof was not Victoria Calhoun. He did not have a poorly boy in his back bedroom. If he didn't prepare, his rental business would go bust in its first week. The obvious solution was to phone up Victoria and get her young Archie to hurry over. But Clovenhoof was cleverer than that. He knew that the most obvious solution was rarely the most fun one.

He made another call.

"Hi, Alice. Jeremy here. It's going to be a flying visit this afternoon. Something's come up. Do you, by any chance, have some women's clothing in my size?"

Joan and Rutspud sat at a table in a Large Mike's fish and chip restaurant with the man called Festering Ken who Joan was convinced was also Kenneth Iscansus the previously missing bishop of Birmingham. It wasn't the first placed they had tried to get served but staff at three coffee shops and a pizzeria had all taken one look at the grubby and unwashed Ken and told him to get out.

But the folks at Large Mike's were less fussy and, in fact, seemed to know Ken sufficiently that the woman at the counter gave his order an extra portion of chips. Rutspud tucked into his fish and chips hungrily.

"Better than bloody Marmite on toast."

"You can't beat a good honest piece of fish," agreed Ken, broke his open with his fingers and doused its steaming innards with vinegar.

Rutspud was less enamoured by the fish but the chips were greasy bags of delicious white pus and the fish batter was crunchier than toenails. Joan nibbled at hers politely but clearly had mixed feelings.

Ken looked out at the sudden and heavy rain that had just started up outside. A woman came in, trying to shelter her hair beneath her handbag. She shook herself momentarily like a dog, saw the demon, saint and homeless man watching her and stalked over to the counter.

"I blame the Peter Principle," said Ken.

Joan frowned at Rutspud.

"Medieval heretical group, I think," said Rutspud.

"You know why I became a priest?" said Ken.

"Those who can do, those who can't preach?" suggested Rutspud.

"You had a calling," said Joan simply.

"I did. I did. I wanted to serve the Lord and my local community. You know why I became a bishop? Because they told me I could."

Joan nodded in understanding.

"You seized too much power," said Rutspud. "Put your head above the parapet."

"Ha! Built my own ivory tower and shut myself away from what I cared about," grunted Ken. "I had one of those, thingamies, moments of clarity. I was in a financial accounts meeting, listening to some dullard called Okra Boddington droning on and on about our investment portfolio and I realised I wasn't involved in religious ministry. I was an executive in a multi-million-pound company. And I just stood up and do you know what I said?"

"'I didn't sign up for this'?" said Rutspud.

"Exactly that," said Ken, pointing at him with a chip before eating it. "I now preach to the pigeons and the squirrels and do my little experiments. It's not as fulfilling as it sounds if I'm honest with you."

"It doesn't sound very fulfilling at all."

"And it's less fulfilling than that."

The woman with the handbag sat at a table in the far corner with a coffee in a take-out cup and played on her phone.

"Have you been offering to give confession or absolution recently?" Joan asked the homeless bishop.

"To the pigeons and squirrels?" said Ken. He shook his head. "They're not keen on sinning as far as I can tell and even less keen to confess what they have done."

"We meant people," she said. "We're investigating a... significant number of absolutions granted in your name."

Ken shook his head again and concentrated on getting as many calories down his throat as quickly as possible. Rutspud didn't know what to make of that. Here was the bishop, of that he was certain. He couldn't imagine many of the faithful would rush to Ken for absolution but the detector in front of him was going click-click-click.

"Yes, mummy," said the woman in the corner, now conversing on her phone. "I did meet him. He's a peculiar sort and that's an understatement. But – no, I rented a corner of a bedroom from him. Already used the address to make the application. Yes, very helpful. What? Say that again? Can he have some of my old clothes?

Whatever for?" She stared at the phone. "He and I are *not* the same size. Well, really!"

The woman put the phone down.

"Crazy old bat!" she grumbled loudly and then, Rutspud could see, her expression immediately relenting. The woman picked up the phone again and tapped at it.

Rutspud grabbed Joan's arm. The needle on the detector had leapt up higher than ever before, just for a few seconds and was now settling down again.

"Oscillating between two points very close together," Rutspud said to himself.

"You just forgave someone," Joan said to Ken.

"'id uh?" he said around a mouthful of fried food.

"Something happened," said Rutspud. He slid out of his chair and hurried over to the woman in the corner.

She gave him a look that was both fearful and suspicious.

"What did you just do?" asked Rutspud.

The woman was perplexed. She held up her coffee cup. "It's a latte."

"No, just now," said Rutspud. "You did something, something on your phone."

"I was talking to my mother if it's any of your business which it is not."

"No, after that. Just now. Just, just now."

The woman was recoiling into the corner of her seat. Joan appeared beside Rutspud.

"Please, you might be able to help us," she said.

"Are you the police?" asked the woman.

"Near enough but you're not in any trouble."

The woman wordlessly turned her phone around to show them. An app on the screen showed a big blue tick. Above it were the words 'Negative thoughts about a loved one.' Below the tick were the words 'Go in Peace!' and a tiny animated angel which appeared to be doing a little rumba dance.

"What the Hell...?" said Rutspud.

"It's PrayPal," said the woman. "It's free to download."

"I am confused," said Joan bluntly. "Am I an idiot or am I right to be confused?"

"It's very simple," said the woman. She hit the back button and typed in a search box until she found a listing entitled 'Discourteous to a stranger'. "That'll do," she said and hit a submit button. The big blue tick came up again and Rutspud's detector gave an excited leap. "It's very freeing," said the woman. "You know, emotionally and spiritually. And the PrayPal does all sins, big and small."

Over at the other table, Ken gave a sudden cry. His hands were raised in enthusiastic surprise.

"I did that!" he said.

"That?" said Rutspud and pointed at the app on the woman's screen.

"That! That's a thing I did!"

Joan listened as Bishop Kenneth Iscansus attempted to explain the origins of PrayPal. She hoped Rutspud understood what he was saying because half of it was just flying over her head.

"And we did it here!" said Ken, delighted.

"Here? Here where?"

"This delightful chip shop," said Ken. "The three of us."

"You and...?"

"The shifty chap and the lad with the computer."

"Names?"

Ken's mouth went through several experimental shapes before he gave up. "Don't get to exchange names with people so much these days," he said. "But the shifty one. He lives on the Chester Road. Offered me a suck on his hairy sweet the other day."

Joan had no idea what item of slang that was. She didn't want to think about it.

"Chester Road is near here," said Rutspud, already looking it up on his tablet. "A long road but we could go knock on doors."

"He was the one who came up with the idea," said Bishop Ken.

"The shifty one?"

Ken nodded. "He came in and ordered a round for everyone."

"A round of fish and chips?" said Joan.

"I think he might have been drunk," said Ken thoughtfully. "But generous. We got to talking. He knew who I was, don't know how. I had been on the streets for a few weeks by then. Din't look like a bishop. Who does without the vestments? We might as well be empty robes."

Ken's gaze drifted off to an empty and introspective place. Rutspud clicked his fingers in front of his face to bring him back.

"The shifty one with no name," clarified Rutspud, "came up with the idea for a mobile phone application that automatically provides the user with forgiveness at the click of a button. And you put your name, your metaphorical seal to it?"

"And the lad with the computer said he'd make it work. Said we'd all have a share in the proceeds. Advertising revenues or something. I wasn't interested in that. It was just a conversation, a bit of chit-chat while I ate a free tray of chips."

Rutspud blinked. Joan could see a faint smile forming on his lips.

"Does this make sense to you?" she asked.

"It explains the recorded facts," said the demon. "The thousands of absolutions. The double readings I'm getting; one for the user and one for Ken here."

"So we can stop it?" she said.

Rutspud grimaced.

"Stop what?" said Ken.

Rutspud tapped at his tablet for a minute.

"PrayPal. Produced by WinkyCat Studios. Shareholders... only two listed. One Kenneth Iscansus and one Jeremy Clovenhoof."

"Oh, no," said Joan, her heart sinking.

"What?" said Rutspud. "You know this Clovenhoof character?"

She blew out the sudden tension that had risen in her chest. "Yes. I do know him. And you know him too?"

"Don't think I do," said the demon, none the wiser.

"What's more I know where he lives. I was briefly on the committee that relocated him when he was sent to earth."

162

"Re...?" Rutspud looked up at her. "You mean, the old boss?"

"Did you never wonder where they sent Satan after they fired him?"

CHAPTER TWENTY-SIX

Clovenhoof knocked on the door to Nerys's second floor flat. The door opened a fraction and Twinkle came out and sniffed critically at Jeremy's hoofs.

"I'm impressed by any dog that can open doors but how do you even reach the handle?" he asked the Yorkshire terrier.

"I'm here," said Nerys, angling the door open with her knee as she took a shoe off with one hand and the opposite earring with the other. "Just in from work. What do you want?"

"Do you have boobs?" he asked.

Nerys stared at him for a long time and then, bereft of words, grabbed her own breasts. Living with the devil as a neighbour had engendered a certain brutal honesty in Nerys.

"I meant for me," said Clovenhoof.

Nerys looked him up and down.

"You know, any other person would ask why you're wearing a woman's blouse and skirt but I haven't got the energy."

"It's for an important reason," he said.

"Are you sure? Because you seem to find quite a number of 'important reasons' to dress up as a woman. You know, you don't have to make up reasons to dress in whatever way you feel is comfortable. Whatever lifestyle choices you wish to adopt, no one's going to judge you."

"You judge me all the time," said Clovenhoof.

"Yeah, that's because you're a dick," she said. "What makes you think I've got false breasts lying around the house?"

"I know you've got a bunch of dressing up things, even though you've shown no interest in the theatrical arts."

"Those are for personal entertainment."

"And private performances, sure. Boobs, please."

Ten minutes later, after a briefing ransacking of Nerys's suitcase of roleplay get up (and the fruit bowl), Nerys had equipped him with a passable brunette wig and a pair of citrus tits.

"They're not very pert," he said.

"Take a look at your face, mate," she said. "A woman your age does not do pert. In fact, I should squeeze the juice out of them a bit."

"Don't you dare," he said, clutching his cleavage.

The front door bell rang. Clovenhoof looked at the clock. It was barely half past two.

"She's early!" he said.

"Who?"

"I'm not ready. I texted Spartacus but he's not got back to me."

"About what?" she asked but Clovenhoof was already running out of the flat and barrelling down the stairs.

As he came to the hallway he slowed, smoothed down his blouse and put on a little feminine sashay. He had the clothes, the hair, the anatomical accessories. He'd even taken the time to apply a little make up and nail polish. This admissions officer had better be appreciative of the effort he was putting in.

He opened the door and was about to offer Miss O'Brien a ladylike greeting when he saw it wasn't her.

"Oh, it's you," he said.

"I'm sorry," said Narinda, confused. She looked at Clovenhoof then at the house number to the side of the door and then back to Clovenhoof. "Jeremy?"

"You've caught me in the middle of something," he said.

"Evidently," she replied.

Clovenhoof looked up and down the street to check no one else was coming along and then dragged Narinda inside.

"I don't have time to discuss trivial tax matters today," he said.

"It was Ben who invited me round."

Oh. He said you two hit it off the other night."

"I don't know about that, Jeremy," she said in a strict tone. "But he clearly takes a more mature attitude to fiscal responsibility than you do and wants me to go over some particulars." She picked up the morning's post which had managed to travel from the doormat to the little side table. She waved the Sutton Railway Building Society letter. "Is this a dirty hoof print?" she said.

"Maybe," said Clovenhoof.

"Do you have a cow living in the flat?"

"Goat actually. No. Shall we?"

He led the way.

"Can you see up my skirt if I go ahead of you?" he asked.

"No."

"What about if I hitch it up like..."

"Aagh! No! Put it away! Them! It! Just..."

Narinda was rubbing her eyes when they reached the first floor. Clovenhoof rapped on Ben's door. Nerys was descending the stairs.

"Ooh, Narinda," she said. "Come to see our Ben again."

"Just to go over some of his particulars," said Narinda.

"Ooh. You two are getting serious then?"

"They're really not," said Clovenhoof. "Or rather, they really are but in an incredibly boring way."

The doorbell downstairs rang as Ben opened the door.

On the wall of Ben's flat, Clovenhoof could see that the geeky bookseller had created a map of financial data with letters, statements, string and drawing pins. It looked like a prop from a cop show, a cop show where the evil serial killer was targeting bank accounts.

"My, you have been busy," said Narinda, nodding.

"Right," said Clovenhoof, shoving Narinda into Ben's flat and arms. "You two, shush. Keep the noise down. I'm a perfectly ordinary housewife and there's meant to be no one else at home except my bedbound son."

"You have a son?" said Ben.

"What part of 'shush' did you not understand?" said Clovenhoof and ran downstairs again.

He opened the front door.

"Mrs Calhoun?" said the small woman with square glasses and thin lips.

"Miss O'Brien?" said Clovenhoof.

"I'm a little early," said Linda.

"I noticed. Come in. What lovely shoes! What are they?"

"Orthopaedic."

"Scandinavian. How exotic."

She walked slowly up the stairs, not because she had any difficulty but because she was taking in her surroundings. Perhaps she was counting the cobwebs. Clovenhoof had no idea.

"You own the whole house?" asked Linda.

"Er, yes," said Clovenhoof, not sure what answer was best.

"It looks like it's been sub-divided into flats."

"It has. It was. I own it all though. Every bit. Just me and my merry brood here."

On the first floor landing, Nerys stood with her ear to Ben's door and a hopeful leer on her face.

"This," said Clovenhoof, "is my... sister, Nerys."

"Much younger sister," said Nerys.

"Let's put the kettle on," said Clovenhoof, steering her towards his flat.

"Who lives in that one?" said Linda, pointing at Ben's door.

"No one," said Clovenhoof.

"Then what were you listening for?"

"Ghosts," said Clovenhoof.

"Mice," said Nerys at the same time.

"Ghost mice," said Clovenhoof. "They might be. We definitely get a spooky aroma of cheese, don't we, Nerys?"

Nerys took a deep sniff to demonstrate. Linda sniffed too. Her expression was of a person who definitely smelled something.

Clovenhoof propelled the schools admissions woman into his flat.

"Cup of tea?"

"I can't stay long," said Linda. "I just have some questions I need to go over."

"Fire away," said Clovenhoof.

"Are these your children?" said Linda, drifting towards the intensely clustered selection of framed photos in the window.

"Most of them, yes."

"The pictures look very professional."

"Thank you, I do try," said Clovenhoof, who had spent an entertaining half hour earlier with a clothing catalogue and a pair of scissors.

"And this is your son, Archie?"

"Yes. Yes."

"And this boy?" she said, pointing to another picture.

"Is that not Archie too? No, clearly it's a different boy," said Clovenhoof. "That's his brother."

"Ben?"

"Yes. Ben."

Linda peered at the cutely posed young lad more closely. "Younger brother or older?"

"Let's say older," said Clovenhoof.

"This boy looks younger than Archie."

Clovenhoof was ready for such an obvious question. "It's an old photo."

"Ah," said Linda. "Makes sense. Now, I would very much like a word with Archie. Is the bedroom this way?"

Clovenhoof stepped smartly in front of her. "No. You can't."

"Can't?"

"He's sleeping. Drugged up. He's got mumps."

"Mumps?"

"Oh, yes," said Clovenhoof. "All swollen up. His glands. Horrible."

"I'm only going to pop my head round the door," said Linda pleasantly. "I'll be quiet as a mouse. A ghost mouse, even."

Clovenhoof panicked. "You can't! He's out!"

"Out?" She frowned. "Out where?"

"The, er, chemist. I sent him to get some medicine. I meant to say that he's *going to be* sleeping because he *will be* drugged up when he's got the medicine from the chemist. Sorry. I'm terrible with tenses. I do it all the time. I mean, I will be having done it all the time."

"I never noticed before."

"It comes and goes – that is, will come and has gone."

"You sent a poorly ten-year-old boy to the shops by himself to get a prescription?" asked Linda.

169

"His brother went with him. His older brother. They're both out. That's why they're not here. The house is completely empty."

At that, there was a thump and an excited burst of conversation from Ben's flat.

"Then what was that?" said Linda. She pushed past Clovenhoof and out onto the landing.

"It was probably just my sister, Nerys," he said.

"What was probably just Nerys?" asked Nerys, coming downstairs from her flat.

"Ghost mice!" declared Clovenhoof loudly.

The doorbell downstairs rang.

"The mysterious children returned?" said Linda sarcastically.

"No. Archie has a very distinctive ring. Not him. Nerys, dear, would you go down and see who that is?" He turned Linda around and shoved her back into his flat before grabbing Nerys's arm and whispering urgently, "I'm lacking children!"

"Children?"

"School kids. I needed to get some."

"What? Like order some over the internet?" she said.

"Brilliant idea!" he said, totally unaware that one could actually do such a thing but glad that she was willing to give it a go.

"Where from?" said Nerys. "Like a talent agency?"

Clovenhoof gave her a massive thumbs-up. Nerys could be quite resourceful at times.

He dashed back into his flat to mollify Miss O'Brien until the kids turned up.

"Right, where were we? I mean, where will we would have been?"

CHAPTER TWENTY-SEVEN

Joan rang the doorbell of four-hundred-and-something Chester Road again.

"I assume he still lives here," she said.

Next to her, Rutspud was hopping from foot to foot.

"Do you need the lavatory?" she said.

"Demons don't go to the lavatory," he said. "Unless it's part of an individual's Personal Torture Plan. Or, you know, if we just want to. For fun."

"Then why are you jiggling about?" she asked.

Rutspud stopped at once, but only for a second, and then clapped his hands like an excited four-year-old.

"I wonder if he remembers me. We've met. Obviously we've met. He created me. Kicked me out of the dirt himself. But there have been so many demons since." He gave her a look of nervous excitement. "Do you think he remembers me?"

Joan sighed. "There's a saying. Never meet your heroes."

Rutspud was instantly still.

"Satan isn't my hero," he said stiffly. "Of course, he's the devil – *the* devil – but I think I aspire to something a bit different. Not getting fired for one thing. But he's... he's my creator. Which makes him like a father. A distant, aloof father who never visits and would just as soon turn you into mincemeat as look at you."

"I see."

"But a father nonetheless."

The door was opened by a sharp-faced woman in an outfit that was not so much revealing as attention-seeking. Joan knew modern women were fairly shameless in their attire but this woman was clearly at the leading edge. What was more shocking was that Joan thought she recognised the woman. The name Nerys leapt to mind.

Nerys looked at the young saint and the short demon. "Are you school kids?"

"What?" said Rutspud.

"He said he'd ordered some. I didn't believe you could."

"We were looking for Jeremy Clovenhoof," said Joan.

"Yes, yes. That's the man," said Nerys. "In you come."

She hurried them into the hallway. She frowned at Joan's plate armour. "You're perhaps on your way back from another job? These outfits won't do."

"Won't do?" said Rutspud.

"I've got a suitcase of, um, dress-up clothes upstairs," said Nerys. "There's definitely some school uniform bits in there. Some blokes they like the whole naughty schoolgirl thing." She paused reflectively for a moment. "Or is that out of fashion now? From Britney Spears to Operation Yewtree. It's hard to keep up, isn't it?"

"Yes, it is," said Joan, having no idea what the woman was on about.

Nerys glanced upstairs. "Wait here. I'll get the clothes."

She ran upstairs, leaving the two bewildered people in the hallway.

"Is everyone in this city mad?" asked Rutspud.

"On the basis of available evidence..." said Joan.

Nerys came flying down with a suitcase.

"There!" she said, flinging it into Joan's arms. "School kids. As quick as you like. Are we expecting any more of you?"

"More?" said Joan.

"I don't know how many he's asked for. It's to fool the school inspector woman. If any do come –"

"I think there's been some confusion," said Joan.

"Ha! Tell me about it," said Nerys, breaking into a manic grin. "It's very simple. Sort of. Jeremy is upstairs. He's Mrs Calhoun. That's the younger Mrs Calhoun, the daughter of the one he's being a pretend husband for."

"He's pretending to be the husband of his own mother," said Rutspud.

"Er, yes. Yes," said Nerys. "You are his children. Not Mr Calhoun's. Mrs Calhoun's, the younger one. And one of you – I suppose that would be you – are a ten year old boy called Archie. I think that's it. Got it?"

"And who am I?" said Joan.

Nerys looked at her and there was a glimmer of recognition in Nerys's eyes, a trace of smile on her lips.

"I don't have a name for you yet," she said then added, "You have really nice hair. Love that page boy look." And the glimmer was gone. "To recap. He's Mrs Calhoun, you're the little Calhouns. If anyone else turns up, they're little Calhouns too. You're to say nothing. The inspector can't know the truth. Got it?"

"Definitely not," said Rutspud honestly.

"Tough," said Nerys. "Now, I've got to tell Ben and Narinda to keep the noise down. Don't matter how high their passions are running. Theirs will have to be a love that dare not raise its voice."

And she was gone, up the stairs again.

"I am confused," said Rutspud bluntly. "Am I an idiot or am I right to be confused?"

"No, I think confused is a fair place to be at the moment," said Joan.

Rutspud opened the case and started pulling out clothes. There was a surprising range of items: nurses uniforms, corsets, part of a nun's habit, frilly garments that Rutspud couldn't match up to any part of human anatomy. He suspected that these clothes all had something to do with sex, the most tedious aspect of human life in his opinion.

"Here," said Joan, flinging a stripy tie at him. "School boy."

"We're actually doing this?" he said.

Joan unbuckled her shoulder plates and arm greaves. "It's a small cosmos, isn't it?"

"How so?" said Rutspud.

"I've met that woman before. In the Celestial City."

"But she's not dead."

"She was at the time. She and I helped Clovenhoof break into Heaven by the back door."

"You're a bad girl, Joan of Arc!" grinned Rutspud. "She doesn't seem to remember you though."

Joan gave it some thought as she slipped off her chainmail and swapped it for a tight-fitting white blouse.

"The Almighty sent her back down to her rightful place on earth afterwards. Maybe the act of resurrection affects the mind."

"That would go a long way to explaining this precise situation..."

Linda grunted in satisfaction as she inspected the gaggle of fake family pictures once more.

"I knew there was something not quite right with this one," she said.

Clovenhoof wondered if he'd neglected to snip out the price when he'd cut it from the catalogue. Having a child with a price tag on would take some explaining.

"This toddler is Archie's older brother, Ben?" she said.

"He's not for sale!" he blurted.

"What?"

"In case, you wanted to buy him," said Clovenhoof lamely.

"When was this photo taken?"

"When he was younger than Archie is now."

"He's wearing a Toy Story 4 T-shirt. That film's not even out yet. So it has to be recent."

Clovenhoof was impressed. Good detective skills by Linda O'Brien! He wondered if all school admissions officers were eagle-eyed lady sleuths. Now, he could explain it by saying the T-shirt was given to Ben by a friendly time-traveller or...

"Yes. It is recent," he said. "I don't know why I lied. Silly female brain of mine. It's the shame you see. Ben is older but he suffers with a rare growth disorder which means he's locked in the body of a toddler. We've tried growth hormone therapy but –"

"Mrs Calhoun," said Linda fiercely. "Let me be honest and I hope you'll do me the same return favour. I have received today alone, three applications for St Michael's Secondary School, giving this address as the families' home address."

"Oh."

"I thought I would pay a visit in case there was some unusual but nonetheless valid reason for this state of affairs. But every question I've asked, your answers have become more and more outlandish. And I've not yet seen a single child."

"But you will soon, I promise," said Clovenhoof. "Let me go see if Nerys has managed to round them up."

He went to the door, subtly repositioning a breast which was leaking citrus juices. Linda, unwilling to let him get far from her sight, followed him close behind onto the landing.

Nerys was in the ajar doorway to Ben's flat telling him to keep quiet.

"And who are you talking to now?" said Linda stridently. "Phantom rats?"

"Er, no," said Nerys but Linda pushed past her and into Ben's flat.

Clovenhoof nearly tripped on his skirt as he hurried after her.

"What is this?" demanded Linda.

The wall of Ben's flat was a riot of pinned documents and colourful thread, a pictorial web of money transfers, bank accounts, loans and financial curios. It all certainly looked very impressive to Clovenhoof. He didn't understand any of it though. As much as he could tell, the display could have been created by a genius, a lunatic or nerdy dweebs with too much time on their hands. Looking at Narinda and Ben, he suspected that it was a pinch of this and a dab of that.

"Why are you grinning like a coked-up child, Ben?" asked Clovenhoof. "Why are you both grinning?"

Ben opened his mouth to answer, sniggered and then tapped Narinda playfully on the arm. "Go on, you tell him."

"Tell me what?"

"We cracked it!" said Narinda. "We know where the money is."

Clovenhoof sighed. "You are excited because you've done your sums?"

"It's more than that," said Narinda, inexplicably ecstatic. "Ben found a letter and then a pile of statements."

"You see," said Ben, "there's this app called PrayPal and –"

"Wait a minute," said Linda. "Ben? This is Ben? The boy...?"

"Yes," said Clovenhoof, thinking fast. "The growth hormones, they really worked didn't they. Kind of overshot the mark a little but if you look closely at him you can see he's not really a grown man just a really big boy. Not a single hair on his body."

"They hurt me," said Ben, wincing. "They hurt me a lot."

Linda frowned and wheeled on Nerys. "So, this individual is your nephew?"

Nerys had no idea what to say.

"Technically, she's my sister-in-law," said Ben helpfully.

"You know what I'm seeing here?" said Linda. "I'm seeing a smorgasbord of evidence pointing towards some sort of fraudulent activity."

"What?" said Ben.

Linda flung an arm out at the financial papers. "I don't know what this represents – Benefits fraud? Child farming? An electoral register scam? – but I'm calling the police."

Linda pulled out her phone. Clovenhoof made an instinctive move towards her.

"Don't you touch me, lady!" she growled, clutching her identity lanyard, "or I'll press my emergency alarm and you'll have a SWAT team swooping on this house before you can spit!"

"Really!" said Clovenhoof, stepping back. "And after I said such nice things about your shoes!"

Narinda sidled over to Ben. "Can you tell me what's actually going on here?" she said, out of the corner of her mouth.

"Absolutely no idea," he replied.

"Perhaps I ought to explain," Narinda said to the schools admissions woman. "I am an employee of Her Majesty's Revenue and Customs."

"Enough with the lies," said Linda and began to dial.

The doorbell rang.

"Maybe that's the children!" said Clovenhoof. He said it very loudly in the hope that it would somehow make it more believable.

Rutspud opened the front door.

The unshaven and jowly man in a suit looked down at him.

"Mr Calhoun?"

Rutspud did his best to recall the garbled information he'd been given.

"No, I'm one of the little Calhouns. I'm a ten-year-old boy called Archie."

"Is Mr Calhoun in? Or Mr Clovenhoof perhaps?"

The man sniffed and made a show of looking past Rutspud.

"Getting dressed here!" said Joan, down the hallway.

"Why are you doing that in the hall?" asked the man.

Rutspud was about to put the man straight on who precisely was who and who they were pretending to be when the man produced a photo ID in a little black wallet.

"Detective Inspector Gough, West Midlands Police Fraud Office."

The inspector can't know the truth, the woman had said, hadn't she?

"I don't think Mr Calhoun is in," said Rutspud. "But Mrs Calhoun, his daughter is upstairs."

Inspector Gough stepped inside and made for the stairs.

"You can't go yet!" said Rutspud. "Joan."

Joan zipped up the very short pleated school skirt and rifled through the case for something for the man to wear. "I really don't think we have anything in your size."

"What are you doing?" asked Gough.

"You're one of the little Calhouns like us," said Rutspud.

"What? I'm a police officer!"

Rutspud and Joan looked at each other.

"We weren't given those script notes," said Rutspud.

"There's some police uniform bits in here," said Joan and placed a peaked cap on the man's head. She pushed a pair of plastic handcuffs and a rubber truncheon into his hand.

"Here's a police ID badge," said Rutspud and stuffed it into the gap in his jacket.

"Get off me," said Gough, pulling away. "You're in serious danger of wasting police time." He threw down handcuffs and ID and went to the stairs, realised he was still holding the rubber truncheon, cast that down too and stomped up. "Up here?" he said, gruffly.

Rutspud looked at Joan.

"Are we meant to go too?"

She shrugged. "Let's go be little Calhouns and see if we can find Clovenhoof."

CHAPTER TWENTY-EIGHT

Clovenhoof heard the heavy footsteps on the stairs and went out to greet what he hoped were a convenient tribe of children who he could pass off as his own. He was therefore distinctly disappointed to find a stubbly bloke in a rumpled suit come up to him.

"Mrs Calhoun?" he said.

"You're not one of my children, are you?" said Clovenhoof.

"They're downstairs, playing silly beggars in the hall."

"Really?" Clovenhoof leaned over the bannister. "Come up, children! The lady wants to see you!" He turned to the man. "So, who are you?"

"Inspector Gough. We in here?"

He stepped past and through Ben's open flat door.

Linda was still on the phone, apparently on hold.

"Are you going to pretend that this is one of your children now?" said Linda, derisively.

"I'm Inspector Gough, West Midlands Police Fraud Office," said the man.

"Ha! No, you're not!" spat the admissions woman. "I've not even got through to them. And there's certainly not been any time for them to send someone over. This is a cheap and pathetic trick, Mrs Calhoun."

"I can assure you I am a police officer," said Gough, searching one pocket and then another for his ID.

"Oh, yes, just like this woman claims to be a tax inspector."

"I've presented you with my credentials," said Narinda but Linda just sneered.

Gough finally found his ID wallet and passed it to Linda.

"Tax, eh?" he said, strolling over to the wall of financial documents. "I'm here because someone is using this property to do business under an invented alias. This so-called Mr 'Jeremy

Clovenhoof' has accrued thousands of pounds of debt at this address."

"But he hasn't!" said Ben. "That's what we've been telling them. We've found the missing paperwork. Jeremy is a major shareholder in a company called WinkyCat Studios and –"

"Jeremy Clovenhoof!" said Gough, spotting the name on a letterhead and ramming it with his fingertip. "So, he is real."

"More than you," said Linda, holding up the ID she'd been passed. "This badge says you're a Private Dick and a licensed Boob Inspector!"

"What?" said Gough. He snatched back the ID and scrutinised it. "The children! They must have swapped it with one from the case!"

"This is very entertaining," said Clovenhoof who was having the best time ever. "I can't see how it can get any better."

At that moment, Joan of Arc and a demon – Rustpot? Rudbud? Clovenhoof was sure it was something like that – entered the room. Both were dressed in a selection of clothes that, if you were incredibly inobservant, you might think were items of school uniform.

"I don't even know why you're here!" said Clovenhoof, entranced by the random turn of events. "What's your name?" he asked the demon, desperate to remember.

The demon cleared his throat theatrically. "I am a ten-year-old boy called Archie Calhoun."

"I am also one of the little Calhouns," said Joan of Arc.

"Oh, my God!" yelled Linda. "Would everyone just stop lying! Is no one here who they actually claim to be?"

"Madam, I'm going to have to ask you to calm down," said Gough.

"Stop pretending!" she screamed.

"You are being hysterical and need to calm down or I will be forced to arrest you for public order offences."

"Calm down? You're all mad!" she shouted and gave Gough a two-handed shove.

The policeman took hold of her wrist, turned and seconds later had her in handcuffs.

"Kidnap! Kidnap!" yelled the schools admissions woman and began kicking anything in range which by chance happened to be Ben. He went down, clutching his knee.

Gough restrained her and pulled her towards the door. "Madam! You will accompany me downstairs where I will find my proper identification whereupon I shall arrest you for..." He thought about it. "We'll work it out when we get down there."

Gough bundled the screaming woman away.

A beautiful, stunned silence filled Ben's flat broken eventually by Clovenhoof declaring, "That was awesome! Seriously. I can't picture that having gone any better." He slapped his forehead. "Rutspud!"

"Yes!" cried the demon, delighted to be recognised.

"Sixth circle!" said Clovenhoof. "Working for that self-important prig. What was his name? Scabular? Scraper?"

"Scabass. That's him! Got out from under him ages ago."

Nerys's eyes widened. "You mean he's a.... And you're...!" She gasped as she pointed at Joan.

A look, both furious and panicked, came over her face.

"You, you and you!" she said to Clovenhoof, Rutspud and Joan. "Pub! Now! And not another word!"

She marched them out, leaving a mightily perplexed Ben and Narinda behind.

Rutspud was in a pub for the first time in his existence.

Rutspud was having *a beer* in a pub.

Rutspud was having a beer in a pub *with his creator and master*, talking back and forth like they were just a pair of regular demons chatting by the lava fountain on their work break.

Rutspud had a general contempt for the goings-on in Hell and had an especial contempt for the vile hierarchy of the underworld but, despite all that, going for a beer with Satan himself was so exciting that he had to squash his lips together to prevent any involuntary squeals of joy bursting out.

Rutspud sipped at his beer (which tasted like bread-gone-wrong but wasn't as vile as Marmite). Clovenhoof sipped at his 'Lambrini' (which looked like fizzy piss and far more appealing). The Nerys woman had a white wine spritzer and had bought Joan the same. Joan nursed her drink unenthusiastically and kept looking enviously at Rutspud's pint. He wondered if he should offer to swap.

Nerys was trying to get her facts straight.

"So, Heaven and Hell have teamed up and sent you two here – you're not here permanently?" she asked fearfully.

"Heaven forfend," said Nerys.

"Good," she said, "because although I know that goaty-boy here is the Fallen One, no one else does."

"Apart from Lennox," said Clovenhoof, hitching a thumb at the bar.

"And Lennox. Point is, *Ben* does not know and he's a delicate little beta male who won't be able to cope with discovering that his housemate is the devil and even more of a shitty villain than he already thinks you are."

"I've always cast myself as more of an anti-hero," sniffed Clovenhoof.

"Having Joan of frigging Arc and one of Hell's demons turn up is going to make it tricky to keep your secret, so whatever you're doing here, it needs to be kept at a low, low profile."

"Not a problem," said Rutspud. "We'll fix this problem and – bam! – we'll be off. That is, after spending some quality time with the boss here," he grinned.

"How is the Old Place?" said Clovenhoof. "Missing me?"

"Like you wouldn't believe, sir."

"I bet that doofus Peter has redecorated my Fortress of Nameless Dread in sickly pastel shades."

Rutspud pulled a face.

"He has?" said Clovenhoof.

"Actually, boss, it was destroyed."

"He demolished it?"

"No. It was kinda swept away in a flood."

"How in Hell could there be flood? In Hell," said Clovenhoof.

"We had an over-heating problem. And there was this magic wardrobe..."

Clovenhoof threw up his hands.

"You turn your back for five minutes and everything goes to pot."

"Lord Peter now operates out of the Portakabin of Nameless Dread while they're doing the rebuild."

At least that made Clovenhoof laugh.

"Shut up. The pair of you," said Nerys. "Reminisce when we haven't got more important things to worry about."

"Like the PrayPal app causing a serious imbalance in the numbers being sent to Heaven and Hell," said Joan.

"Right, Joan. So, what the heck is that about?"

"His former infernal majesty here invented it, along with a mad bishop and a computer programmer we have yet to locate. I'm sure you had the best of motives when you decided to do that but –"

"That?" snorted Clovenhoof. "Just some bullshit me and a couple of guys were chatting one night."

"When was this?" said Nerys.

"Months ago. I was out on the town, toasting my own crapulence and pulling the birds."

It was Nerys's turn to snort. "When did you last pull a... a woman?"

"They are frequently intimidated by my aura of powerful masculinity," he conceded, "but you don't know what I get up to in my free time."

"You tell us. Loudly."

"Anyway, I walked into this classy bar and I was in a good mood so I told the barmaid to buy a round for everyone there. Weirdly, she took that to mean getting everyone a plate of chips."

"It was a fish and chip shop," said Joan.

"And that now makes sense," continued Clovenhoof. "I ate my chips and told everyone tales of my sexual conquests and brilliant business plans – I was just winding down my animal cremation business and looking for new ventures and –" He paused and he stared off in thought. "I got to talking with these two guys:

Festering Ken and this entertaining geeky guy, lots of curly hair. I can't remember his name. I want to say it's Wank Stain but I'm possibly misremembering."

"Possibly," said Nerys.

Clovenhoof shrugged and slurped his drink. "I just said that wouldn't it make sense, in this day and age, if people didn't have to physically go to church to get blessed and all that shit? They should be able to do it over the internet. I mean you can do everything else over the internet these days – shopping, dating, and with recent advances in wireless dildonics..."

"Getting off topic," said Nerys.

"Yeah," said Clovenhoof, "but that was it. The geek was very excited, making notes; Ken obviously had input. I knew who he was. You can take the bishop out of the cathedral, but you can't take the cathedral out of the... Well, something like that. The kid told us we were going to be rich, but Ken and I are older and wiser and knew nothing was going to come of it. But the kid – it's not Wank Stain. It's..." Clovenhoof growled, unable to recall. "He took our details. Names and addresses. Well, my name and address. Ken's sort of lacking a fixed abode at the moment. And that was it." Clovenhoof sat back. "We finished our chips. I bid them a fond adieu, went down the Boldmere Oak for the tail end of the Grab-a-Granny night and got a knee in the nads for some unwanted granny-grabbing."

There was a hopeful look on Joan's face.

"That's it then. Case closed. It's your app."

"I guess," said Clovenhoof.

"Then sort it out. Call them up. Log on. Whatever it is you're supposed to do. Shut it down."

"Why should I do all that?"

"Because you're sending the afterlife all out of whack, sir," said Rutspud. "Millions of people are being forgiven every day through the power of PrayPal and the sanctioned power of Bishop Iscansus which is written into its code. The Celestial City is filling up with scumbags scraping in on a technicality and there's some exquisite ironic punishments going to waste in Hell because there's no one there to inflict them on."

Clovenhoof gave this some thought.

"I like you, Rutspud," he said.

"Thank you, sir."

"And if you want to go sort this mess out yourself, then I'm not going to stop you."

"But?" said Joan. "There's a 'but'."

"But I'm not going to solve this thing for you."

"Why not?" said Rutspud.

"Because, numero uno, I don't know how. I'm an ideas guy. I didn't write an app. That's something nerds do. You should ask the Archangel Michael, when he gets out of prison and gets back here. I don't know anything about this PrayPal thing. I don't know the programmer and I don't know how to contact him. I haven't seen any paperwork and I certainly haven't seen any money."

Nerys put an envelope on the table in front of Clovenhoof. There was a dirty hoof print on it. It had already been opened.

"What's this?" he said.

"Ben gave it to me."

Clovenhoof opened it. It was a letter from the Sutton Railway Building Society. Clovenhoof scanned it for significant details but it was an irritatingly vague request to come in and discuss what he would like to do with his funds as the regular savings account he had his money in was perhaps 'unsuitable'. There was a post-it note attached to the letter:

This is where your taxable income has been deposited! – *Narinda*
You are NOT in debt.

"Well, I hope that this PrayPal has made me a quid or two," said Clovenhoof, went to tuck the letter inside his jacket, realised he was still wearing women's clothing and so stuffed it down his fruity cleavage.

"Does that help us?" said Joan.

Clovenhoof ignored her, drained the last trickle from his Lambrini and stood up.

"Come on, Nerys. Home time."

"What?" said Nerys. "It's not even eight o'clock. We've got hours of drinking time left."

"Yes, but I want to flounce out dramatically," he said, "because even if I could fix things like that for Joan here –" He clicked his fingers. "– I won't."

"Why not?" said Joan.

"Because – numero dos, my friends – you knocked down my Fortress of Nameless Dread! In a flood! Nerys! Flouncing time!"

Nerys gave the pair of them an apologetic wave, downed her drink and followed Clovenhoof out. His former Satanic majesty could flounce really well in a skirt, Rutspud noted.

Joan punched Rutspud in the shoulder. Hard.

"Ow! What did you do that for?" he said.

"You told him about the flood. Did you have to tell him?" she said, peeved.

Rutspud sighed.

"Want to swap drinks?"

"Yes, please," said Joan.

PART TWO –
ARISE HOOFLANDIA!

CHAPTER TWENTY-NINE

Armed with his letter, and its irritatingly vague invitation about discussing his funds, Clovenhoof walked to the town centre in search of the Sutton Railway Building Society.

The reason Clovenhoof walked everywhere was twofold. Firstly, the powers-that-be (both spiritual and temporal) refused to give him a free old fogey's bus pass even though, at his age, he clearly qualified. Secondly, it turned out that hoofs were less than ideal for working pedals – both bicycle pedals and car foot controls. Clovenhoof had tried to learn to drive. He'd booked lessons with a dozen different instructors. None of them had managed more than one lesson with him: most had told him that they could no longer teach him, one had stopped the lesson partway through, kicked him out, yelled at him for a full ten minutes and then chased him down Boldmere high street, mounting the pavement in her Fiat 500 several times, and one, after the car had finally come to rest in the shallow end of the Sutton Coldfield swimming pool, moved to the West Country and became a druid called Gwyddion Longstaff. Having hoofs was brilliant for a whole range of reasons but, for the purposes of driving, they were a decided handicap and Clovenhoof felt that people should really take that into consideration when trying to teach him. He did briefly consider getting one of those cars specially adapted for people with no legs and he even took one for a test drive but, when he got back, the man with no legs he'd stolen it from wasn't very understanding and he'd not pursued the matter further.

Clovenhoof walked and looked for the Sutton Railway Building Society. He'd never seen a branch before, hadn't even heard of the company, and it was only after getting a set of directions from an old dear who was convinced that the place had closed down years ago, that he found the place not far from the town railway station, squashed between a 'drop and shop' car valeting business and the Station pub. It was a narrow building with Roman columns on its steps and a carved stone frieze above the door depicting stolid men of Sutton Coldfield engaged in some form of unspecified honest labour and the date the building society was opened (which, eroded by time and the elements, might have been 1806, 1886 or, as an outside possibility 1006). This tiny but grandiose institution was clearly founded by people whose dreams were bigger than their wallets and who were rightly shown up by history for the fools they were. Clovenhoof loved it already.

Clovenhoof bounded up the stone steps and veritably leapt through the door, nearly causing the rotund middle-aged woman behind the wooden counter to have a heart attack.

"Can I help you, sir?" she asked, in the tones of one who was rarely asked to help people and probably wasn't up to the job anyway.

"I'm sure you can..." He leaned over the counter and peered at the name badge pinned to her patterned lilac blouse, "Penny. Ha! A Penny in a building society. I bet that never gets old. Any other colleagues with money-based names lurking back there?"

"My uncle went to school with a boy called Bobby Tanner," said Penny, "but that was old money and only worked as a joke pre-decimalisation."

"Indeed," said Clovenhoof, who had no idea what she was on about.

"If you want change for the parking meter outside, I'm afraid we're only allowed to open the tills for customers."

"Nope. No parking meter change for me. No car. Hoofs, you see. They're a curse and a blessing. No, Penny dear, I'm a customer and I'm here to collect my money."

"Ooh."

In that single syllable, Clovenhoof grasped that the number of customers who came in to make withdrawals (or who came in at all) could be tallied by circling dates on a calendar. There were other clues to the general lack of custom in this place. The dust motes that hung heavily in the shafts of light from the bank's high windows. The lack of glass shields and other security measures between the plushly carpeted customer area and the decidedly Victorian-looking back office. The poster on the wall that reminded customers to bring in their green pound notes in preparation for the switch to the new one pound coin.

"Withdrawal, right," said Penny. "Do you have your account details, sir?"

Clovenhoof presented her with the letter.

"I think you'll find everything in order," he said. "Ignore that. That's just where I used it as a coaster. And there. I was having drinks and nibbles last night."

"Chocolate, sir?" she said.

"Yes. Let's say it was chocolate. Why not?"

Penny the cashier copied some details down onto a form and tapped for a minute into a device which was to a modern computer what primordial slime was to modern humans: in other words, utterly indistinguishable in Clovenhoof's eyes.

"A withdrawal, sir?" she said. "How much would you like to take out?"

"All of it. Obviously," said Clovenhoof and did a little tap dance.

"All...?" Penny tippy-typed some more, looked at Clovenhoof, looked at the paperwork and then picked up the chunky telephone at her counter. She spoke at length to the person on the other end, mostly in whispers, frequently glancing up at Clovenhoof. Clovenhoof started to get bored. It was no wonder so many people were getting into debt with those unscrupulous lending companies on the telly if it took this long to get their hands on their own actual money.

Eventually, she put the phone down.

"Mr Clovenhoof, I've just spoken to the manager. Unfortunately, we can't give you all of the money over the counter today. There are certain regulations and procedures, I'm sure you understand."

"Are you? That's flattering. Wrong, but flattering."

"But we can give you a quantity today and arrange for the rest to be sent to you. Someone will be in touch."

"Well, I'm not very happy."

"I'm sorry, sir. It's the regulations."

"I meant just generally. My therapist said it was because I had unrealistic expectations of life. I think it's because I don't drink enough."

"Um. Okay," said Penny and then smiled with relief when a shaven-headed bloke in a jumper with epaulettes came through from the back office with a small silver suitcase. "It's for Mr Clovenhoof here, Claude."

Claude gave Clovenhoof a most deeply distrustful look.

"You'll have to sign here," said Penny.

Clovenhoof signed the document. He put a smiley face in one of the 'o's in Clovenhoof and drew little devil horns on it. Claude passed the suitcase over. It was very heavy.

"And, as I said, someone will be in touch about the rest," said Penny.

"Oh, they'd better be," said Clovenhoof, grinning nonetheless.

Clovenhoof knew it would be wise to wait until he was in the safety of his own flat or at least a corner booth of the Boldmere Oak before opening the case to look at his money. He lasted less than a dozen yards and, in fact, sat on the steps of the 'drop and shop' car valeting place, put the case on his knee and lifted the lid.

Banknotes in pristine blocks, bound with paper bands, stacked in an overlapping pattern to make a solid block of cash. Clovenhoof took out one of the neat little bundles and riffled through it with his thumb. He breathed deeply. Oh, yes. Even with such clean, unsullied money, there was the deliciously earthy smell of cash. It sent a devilish shiver through him.

The devil knew numbers better than almost any other being in creation. Numbers were details and the devil was famous for being up in that jam and down with that shit. One thumb riffle and Clovenhoof knew the block contained a thousand pounds. He did a mental count of the number of cash blocks and found himself unavoidably aroused.

"Oh, money. It's been a long time, my friend," he sighed happily. "Let's see how long you last this time."

He stuffed ten thousand pounds down the front of his underpants - If anyone asked him, he would have possibly told them it was to keep it safe and hidden but he did it because he wanted to stuff ten thousand pounds down the front of his underpants – and then, with a bulging crotch and a happy swagger, strolled home.

As a small reward, he bought himself a little something on the way home. It was totally worth it and it made the case a little lighter.

At home, Clovenhoof lay on the living room floor and phoned Narinda Shah.

"I've got it," he said.

"Got what?" said Narinda. "And who is this?"

"I've got your money, babe. Cold hard cash. Well, I've warmed it up a bit now. You know that thing where people throw money in the air and roll around naked on it?"

"Jeremy Clovenhoof," said Narinda in weary recognition.

"Well, it doesn't work with those new plastic bank notes. They're really quite prickly and I've got a couple of papercuts in some of the less obvious places. Still, I suppose they're wipe-clean which has got to be good for people who believe in hygiene and all that."

"Are you saying you have the money, Jeremy?"

"Yup. Ooh. There's one right up my..." He grunted and glared at the offending bank note and then gave it an experimental sniff. "Yup. Every last bit to pay off your tax bribe thingy."

"It's a bill, not a bribe, Jeremy."

"But I pay it to you..."

"To Her Majesty's Revenue and Customs."

"To stop you pestering me for another year."

"We never pester, Jeremy."

"Sounds like a bribe to me."

There was silence on the phone for a long second.

"You have it in cash?" said Narinda.

"Yes," said Clovenhoof.

"There, with you, at your home?"

"Yes."

Another long second of silence.

"I will come round tomorrow. As soon as I can. Do *not* spend it all before I get there."

"Ooh, that sounds like a challenge!"

"It is not, Jeremy. Jeremy? Don't spend it. You hear me?"

"Well, maybe I will, maybe I won't. It's like that cat in the box. Until you open the box, you don't know who killed it?"

"What?"

Clovenhoof killed the call and laid back on his bed of cash.

"Milo!" he called.

"Yes, boss!" came the shouted reply from the kitchen.

"How's the cooking coming on?"

"I'm just grinding down the ciabatta for the breadcrumbs and grating Parmigiano for the sauce."

"Okay," said Clovenhoof. "As long as it tastes like the original, you hear?"

"Better than the original."

Clovenhoof scoffed. "You can't improve on perfection, Milo."

The smells coming from the kitchen were certainly enticing, particularly that guffy note you only got from the most expensive of cheeses. Bored by rolling naked in cash, Clovenhoof got to his feet, put on his game night smoking jacket – Black-Jack-table green embroidered with gold dice – and went down to flat 1b with his silver suitcase of cash.

He unlocked and removed his padlock and then spent thirty minutes fiddling around inside the others with a paperclip in a manner that he felt looked really professional and cool and just like a lock-picking thief on a TV show before giving up and using teeth, hoofs and horns to wrench padlocks and brackets from the door frame.

He had just finished setting up when Ben and Nerys arrived.

"What the hell, Jeremy!" said Nerys angrily.

"I just wanted to prepare a little surprise," said Clovenhoof.

"You've ripped the padlocks off the door."

"This is a total infringement of the game rules," said Ben.

"What are you talking about?" said Clovenhoof. "You two cheat all the time."

"Oh, but there's a scale," said Nerys. "The footballer might take a cheeky dive when he's been tackled but he doesn't pick up the ball and run with it."

"She's using sporting analogies," said Ben. "I've no idea."

"I just wanted to make some exciting little changes," said Clovenhoof and spread his hands over their cluttered gaming spaces.

"The money!" said Nerys. "He's switched it around."

Ben plonked himself in his seat and ran his fingers over the piles of notes that stood where his printed toy money had once been. He tested the top note between thumb and forefinger.

"What do you reckon, huh?"

"Bit plasticky," said Ben. "Where'd you get this? Poundland?"

"It's real!" said Clovenhoof.

Nerys smirked. "A lot of the modern notes look like toy money anyway. These look realistic enough. Maybe we will play with real money one day."

"It is real!" insisted Clovenhoof.

"Whatever." Nerys sat down. "I declare it's Malibu-and-Coke o'clock. Let's set up drinks and it is my go, I believe."

"But it's real money!" said Clovenhoof.

"Uh-huh. Of course, Jeremy." She looked to Ben. "It's happened. Dementia's set in."

"You said it would be syphilis-induced madness," said Ben.

"Whatever. Let's break out those retirement home brochures."

There was a knock on the flat door. "Boss? Are you in here?"

"In here, Milo."

Clovenhoof's newly appointed personal chef entered the flat, bearing a tray of steaming baked goods.

"Is that Milo Finn-Frouer?" whispered Nerys.

"Who?" whispered Ben.

"The chef at Charretier's, that swanky restaurant on the high street."

"I'm more of a Nando's person," said Ben.

Trying not to grimace at Ben's comment, the burly chef leaned forward and offered his creation for inspection.

"Here, we have a light confection of diced York ham in a combination of Schabziger and Parmigiano cheese, lightly spiced with turmeric and paprika, wrapped in a blanket of buckwheat crepe and baked in a crumb coating of authentic Italian ciabatta."

Clovenhoof took one of the golden crescent-shaped items and broke it open. Steam burst forth in fragrant clouds.

"That smells delicious," said Nerys.

"It smells a bit like..." Ben sniffed. "Hang on. Are those just Findus crispy pancakes?"

"They are *my* crispy pancakes," said Milo Finn-Frouer.

Clovenhoof bit deeply, eyes closed. Melted cheese and meaty juices welled in his mouth. He was about to declare them a success but something made him hold back. There was something wrong, something missing. He chewed thoughtfully, stuck his tongue out and ejected the mushy mass into the palm of his hand.

Ben recoiled in disgust. Nerys pushed her chair back.

"You don't like it?" said Milo, shocked.

"No, Milo, I do not," said Clovenhoof. "Where's the glucose syrup? Where's the sunflower oil? Where's the added salt? Where, for Hell's sake, are the antioxidants?"

"Boss," said the chef, "I was trying to recreate the best aspects of the original recipe and present an interpretation of –"

"No, Milo," said Clovenhoof, disappointed, pouring the slop back onto the chef's tray. "This... this... forgery is like... a Christmas present from Ben."

"Eh?" said Ben and Milo as one.

"Oh, it's all shiny and seductive on the outside and then..." Clovenhoof stuck a finger in the chewed gloop. "It's a pair of socks."

"A pair of socks?" said Milo, affronted.

"A perfectly decent gift," said Ben sniffily.

"Horrible," said Clovenhoof. "It's back to the kitchen for you, Mil-i-o. I want the real crispy pancake experience. You're not inventing. You're rediscovering."

"Rediscovering," said the chef. "Sure. Back to basics. Reverse engineered."

"Yeah, that. Whatever that is," agreed Clovenhoof.

Milo retreated slowly, deep in thought.

"What the hell?" said Nerys when he was gone.

"I know," said Clovenhoof. "That tasted like rubber. And not the good kind neither."

"That was Milo Finn-Frouer!" said Nerys. "He's got a Michelin star!"

"Maybe that's why it tasted like old tyres."

"Why's he working for you?" said Nerys.

"And re-inventing the crispy pancake?" said Ben.

"Not re-inventing, dear Kitchen. Rediscovering. The company changed the recipe a while back. I wasn't totally happy with the changes. Frankly, I should have been consulted –"

"But how did you get him to do it?" said Nerys.

"I paid him," said Clovenhoof simply.

"With what?"

"I. paid. him."

Sometimes, thought Clovenhoof, people just didn't know happiness until he entered their lives. It was like that time he'd shown the fruit to that cute naked couple, like that time he'd taught Onan that one didn't have to be the loneliest number you could ever do. Realisation dawned on their faces as growing smiles and widening eyes.

Ben ran his fingers over the pile of cash.

"Real money?"

Clovenhoof nodded.

"And you've replaced like for like?" said Nerys, apparently trying to remember how much her toy money stash had been worth.

Clovenhoof nodded.

"And this is for us?" she said.

Clovenhoof shrugged. "But if you spend it, it's gone."

"We're playing for real now?" said Ben, oscillating rapidly between excitement and worry.

"We were always playing for real," said Clovenhoof.

Nerys's hands hovered over the pile, caught in a moment of indecision, and then she snatched up the top inch and dashed for the door, stumbling over the quote-deciding hamster ball and an unfinished Lego ring road on her way. The front door of the house opened and slammed shut a moment later.

"Keen to spend it, isn't she?" said Clovenhoof.

"Not one of life's deferred gratification types," said Ben, rising and going to the window to look out.

"What's she up to?" said Clovenhoof.

"Um. She's running around." He pushed the curtain further aside. "Nope. She's seen Victoria Calhoun. Ah, and is offering her some money for that Hermès handbag."

"Is Victoria selling?"

Ben pulled a face.

"Hard to say. Either that or we're witnessing the world's first mugger to pay their victim in thanks."

CHAPTER THIRTY

There was no lovelier sight to behold from one's bathroom window than that of a man in his dressing gown in the middle of a nervous breakdown. Clovenhoof had been polishing his horns with an electric shoe buffer he'd bought off the shopping channel with Nerys's credit card – a shoe buffer with a spinning duster disk that not only doubled as a horn buffer but also as a hoof buffer and, on days when he felt bold, a powerfully dangerous toothbrush. He was polishing his horns to a minty-fresh shine (there was still a residue of toothpaste on them) when he looked down at the back garden of four-hundred-and-something Chester Road and saw Ben, in his dressing gown, pants and a 'miniature wargamers do it on your table' t-shirt hastily digging a hole in the middle of the lawn.

"What are you doing, Kitchen?" he shouted down.

Ben looked up, spade in hand, a look of guilty alarm on his face. Clovenhoof saw there was a bulging carrier bag on the ground next to him.

"Did you kill one of the neighbours' cats with a model ballista again?" shouted Clovenhoof.

"No," hissed Ben. "And I didn't kill it, I only stunned it. *And* it wasn't a cat, it was one of their children. *And* could you please cover yourself up. Most people have frosted glass in their bathroom windows."

"Nothing wrong with showing off the body God gave you. I mean literally. This body. His design choices all the way. And they say He doesn't have a sense of humour. So, what are you doing?"

Ben looked round nervously.

"I stayed up last night, researching on the internet."

"It's not called researching if you do it one-handed, Nerys says."

"Researching how to invest my money."

"Ah."

"But we live in such uncertain times..."

"You thought you'd just bury your share of the cash."

Ben shushed him. "Not so loud! You don't know who's listening."

Clovenhoof sighed.

"You can't take it with you when you die, Ben. Trust me. I've met people who've tried. Spend it. Live a little or, if you can, live a lot."

Clovenhoof wrapped a towel around his waist, hula-danced into his bedroom and dressed for the day. There were several windows open on his computer browser. He'd been doing some internet research of his own (and not all of it one-handed) but with a more of a focus on spending his cash, rather than saving it.

Nerys entered his flat without knocking and strode purposefully through the living room, pouted at a non-existent audience, turned and strode back.

"And here is Nerys Thomas," she said, "wearing a dress by Roland Mouret, shoes from Jimmy Choo and earrings and necklace from Alexander McQueen."

"And since when did Nerys Thomas speak about herself in the third person?" asked Clovenhoof.

"Ever since she became bloody minted."

"Ah, Clovenhoof was wondering."

"Nerys is glad to help."

"Then Clovenhoof wonders if Nerys could help with something else."

"Nerys is listening."

Clovenhoof gesticulated at his computer. "Why is it so bloody hard for me to spend my money?"

"What do you mean?"

"I have money. I have oodles of money. I have shitting oodles of money with knobs on. And I know what I want. And I'm prepared to pay for it. But can I find the things I want? I can't."

Nerys glanced over the browser tabs. Buy-a-yacht.com, Robots4u.co.jp...

"The Drugs Advice Centre?" she said.

"Who aren't apparently interested in advising on where to buy the best disco biscuits. False advertising."

Nerys nodded in understanding. "You need a personal shopper."

"Ah!" he cried. "Ah! I tried that. All that means is someone from some department store tries to get you to buy stuff from their shop. And John Lewis's don't do class A giggle-cakes or the necessary goods for my planned boats 'n' hoes weekender."

"Hoes?"

"Boats 'n', yes."

Nerys gave this some thought.

"I know someone who could be your bespoke personal shopper. For a price."

Clovenhoof narrowed his eyes. "Would that be you?"

"It might," she said.

"Why do you need to sell your services? I gave you a wad of notes."

"But unlike some people, I know how to spend it. And only charge a very reasonable ten percent fee."

Satan's balls, the woman was mercenary. It was one of the few qualities he admired in her. He thrust a scribbled list into her hand.

"That lot. I want that lot."

Nerys read, her eyes widening.

"Self-driving car?"

"I'm tired of walking everywhere."

"A yacht?"

"Boats 'n' hoes, remember?"

There was a sharp rap at the front door downstairs.

"Get that," said Clovenhoof.

"I'm your personal shopper, not personal slave," said Nerys.

"Ooh, add personal slave to the list on your way down."

"Cock," said Nerys and left.

While Clovenhoof was picking the best cravat to accompany today's clothing ensemble, the phone rang. He made a mental note to employ a 'personal phone answerer' and picked it up.

"Mr Clovenhoof?" said a voice.

"Yes?"

"Hold for Maldon Ferret."

"Not usually," said Clovenhoof but the voice was gone.

"Clovenhoof, is it, eh?" came a new voice, as rich and self-assured as a TV advert voice-over. "Jerry Jerry Jezza, is it? Maldon Ferret."

"I heard." It was definitely the same Maldon Ferret whose father's funeral he'd attended. Clovenhoof briefly wondered if he was calling to charge him for eating so many cheap sandwiches.

"Queer Nigel down at head office asked me to give you a call. Lovely chap. Cracking wife. Goes like a broken gate in a hurricane if you get a couple of gins inside her."

"Does she?"

"Seems you've come into a spot of lolly and are all too keen to raid the piggy bank. Yum-yum, eh? As one of the major shareholders of Sutton Railway Building Society thought I'd drop you a tinkle and share some pearls of wisdom."

"Oh, it's about my money," said Clovenhoof, suddenly understanding.

"Indeedy-do, Jezza," said Maldon Ferret. "Your money and – I'm guessing here – you've not had much of it before. No, don't apologise. We've all been there. Once found myself penniless and near buck naked in Chamonix and was faced with having to spend the rest of the month sans après-ski or make some moolah fast. Of course, I'm much better at doing chalet girls than being one but, fortunately, there was a rugby team on tour who were all willing to pay for some public school specials – scrum fumble! – so it was prayer positions, Handy Andys and fizzy pop all the way after that. No, we've all been there, Jezza."

Clovenhoof had no idea if the man meant Chamonix or in a scrum or something else and didn't care to ask.

"No," said Maldon, "you're like a man lost in the desert who's found himself suddenly at the bar of one of the finer London clubs. Not my club, obviously, but one of the others. And you've got a raging thirst. You want to drink the bar dry. Totally understandable, Jezza. But you drink it all and it'll be chunderbirds are go before tea-time and you'll be back out in that desert. So, consider me the voice of prudence."

"Hello, Prudence," said Clovenhoof bewildered.

"Ha! Cracking humour, Jezza. I see we're going to get on like Fortnum and Mason. Tell you what, I'm having a little shindig at my place this evening. Popped my old man in the crypt recently and a bunch of the boys from the Square Mile are up for drinks – mostly to check that he's brown bread."

Maldon laughed raucously at that though Clovenhoof couldn't be sure why. He also wasn't sure if the old man was Maldon's father or his penis.

"Look, I'll send a car for you at six," said Maldon. "I'll introduce you to some investment chaps. A right load of bankers, eh? Ha! And let's get that money working for you. Ciao, bambino!" cried Maldon and was gone.

Clovenhoof stared at the phone. He wasn't sure what had just happened and he might need a breakfast Lambrini to help him decode it.

"I knocked," said a voice at the door.

Clovenhoof turned. It was Narinda Shah, his friendly neighbourhood tax collector. Grey suit, dinky briefcase held in both hands.

"I said I would come as soon as I could," she said.

"You did," he said. "I'm just about to have breakfast. Care for a Findus crispy pop tart."

"They do pop tarts?"

"It's just a crispy pancake with treacle on it and then put in the toaster. Set the fire alarm off three times last week but that's just a sign that you're really searing the flavours in."

"Jeremy, I've come to talk to about your overdue payment."

"Yes, yes," he said, wandering into the kitchen to look for breakfast. "Tell me, if I said I'd popped my old man in the crypt, what would you think I meant?"

"Is this relevant, Jeremy? I'm only interested in facts pertaining to your recent tax assessment."

"Ever the professional," said Clovenhoof. Milo Finn-Frouer had left Clovenhoof's kitchen worktop covered in a complex arrangement of alembics, muslin sieves, rubber tubing and pressurised containers. It looked like the chef had been engaged in wild science experiments rather than cooking. As long as today's attempts at recreating the perfect crispy pancake were better than yesterday's Clovenhoof didn't mind but, in the meantime, Clovenhoof was struggling to find anything resembling food. In the end, he settled for a bottle of Lambrini. Breakfast power drinks were all the rage with young wealthy types, weren't they?

He went back into the living room, swigging from the bottle like the cool dude he knew himself to be.

"You said you had some or all of the money you owe," said Narinda.

"If someone was said to go like a broken gate in a hurricane, would you know what that meant?"

"Could we *please* focus on the matter in hand."

"Perhaps if I added gin to the equation, would that help?"

"Jeremy Clovenhoof!" she said sternly. "I came here to talk about the very serious matter of your tax assessment, not to be propositioned with gin and your 'old man'."

"Ah, I thought as much. Yes, Miss Shah. I do have your money. All of it. In cash. Not a word of a lie."

"Then I would very much like to have it," said Narinda.

"I bet you would. Now let me see..." Clovenhoof scouted about for the location of his case of money.

Nerys appeared at the doorway, hand cupped over the phone she held.

"Jeremy."

"Yo."

"Yacht. Forty foot or eighty foot?"

"Which is better?" he said.

"Bigger is better," she said, as though it was the most obvious thing in the world.

"Eighty then."

"They can reserve one today with a ten percent deposit." Her phone warbled. She put it to her ear and nodded. "They'll take twenty thousand for now."

Clovenhoof retrieved the metal suitcase from under the sofa, opened it and, after a quick count, passed Nerys much of what remained.

"Thank you," she said. "I've already made enquiries about other purchases. And I've sub-contracted some to Ben. You know, the nerdy stuff. I asked him about self-driving cars and he started waffling on about Google-somethings and that SpaceX science guy.

I left it with him." She walked off, cash in hand, chatting on her phone.

Narinda stared at Nerys and then stared at the suitcase.

"I told you not to spend it, Jeremy," she said.

He raised a finger to correct her. "You told me not to spend it *all*."

Narinda approached the money and with a nod from Clovenhoof began to count what remained.

"Well, it doesn't appear to be the full amount," she said as she efficiently stacked and arranged the notes, "but it would certainly represent a gesture of good faith on your behalf. Her Majesty's Revenue and Customs will look much more kindly upon your case if I can take this with me and –"

"I can't let you have it all, obviously," said Clovenhoof.

"Obviously?"

"I've got some personal expenses that need settling, Ben is buying me one of those computerised cars as we speak and I've got to buy a new suit for tonight's party."

"Party?"

"Yes. Some bloke from the building society, Maldon Ferret, has invited me to his shindig."

"Maldon Ferret?"

"Yes, he's going to introduce me to some people who will tell me how to invest the rest of my money."

"*Lord* Maldon Ferret?"

"Can't say I know him that well. He's sending a car for us later."

"And what do you mean, the rest of your money?"

"This?" He tapped the case with his hoof. "Tip of the iceberg, babe."

"And Lord Maldon Ferret is helping you invest the rest?"

"Hey!" he said. "You should come with us."

"To the party?"

"To the party. Reckon you could do to let your hair down. Do tax collectors let their hair down? Do tax collectors get invited to parties?"

She gave him a firm glare. "Jeremy, I am surprised that you get invited to parties at all, particularly ones with such distinguished hosts."

He scoffed. "I'm the king of parties. In fact, now I own a boat, I'm the captain of parties. Set a course for fun!" He frowned. "Darn it. I'm going to need a captain's hat."

Clovenhoof spent the afternoon trying on different clothing combinations for the evening party at Maldon Ferret's. He owned some of the finest and most visually offensive smoking jackets that the internet could offer but really wanted to create an ensemble that went beyond the merely eye-watering to speak at a deeper level to anyone who saw it. He wanted it to say, 'Here is a creature of infinite power and intelligence who is so wealthy he could wear the fashion equivalent of a pavement vomit explosion and still have all the honeys flocking round him.' It was a big ask of Clovenhoof's wardrobe but he was nothing if not determined.

Meanwhile, Milo Finn-Frouer beavered away in the kitchen, creating the new (old) crispy pancake. The man was certainly going about his business with a passion. When the chef came through from the hallway with a gas cannister labelled 'liquid oxygen', Clovenhoof didn't stop or question him. Anyone willing to bring dangerous chemicals into the home should simply be applauded and allowed to get on with it.

As evening fell and Clovenhoof was considering whether wearing no trousers at all was a fashion statement too far, Ben came into the flat, phone in hand.

"Nice tux," said Clovenhoof.

Ben grimaced. "Nerys told me I had to buy a suit because we're going to some party. Two hundred quid this cost me," he said, disgusted. "You know if I wanted to spend a lot of money on a suit, it'd be a historically accurate suit of plate mail."

"A man who turned up to a party in plate mail armour would definitely make an impression," said Clovenhoof, entirely in favour of the idea.

Ben held out the phone.

"Could you do me a favour and talk to this guy," said Ben, waggling the phone.

"I don't do favours anymore. I'm rich, don't you know."

"I'll give you a hundred quid."

"Done. What is it?"

"These Eddy-Cab guys. They've taken the deposit. They've got six of them coming down from their Manchester factory today but, apparently, there are other people on the waiting list. I'm not good at being forceful with people."

"You want me to sort him out?" said Clovenhoof.

"Just make our case," said Ben and handed the phone over. "Polite but firm."

Clovenhoof gave him a knowing wink and put the phone to his ear.

"Listen to me, you goat-sucking inbreds!" he yelled. "What the hell do you mean you can't make the delivery today?"

There was a worried silence. "Er, who is this?" said a confused voice.

"Never mind who this is!" Clovenhoof bellowed. "I don't have time to discuss who I am or what infectious diseases I'm carrying when you're dilly-dallying and giving my friend, business partner and intimate companion, Ben Kitchen the runaround! I'll not have it! You hear? You hear?"

Another silence. This was good. Clovenhoof had them on the back foot.

"I did try to explain to Ben that –"

"That's Mr Kitchen to you, buster!"

" – to Mr Kitchen that we have a waiting list for the Eddy-Cab 900 and while we're grateful for his custom –"

"Grateful?" roared Clovenhoof. "You should be licking the ground we walk on, sunshine! Break out the red carpet. Throw a path of roses before me. Do you know who I am? Do you? Do you?!"

"No, sir. You said it didn't –"

"But you think it's okay to bamboozle my Ben with your excuses? I know this man! Like brothers we are! You don't know a man until you've buried a body together! That's an unbreakable bond!"

"Er, Jeremy?" said Ben uneasily.

Clovenhoof gave him a big thumbs up.

"Sir," said the man on the line, "I told Ben – I mean Mr Kitchen – that we do have six being transported down today but –"

"We'll take them," said Clovenhoof.

"Take them?"

"Take them all, yes." Clovenhoof had no idea what Ben was buying but six was always better than one. "And have them delivered directly to me. Cash in hand. No questions asked. There's an offer you can't refuse."

"An offer I can't refuse..."

"Or do you need me to come there and repeat myself in person? Huh?"

There was a reflective silence.

"No. No, I think that will be fine."

"Damn straight it will!" growled Clovenhoof and, with a cheeky grin, passed the phone back to Ben.

CHAPTER THIRTY-ONE

Rutspud was still adjusting to operating in daylight hours, so it was long past noon when he and Joan sat down for breakfast in the kitchen diner of the Mission Society of the Thrown Voice. Rutspud stared with interest at the confection that Sister Anne had put in front of him.

"So," he said, "these are grains of semi-aquatic grass from distant Asia, baked until they go all fluffy and dry, and then served in a bowl of the glandular secretions of an animal called a cow."

Tommy Chuckles rolled his eyes. "It's Rice Krispies is what it is, sunshine."

Rutspud picked up his spoon and stirred the unappetising mass.

"Give it a try," said Joan, shoving a spoonful in her mouth. "When are you going to get another chance?"

"Ah, the 'give it a go because you can' philosophy," said Rutspud. "Fine advice from a saint."

Joan glared at him but Sister Anne and Tommy Chuckles had moved away to do the washing up.

"I was thinking," said Rutspud.

"Yes?" said Joan.

"The PrayPal app is offering indulgences and absolution in the name of Bishop Iscansus."

"Yes."

"It is, in practical terms, as if he is personally absolving the individual each time they press the 'submit' button."

"Yes."

"But absolution can only be given by a living priest."

"Er..."

"A priest can't forgive someone post-mortem."

"I see where you're heading with this, Rutspud."

He offered her a grin and a twinkle of his very expressive eyes. "I'm not even going to ask you to get your sword dirty. Just give me a dark alleyway and half a brick. He'll be dead and knocking on Heaven's door before the day is out. Problem solved."

Joan put down her spoon. "We are not murdering Bishop Iscansus."

Rutspud sighed dispiritedly. "What's your idea then?"

"We need to shut down the app at source."

"Meaning?"

"We find the man who crafted it."

"The programmer."

"And we tell him to turn it off."

"And how do we find him?"

Joan pulled a face and ate another mouthful of Rice Krispies thoughtfully.

"We could have a bit of a pray."

"Oh, right. Cos Heaven has all the answers," he snarked and then thought. "We could contact Belphegor. He might be able to help us with that."

"Will he?"

"Yes, let's do it. Come on."

As Rutspud made for the door, Tommy Chuckles' head turned to look at him while Sister Anne continued to diligently wash up the pots one-handed.

"Have you eaten all your cereal, young man?"

"Yes, Sister Anne. The crisped rice were, er, delicious."

"My name is Tommy Chuckles," said the puppet firmly.

"Yes. Course it is. Sorry."

"Where are we going?" said Joan.

"This way," said Rutspud, pointing north towards the town centre and setting off without further explanation.

The shops in the pedestrianised high street were busy. A sign in a department store window read, 'Buy it now on credit – it's better to ask for forgiveness than permission.'

"I've got to make a note of some of these," said Rutspud.

"Some of what?" said Joan.

"Do you not notice?" said the demon. "Every sign, every advert, it's all 'buy now, pay later', 'live for today, forget about tomorrow.'"

"Act in haste, repent at leisure?"

"Exactly. Look."

Rutspud pointed at an A-frame advert outside a café. 'Eat cake. It's been scientifically proven that fat people are harder to kidnap.'

"It's just a humorous little quip," said Joan.

He laughed. "Only the virtuous could be so blind. The road to Hell might be paved with good intentions but this stuff should be on the advertising hoardings on the roadside. This country is sliding into decadent short-term hedonism."

He cocked his head at a poster in a doorway.

"'Swinging – How do you know you don't like it if you haven't tried it?'" he read. "I'm sure someone was trying to get me to eat crisped rice with a similar line earlier."

Joan grunted a reluctant acknowledgement. "And is 'swinging' what I think it is?"

Rutspud gave her an appraising look.

"I shouldn't think so. Not in this context. I recall an ex-politician explaining it to me. This was in the Pit of People Who Died During Embarrassing Sexual Acts."

"Oh, it's a moral perversion," said Joan quickly. "Say no more, Rutspud."

"Don't you want to be educated, Joan? How can you understand the ways of sin if you don't know your swinging from your dogging, your fisting from your tea-bagging?"

Joan tutted and inspected the poster more closely. "You can't just stick '-ing' on the end of an innocent noun and pretend it's a sexual act. I'm not that naïve. So, you can keep your, um, fingering, pegging and cupping, and just be honest enough to admit you don't know something rather than making it up. What's this?"

Rutspud stood on tiptoes to get a better look at the poster. "'We're an informal group that meets on alternate Tuesdays for fun and games'?"

"No. This bit underneath. 'In-house moral cleansing service provided.' And there's the little picture of a winking cat."

"It's called an icon."

"Icons are religious images of devotion," said Joan.

"And little computer images too," said Rutspud. "They're using the PrayPal app. You see? People aren't just using the app to forgive what they have done. They're planning their sins in advance, knowing they can buy absolution."

"This is serious," she said.

"You're telling me."

She frowned. "Yes. I just did."

"Come on. Since you've vetoed bashing the bishop's head in, we need Belphegor's help in finding the programmer."

Rutspud set off down the street.

"And where are we going?" said Joan.

Rutspud pointed at a spire in the middle distance. "We're going to church."

"What for?"

"It's a secret," he grinned.

"We're meant to be partners, Rutspud."

"Well, as long as you promise not to tell anyone," he said.

"Tell anyone what?"

Rutspud stopped and faced her.

"Promise."

She shrugged and raised her hand. "Sure, I promise."

"Good. So, your side use prayer to communicate from earth to Heaven."

"Yes?"

"And prayers are felt more strongly if offered in places of worship."

"That 'spiritual desire paths' thing you mentioned?"

"Spiritual desire lines," said Rutspud. "Right. The best communication routes to the afterlife start here. Churches and such are like mobile phone masts, like telephone exchanges for that hotline to the Almighty."

"I see," she said.

"Well, those desire lines, those exchanges... We hacked 'em."

"Did what?"

"Us lot in Hell hacked 'em for our own use."

CHAPTER THIRTY-TWO

The limo turned up at six o'clock precisely. There was room for a small party in the back, which was a good thing because, despite the driver's insistence that he had only come to collect one Jeremy Clovenhoof, four of them got in.

Ben pulled awkwardly at the collar of his new suit. Neither suits nor parties were really his thing, but Clovenhoof had insisted that, as one of the newly rich, Ben must now enjoy the good things in life whether he wanted to or not. Nerys planned to enjoy the evening, come what may, and was wearing a black dress constructed from barely enough fabric to make a hat. Narinda Shah (who had followed along to make sure Clovenhoof didn't "spend all of his money in one evening") was dressed far more modestly. When Ben complimented Narinda on her dress, Nerys shot him a look of such indignant malevolence that, if its energy could be harnessed, it could be used to blow up planets.

The limo was wending its way through the hedge-lined roads on the outskirts of Sutton Coldfield.

"Where are we?" said Clovenhoof.

"Lord Ferret's estate covers several hundred acres around the village of Floxton Magor," said Narinda.

"Does it now?" said Nerys. "And this lord, is he married?"

"I'm sure I wouldn't know," said Narinda primly.

They turned into a driveway flanked by ancient stone pillars and up a long driveway to a wide-fronted house with high windows and the kind of overly ostentatious neo-classical pillars that suggested the same architect had worked on this grand home as on the frontage of the Sutton Railway Building Society building. Open braziers all along the front of the building threw orange shapes against the house in the deepening dusk.

A flunky stepped down to open the door as they drew to a stop.

"Mr Clovenhoof," said the flunky in unctuous greeting. "And friends," he noted as the others slipped out behind Jeremy. "Welcome to Floxton House. The entrance is this way."

"Just point me towards the drinks, my good man," said Clovenhoof.

The flunky raised his hand to gesture.

"I'm only joking," said Clovenhoof and grinned. "I don't need help finding the alcohol."

Through the entrance hall and not one, not two but three halls, guests were already gathered, chatting in clusters, striking up conversations, filling the air with inanities, murmurings and exaggerated laughter.

"Right, team. Time for Operation Mingle."

"Mingle?" said Ben nervously. "You know I'm not one of life's minglers."

"Everyone can mingle," said Nerys.

"Not me," said Ben. "I don't mingle. I'm excused from mingling. I've got a note from my mum and everything."

"This is an ideal opportunity for you to alpha-up, Ben," said Nerys.

"Whatever, kids," said Clovenhoof. "Skedaddle. Don't want you cramping my style."

Nerys snorted. "Your style consists of replacing your belt with a string of sausages and pulling them through your flies to the tune of *New Pork New Pork*."

"Well, I'm sticking by your side, Jeremy," said Narinda. "I'm going to be your shoulder angel for the evening."

"I hate those fuckers," said Clovenhoof. "Very well. Then I insist I get you a drink, toots." He led her through the throng towards a bar, leaving Ben and Nerys to their own devices. "So, you're an accountant, yeah?"

"A qualified tax assessor, yes."

"The joke works anyway. What do tax assessors do when they're constipated?"

"Do they, by any chance, work it out with a pencil, Jeremy?"

"Maybe," said Clovenhoof. "You know, it's polite to pretend you've not heard a joke."

"I'm not going to lie to you, Jeremy," she said. "I've heard it and it's not a good joke."

"Well, that's just rude."

"Honest," she said. "Shoulder angel, yeah?"

He gave her a little frown.

"And this shoulder angel would like a brightly coloured cocktail with an umbrella in it."

"Now you're talking," he grinned.

Soon enough, Clovenhoof found himself on the rear terrace, drink in hand, peering into a large fish pond and wondering if there were any piranhas in it. He had explored much of the house. There were stylish furnishings throughout and a range of tall and gorgeous females draped over much of those furnishings. Men in sharp suits, looking like upper-class Reservoir Dogs, held court or held furtive conversations. Security were evident everywhere, although Clovenhoof wasn't sure if they were there to protect the wealthy partygoers or the fine art on the walls. Based on what Clovenhoof had learned from TV and movies, this was clearly the home of an international supervillain. There was probably a secret bunker under the house where at this moment a secret agent was being bisected by a high-powered laser.

A shape briefly broke the surface of the water.

"Koi," said Narinda joining him at the balustrade with her cocktail with a little umbrella in it.

"Not piranha then?" said Clovenhoof.

Narinda smiled tolerantly and raised her glass.

"No. Ferret keeps those in his secret volcano base. Here he disposes of his enemies by cannon."

She indicated the half dozen small cannons arranged along the edge of the terrace.

"Surely they're just decorative," said Clovenhoof.

She tilted her head. "Unused but very real. I was told by one of the more elderly Ferret relatives that they date from the time this was a royalist command base in the civil war."

Clovenhoof contemplated the idea that you could own cannons for several hundred years and not be tempted to use them. It had to be a mistake.

"Have you seen any other unused weaponry around the place, Narinda?" he asked. "I wonder if these Koi are hiding a small nuclear submarine at the bottom of their pond? Where do you suppose they keep the ground-to-air missiles?"

"I'm sure I heard Nerys asking the barman for a heat seeker," said Narinda with a mischievous smile, "but I assumed it was a cocktail."

"You can never be completely sure with Nerys," said Clovenhoof. "She sent me a text just now saying that I should look at the amazing pergola but to watch out for the ha-ha. I think she's drunk."

"No, those are things that you find in a large garden. A ha-ha is a ditch, and the pergola is a timber construction with plants growing over it. I saw the one she means, and it is spectacular."

Clovenhoof looked at her with stark disbelief. "We have timber with plants growing over it in our garden after the shed had an unfortunate accident. Nature's wonderful and all that, but I'd never thought of showing it off as a feature."

Narinda ushered him out to the garden. "No, it's not a weed-covered wreckage, it's a rather lovely bespoke construction dripping with wisteria. Come and see."

"Now that sounds like something I could appreciate," said Clovenhoof, following her. "By the way, it's pronounced 'viscera'."

Clovenhoof was disappointed to find that the pergola was just a fancy shed with no roof that seemed to exist only for flowers to grow on. In that respect it really wasn't so different to the fecund wilderness at the back of their house. Nerys sat at the centre on a bench with a tall man who was so limp and rangy he could have been replaced by a dishcloth (if you'd sent the dishcloth to Eton and taught it how to wear a suit). Clovenhoof recognised in Nerys the signs of a predator that had trapped its prey.

"New toy, Nerys?" he asked breezily.

"This is Okra Boddington," said Nerys, stroking the pinstriped arm. Okra's face looked like a gazelle who'd currently got a lion's paw upon its head. He wore an expression that tried really hard to be neutral, but which fell short and settled into swivel-eyed panic instead. "Okra manages the investment portfolio for one of the largest landowners in the country."

"The National Trust?" asked Clovenhoof.

"W-w-w-well," burbled Okra. "The f-fact of the matter is –"

Nerys silenced him with a pat on the thigh that sort of missed and was more of a gentle groin squeeze. "Okra is disappointed that his client has lost considerable ground in recent years to organisations like the National Trust."

"And does Okra not like to speak for himself, or is it just that you like speaking too much?" Clovenhoof asked Nerys.

"N-n-not at all," began Okra nervously before being cut short by Nerys.

"Shush now, darling." She smiled at Clovenhoof.

"He manages the investment portfolio for the Church of England," said Narinda.

"See, darling, you're famous," said Nerys, patting his thigh again and missing as badly as before. Okra moaned in delighted confusion.

"No," said Narinda. "I just heard him chatting over there – before all the blood ran away from his vocal cords – about how the Church could make some serious money if only it was prepared to invest in a few wars now and then."

"N-not quite..." said Okra.

"Apparently, Church Commissioners are weirdly cagey about war, slavery and regime change," explained Nerys.

"Weird," said Narinda, deadpan.

"I have a lot of experience in regime change," said Clovenhoof. "Attempted regime change, at least."

"Really, Jeremy?" said Narinda sounding cynical.

"Pretty much the first job I had," he said, sighing wistfully. "Maybe I should invest some of my newfound wealth in that direction."

"Jeremy?" said Okra. "Jeremy Clovenhoof?" He caught a glance from Nerys and then leaned over and whispered in her ear.

"Oh, yes!" said Nerys. "The host of this lovely party is very keen to meet you, Jeremy."

CHAPTER THIRTY-THREE

Finding a church that was actually open had proved a more difficult task than either Rutspud or Joan had expected. It wasn't Sunday certainly but, in Joan's eyes, every day was a day for collective worship. They had tried handles and rapped on doors.

"Why would anyone lock a church door?" Joan had said.

"I know," Rutspud had replied. "Churches haven't had anything worth nicking since the Reformation. Seriously. The Pit of Church Thieves has seen a real tail-off in the last five hundred years."

By evening, they were still looking, having wandered far from the town centre.

"That one," said Rutspud, pointing.

"You think it will be open?" said Joan.

"The lights are on."

"But maybe no one's at home."

"A metaphor for the priesthood if ever there was one," grinned the demon.

Joan gave him an admonishing shove but not a big one. She'd met priests and, certainly in her earthly lifetime, it was rarely the brightest son of the family who was sent into the priesthood.

Joan pushed open the door of St Jude's parish church. "Hello?"

She watched Rutspud hesitate in the doorway before stepping across the threshold as though he might be banished back to hell just for stepping on consecrated ground. She knew he'd been in churches before but she guessed it was just force of habit.

"Hello!" came a rather strained reply from within the church.

"Friendly Christian folk here," said Joan, walking through.

"Just want to piggyback off your holy Wi-Fi," added Rutspud.

Around the corner, towards the rear of the church, Joan found a red-faced little vicar, red-faced because he was hauling on the long rope that ran up the spire. Initially thinking that he was ringing the church bells, Joan realised her mistake. The rope was indeed connected to a bell high above but by a sturdily fixed pulley system. The vicar followed her gaze up.

"It's a tragedy really, isn't it?" he said.

"What is?"

He jerked his head upwards, keeping both hands firmly on the rope.

"Got to make financial cuts somewhere. And we'll get six grand for this one at least."

Rutspud was wandering up the aisle towards the altar, waving his sin-detecting Geiger counter around as though casually searching for a nuclear bomb.

"Do you need a hand with that?" said Joan, offering to take the rope.

"I couldn't impose," said the vicar.

"I'm stronger than I look," said Joan.

"I'm sure you are. I've been terribly let down by Rick the builder but it's national throw-a-sicky day and the buyer's truck is coming tomorrow. So, I've got to get it down. I don't know how the truck's going to fit down the lane but that's their problem. As long as they don't knock any more masonry off the side of the building like that lorry did last year. I've put up signs, you know."

Joan took the strain on the pulley rope. "What's a sicky?"

"A day off from work," said the vicar. "Phone in. Pretend to be ill."

"When you're not?" said Joan.

"Quite."

"And that's an annual event, is it?"

"I think it's moved to a monthly event," said the vicar. "The argument is that your work is obliged to cover you for a number of sick days a year so you might as well take them as holiday."

"But that's lying."

"Haven't you heard? Absolution is only a click away. I think some of the vergers and ministers of other local churches have taken a similar attitude."

Joan thought of all the closed churches they had passed. Was it coincidental?

Joan and the vicar worked on the rope hand over hand, bringing the giant brass slowly down. Shifting several hundred pounds of church bell was not easy.

"It's a crying shame," said the vicar. "This used to be a wealthy parish. This church was the owner and landlord of much the land hereabouts but much of that has been taken by the Ferret estate. Now times are hard and takings are down. The bells are near useless now anyway, since the volunteer bell-ringers all had to be let go."

"Let go?"

"They were using the bell-tower for... unseemly behaviour," said the vicar, going a little redder than before. "The chief bell-ringer tried to argue that flagellation was a historical Christian tradition and the ropes were already up there..."

"But how are you going to call the faithful to worship without bells or bell-ringers?" said Joan.

"Ah," said the vicar, with a grin. "I should show you. Take the strain."

Joan did and the vicar tied off the rope with a braking mechanism.

"If you're interested of course. Here's you and your..." He looked at the demon Rutspud. *"friend*? – come into the sanctuary of our humble church and here's me pressganging you into labour and wittering on about bells and our new all-electric system."

"I find it fascinating, father."

He smiled nervously. "It's not father. We're not part of the papist crowd here. Although, nothing against them," he added quickly. "Sterling chaps. I'm in the same yoga class as Father Paul from St Nicholas's. Justin."

It took Joan a moment to realise that Justin was his name and that Father Paul didn't work at a place called 'St Nicholas is just in', by which time the vicar was gesturing her to come and look at a cabinet near the base of the tower.

"State of the art electronic chime-management system," said the vicar, flinging the cabinet open. "We've got five resonating panels up in the belfry. A normal person would call them speakers but that's what they're called."

He flicked a switch and a computer screen awoke.

"All controlled from here," said the vicar. "Totally programmable."

Joan watched as the vicar tapped at the touch screen and then she realised what she was looking at.

"Rutspud," she called.

"Pardon?" said the vicar.

"My friend," said Joan. "It's a traditional, um, Saracen surname. Rutspud!"

"Kinda busy here, Joan!" replied the demon. "Struggling to locate a decent hotspot."

"You need to see this," she said.

"But –"

"You *really* need to see this."

Clovenhoof and Narinda followed Nerys and Okra through the crowd on the terrace. Okra towered above Nerys but continued to silently exist in her slipstream. Whenever he looked in danger of drifting away or offering any personal opinion, she brought him into line with a brazen bit of crotch massage. It was an admirable piece of Nerys's tactics. Whatever old adages might erroneously state, the quickest way to a man's heart was through his flies.

"You're buzzing," Narinda said to Clovenhoof.

"I've barely had two drinks," he argued.

"Your phone."

Clovenhoof reached into his pocket, didn't recognise the number but answered anyway.

"Go for the Hoof," he said.

"Mr Clovenhoof? Hi, it's Damo from Eddy-Cab. I've got a transporter with six Eddy-Cabs on it for you."

"Have you?" said Clovenhoof and then remembered. The people Ben asked him to shout at earlier. "Oh, right. Transporter?"

"That's right, sir. And Glen in the office said it was very important that we deliver them directly to you. Cash in hand?"

"That's what I said. Well, where are they, huh?"

"That's why I'm phoning, sir. I'm just coming up to the M42 turning and I was wondering where you'd like them delivered."

"To me, of course."

"And you are...?"

Clovenhoof looked around, at the long lawns, the wooded landscape and tried to remember.

"The Ferret estate. Um, Floxton House."

"Floxton House. Got it. Just putting it in the old sat–"

Clovenhoof killed the call.

Nerys led them down a torch-lined colonnade to a courtyard in the depths of the gardens, where a small number of guests had gathered on a patio framed with arches.

"I'm back boys. Did you miss me?" said Nerys.

Clovenhoof nearly laughed. Not only had she already bagged herself an upper-class drip, she had a few others simmering in case this one went off the boil.

"You were telling us about a novel you are working on..." said a short man with a tiny beard.

"Maybe a novel, maybe a screenplay," said Nerys airily. "It's about a sexy devil who comes up from Hell to have his wicked way with anyone and everyone." She glanced over and saw Clovenhoof looking at her. "Of course, it's not based on anyone real," she said loudly.

Clovenhoof winked at her.

"That's Maldon there," Narinda whispered.

A man turned from his circle of friends and looked at Clovenhoof. He was of middle years, with an athlete's body that was slowly but certainly turning to fat and a film star's good looks that were slowly but certainly letting him down under a receding hairline. He gave Clovenhoof a gleeful look.

"Jezza? Jerry Jerry Jezza!" He grabbed Clovenhoof's hand and pumped it. "Maldon Ferret. Been waiting for you all evening!

223

Everyone! This here is Jezza Clovenhoof, new best friend of mine, shooting star in the financial world."

There were drunken cheers, raised glasses and a few laughs as well.

Maldon looked past Clovenhoof to Narinda.

"And you've brought a filly with you. Fine filly."

"I'm not a filly, Lord Ferret," said Narinda coldly. "I'm Jeremy's... financial adviser for the evening."

"A filly who can count!" said Maldon merrily. "Hear that, Paisley? Well, if you're this young buck's financial advisor, I guess you'd best take a look at the numbers."

He clicked his fingers and a piece of paper was immediately placed in his hands. He passed it to Clovenhoof and Narinda deftly took it.

"A lot of zeroes there," said Maldon. "That's why money makes the ladies go 'ooooo'."

He cackled at his own joke.

"Is it a lot?" said Clovenhoof.

Narinda took a moment to find her voice. "Yes. I can safely say it is a lot. Certainly, enough to settle your tax issues."

"What?" said Maldon. "Did I hear someone say, 'tax'?"

There were loud boos and laughs all round.

"Naughty filly, bad filly," said Maldon. "We don't approve of tax round here, do we, boys?"

"No!" yelled several voices.

"Taxation is taking away from the earners and giving to the lazy, right? What was it Darwin said, eh? Survival of the fittest? And he was one of our finest science minds, wasn't he?" He shook his head at Narinda. "Are you trying to break the laws of science, little lady?"

Narinda kept her cool. "Jeremy has some outstanding debts to Her Majesty's Rev –"

"I've got friends who can sort that out for him," said Maldon. "Don't worry your pretty head. Money isn't for paying tax and bills and boring stuff. Money is for having fun!"

Clovenhoof, who had been watching the ping-pong between the two of them with barely any comprehension, latched onto the one thing he understood.

"Fun?"

"Absolutement, my handsome fellow! My father – God rest his beautiful soul – was a big fan of fun. In fact, it was in this space that he invented his favourite game. Want to play?"

"I like games," Clovenhoof agreed.

"Oh, shit," muttered Nerys in the corner.

"It's simple, really," said Maldon. "We sit in these chairs here and watch the skies. Night falls and the birds – the feathered kind – are coming in to roost. And we bet on which arch out of these four we see the next bird fly through. This seat, yes. Gufty Bernard's been sat in yours, warmed it up no doubt. You're a disgusting man, Gufty, and if you weren't nephew to the hottest milf in England, I'd have you beaten and thrown to the dogs."

Clovenhoof sat. Maldon clicked for drinks.

"A whisky sour for me. Jezza, name your tipple du soir."

"I don't think your bar does Lambrini," Clovenhoof said.

Maldon gave him a surprisingly passionate look. "My bar will get you what you want, sirrah! A Lambrini for the man!" As the waiter silently vanished, Maldon gestured at the courtyard arches before them. "Choose your weapon."

Clovenhoof hesitated but a moment. "That one."

"Then I will take that one," said Maldon. "Shall we say ten thou?"

"Jeremy!" hissed Narinda, coming in close behind him. "I strongly suggest –"

"Oh!" said Maldon loudly. "I see the filly is actually here to hold your purse strings. Or is it your ball sack?"

Narinda didn't allow the laughter to cow her. "Do not do this," she whispered to him. "You could lose your money before you've even got it."

Clovenhoof waved her away. "Ten K is a drop in the bucket. And, besides, I practically invented gambling. I can't lose."

"The certainty of a born winner!" said Maldon. "Game on! The chips are down. We're locked in. Watch for the birdie everyone."

A few minutes later, as the waiter presented Maldon with his whisky sour and Clovenhoof with a chilled glass of the finest Lambrini, a guest gave a cry.

"There! There!"

Maldon leaned and squinted at the two flapping silhouettes.

"Ten thou to you. You *are* a born winner, Jerry!" he declared. "Nigel? You keep score."

"As will I," said Narinda.

"Pick your arch, Jezza. Let me know when ten grand becomes passé."

CHAPTER THIRTY-FOUR

Rutspud feigned interest as the vicar talked them through the workings of the wonderful electronic chime-management system.

"And I can use this app to programme the bells," he said. "Mostly I keep it set to the hourly chimes. Only allowed to use them four times a day due to noise pollution regulations but I do think it's nice to hear them. But I can programme it with any tune. I cheekily created a file to play *Bat out of Hell* but I've not had the courage to run it."

"Oh, you should," suggested Rutspud.

Joan tapped him.

"Sorry, reflex action," said the demon.

Joan put her mouth to Rutspud's cavernous ear. "You see it?"

He nodded. He'd spotted the winky cat icon the moment he looked at the screen. WinkyCat Studios. The computer programmer.

"Tell me, Justin, who put this system in for you? It's some seriously hi-tech affair."

"Oh, some local lad."

"A computer programmer?"

"Yes. Felix."

"You wouldn't happen to know where we could find him?"

The vicar gave them a pained look. "Afraid not. Met the lad one day in a chip shop. He did the job for me at practically cost. He gave me his e-mail address on a bit of paper but I've lost that. Put it on the cabinet one day and then..." He shrugged. "I'd blame the cleaners, but they've been throwing sickies so often that I don't think I've seen them in a month."

"I could have a little look round for it," suggested Rutspud.

"Really? Why?" said the confused vicar.

"While I help you bring that bell down," said Joan.

"Well, if you're sure..."

"Just being good Christians," said Joan.

"That's right," muttered Rutspud. "we'll sing a few kumbayas while we do it."

The vicar looked deeply grateful. It was funny, thought Rutspud, that in a crapbucket world, you only had to offer a glimmer of niceness to make the terminally good smile.

"And if you hang around until the top of the hour," said the vicar, "you'll hear the final chimes of the day. Just the chimes, no *Bat out of Hell*. The bells might be gone but the resonating panels are mighty powerful. Sends the local birds into a right flap."

Maldon casually looked at his watch.

"Well, you've got me backed into a corner here, Jezza. Like office totty in the stationery cupboard with one of the board. Let's say a hundred and sixty thousand on the next one. Give me a chance of winning some back?"

"Sounds more than fair," said Clovenhoof. He downed his second Lambrini and waved the empty at the waiter. "I wouldn't want to rob our host of everything."

Maldon laughed.

There were manly, encouraging pats on Clovenhoof's shoulders from the other guests but he could see something different in the eyes of those gathered round. There was coldness, a condescension, like punters round a bear-baiting pit. Clovenhoof wasn't surprised. He was a winner and, despite what anyone else might say, no one loved a winner. That's why he got his face on all those Heavy Metal album covers and the Other Guy didn't get to appear on a single one.

Narinda had to force herself between two men to get close to Clovenhoof.

"You need to stop. He's playing 'double or quits', increasing the bet every time. He only needs to win once and you're sunk."

"I am aware," said Clovenhoof.

He had placed the inventor of the martingale 'double or quits' system in the Pit of Bad Mathematicians over two hundred years ago and offered the idiot a chance to win his way out on a coin toss – double or nothing. The last time he'd checked, the man owed Hell two trillion eternities of torture. And still he kept playing, the silly tosser.

"Nerys says it's a sting," Narinda whispered.

"What does she know?"

"Because they were talking about fleecing some nouveau riche oik before you got here. A trick. Something to do with the local church."

"Coincidence," he scoffed, as his phone vibrated in his pocket. "This is a simple game between new friends and I'm the king of gamblers. Now back off." He answered the phone. "Yes?"

"Mr Clovenhoof, sir. It's Damo from Eddy-Cab."

"Who?"

"With the cars, sir. Just wanted to check that it's okay to bring the transporter down through Floxton Magor. Some of these lanes are –"

"Dammit, man!" he yelled. "Bring them to the home of my good friend Lord Maldon Ferret now or there will be consequences on a Biblical scale!" He killed the call with a vicious finger jab that nearly cracked the screen.

"Everything okay, Jezster?" said Maldon.

"Peachy, Maldo," he replied. "A hundred and sixty thousand, you say? We could just call it a cool million."

Maldon's surprise lasted only a heartbeat before his face cracked into a wide and avaricious smile.

"Now, you're talking! Let's get a round of shotskies in, up the ante and, if we're in the mood, try and get one up Gufty's aunty later too. Pick an arch, Jezza."

No sooner had they settled down with drinks to watch than one of Maldon's cronies pointed through Clovenhoof's selected arch.

"There!"

Clovenhoof looked, but he'd had more than a few drinks and his eyes failed to catch sight of a bird. "You sure?"

"Definitely," said Maldon with a sad shake of his head. "Two million on the next one?"

"Make it three," said Clovenhoof breezily and then merely smiled smugly when someone shouted that he'd won again.

Two drinks and several bets later, Maldon gave a cry of anguish as the latest bird failed to favour his archway.

"Damn it all to hell! How much have I lost to this god among men?"

"Seven hundred and forty million pounds," said the tally-keeper, Nigel. Narinda nodded in grim agreement.

"That is a pretty penny, isn't it?" said Clovenhoof.

"One last bet. One last bet!" pleaded Maldon. "Double or quits?"

Clovenhoof nodded genially and sipped his Lambrini.

"Er, Lord Ferret," said Nigel, "I'm sorry to point out that Mr Clovenhoof's current winnings and original pot would not cover a bet that size."

"It's okay, I'm good for it," said Clovenhoof.

"He is not!" said Narinda.

Maldon hung his head. "Please, Jezza, won't you give an Old Etonian a chance? Tell you what, eh, old chap? We'll stake everything you've got against..." He sucked his breath in as though in thought. "A billion pounds?"

"Billion pounds!" squeaked Nerys.

"A billion, eh?" said Clovenhoof.

"I mean I'd have to sell a castle or two to cover it but at least I'd have a chance to regain my honour." Maldon was doing a great impression of a broken man. "Let me make it more enticing. You can have all three of those bally arches. All three. And I'll have that one, the one with the church."

Narinda was waving her hands and mouthing 'Don't do it!' loud enough for someone a mile away to read.

"Three arches to one?" said Clovenhoof. "Everything I own against a cool billion?" He held out his hand.

Maldon shook it solemnly and was suddenly a composed gentleman once more. He glanced at his watch.

"Everyone, keep your eyes on that arch," he said. "Nigel? You filming this?"

Rutspud surreptitiously climbed on top of the chime-management cabinet to see if the paper with the programmer's e-mail address had slipped down the back. He recognised, of course, that there was virtually no way to climb on large fixtures and fittings whilst remaining surreptitious and had instructed Joan to cough and engage the vicar in loud conversation every time the man was in danger of looking round.

"So," she grunted as they worked the pulley rope hand over hand, "these bells must have been part of the church's history for hundreds of years."

"These ones were installed in the 1860s," said the vicar. "This one was the biggest of them."

"Yes. Weighs plenty," she agreed.

Rutspud waggled his hand down the back of the unit, forcing his dextrous fingers into the gap between metal cabinet and stone wall. A disturbed spider ran over his knuckles and away. If he'd had the time, he might have snagged it and eaten it. Even a spider was an improvement on those crispied rice things. But he didn't have the time. He jammed his hand further down and felt around.

"Weighs close to eight hundred pounds, this one," said the vicar. "Although, judging by your accent, you'd prefer it in metric."

"I'm an old-fashioned girl," smiled Joan. "Pounds I understand."

"*Chimes commencing in thirty seconds,*" said the machine beneath Rutspud.

"Oh, you must listen," said the vicar. He looked up at the bell, still hanging a good twenty feet above them. "I'm sure your friend would –"

The vicar stared at Rutspud at the same moment as Rutspud realised his hand was not only jammed down the back of the cabinet but well and truly jammed.

"What are you doing?" demanded the vicar.

"Um. Joan?" He yanked his arm but his wrist was caught against something.

There was the honk of air brakes and the loud rumble of an engine outside. Joan was opening her mouth to offer some excuse but the vicar was scurrying to the door, his black cassock flapping.

"No, no, no. Too fast, too near. I put up signs!"

A shuddering crunch against the wall right behind the cabinet shook Rutspud and set his scraped hand free. Up above, stonework trembled and something somewhere went snap.

The rope flew from Joan's hand. She yelled something very unsaintly and grabbed for it again.

The bell tumbled. The vicar screamed. Joan flew up with the rope. Rutspud tottered on the top of the cabinet. He could see that in roughly half a second, Joan was about to get clouted on the head by the bell and, in short order, would experience a brief ringing in the ears before becoming the world's first two-dimensional saint.

Rutspud half-leapt and half-fell from his vantage point. He slapped against the rim of the bell with sufficient force to turn its downward plummet into an elliptical swing.

The descending bell missed Joan of Arc by millimetres (or *lignes* if the old fashioned French girl preferred). Her rising weight slowed it as it and Rutspud swung round and back...

"Oh, bollocks," said Rutspud.

"Chimes commencing in five –"

Rutspud was aware of the phrase 'between a rock and a hard place'. Between a bell and a stone wall didn't have the same poetry to it but that was where the chime-management cabinet found itself. Briefly.

On the Ferret estate, dozens of eyes were fixed on an archway with a commanding view of the darkening gardens and the nearby village church.

"Any moment now," said Maldon and consulted his watch again.

"Maybe they've all gone to bed," said Clovenhoof nonchalantly.

"No," said Maldon softly. "It should... The birds in the belfry. The chimes."

He tapped his watch.

"There!" shouted Nerys, pointing.

Clovenhoof looked. A dim shape, a hunting owl perhaps, flapped above distant woodland. And it was most definitely in one of Clovenhoof's arches.

"Did you see that?" said Nerys.

"I'm not sure any of us saw anything," said Maldon unconvincingly. "It's getting dark after all."

"Perhaps Nigel filmed it," suggested Clovenhoof.

"I did," said Nerys.

"Jeremy won?" said Nerys.

"Um," said Lord Maldon Ferret.

He looked round at his guests. Many were as stunned as him. He saw shock on a lot of faces but there was also plenty of amusement and contempt. People might hate winners, but they also hate total losers.

Maldon's mouth worked silently, as if searching for a way to back out of the bet, to claim that it had all been in jest. But Clovenhoof had met (and tortured) a lot of rich people and knew that it wasn't enough for them to have lots of money, they had to pretend that they didn't care they had lots of money. To plead for his money just wasn't in Maldon's nature.

"I take cash or cheque," said Clovenhoof. "Cash preferably. I like to roll in it and shove it down my pants."

Maldon's mouth continued to work silently.

"That will be one point seven four billion pounds please," said Narinda, "in addition to the money held in your building society."

"Fuck me," whispered Nerys, astounded and delighted. She nudged Okra in the ribs. "Seriously. I'm feeling generous."

"But..." managed Maldon.

"Nigel," said Narinda, "fetch his lordship's chequebook."

"Unless he'd rather see a soon-to-be viral YouTube video of him welching on a bet," said Nerys.

Clovenhoof gave the shell-shocked lord a consolatory pat on the shoulder. "Never mind, eh, Maldo-mate. Tell you what, I took a shine to those cannons of yours up on the terrace. I'll buy them off you. Million a pop. They'd look great on my yacht. And maybe we can find you a rugby team somewhere willing to pay for some public-school specials, earn you a little extra cash."

Clovenhoof turned, arms outspread to the guests and what he reckoned would suddenly turn out to be his new best buddies.

"Scrum fumbles are on Maldon. Drinks are on me. To the bar everyone!"

To whoops and cheers, he led the way back up to the house.

"Okra would really like to have a chat with you as soon as possible about some lucrative business opportunities," said Nerys, steering her new boyfriend along with them.

"Have his people call my people," he said, draping an arm over Nerys's and Narinda's shoulders. "I think it's going to be a busy week."

"I can't believe that just happened," said Nerys.

"You are a reckless man," said Narinda sternly.

"King of gamblers," he grinned.

Joan found Rutspud next to but fortunately not amongst the wreckage of the cabinet of electronics.

"Are you unhurt?" she asked, helping him to his feet.

Rutspud corrected an arm that was bending the wrong way and noisily cricked his spine.

"There was that remark about us both being good Christians," he said, "but I'll get over it."

Both limping slightly, they headed outside.

A lorry with a long trailer filled the road outside the church, the back end of the trailer stuck in a hedge on the bend, the top front edge crumpled against the church wall.

The driver struggled to get out of his cab in the narrow lane. He looked up at the damage the trailer and wall had made of each other and, putting his hand to his head, winced.

"Are you hurt?" said the vicar.

"No," said the driver despondently, "but I think I soon might be. Mr Clovenhoof was really insistent about getting these self-driving cars delivered."

Joan looked at the half dozen sleek vehicles on the split level trailer.

"Self-driving?"

"Top of the line."

"And is your lorry self-driving?" said the vicar, his withering tone unmistakeable.

"No," said the driver. "Sorry, father."

As the vicar began to educate the lorry driver on both the difference between Anglican and Catholic priests and on the existence of certain signs he had put up along the lane, Rutspud put a piece of paper in Joan's hand.

She unfurled it. It was a long printed ticket, torn at both ends and apparently for something called National Express West Midlands.

"What is it?"

"Turn it over," said Rutspud.

She did. "The programmer's e-mail address. Can we use this to find him?"

"We can use this to contact him," said Rutspud. "All we need is a computer. Come on."

CHAPTER THIRTY-FIVE

It was the morning after the night before, but no one had slept.

Clovenhoof, Ben, Nerys and Narinda were all in the games room, but The Game was ignored as they all tried to absorb how rich Clovenhoof actually was. Clovenhoof lounged dreamily on his favourite chair. Narinda sat primly at the table. Ben was wedged in a corner as though the prospect of fabulous wealth was the most terrifying thing in the world.

Nerys leaned against the filing cabinet filled with The Game's rules.

"Sit down," Ben said to her, nervously. "You're making the place look... cluttered."

"I'm too buzzed to sit," she said.

"Ah, I thought you might be too sore," said Clovenhoof. "You and your catch were noisy in your celebrations last night."

"Okra was very energetic," she commented, shamelessly. "He's sleeping it off upstairs. And you are a dirty old man."

"Unh-uh," said Clovenhoof, wagging a finger. "I'm filthy rich now, so I'm a 'character' or a 'card' if you will."

Narinda ended the call on her phone and put it meaningfully on the table.

"It's done," she said.

"Done."

"The money has been transferred. Maldon honoured the bet."

"Good God!" breathed Ben, stunned.

"That's an opinion," said Clovenhoof. "So, I've got questions."

"Of course," said Narinda.

"First up, if I stacked all my money in tenners, would I need a fork lift truck to move it around?" he asked Narinda.

"That's the question you really wanted to ask?" said Nerys.

Narinda tapped on her phone. "You would need a fork lift truck and several days. Seriously, you would need more than fifty trucks to move it around."

"What about gold bars? Could I build a house?"

Narinda spent a little longer tapping. "Around six thousand bricks in a house. Gold bars are smaller than house bricks, so I'm going to say you'll need fifteen thousand, although I have no idea how you'd construct this house. Let's check the current price of gold – yup, you could afford to build a house from gold bars."

"Maybe I should do that?" mused Clovenhoof.

"It would be a very insecure way to hold funds," said Narinda.

"I suppose it would be handy for paying the window cleaner," said Ben. "You could just carve a chunk off the wall if you were short of cash."

"Window cleaner?" said Clovenhoof, who was always suspicious of any kind of cleaning. "Surely you mean wall polisher? I want to be able to see my reflection in my golden wall as I rub myself along its length."

Narinda pulled a face. "The first thing that we need to do is establish your tax position."

"Oh, Narinda," said Clovenhoof shaking his head. "That is absolutely not the first thing we need to do. I'm not even sure it makes the top hundred." He pulled out a ragged envelope he'd been scribbling on. "Nope. It doesn't."

Nerys walked over and took the list from Clovenhoof. He noticed that she was still in catwalk mode, placing her feet carefully in line and sashaying her hips for the invisible audience. She scanned down the list. "Uh-huh. Yep. On it. Oh, right. This one here, about being famous? You're having a press conference in five minutes."

"I have?"

"You asked. I made phone calls. It's a great news narrative."

"My rags to riches tale, of course it is."

"I think they're more interested in Maldon Ferret's riches to, well, much smaller riches tale. The British press do like to kick the rich and powerful when they're down."

Narinda sighed. "I would strongly suggest that you take a while to properly evaluate your situation. The tax office can help you to ensure that your obligations are clarified."

"But you said that bets aren't taxable," said Clovenhoof.

"That is correct, but we will need to provide assurances that this was not staged in order to disguise a gift, especially given the sums of money we're talking about. And I should remind you that your original tax bill is still outstanding."

"Narinda, Narinda, you worry too much," said Clovenhoof, pulling a wad of cash from inside his smoking jacket. "Give them this to tide them over and we can sort it all out later. In the meantime, I have a press conference to give. My audience awaits."

Clovenhoof led the way out of the ground floor games room and opened the front door to find a crowd of people facing him. They stood in the small front garden and spilled onto the pavement. One or two of them seemed to be standing on top of the hedge, which was a good trick, but then he realised that they had step ladders and stood on top to take photographs. Out of the corner of his eye, Clovenhoof could see Nerys shifting position so she could pout at the camera. He struck a pose in his smoking jacket, while journalists crowded forward and stuck microphones in his face.

"Is it true that you won millions in a bet?"

"How rich are you?"

"Do all of these Eddy-Cabs belong to you?"

Clovenhoof held his hands in the air and beamed at them all. "It's true that I am unbelievably rich and that you should now all be fascinated by the details of my life. Luckily for you, I've been keeping careful records of my bowel movements for some time now. Photos too! My assistant can send those out in a press pack later today."

Nerys elbowed forwards. "As you've just heard, Mr Clovenhoof is a hilarious rogue with a fascinating life story. We'll be taking bids for the serialisation rights in a short while. In the meantime, he will take a few questions. You, there."

"You've made several fortunes recently, Mr Clovenhoof. Have you got any financial tips for our readers?" asked a woman wearing a hot pink suit.

Clovenhoof ignored Narinda gently shaking her head beside him. "Money. Hm, let me tell you about money. Money is like water," declared Clovenhoof. "Dirty, smelly, delicious water. It flows from one place to another and if you try to hold it in your hands it will run through your fingers. The best thing that you can hope for is to fall into a lake and then go splashing around while you can. My tips for you are: make sure you get good and wet; never use an umbrella; and swallow, don't spit."

The journalists nodded and scribbled, and if they were confused by his nonsensical declarations they pretended not to be.

"Next question?" shouted Nerys. "You in the tweed."

"Ah, I am actually a representative of the Sutton Railway Building Society. I was hoping, Mr Clovenhoof, that you'd be able to provide assurances that you'll be leaving your funds in our organisation?"

Clovenhoof's eyes widened. "Why on earth would I do that?" he asked.

"Because it is a long-standing cornerstone of Sutton Coldfield. Part of its heritage, you might say," said the man in the tweed.

"What's that got to do with me leaving funds in there?" asked Clovenhoof.

"Because you now control all of the funds available to our venerable institution. Jobs and livelihoods depend upon your sense of responsibility towards it."

Clovenhoof nodded. "Yes, I've met Penny. If you ask me, she could do with a change of scenery, so I'll be in touch about an alternative position for her."

The man blanched. "So you'll be withdrawing your funds?" he asked.

"Didn't you just hear my eloquent speech about money being like water? I have big plans for my money, and none of them involve leaving it where it is."

"I have a question," said a woman with a strident voice. "Your PrayPal has been responsible for a significant decline in church attendance."

"Has it?"

"It has. What are you going to do about it?"

Clovenhoof gave her a smile. "Do you want me to answer that question truthfully? Tell you what, why don't you explain why that bothers you?"

The woman straightened her jacket and looked defensive. "Well it's a social hub for some people. We like the sense of community. Now that's all gone."

"Easy!" said Clovenhoof. "PrayPal has a social forum. People can chat and swap cake recipes or whatever it is you Jesus freaks like doing."

"It's not the same. A proper social life can't be replaced by a thingy on a phone. What about the singing and the playgroups and the coffee mornings."

"You can use PrayPal to organise some singing sessions somewhere a bit more convenient, like the pub."

"That's not an answer, Mr Clovenhoof."

"But, you have, in fact, given me a great idea. I'm going to organise the biggest social get-together this town has ever seen. If the church can't create social joy and cohesion then I guess it's up to the marvellous Mr Clovenhoof to provide. Give me a few days and I will announce the details."

The woman fell short of smiling at Clovenhoof's answer, but her scowl diminished slightly.

"Next," said Nerys. "You!"

"You gunna be one of them tax dodgers who puts their millions in a tax haven?" asked an oily-haired fellow.

"Apparently I don't pay tax on money I won in a bet. It's all mine," said Clovenhoof triumphantly.

"Yeah, but you're earning interest every day on that money. Government are gunna want to tax that," said the man.

"Is this true?" Clovenhoof whirled on Narinda.

"Well, yes –" started Narinda, but Clovenhoof turned his attention back to the man with the oily hair.

"But I can avoid that? What's a tax haven?" he asked.

"It's where you put your money in a country wiv diff'rent tax rules, so's you get to keep more of it. Or there's loads of other things that rich folks do like –"

"Mr Clovenhoof will not be avoiding tax," said Narinda, cutting in front of him, "as he is a fine upstanding citizen who intends to play by the rules."

Clovenhoof spluttered with rage. "I've been accused of some things in my time," he yelled, "but that is just *rude*. How dare you!"

Nerys pointed again. "You, next question."

"Is it true that Jeremy Clovenhoof is a fake identity, cooked up a few years ago and you're currently under investigation by the Fraud Squad," called out a man who might or might not have been Inspector Gough of the fraud office putting on a voice.

"And who's that naked man?" asked a woman, pointing upwards.

Everyone looked. A naked dishcloth of a man stood dazedly at a second floor window.

"Put some clothes on, Okra!" Nerys shouted.

"This press conference is over!" said Clovenhoof and went inside.

Joan watched Rutspud's fingers fly across the tablet. She'd stopped asking about how he knew how to work these gadgets. Rutspud had explained emails to her. They were letters that you sent using this new-fangled wizardry and they got delivered instantly. Joan was thrilled by this. They would send a message and the programmer would help them with their mission. They had decided on a brief and truthful note.

Dear Winkycat,
We are agents of a higher power. The PrayPal that you created is causing a spiritual imbalance in the afterlife and we need you to turn it off. Please let us know when you have done it.
Joan of Arc (Heaven) and Rutspud (Hell).

Unfortunately, since they'd sent the message the previous night there had been no response.

So, Joan and Rutspud now sat in the living room of the Mission Society of the Thrown Voice doing further internet research. On the upper walls of the living room, glove puppets of deceased society members hung from pegs above little plaques detailing who they had belonged to. Joan struggled to articulate her feelings about this display of dangling mannequins but when Rutspud vulgarly declared it to be "creepy as fuck" she could not disagree.

The door swung open silently and Tommy Chuckles' over-sized head peered round the door frame. Joan's natural instinct was to kill it and then burn it with fire and, much to her shame, she realised her hand was already on the hilt of her sword. She let it go and smiled at the puppet.

"Hello, Tommy."

"Morning, young uns," he said. "Me and Sister Anne is off into town for an emergency meeting with the regional abbeys, holy houses and religious retreats."

"Emergency meeting. Oh."

"That jumped-up and godless billionaire Jeremy Clovenhoof thinks he can supplant the work of the church with a tacky street party and we're going to do something about it."

"Have a bit of a pray," suggested Rutspud with expertly subtle sarcasm.

"We're going to do a lot more than that. We'll have a million nuns marching on his doorstep and what'll he think then?"

"There's a *Sound of Music* sing-a-long?"

Tommy Chuckles' face screwed up in a puppety frown and was gone.

"There was no need to be rude," said Joan.

"We've got work to do," said Rutspud, and resumed his dextrously speedy typing.

"Do you think that Winkycat is the programmer's real name?" asked Joan, looking over his shoulder.

"No, it's a nickname," said Rutspud. "I found an older account using the same nickname though, and it was someone based in

Birmingham, so I think it might be the same person. Look, there's a photo."

Rutspud enlarged the picture. It was a young man. He didn't look much older than Joan. He wore a chunky woollen sweater with a zip up the front and had a thick crop of curly hair. He sat on a low wall, his hands buried in the pockets of the sweater.

"It would be good if we could work out where this picture was taken," said Rutspud.

"Is that a shop in the background?" said Joan. "That big glass window behind him."

Rutspud enlarged the picture. "Yes, there's a sign saying *OAP Specials on Wednesday.*"

"So, we just need to find a shop that sells OAPs," said Joan. "Why don't you use the laptop to find out?"

Rutspud gave her a look. "OAP is shorthand for an old aged pensioner. That sign means they sell something cheap for old people on Wednesdays. I think it might be food. Look, you can see the edge of the sign at the top."

"Oh, wait. Is that Large Mikes?" said Joan, poking the screen with her finger. "That name keeps coming up. We need to go there."

"Let's kidnap an OAP on the way there and claim the special!" said Rutspud, closing the laptop and jumping up. He laughed as Joan glared at him. "That was a joke by the way. You should see your face."

CHAPTER THIRTY-SIX

Clovenhoof sat in the Eddy-Cab and grinned at the world. He had been filthy rich for less than a week, was still getting used it, and was currently having some fun on the dual carriageway, putting his feet up on the dashboard and catching the eye of other motorists as he overtook them in the fast lane. He had no idea how this car was a more capable driver than the humans who swerved and honked at the slightest excitement, but it was and he loved it. This car was possibly the best invention since the crispy pancake. On the subject of crispy pancakes...

"Kylie, send a text to Milo asking how his latest pancake is coming along," he said.

"Texting Milo asking how his latest pancake is coming along," said the automated voice of the car. He had set its name to be Kylie because it reminded him of the dinky Australian singer, in that it was low to the floor, with a shimmering airbrushed finish and it was way out of his league. Except now he had twelve of them. He had yet to try to drive them all at once...

"Kylie, text Nerys and tell her to buy me a new loudhailer. Then set destination for the Boldmere Oak."

"Text sent," said Kylie and then pulled smoothly into the left lane to turn off.

On the road outside the Boldmere Oak, Spartacus Wilson and his gang were charging up and down in their shopping trolleys. To the inobservant viewer it might have simply appeared to be a bunch of lads messing about but there was a studied precision to their manoeuvres, like a ballet for daleks.

"Window, Kylie," said Clovenhoof. "Oi! Spartacus!"

The teen menace wheeled over.

"Kerb-crawling now, are you?" he said.

Clovenhoof waved at the choreographed trolley action.

"You guys are getting good at that."

Spartacus sniffed. "I heard you're stinking rich now, you can sponsor us, yeah?"

"You reckon you could do a demonstration of your trolley stunt –"

"Street polo."

"– for my Family Bumper Fun Day?"

"Maybe," said Spartacus. "Where is that going to be?"

"Right here," said Clovenhoof, pointing at the pub. "You're looking at the pub I just bought. I bought a few bits and pieces around it too, so I can fulfil the more ambitious parts of my vision."

"Like what?" asked Spartacus.

"Well, as well as being the fun venue of choice for amazing gatherings like the one we're about to have, this is also going to house the Clovenhoof Lifestyle Academy where people can learn to be more like me. But first, we'll be building a moat all the way round the place. The diggers are coming today."

"What you need a moat for?"

"Two things. I have a sizeable yacht and I plan to moor it here. Second reason is that I am creating a moat around my tax haven."

"Tax what?"

"The nation state of Hooflandia will be contained within that moat."

"Like a foreign country?"

"Yes, indeed."

"So, what, you'll be like, abroad?"

"That is correct, Spartacus. You can come on your holidays. Provided you get your passport and exchange your currency, of course," said Clovenhoof.

He went inside the pub-recently-turned-country to find Lennox tapping on a laptop in the saloon bar.

"Yo, Lennox, my man! I mean that literally by the way, given that you now work for me."

"I will overlook that arrogant remark since you're Old Nick himself and have recently given me a million quid for this old ruin, sir," said Lennox. Lennox was one of less than a handful of humans who knew Clovenhoof's true identity. No one had ever told Lennox that Clovenhoof was Satan. Jeremy just reckoned that, as a seasoned barman, Lennox saw through bullshit instantly and no amount of heavenly hocus pocus was going to blind him to Jeremy's horns and hoofs.

"A million was twice the asking price," said Clovenhoof, "so I'll have less sass from you. But don't call me sir, Lennox. Landlords only call people sir when they're about to tell them they've had too much to drink. Have you made progress with my army yet?"

Lennox called out towards the back. "Florence, get your brothers out here!"

A group emerged from the back. Florence was clearly in charge of the three tall youths and made strange swooping attacks upon their clothing with pins as they walked.

"My niece and nephews," Lennox explained. "Florence is working on the uniforms."

"You want lots of gold braid on the dress uniforms, yeah?" queried Florence, through a mouthful of pins. "You want desert camo or jungle camo for the combat fatigues?"

"Just make them look kick-ass. Use your judgement," said Clovenhoof. "Lennox, I want more people in this army. You still recruiting?"

"Sure! This is just the first set to get through basic training," said Lennox.

"And what is the basic training? Sniper rifles? Knife fighting?"

"Since Hooflandia currently has no actual weapons our army's mostly ceremonial so we focused on relevant skills."

"Changing of the guard? Silly marches?"

"No, that's advanced training. We've just focused on the basic standing still and looking fierce but reassuring."

The three conscripts stood to attention and did their best fierce-but-reassuring looks, looks which Clovenhoof would have otherwise described as 'doing a difficult poo.'

"Very good," he said, unconvinced.

Florence continued chasing and pinning as the army went back to their quarters.

"You can show me to my presidential suite now, Lennox," said Clovenhoof. "Or should I say, Prime Minister?"

Lennox smiled. Clovenhoof decided that he would need to start with Lennox when it came to coaching the world on being more Clovenhoof. Lennox still moved in a gentle, laid-back way. He was the prime minister of a brand new country now, he might want to learn to strut and swagger.

"Come and take a look," said Lennox.

They went up the stairs. Clovenhoof was hazy on whether this upstairs room was new or extended, but the important question was simply this: did it ooze vulgar excess?

He went through the double door with side columns supported by golden cherubs. The space that he entered was vast. Somehow it must extend further back than the pub itself. This was excellent! Velvet was gathered artfully on the walls into complicated sculptural arrangements. There were chaises longues covered in leopard skin fabric. There was a television the size of a cinema screen and a bar padded with leather and topped with beaten copper. He could see the Lambrini lined up on glass shelves.

Small water features dotted throughout the room had more of the golden cherubs. This must be Nerys's doing, she knew how much he enjoyed poking the bare bottoms of cherubs with anything sharp – it helped him to think. He breathed deeply, enjoying his first sight of his new favourite place.

"Needs some mood lighting," said Clovenhoof. Lennox flipped a switch by the bar and lamps burst into life along the walls. They had flickering bulbs that looked like flames. As Lennox turned the controller the colour of the flames turned from white, through a soft apricot to a Hellish red.

"Smart bulbs. We can change the presets to be any brightness and colour saturation that you want," said Lennox.

"Reminds me of the Old Place," said Clovenhoof approvingly.

"By the way," said Lennox, coughing uncomfortably, "I do want to make it clear that, just because I'm your employee now, I do not consider myself a servant of Hell." He directed half of this in a generally upward direction as though Heaven itself might be listening in. "I consider myself to be a... a shoulder angel of sorts. Just one on the payroll as it were."

"Bloody shoulder angels everywhere," sighed Clovenhoof. "And now I'm paying for them. Ooh, talking of money..."

"Ah, yes." Lennox went behind the copper-topped bar, pulled out a courier's box and placed it on the counter. "We have some samples of your new currency, the Hooflandian pound."

"Are they as I requested?"

"Pretty much."

"Only pretty much?"

"Yes. I chatted with some legal people and, apparently, having, um, vulgar anatomy as the main image on each banknote would make it extremely unlikely they would ever be accepted as a recognised currency."

"But I've already started practising calling a ten pound note a 'titty'."

"I'm sorry to hear that but –"

"As in, 'cool hat, I'll give you a titty for it.'"

"Yes, I'm –"

"Or 'I'd like to put two titties on a horse in the three fifteen.'"

"Very droll."

"And then there's the other notes. The snatch. The ass. The dong. Hey. How come those foreign lot can get away with calling their money the dong and I can't?"

"I think it means something different in Vietnamese," said Lennox.

"Excuses. Let's have a look then."

As Lennox pulled out piles of notes and stacks of coins, Nerys and Ben arrived.

"This is where you two are hiding?" said Nerys.

Ben pulled a face at the décor. "Is this place meant to look like a tart's boudoir?"

"And how would you know what a tart's boudoir looks like?" said Nerys.

"Or any boudoir for that matter," said Clovenhoof.

"Boudoir," said Lennox.

Everyone looked at him.

"It's a fun word to say," he said. "I just wanted to join in."

"Boudoir," agreed Ben. "You serving, Lennox?" he asked and the barman was already pouring their usuals before he'd even got to the question mark.

"Diggers are all set to excavate the moat," Nerys said to Clovenhoof. "We need to talk about the border wall that you wanted as well."

"Oh yeah, an absolute must-have," said Clovenhoof.

"What's it for?" asked Ben.

"Well, we need to clamp down on the movement of drugs," said Clovenhoof.

"Oh, fair point," said Ben, taking receipt of his cider and black and giving Lennox a twenty. "Are people going to try to smuggle drugs into Hooflandia?"

"No, no, no! I need to stop drugs going *out*," said Clovenhoof. "If there are drugs in here then they're mine and I don't want them leaving."

"Um, what's this?" said Ben, looking at the coins and notes in his outstretched hand as though Lennox had just spat in it.

"Hooflandia's exchange system," said Lennox. "The pub takes payments in British pounds and gives change in Hooflandian."

Nerys took a jagged edged coin from Ben's hand.

"Are these jigsaw pieces?" she asked.

"Part of our plan to encourage saving," said Clovenhoof. "The fifty pences are cut in jigsaw shapes and, if you collect enough, it will build up into a two-thousand-piece jigsaw."

"Of what?"

"Might be a tasteful picture of your Hooflandian president. Might be Her Maj, Queen Elizabeth, topless. Who can say?"

"And these?" said Ben, holding up a thick and shiny brown coin.

"A stroke of genius," said Lennox. "I told Jeremy here that old wise saying about once all the trees and fish have gone that people will discover they can't eat money."

"And I decided to change all that," said Clovenhoof. "That's why the Hooflandian pound coin is a densely compacted cup-a-soup. Pop that in a cup of hot water and you'll have a nice oxtail soup."

"And dysentery," said Nerys, "considering all the grubby hands and pockets it will have been in. What was it they say about the amount of urine on the average coin?"

"Which brings us to the notes," said Clovenhoof.

"Yes," said Lennox. "Jeremy doesn't like the new plastic British notes."

"Too shiny. Too clean," shuddered Clovenhoof.

"So, we've taken a retro step with the Hooflandian notes," said Lennox. "They're designed to retain the chemical essence of anything they touch."

"Super absorbent," said Clovenhoof.

"Easily stained."

"It gives them character."

"A unique feel."

"And I pissed on every hundredth bank note just to get the ball rolling."

Ben dropped the money in disgust.

"Can we talk about this wall, please," said Nerys.

"What's the problem? I want a wall. A bigly wall. Tall, proud –"

"See-through?" said Nerys.

"Absolutely. I want people to be able to see into Hooflandia and be all jealous that they're on the wrong side."

"So, looking in at the nudist beach?"

"Nudist beach!" said Ben. "Are you nuts? This is Boldmere, not... not Brighton!"

"Not any more, Ben. It's Hooflandia and all things are possible," said Clovenhoof. "It will be a normal beach for the Family Bumper Fun Day, then we'll change it to a nudist beach later on. Part of my exclusive club and lifestyle coaching centre. It saves me having to buy a private island. I'm building my own island paradise right here in Hooflandia."

"We'll get the sand for the beach delivered with the wall materials," said Nerys. "But I think it's going to be a simple brick and concrete wall, sorry."

Oh. Your weird friends are here," said Ben. "The Calhoun children, was it?"

Joan and Rutspud had entered the presidential suite. Rutspud was nodding approvingly. Joan's face suggested she was less impressed but she was French and they famously had no taste in décor. They'd built the Pompidou Centre for one thing.

"This place looks like a tart's boudoir," said Joan.

"Thank you," said Ben, vindicated.

"Boudoir," said Lennox.

"Sure," said Clovenhoof. He reclined on a chaise longue and invited Joan and Rutspud to grab their own. Joan sat primly on the edge of another chaise longue, and Rutspud bounced gently on the springs of his. "Are you two coming to the Family Bumper Fun Day?"

He caught a look between Joan and Rutspud.

"What?" he asked.

"Nothing," said Rutspud.

"Spit it out," said Clovenhoof, "what's up?"

"Apparently there's to be a protest march at the same time as your Family Bumper Fun Day," said Joan. "Church solidarity against PrayPal. Some people we know are going on it."

"Some people?"

"Nuns," said Joan.

"Lots of nuns," said Rutspud.

Clovenhoof clapped his hands with glee. "The looks on your faces! I thought it might be bad news, but that sounds like great fun. How many nuns?"

"Tommy Chuckles said a million, but he might be exaggerating."

"And he's also a puppet," said Joan, "so I don't know how much we can trust his word."

"A million nuns! Thank you, guys. Well, if that's all you've got to tell me..."

"No," said Joan. "We've come to ask for assistance."

"We need your help," said Rutspud.

"I told you, I'm not helping you fortress-wreckers."

"We've made some progress finding the programmer who wrote your app," said Joan.

"That's swell but –"

"And we think he hangs out at a Large Mike's chip shop."

Clovenhoof paused, licking his lips at the thought of fast food. "Of course, I could have told you that. That's where he and me and Festering Ken cooked up the idea."

"So that's our main line of enquiry at the moment," said Joan and began to explain their current plans, but Clovenhoof wasn't listening. He was thinking about a kebab – steaming fragrant meat, topped with chilli sauce that could blow your socks off, grease all over his face as he tried to eat it and not caring in the slightest... He licked his lips.

"– a chain of about twenty and we just can't get round them all," said Joan.

Clovenhoof held up an Eddy-Cab security fob. "Take Kylie."

"What?" said Rutspud.

"The car. She does what you need if you just talk to her. You'll get round the chip shops no problem with that. One condition though."

"What?" asked Joan, as Rutspud gleefully grabbed the key.

"Bring me back a kebab from the first one you get to."

CHAPTER THIRTY-SEVEN

Joan and Rutspud went out to the street.

"There," said Rutspud.

"Ah, it's one of those," said Joan, recognising the sleek curves of the cars they'd seen on the transporter. Why did they look more like fish than mechanical conveyances? Like fish with the disturbingly anatomical curves of the human body... Joan felt a little sordid just looking at it.

She stood at a respectful distance.

"Hello, Kylie."

The car said nothing.

"Can we get in please?" she asked.

Rutspud stepped forward and pressed something on the key fob. The doors unlocked with a well-engineered 'ka-thunk'.

"Shall I drive?"

"You know you want to," said Joan.

In the driver's seat, Rutspud examined the controls with a huge grin on his face.

"Check this out! It's got an AR-compatible HUD, a Warp Ten acceleration mode, multi-variable suspension lifting and three sixty parking globe vision."

"You sound excited, so I assume they're good things."

"Oh, momma, you've no idea," said the demon gleefully. "Start her up, Kylie. Whack her in Warp Ten and plot a course for Large Mike's."

"I'm sorry," said a sweetly unflappable computer voice. "The law requires an adult with a full driving licence to control this vehicle at all times when it is in operation."

"What?"

"The law requires an adult –"

"I am an adult."

"The weight on the seat is below the minimum weight permitted. I can contact Eddy-Cab support if you wish –"

"It thinks I'm a child!" he hissed.

Joan couldn't help a small laugh when she saw Rutspud's look of horror. He bounced in the seat. "That's just rude you stupid machine. Do you have any idea how old I really am?"

"I'm not equipped to answer that question," said Kylie, "but the weight on the seat is below the minimum –"

"Screw you, Kylie!"

Rutspud sat and glared for a full minute before Joan broke the silence. "Shall we swap seats?"

Rutspud sulkily slid across while Joan went around. She popped her broadsword onto the back seat so that she could hold the steering wheel.

"How's that, Kylie?"

"How is what?" asked Kylie.

"Am I heavy enough to drive this car?"

"The weight on the seat meets the minimum required."

"Fat heffalump," scowled Rutspud but Joan ignored him.

"Please state your destination," said Kylie.

Rutspud huffed and grumbled while Joan gave Kylie the first address. He leaned across to try and see the heads-up display and Joan swatted at him.

"I'm driving, Rutspud," she said.

"No, you're not, the car is," he said. "You don't even know how to drive."

"But I'm supposed to be in control, just in case," said Joan, taking a firm grip on the steering wheel.

"Don't even know how cars work," he muttered.

"I imagine it's not too different to a horse and carriage from my day."

"Sure," he sneered. "Exactly the same. But where are the horses, huh?"

"They're... internal."

"Internal?"

"Internal, yes."

Ten minutes' later, they pulled up outside a Large Mike's chip shop.

As they stepped out, Rutspud inhaled deeply as he had at the previous ones they'd visited. "Mmm, that smells good."

"You say that every time," said Joan.

"To which you reply by mithering on about the English habit of frying everything in oil."

"It's disgusting and unhealthy."

"Which is why it smells good. Let's go and get kebabs and see what they know."

They went inside and to the glass-fronted counter, which was filled with various things coated in batter and golden from the fryer.

"What can I get you, bab?" asked the middle-aged serving woman.

"Just deciding," said Rutspud, studying the menu displays overhead.

"But I wondered if you could take a look at this picture," said Joan. "Do you recognise this person?"

The woman gave a half second glance to the picture they had printed off the internet.

"Perhaps, he works here or lives nearby?" said Joan,

"No, don't know him, bab. Have you decided what you want?"

"Three kebabs, with everything on," said Rutspud.

"I don't want one," said Joan to Rutspud.

"That's good then, because I'm having two and we'll take one back for Mr Clovenhoof."

Rutspud watched the woman as she carved strips off the rotating spindle of kebab meat. "It's a lot like our team-building exercises back home," he observed, "taking all the bits that nobody wants and recycling them."

Joan looked at him. "You mean... oh yuck!"

"It's not that bad," he said. "I won these legs in a team-building game in, oh, must be before they started numbering years."

"That sounds barbaric."

"Tough but effective business practice. Encourages ambition and independent effort. A demon's gotta stand on his own two feet. Or someone else's."

"I'll be outside when you're done," said Joan.

Joan went outside where the air wasn't thick with hot oil and greasy kebab meat. She looked around the outside of the shop and tried to compare it with what was on the photo. She wasn't sure if it was a match or not. The sign about OAPs wasn't there, but maybe that offer had been replaced. Rutspud returned a few minutes later, shovelling hot food into his mouth and making appreciative chomping sounds.

"This is so good," he said. "It's got all the flavours you want in a dish."

Joan couldn't help herself. "Like what?"

"Neglect, desperation and suffering," said Rutspud, smacking his lips.

Joan decided not to ask whose suffering that might be.

They both looked up as a bus drove by. Rutspud paused, his kebab partway to his mouth.

"Why would a bus need Wi-Fi?" said Joan, reading the promotional lettering on the side of the bus.

"Because it's cool," said Rutspud in that distant voice of those who are thinking about something else entirely. "Why put cupholders in chairs? Why spear your earlobes with pieces of decorative metal? Why combine swimming and dancing and pretend it's a sport? Humans stick stuff together for a million stupid rea –" Rutspud made an odd, strangled noise. His eyes bulged.

"What is it?" she said, alarmed. "Too many kebabs? Is it that chili sauce?"

Rutspud appeared to be choking. Maybe kebabs were incompatible with demon biology or maybe he just had wind. Would he explode in fleshy gobbets or fart?

Rutspud turned to her and clawed at her breastplate. Joan was shocked and then instantly angry. She slapped him hard but that didn't stop him. He took a deep wheezing breath.

"The ticket! The ticket!"

"What ticket?" she said.

"The bus ticket!" he cried. "The one with the e-mail address on it!"

Joan pushed him away. "You're looking in the wrong place," she said and pulled it out from the leg greave in which she had stored it.

Rutspud snatched it from her. "Look!"

She looked, but it took her a moment or two to see. A number eleven on the ticket. A number eleven bus.

"That's it!" spluttered Rutspud. "He wrote his e-mail on *his* bus ticket. It's where our guy hangs out. It's the number eleven, which is a circular bus route, so he can spend hours just going round using his computer. It's his office."

"So, all we have to do is get on the bus and look for him?" said Joan.

At that moment another number eleven bus pulled up behind the first.

"All we have to do is get on the *right* bus," said Rutspud.

Clovenhoof twirled around so that he could properly absorb how gobsmackingly brilliant his family fun day was going to be. What had started as a flippant remark at the press conference five short days ago, a response to the supposed failings of his PrayPal to replicate something as pathetic as the church coffee morning, was now burgeoning into what could only be described as an absolutely kick-ass party.

According to Nerys, they were expecting over five thousand people at this event, which would elevate the humble coffee morning to something that would make everyone sit up and take notice. The coffee part of it would be serviced by the team of baristas with state of the art coffee machines that looked as though they might also be able to navigate to far-flung galaxies or perhaps control a nuclear power station, but Clovenhoof had definitely seen them create coffee so that was okay. Biscuits were piled high into vast constructions that Milo Finn-Frouer had called

Croquembouches Biscuit but which looked like Christmas trees constructed from biscuits. They were crying out for someone to eat a biscuit from the bottom layer, prompting a catastrophic collapse. Clovenhoof magnanimously decided to leave that treat for his guests.

He strolled down to the edge of his new lake. The diggers had moved vast amounts of soil, but it turned out that transporting soil away from an urban site was a tricky and time-consuming task, as it all had to be loaded into lorries and taken elsewhere. His moat did not yet encircle the whole of Hooflandia, but as his yacht was arriving today it was being filled with water by a team of engineers with pumps and hoses.

Nerys appeared with a clipboard and a swagger. Ben trailed behind, carrying a bottle of fizzy plonk.

"I do like pumps and hoses," said Clovenhoof to the world at large.

"Makes me want to go to the toilet just looking at it," said Ben.

"Me too," said Clovenhoof. "And isn't pissing one of life's great pleasures?"

"A relief perhaps," said Nerys uncertainly.

"Yes, but the beauty of it is there are so many things and persons one can piss *on*. New dress?" Clovenhoof asked.

"Yes," said Nerys, doing a twirl. "It's one of a kind. Isn't it fabulous?"

"It looks as though it's made from Capri Sun wrappers."

"It is," said Ben with a baffled shake of his head.

"Winnebago Kisskiss is a hot new fashion designer," said Nerys. "He makes one-off pieces from unexpected materials. I wanted something avant-garde and memorable for today."

Clovenhoof nodded. "Make a note to ask him about a new smoking jacket for me."

"Will do. Right, I think we're almost ready with everything."

"Everything?"

Nerys checked her clipboard.

"Buffet with Hooflandia flags in all the sandwiches. Check. Screening of the Hooflandia community vision and corporate opportunities on loop in the presidential suite. Check. Fairground rides, programme of entertainment, customer advice desk for PrayPal users. Check, check, check."

"And they do look marvellous," Clovenhoof agreed, "but surely one of the many climaxes of the day – I do love a multiple climax – is the launching of the presidential yacht into the Hooflandian lagoon while the crowds gaze on from the beach. I cannot help but notice the lack of a yacht, a lagoon and, quite tellingly, a beach."

"Fear not, Jeremy," said Nerys smoothly. "The yacht should be here within the hour. The moat – sorry, the lagoon, should be filled in..."

"Two point six hours," said Ben, glancing over at the engineers.

"And here comes the beach now," said Nerys and pointed ahead.

"Those are lorries, not a beach," said Clovenhoof. "Just because I'm rich, doesn't mean I'm gullible."

"Says the man who wants a smoking jacket made out of orange squash packets," muttered Ben.

"That's the sand. They're going to just dump it and go," said Nerys.

"Won't it need levelling out? Raking?" said Ben.

"Sand dunes," shrugged Clovenhoof. "So, we've got the beach. The lagoon will be full in..."

"Two point five five hours," said Ben.

"The yacht comes in. We get it on the slipway. I do my keynote speech and then smash – champagne christening and the SS Watery Cock-Extension slips into the lagoon."

Ben held out the bottle of plonk to Clovenhoof. Clovenhoof looked at it but did not touch it.

"I hope you're about to say, 'Have a refreshing breakfast tipple while I tell you about the fricking mahoosive bottle of fizz you're gonna use to launch your yacht.'"

"What?" said Ben. "It's a bottle."

"I'm launching a bloody ship, Ben! I want to smash a bottle off its prow that they can see from space."

"I'll get onto it," said Nerys. "How big do you want it?"

"The biggest!" said Clovenhoof.

261

"That'll be a Melchizedek of champers then."

"I knew Melchizedek of old," said Clovenhoof. "We're talking Biblical times. Smug git. Fancied himself as a bit of Christ figure. Even wanted the job. I told him. 'Melchy,' I said, 'don't even get your hopes up. In this business, it's not what you know, it's who you know.' Bloody nepotism."

"Oi, mate!" shouted a lorry driver in a hard hat. "Where do want this lot?"

Clovenhoof turned to tell Nerys to deal with it but she was on the phone now, taking wine with someone.

"Fine, I'll sort my own beach," said Clovenhoof.

Ben walked with him towards the convoy of nine dumper trucks. "It's just a bottle," he said.

"I need to make a statement today," said Clovenhoof, "and that statement is I've got a fricking huge bottle of champagne."

"Size doesn't matter," said Ben

"There speaks a man in denial. You should get yourself a watery cock-extension like me. Tell you what, later on you can take her out for a spin."

"No thanks, I get seasick on anything larger than a pedalo."

A bent figure in kitchen white and chequered trousers scampered over.

"Boss! Boss!" called Milo the chef. He held a silver platter aloft to Clovenhoof, like a tribute to the gods.

Clovenhoof regarded the golden half-moons on offer.

"The latest batch," said Milo. "I think I've cracked it. I found a man who worked on the original development team and I took notes – oh, the amount of notes I took..."

Clovenhoof picked one up and sniffed it. Ben picked one up too. Milo flashed him a look of pure contempt as though he were not worthy of sampling his wares.

Clovenhoof bit deeply. There was definitely a satisfying crunch.

"They're very cheesy," he said, spitting crumbs.

"Too cheesy, boss?"

"No, definitely the right amount of cheese. But..."

"But?" Milo's face froze in horrified anticipation, a rollercoaster rider coming to the brow of the hill, seeing only a plummet into the abyss on the other side.

"Is the mix of spices, right?" said Clovenhoof.

"No," whispered Milo.

"It's an open question. I was just wondering..."

Milo cast his silver platter of pancakes aside. He snatched the one from Ben's hand and stamped it into the ground. "I have failed. I have failed *you*, boss."

"They were very close," said Clovenhoof kindly but Milo was already scampering away, shamefaced.

"I will fix it!" he wept as he ran. "I will do it right, boss!"

"What a strange man," said Ben as they moved on. He waved at the nearest lorry driver. "Is this the beach?" he asked.

The driver jerked his thumb back at the convoy of trucks behind him. "Twenty tonnes of fine grade sand. Fifteen tonnes of aggregate. Eight tonnes of cement."

"Cement?"

"Yeah." The man opened his paper docket. "We're laying the foundations for a wall or something tomorrow."

Clovenhoof rubbed his hands together in glee.

"A fun day in the sun. An imposing and brutalist wall. It's like a dream come true."

"Mixed messages more like," said Ben.

"This is just the start," said Clovenhoof. "Next week, theme park rides and underground torture chambers."

"So where do you want it?" said the driver.

"Probably over there," said Clovenhoof, pointing at an unexploited corner of Hooflandia. "We don't have much room so we might have to combine them. The Hooflandia Log Flume and Waterboarding Centre."

"So, the sand, aggregate and cement over there?"

"No," said Ben. "He was wittering about something else. We want the sand and that over here, on the beach."

"Beach?" said the driver.

"Well, it isn't one yet. But not the cement. That will need putting out of the way."

"Surely, the beach should be on the inner edge of the lagoon," said Clovenhoof.

"Right," said Ben, "so over there. And the cement on the scrubby land next to where the trucks have dumped the soil from the moat."

Nerys approached, ending her phone call.

"When in doubt, call a crook," she said. "Animal Ed says he can rustle up a Melchizedek of champagne in half an hour. I told him you'd collect it, Ben."

"Why me?"

"Because I'm happy to do a deal with that man but I don't want to spend any time in his company. That pet shop of his smells and he's a little too handy and familiar when I'm around."

"You don't mind men getting handy and familiar most of the time," said Clovenhoof.

"Yeah, but he spends his day handling bird poop and lizards." She shuddered.

"I don't see why having a big bottle is important," said Ben. "And what kind of message about alcohol is that sending to the kids at this fun day?"

"There is no evidence at all that large quantities of alcohol do anyone serious harm," said Clovenhoof.

"Hmmm. And how big is a Melchizi-whatsit?" said Ben.

"It holds forty bottles of wine."

"Oh, and I'm supposed to collect it? I can't even say it, let alone carry it."

"Improvise. Commandeer a vehicle. There's enough of them around this place."

Ben cast about.

"Hey! Spartacus! Can I borrow you a minute?" he called and went off.

"Right," said Nerys. "Are we sorted here?"

The truck driver pointed to the inner edge of the moat. "We're going to dump the first four loads on that area there to create a beach and the rest is going on the scrub land."

"Two beaches?" said Nerys.

"No, just one," said Clovenhoof.

"That's what I thought. When that's all down we'll put out some brightly coloured parasols and some deckchairs. Everything about today is going to be big and bright."

"Cool," said Clovenhoof.

"Apparently, the Military Wives Flashmob Choir who'll be on before your speech will all be wearing fluorescent jumpsuits. Sounds good?"

"Lambrini hula girls might help as well," said Clovenhoof.

"To brighten the place up a bit?"

"No, just generally," said Clovenhoof dreamily. He gazed at the hoses that were slowly filling his beautiful moat. "He's right," he said. "It does make you want to piss."

Clovenhoof strode to the edge of the moat and unzipped his fly.

"Seriously?" said Nerys. "Here?"

"Every drop helps."

Nerys made a scoff of disgust and turned to give the lead truck driver clear instructions on where the sand needed to go.

CHAPTER THIRTY-EIGHT

Joan and Rutspud stood at a bus stop, about to board the next number eleven.

"Ready, Ticket Inspector Joan?" said Rutspud.

"Ready, Ticket Inspector Rutspud?" said Joan.

"Got me hi-vis vest. Got me peaked cap."

"I've got my clipboard. I've got my pen. If people knew this was all you needed to ride buses for free I'm sure more people would do it."

"As cover to have a little search of each bus, it's ideal," agreed Rutspud.

"Of course, there's only really one thing that could go wrong with a plan like that," observed Joan, looking over Rutspud's shoulder.

"What's that?"

"If a real ticket inspector appeared," said Joan, nodding towards the man who was walking towards them. He, like them, was wearing a hi-vis jacket, an official looking hat and an expression of mild confusion.

"Not seen your faces before," said the real ticket inspector to Joan and Rutspud.

"No, we're new," said Joan. She noticed that he was eyeing her sword and armour.

"Have you confiscated that weapon?" he asked her.

"Yes," said Rutspud, before Joan had weighed the relatively minor sin of lying against the greater good that their mission would surely represent. While Joan pondered the question, Rutspud was embellishing the lie. "There are cosplayers all over the place today. There's a protest march." He held out the flyer that Sister Anne had given them. "Watch out for the nuns. They've got martial arts weapons concealed under their robes."

"No! Nuns? Surely not?"

Rutspud nodded, his eyes melting pools of utter sincerity. "It's true. Nunchucks. They have terrible habits."

Both Joan and the genuine ticket inspector turned to Rutspud, incredulous.

He shrugged and gave Joan a small grin. "Sorry."

Joan glared at him. "That could have worked. That could *actually* have worked but you had to go and be extra clever."

"Sorry?" said the ticket inspector, as the next bus pulled up. "Do you mean that you're not real ticket inspectors?"

"We're unreal ticket inspectors," said Rutspud.

"Look, excuse me, I think I need to –"

"We'll take this bus, you do the next one," said the demon and bundled Joan aboard before the inspector could complain further.

A nod to the driver and then a purposeful walk up and down the bus, using the pretence of inspecting tickets and passes to carefully scrutinise each passenger. They jumped off at the next stop and then waited for the next bus.

Halfway along the upper deck of the fourth bus they tried to approach a man tapping on a laptop. He wore a sports top rather than the chunky knitwear in the photo, but the curly hair was exactly the same. Joan met Rutspud's eye and saw that he had come to the same conclusion.

"Ticket please," said Joan.

The young man passed his travel card over without even looking up. Joan looked at it to confirm that, yes, this was the man from the internet picture. His name was printed underneath. She wasn't sure why she felt comparing two pictures was proof when she had the actual man right in front of her but it was him nonetheless.

"Felix Winkstein?"

"Yes?" he said.

"You're the creator of PrayPal," said Rutspud.

"We really need to talk to you about it," said Joan.

Felix's eyes went from Rutspud to Joan. He snapped his laptop shut and stood up. "Sure. Happy to chat. Hold this for a second, will you?"

He held a folded umbrella out, and Joan put out a hand to take it. Felix gave a sudden shove with it, heaving Joan into Rutspud as the spring-loaded umbrella sprang open. He scrambled for the stairs while Joan and Rutspud righted themselves.

Rutspud seemed to be engaged in a life and death struggle with the umbrella. It was like he was being attacked by a wire-frame octopus.

"Go!" he yelled but Joan was already hurling herself down the stairs.

The bus had hissed to a stop and Felix was squeezing through the doors.

Joan pushed past other passengers and followed Felix off the bus. He was already a good way down the road. He was undoubtedly fast on his feet for someone who spent all of his time at a keyboard.

Rutspud literally tumbled down the stairs, fought his way through the passengers inconsiderately blocking the aisle and clawed his way off the bus, only then taking a moment to shake off the umbrella still clinging to his ankle.

Rutspud looked about and thought he had already lost sight of Joan and her quarry but then he caught a glimpse of a hi-vis jacket some distance down the road. He growled in frustration and then realised that this stop was the one where they'd left the self-driving car. It should be parked just over...

"Yes!" There it was. He could follow in that. He had the key and opened the car as he dashed over to it.

He jumped in. "Go, Kylie, we need to follow that woman in the plate armour!"

"I'm sorry," said Kylie. "The law requires an adult with a full driving licence to control this vehicle at all times when it is in operation."

Rutspud jigged in his seat with the frustration. "Right. Right. We need to add some weight to the seat. Hold on."

He got out of the car and stood on the pavement looking up and down the street.

"March for solidarity in support of the church?" said a woman and thrust a leaflet at him. It was a nun. Not a sister of the Mission Society of the Thrown Voice but a nun nonetheless: coif, crown, wimple and all.

Rutspud looked her up and down.

"Sister, how much do you weigh?"

Clovenhoof checked his notes for his keynote speech. His warm-up act was the military wives choir. He wasn't sure if any of them were military wives, but Nerys had suggested that a military wives choir was an established 'thing' and it sounded more appealing than the *mad squawking of a hundred wannabee spice girls* that Clovenhoof had pencilled in to the timetable. On the stage, they were warbling their way through Robbie Williams' *Angels* which he thought proved his point somewhat.

Clovenhoof sighed contentedly. This was easily the best fun day that he'd ever been to and, better still, there was no chance of him being kicked out.

Everything was going brilliantly. Nerys had even managed to find Lambrini hula girls, although one of them looked suspiciously like Tina, her long-time nemesis. He had to hand it to Nerys, she was a master of multi-tasking. She could solve a practical problem and sock it to her enemies at the same time. Tina wiggled her way round the crowds, offering glasses of Lambrini from a tray. She also held up a little sign that said *Ask me how you can buy your own title. Be a Duke or Duchess of Hooflandia!*

Even Clovenhoof's yacht had arrived. Eighty feet of sleek, white, I-got-cash-and-you-ain't shamelessness sat on its trailer next to the performance stage. A team of engineers had jury-rigged a wedge-shaped slide along which the majestic vessel would slip into the water. They'd even been unusually confident that this wouldn't involve the boat snapping in two, spectators on the other side of the moat being impaled on the prow or the whole lorry and trailer being dragged into the water too. Officers from the council and the local police force had made representation, claiming that the very presence of the yacht was an inconvenience to local traffic and contravened any number of by-laws. However, Clovenhoof discovered to little surprise that even moral employees of the state had a price and all had been handsomely paid off.

The only thing missing at the moment was the giant-sized bottle of champagne Clovenhoof was going to use to launch the vessel. The engineers had hung a harness and swing from the rigging of the stage. All it needed was the bottle itself and Clovenhoof was ready to swing, smash, splash and party like never before.

Down in the grassy heart of the fun day, Lennox was showing off the army to the visitors. It had swelled to around forty members now. The dress uniforms were crisp pale blue and sported more embellishments than Clovenhoof had ever seen on an outfit. Gold fringed epaulettes hung down from their shoulders. Bright green and red sashes crossed their bodies. Gold braid snaked across their bodies from their shoulders via the buttons to their waists, and medals filled any space that was still available. Lennox had appointed Florence as drill sergeant, and she bellowed at the new recruits, putting them through their paces using a series of highly personalised threats and insults.

"Excellent work on the army, Lennox. Florence is clearly a natural," said Clovenhoof, wandering over.

"Yeah, I asked Ben first of all. He ought to know loads about the military with his model soldiering, you know? Trouble is, he's just not bossy enough. He kept saying 'please', like it's optional to do what he says. That's when I knew I had to put Florence in charge. Most of these soldiers are already terrified of her, so it's worked out well. But I thought Ben would be here, giving me some pointers."

"He's on a vital national mission at the moment," said Clovenhoof. "The Boldmere Ponies are helping him."

"Who?"

"The boys with the trolleys."

CHAPTER THIRTY-NINE

Sister Genevieve Powell was a professed sister of the Holy Community of St Paul the Apostle in Perry Barr. She had been a nun for seventeen years, was a very generous soul and, most importantly, was two hundred pounds of solid nun.

"I don't understand," said Sister Genevieve. "I don't have a driving licence."

Kylie piped up. "The law requires an adult with a full driving licence to control this vehicle at all –"

"She *does* have a driving licence," said Rutspud, standing in the passenger seat. "Now, belt up, sister. Literally and metaphorically. Kylie, let's go."

"Where would you like to go?" asked Kylie.

"Just drive!" he growled.

"Please repeat the destination," said Kylie's infuriatingly patient voice.

"There is no destination! I want you to go up there!"

"Please repeat –"

"Fine!" snapped Rutspud, scanning the road ahead. "I want to go to, um, the nearest carpet shop."

The car trundled towards the carpet shop, which was about two hundred yards down the road. Before it could slow down, Rutspud sought out the next destination.

"Now I want to go to a petrol station," he said, "and I want to go faster than this."

"Optimum speed is dictated by road conditions and safety considerations," said Kylie, without altering speed.

"Who is talking?" asked Sister Genevieve.

"I am the car's on-board journey management sys –"

"What safety considerations?" cut in Rutspud.

"I am programmed to preserve human life above all else," said Kylie.

"Right, well what if I were to tell you that human life is at risk if you don't go faster?"

"Is it?"

"Probably. Human lives and the entire cosmic balance are currently at stake if we don't catch up with that man."

"I may only use information from my sensors combined with other approved inputs," replied the car, keeping to a gentle, unthreatening speed.

"Wow. Dismissed by a car."

Rutspud seethed and wondered if he could find the processor that controlled the car's logic. All he'd need to do was smash open the dashboard or pull apart the panels where they joined. Of course, one never had a screwdriver to hand when one was needed.

"Sister?"

"Yes."

"That cross you're wearing. Is it gold?"

"I shouldn't think so. Probably just gold-plated tin or something."

"Excellent. May I borrow it?"

The mindlessly charitable nun was halfway through handing it over before she even thought to ask why. The holy symbol fizzed softly against Rutspud's demon fingertips, barely more than a tickle. He rammed it into the gap in the dashboard panels, whacked it hard with the palm of his hand and then levered away the plastic panel.

"What are you doing?" said Sister Genevieve.

"Never mind what I'm doing," said Rutspud. "Just keep giving the car instructions. Always somewhere a bit beyond that running human."

"Which... human?"

"The one with the hair! The one the armour-plated goody-two-shoes is chasing!"

Rutspud put the nun's cross between his teeth (it made them vibrate and sing) and pushed himself headfirst into hole in the dashboard and the inner workings of the car.

Sometimes, Joan forgot what genuine physical exertion was. The Celestial City, her home, operated a shadow copy of the laws of physics – mostly for the convenience of people who were used to time running forwards instead of sideways and preferred 'down' to be in the traditional direction. However, the Celestial City was also, by its nature, a place without suffering. So, it didn't matter how much running, lifting, falling or playing mixed doubles tennis one did in Heaven – it was never painful or exhausting.

Joan was nineteen years old (and had been for over half a millennium). She had been raised on a lean medieval diet and strengthened in the forge of battle. She was, by the standards of any age, an athletic young woman. In a straight sprint, she should have been able to outpace almost anyone. There were, unfortunately, three barriers to her catching Felix Winkstein: first, apart from some minor adventures in France a few years back, she hadn't run in the real world for over five hundred years; second, she was carrying the weight of full plate armour and a broadsword; and third (and most mystifyingly), the fast-food-loving computer nerd had a raw, wiry energy that always kept him a dozen yards ahead of her.

They had circled round the Erdington high street and now Joan was chasing Felix along a wide and busy road. As they approached Boldmere, he narrowly missed being mown down by a shopping trolley loaded with poles and broom handles and a green bottle the size of a fat toddler. It was pushed by a team of six boys who were being harangued by an agitated man that Joan realised she had met before.

She came to a gasping halt next to the trolley and gestured at the enormous bottle.

"What...?" she panted and hoped that the situation itself would fill in the gaps that her breathlessness would not allow her to fill with words.

"It's a Melchi-something of champagne," said Ben Kitchen.

"Why...?"

"To launch Clovenhoof's yacht during his big fun day speech."

"Where...?" She pointed down the road in the general direction Felix had dashed in.

"Yeah, at the Boldmere Oak."

"Hey, babe," said the most roguish-looking of the lads. "You chasing someone or something?"

She waved again. "Winkstein... Programmer... Very dangerous..."

"You want a lift?" said the boy.

"We don't have time for this, Spartacus," said Ben.

"Sure, we do," said the boy. "Hop on my sweet ride, honey."

Spartacus took the poles out of the trolley. Joan didn't hesitate. She climbed in and crouched with her legs either side of the massive bottle.

"PJ, Jefri, take these," said Spartacus. "Everyone else, delta formation."

"We don't have time for this!" cried a distressed Ben but he went ignored as Spartacus and his companions pushed the trolley into a bone-rattling sprint. Joan gripped the bottle tightly.

She became aware that the trolley commander running at her side was staring at her. She pointedly looked back at him.

"I like your... armour," he said. "Very, um, shiny."

"Eyes on the road, driver," she said and her underage chauffeur reluctantly did as he was told.

Nerys stepped through the crowd and grabbed Clovenhoof's elbow.

"Come on. You're up next. You should be backstage already."

"There's no hurry," he said. "It's my party. It's not as if I can miss my slot."

Nerys looked concerned.

"There's a protest march of nuns and other folk not far from here," she said, "apparently they're urging solidarity with the church. Okra's worried about the church's PR."

"You still got that useless posh-boy hanging around?" said Clovenhoof. "You know you're an independently wealthy woman now, Nerys. You don't need a man for a meal ticket."

"Old habits," she shrugged and looked round. "I had him here a moment ago. Anyway, he's beginning to think the Church got bigger problems than they realise with this and your PrayPal app puncturing a hole in their attendance."

"What does solidarity with the church even mean?" said Clovenhoof.

"It means they think people who've turned away from the church really ought to return and they believe the reason for the downturn in church attendance is PrayPal and you, specifically."

"Wow, it is amazing how much blame I get for things round here."

"Anyway, the sooner you've done your bit, the better. Maybe wrap things up before they even get here."

Clovenhoof grinned. "Are you kidding? If there's one thing that could make today more perfect, it would be nuns, especially angry ones. Do you think they might try to gatecrash my fun day?"

"Given that the moat's not a full circle yet, I don't see quite how you would stop them."

Nerys bustled him towards the stage and to stairs at the side.

One of the soldiers – one of *his own* soldiers, he thought with a thrill – saluted him as he neared.

"Got your notes?" said Nerys.

"Oh, yes."

He thought he might break the ice for his speech with the joke about the drunken zookeeper and the bagpipes. Perhaps he might sing a brief medley of hits, then he would share some titbits of his valuable wisdom with the crowd to give them a taste of what they might learn at his lifestyle coaching centre. Florence was lining the army up to form the back and two sides of the temporary stage, near to the dismally grey beach that sloped down into the freshly-filled lake.

"Why is the beach so grey?" said Clovenhoof but Nerys was gone again.

He rubbed his hands in anticipation. A religious march by the church's supporters against those it perceived as the enemy. When had that ever gone wrong?

Clovenhoof pondered that for a second. His grin widened.

"Take me to the nearest florist," said Sister Genevieve. "Now, the nearest charity shop. Now, a petrol station. I don't really understand why I'm doing this."

"We're trying to catch a man," said Rutspud who was currently tucked up inside the confines of the car's dashboard and pulling out circuitry and hastily rewiring things for all he was worth.

"Are you the police?" asked Sister Genevieve.

"Sort of. Not really. Joan's like the police. I'm like..." Rutspud clawed his way out of the hole in the dashboard and onto the passenger seat, his hand clutching a bundle of cables and his tablet. "You ever seen *The Spy Who Loved Me*?"

"I'm sorry?"

"James Bond film. He's a British spy. She's a Russian spy. Together they team up to defeat the bloke with the unrealistic underwater city and – not that Joan and I have got some kind of romance thing going on. Although I can do that thing Roger Moore does with his eyebrow."

"What thing?"

"Act. Anyway, the bloke we're chasing is like that evil villain."

"He has an unrealistic underwater city?" said Sister Genevieve.

"Maybe."

"I really ought to be getting back to my sisters. We're supposed to be marching to protest against that horrid Mr

Clovenhoof and his PrayPal computer thingy. Have you heard about that?"

"Yes! And the guy we're chasing is the guy who created it!"

"Really?" Sister Genevieve leaned forward, suddenly interested.

"Really," said Rutspud, inserting wires into the data ports on his tablet. "We're going to force him to shut PrayPal down. Now, if I've done this right, we can feed any visual input we like to Kylie's processor and get her to speed up."

An orange warning icon flashed on the windscreen Heads Up Display.

"I have suffered a cognition impairment," said Kylie. "Causes may include a malware attack or unexpected bird strike. I must be checked in for service immediately."

That didn't sound right. Rutspud tapped on his tablet and wiggled a loose wire. The orange warning icon disappeared (which was a good thing) but was immediately replaced with a much larger red warning icon (which was a bad thing).

"I have suffered a catastrophic cognition impairment." Kylie's voice wobbled alarmingly. "This car may be under attack from Russian or North Korean hackers."

"That's quite a specific assessment of the situation," said Sister Genevieve.

The car began to slow.

"No! No! Don't do this, you stupid piece of junk!" cried Rutspud but he could do nothing to stop the car's deceleration.

Sister Genevieve peered ahead. "I think we've lost sight of them anyway."

Rutspud looked up. There was indeed no sign of Winkstein or Joan. However, he did see someone he recognised on the pavement. He leaned out the window as they crawled by.

"Hey. Ben, isn't it? You didn't happen to see Joan running by, perhaps chasing a surprisingly agile nerd?"

"Did I?" said the mopey man. "She stole our trolley, our best pushers and a Melchi-something of champagne."

"And which direction did they go in?"

One of the two young humans with him, who were carrying various poles, waved a big stick down the road. "Towards the Boldmere Oak and the fun day."

"You sure?"

"They'd better be," said Ben. "They need that bottle of fizz to launch the yacht."

"Oi, you!" said Rutspud to one of the youngsters. "What's your name?"

"PJ," said the lad in the tones of one who spent much of his life having to explain his name to people and taking remedial action against people who sniggered at it.

"PJ, I need a couple of those pole things that you've got," said Rutspud.

With some help, Rutspud dragged the poles inside the car, the ends hanging out through the windows at each side.

"Right, now we need some pictures of something."

"Pictures of what?" said PJ.

"We need a carrot and a stick." He took one of the flyers from Sister Genevieve.

"What do you want that for?" she asked.

"This is the stick. Kylie will do anything to avoid hitting some innocent nuns. And now I need..."

"What?" said Ben.

"Anything that doesn't look like a busy traffic junction. What have you got?" Rutspud asked Ben.

Ben patted his pockets. "I've got the draft copy of *Hooflandia, living the dream – your island getaway in the heart of the city,*" said Ben. "Why, what do you want it for?"

"Pictures?"

"Yes, it's got the artist's impression of the beach and a picture of a Noble Knight of Hooflandia gazing over the rolling hills."

"Give it here," said Rutspud. He grabbed the leaflet, ripped out the pictures and spat into his hand. "Nothing stickier than demon spit," he cackled.

"What?" said Ben.

"Nothing," said Rutspud, sticking the images onto the ends of the poles.

The light of comprehension suddenly dawned on Ben's face. "Wait, are you doing what I think you're doing? That's unbelievably reckless!"

"You got me banged to rights. Unbelievably reckless it is," said Rutspud.

For several hundred yards, Joan rode the shopping trolley (and the jiggling bottle of champagne) without any sight of Felix. The boys grunted and groaned but, to their credit, they never slackened the pace. They drove pedestrians off the pavement, cut off vehicles at crossings and junctions and thrust Joan recklessly in front of oncoming cars with the kind of bravery that only the young and the foolish could exhibit.

Ahead, Joan saw the helter-skelters and big wheels of some sort of fun fair and suspected they were very close to Clovenhoof's ill-judged fun day event. Nearer to though and much more importantly there was Felix, but only a moment after spotting him, Joan was dismayed to see him plunge into a thick crowd of nuns. This then was the much-touted march against Clovenhoof's immoral ways and irreligious excesses. Not quite a million nuns, Joan noted but there were a heck of a lot of them. They waved placards, shouted slogans and from some point in the gathering a swell of voices sang, *Abide With Me*. It was currently a peaceful protest which was at least something.

"Do you go to hell for mowing down penguins?" shouted Spartacus.

"Slow, don't stop," said Joan, knowing she couldn't afford to lose Felix in this sea of bodies.

The boys dutifully slowed but kept their course down, driving at the nuns. They scattered like birds, grey, black and blue tunics flapping as they fled. Joan caught sight of a suspiciously bulky nun, fixing her robes in place.

"He's trying to blend in!" she shouted.

"What?" said Spartacus.

"Felix! Hiding in plain sight! Keep going!"

As the trolley ploughed on, Joan stood, got up onto the rim of the trolley and leapt right on top of the fake nun. They landed with an *oof* sound and Joan sympathised briefly, knowing that her armour was rather weighty.

She rolled and came up on her feet.

"This has to stop!" she yelled.

The nun slipped and stumbled on the ground. Joan stepped forward and yanked the veil back to look at Felix's face. Except it wasn't Felix, it was an elderly nun who looked winded, bruised and very, very angry.

"Ah," she said.

"Yer tinplated eejit! Wha' do you think –"

"Yes, sorry. You I thought you were a man and –"

Joan was cut off by a placard whacked directly in her face.

It had been a peaceful protest, but Joan had just changed that.

CHAPTER FORTY

The Military Wives Flashmob Choir was massacring its last song when Spartacus Wilson and Kenzie Kelly came running up the backstage steps with a satisfyingly gargantuan bottle of fizz.

"Brilliant!" said Clovenhoof. "And just in time."

"We were extra careful," said Kenzie. "Didn't break it."

"Well done, boys. Now, let's get it hooked up so I can smash that mother off the prow of the presidential yacht. Oi, privates, corporals, whatever your rank is." Clovenhoof whistled and waved a trio of his soldiers over. "Get this in the cradle for the boat launch."

"Yes, sir," said the most eager chap.

"What rank are you fellers anyway?" asked Clovenhoof.

"Ninja, sir," said one.

"Black Ops Decimator," said another.

"Lennox said we could just pick our own ranks until we got a proper hierarchy sorted."

"I like it," said Clovenhoof. He turned and thrust an uncounted quantity of cash in the hands of the two delivery boys.

"Don't spend it all at once. But if you do, spend it here."

On stage, the Military Wives Flashmob Choir's routine came to a rousing and sudden end. Clovenhoof wasn't certain if they had simply finished or someone had cut the mic. Either way, the crowd cheered and clapped now that it was finally over. While the cheering continued, Clovenhoof looked at his speech notes, decided that winging it would be best and took to the stage.

"Hello, Sutton Coldfield!" he yelled. "Let's get on down and cosy on up! I'm the man who put the 'F' in Fun Day, and we're all about effin' fun here!"

A sea of faces stared at him in confusion. Clovenhoof had worked a tough crowd before. He might have to treat them to a strip.

Rutspud and the two boys, PJ and Jefri, stood awkwardly on the front seats and leaned out of the Eddy-Cab's sun roof. Each held a pole in their hands. Rutspud leaned forwards, dangling a picture of open sunny vistas with definitely no inconvenient traffic. PJ and Jefri leaned generally towards the back, presenting images of nuns to the car's rear cameras.

"Like this?" said PJ.

"Whatever," said Rutspud. "I want to hold those against the car's sensors or cameras to make it do what I want. It's programmed not to hurt people, so pictures of nuns coming at it might move it along, I reckon."

"That is by far and away the most dumb-ass thing I have heard all day," said Jefri.

"You don't think it's going to work?" said Rutspud.

"Pfff," shrugged Jefri.

Down in the car, Sister Genevieve made a sceptical noise.

Ben had climbed in the back seat. "I'm coming with you. If I don't get these Street Polo players back in time for their performance, I'll lose my position as Vice Lord Baronet of Hooflandia."

"Hey, Kylie," Rutspud shouted, "we need to move quickly or those speeding nuns are going to hit us!"

"How do we know where the sensors are?" said PJ.

"Just wave the pictures around, we'll work it out," said Rutspud.

Unbelievably, the car began to accelerate. Rutspud hooted with delight. "It's working! Do more of whatever you're doing! Look, Kylie, go towards the lovely country view."

"This could be dangerous for the boys!" warned Ben from the back seat.

"Shut up, old man," said PJ. "We're having fun."

The traffic was backing up ahead of him, waiting to pull out onto the Chester Road. Kylie started to slow down to join the back of the queue. Rutspud waggled his pole, hoping that his assessment of where Kylie's cameras were situated was reasonable.

"Oh look, there's a brand new filter lane on the left, let's go that way."

"Beep your horn, Kylie!" commanded Sister Genevieve.

Kylie blared the horns as they shot out of the junction, into the path of the traffic approaching from left and right. Remarkably, to the accompaniment of many horns honking and the last-minute squealing of brakes, they crossed the junction without being hit. There were whoops of delight from the lads.

"Nuns!" shouted Ben from the backseat.

"On it Ben," said Rutspud. "Kylie's got the message about the nuns, I don't think we'll get her to go any faster than this."

"No! Actual nuns!" said Ben, pointing ahead.

"Oh, shit."

Clovenhoof was well into his performance. He'd made sure that people would gaze adoringly throughout by chucking tenners from the stage at random intervals. He was currently doing a couple of songs. *Do Ya Think I'm Sexy?* was an obvious choice and he'd also cued up the backing track for *Wrecking Ball* on the off chance that he decided to ride on the champagne bottle as he launched it (twerking as he went). He was gratified to hear the crowd murmuring with approval. The murmuring quickly grew to a roar, which was surprising, as he hadn't even got to the part where he took his top off and swung it round his head. Then he realised that the crowd were no longer looking at him, their attention had been captured by a giant brawl with an unmistakeable crowd of nuns at the centre of it.

Clovenhoof knew he could not compete with such a spectacle, so he stopped singing and began chanting "Fight! Fight! Fight!" The crowd immediately joined in, and as fists flew and angry shoves were dealt out, the brawl grew until hundreds of people were fighting.

Joan of Arc emerged from the crowd, chasing a young man who looked genuinely panicked by the commotion. He looked left at Clovenhoof, right at the tables of food and drink and ran straight ahead. Joan reached out to grab him but a band of enraged sisters of mercy leapt upon her and bore her to the ground.

Clovenhoof saw Lennox whisper something into Florence's ear, and Florence bellowed at the army who had been standing to attention around the stage. "Engage with this rabble, soldiers! Hooflandia will not tolerate violence in its streets. Arrest anyone who is fighting!"

In Clovenhoof's assessment that was more or less everyone. The single street of Hooflandia was full to bursting and everyone was fighting with someone. A couple seemed to be fighting with themselves.

"Those without valid travel documents should be ejected from Hooflandia," hollered Florence as she sent them into action.

The soldiers waded into the melee. It wasn't clear how they were going to stop the fighting, but they did manage to eject a fair number of people by working in pairs, grabbing a person's arms and legs and tossing them into the moat. The brave Hooflandian army was massively outnumbered by the regiments of placard-wielding nuns and, within minutes, they were swamped by the vengeful holy ladies. But, then, at their moment of crisis, what could only be described a cavalry charge of boys on shopping trolleys swooped forward with cries of joy, drove a wedge into the nuns' flank and threw them into confusion.

Sadly, Hooflandia did not even come close to the world record for shortest time between a country's inception and its first war. Nonetheless, the day's events proved of exceptional interest to a number of journalists and a select band of crackpot historians and became known as the Battle Of The Four Armies, although it perhaps ought to be properly referred to as the Battle Of The Four

Armies Plus That Unfortunate Bit With The Self-Driving Car And The Yacht (since these last two proved to be the deciding factor in the conflict).

On one side were the nuns. It was difficult to gauge their true numbers, particularly as all that black and white created a zebra-style camouflage effect that made it difficult to distinguish one nun from the next. Sensible estimates ranged from two to seven thousand. It was also later argued that their numbers were swelled by various students, fetishists and musical fans who had come along in fancy dress to join the revels. The nuns were ostensibly the aggressors in the battle but their protest had been a peaceful one until a teenager in medieval battle armour wrestled an elderly nun to the ground and tried to rip off her clothes.

On the other side was the official Hooflandian army. The ranks of self-appointed captains, battle lords, Eagle Strike Warriors and covert agents, were well-disciplined in the art of standing still and looking both stern and reassuring but were less capable on the field of battle. Nonetheless, what they lacked in training they certainly made up for in enthusiasm and impressive uniforms. Two of them – ingenious souls definitely deserving of immediate promotion – had commandeered one of the pumps used to fill the moat and were using the hose to blast away anyone who came near.

In the middle, forming a loose alliance with the Hooflandian forces, were the masses of local folks who saw the nun advance as an attack on their free family fun day. These were people who wished to protect their families, ensure fun was had by all and, most importantly, stopping anyone else taking stuff that was free until they got their own hands on it. Whether they were combatants or merely looters was entirely a matter of perspective.

The Boldmere Ponies were the fourth major force in the battle. The boys, charging at speed on their shopping trolley steeds, had the advantage of agility and height, and used their poles to knock down nuns, soldiers and passers-by like skittles. Their specific goals in the conflict were uncertain and they rampaged across the battlefield more like a force of nature than any coherent military unit.

The battle raged back and forth for several long minutes with no clear winner and it might have raged on for considerably longer if not for the sudden and eventful appearance of a self-driving car.

Clovenhoof had an almost unparalleled view of the carnage from the stage. He took out his phone to film it, certain that future generations would thank him, and simultaneously sidled over to the music desk to put on some thumping accompaniment. To the sounds of *Swords of a Thousand Men* (with *Two Tribes* cued-up to follow), he swung his phone left and right, groaning with frustration that his phone arm was too slow to catch every scene of chaos. There was Nerys and a Hooflandian ninja defending a cake stall from a band of opportunistic locals. Here, a Boldmere Pony wrestled with a rather nubile nun as they sped by together in a shopping trolley. And there – oh, there! – a rather surprising bride of Christ atop a grey sand dune had whipped out what did indeed appear to be a pair of nunchuks and was sending assailant after assailant cartwheeling down into the water.

"How the hell did this happen?" asked Florence, who'd apparently mounted the stage to oversee her troops more effectively.

"Sometimes you just gotta dream big, Florence," said Clovenhoof. "Sometimes, even that bastard Upstairs lets things go your way. Wahey!"

This last was directed at Joan of Arc. The spirited saint had just executed a leapfrog move from a shopping trolley to a rubbish bin to a bouncy castle and was now rebounding up and already running before her feet hit the ground. She sideswiped a feisty nun with the flat of her blade and pushed on in pursuit of a young mopped-hair figure.

"Is that young Felix Wank Stain?" said Clovenhoof, peering.

"Who?" said Florence.

Clovenhoof was about to explain when from off to the right, a roaring vehicle entered Hooflandia at speed. It was Kylie, his beloved self-driving car.

"She's come to protect her daddy!" yelled Clovenhoof.

The sunroof was open and – Clovenhoof squinted – there were two Boldmere Ponies, a demon of the sixth circle and Ben

288

Kitchen all crowded round the opening. The first three were waving great big sticks around as though fishing for some sort of land-based game fish. Ben was screaming his head off in a delightfully alarmed fashion. Clovenhoof had to hand it to Ben: he had rarely demonstrated such creative flair.

"What on earth are they trying to do?" said Nerys, staggering onto the stage with her docile boyfriend who, inexplicably, appeared to have half a Victoria sponge cake smushed against the side of his head.

"Lots of things at once," observed Clovenhoof. "She's coming this way. She senses my presence."

"I'm sensing you're bonkers," said Nerys. "She's coming this way a bit fast."

"Where's she going?" said Florence.

It was clear to Clovenhoof that no one on board the car had any clue where the car was going to end up.

The car slewed in a wide arc across the beach, spraying fine sand in her wake. Her slide cut a path between Felix Winkstein and Joan of Arc who was still in pursuit and clouded the shiny saint in grey dust.

"That's not sand at all, is it?" said Florence.

"Not sure what else it could be," said Nerys.

Joan was left coughing in her own personal cloud. Felix ran on. Kylie fishtailed about wildly.

"She's going to hit the stage!" said Poppy.

"No, the yacht!" said Clovenhoof.

Kylie bounced over a sand dune, nearly decapitating a nunchuk-wielding nun, scraped her wheel arches on the slipway to the moat and then slipped the surly bounds of earth to jump up and clip the rear of the trailer carrying the presidential yacht.

"Was that a nun driving that car?" asked Clovenhoof.

Clovenhoof heard the sounds of disaster before he saw it. The yacht gave a terrible groan and began to move free from the ropes and tethers that held it in place.

"She's launching!" cried Clovenhoof.

"Possibly the least of our worries right now," said Nerys.

"But I haven't christened her yet!"

"What?"

"The bottle! The bottle!"

As the monstrous yacht slowly slid into the moat, Clovenhoof ran for the swing cradle that held the Melchizedek of champagne. The yacht was picking up speed, slowly but surely, like an elephant lumbering into a charge. Clovenhoof grabbed at the release cord which was simply a slipknot tying the bottle in place.

"I bless this ship and all who sail in her!" he cried.

The bottle in its cradle swung out in a long arc.

"It's going to miss," whimpered Clovenhoof but he was wrong.

As the stern of the yacht slipped by, the weighty bottle clipped it heavily but did not break. The Melchizedek spun away past the departing stern and, at the zenith of its swing, snapped free from its cradle and flew out. The yacht's groans increased as the vessel, bottle-struck, wobbled and listed sideways in its final descent. The yacht fell away, hitting the lake with a slap like a sumo-wrestler belly-flopping into a stagnant pond.

A bow wave surged, bounced off the far side of the moat and, as it flowed back, the yacht righted itself and leaned all its weight and momentum behind it.

"Tsunami," whispered Nerys.

"No thanks, I've already eaten," said Clovenhoof.

The tidal wave struck back at the beach. Grey dunes gave way and tumbled in. Soldiers, nuns and the general unfortunate were dragged in with it.

"The sand underneath is yellow," said Nerys. "Why's the sand underneath the top layer yellow?"

Ben staggered onto the stage, his front covered in what appeared to be his own vomit.

"Where did you tell the builders to put the cement?" he said.

"What cement?" said Nerys.

"The cement I originally told them to put on the scrubby land round behind the Boldmere Oak."

"I didn't tell them to put any cement anywhere," she began. "I told them to put everything... ah."

As the waves washed to and fro, churning the grey mire that was now the moat. A multitude of miserably soggy and grey individuals scrambled on the banks where only the vestiges of a beach remained. The heavy dress uniforms of the Hooflandian troops and the many layers of nun habits were clearly equally absorbent and the opposing forces in Hooflandia's brief inaugural war were now indistinguishable mounds of dribbling muck.

"Oh, this is all terrible," said Florence. "My soldiers didn't stand a chance."

"And their uniforms will be ruined," said Nerys.

"Whose fault is that?" said Ben.

"Don't try to pin this on me," she retorted. "You've all seen this beach and not said a word."

"Oh, I think people are finding the words now, Nerys," said Clovenhoof airily. "They might also have questions about whether this is quick-drying cement."

"Still, the boat's in the water," said Ben. "Along with a lot of other stuff, but hey."

The lake was a bizarre tableau. Soldiers climbed stiffly out of the water, which had started to take on a much more solid aspect. At the centre of it all, listing slightly, was Clovenhoof's yacht.

"Well, I've got to say I was worried about my sea sickness on your yacht," said Ben, walking to the front of the stage to inspect the scene. "But I think it's going to be fine. Oh, and another thing..." He beckoned Clovenhoof over.

Clovenhoof came forward. Ben pointed down at the sand to the side of the stage. The Melchizedek of champagne laid, still unbroken, on the ground and, pinned beneath it, was a curly-haired and inert computer whizz of Clovenhoof's acquaintance.

"Unlucky," said Clovenhoof.

Ben stroked his chin thoughtfully. "'There is no evidence at all that large quantities of alcohol do anyone serious harm.' Isn't that what you said to me?"

On the ground, Joan and Rutspud closed in on the trapped Felix Winkstein.

"Some people can't handle the hard stuff," said Clovenhoof.

CHAPTER FORTY-ONE

Joan was a tolerant and charitable individual and believed that there was a place in the Almighty's kingdom for all sorts of people. And though she might have thought the practices of the Mission Society of the Thrown Voice were unorthodox and even, perhaps, preposterous she saw that they were good and Christian folk. However, their behaviour over the days following the fun day fiasco tested her tolerance.

Many of the sisters had returned to the Mission Society house in cement-laden clothes and with cement-laden puppets and with more than a few cuts and bruises. The clothes were put into the washing (which promptly broke under the weight of all that cement), the puppets were washed by hand and the sisters tended to their injuries. Joan, who had suffered no more than a light winding and a thorough dusting with cement powder, helped dress their wounds.

And that should have been that. But then the Mission Society members proceeded to tend to the injuries of their puppet accessories. This did not mean sewing up any nicks or tears they had acquired in the fight (although there were a couple of those). No, the Mission Society sisters created little bandages and plasters for their hand puppets so that they replicated those worn by their human counterparts. So, Sister Valerie's puppet, Gambol the Lamb, was given a little sling for its front paw, Sister Tracey's pink dinosaur, Yazoo, had a splint and bandages on its tiny fingers and Tommy Chuckles was given a head bandage to match the one that now covered Sister Anne's bruised and bloodied eye. Saddest and most bizarre of all was Sister Margaritte, who had broken her right arm in the tousle and now sat silently weeping, staring at the giraffe puppet that she could no longer operate. Occasionally, she would give a little sotto voce cry of "Help me! Help me!" as though the dead puppet was calling to her from beyond the grave.

Joan found herself torn between offering poor Sister Margaritte comforting support and giving her a slap round the chops and pointing out that it was only a bloody puppet. Instead, wisely, she opted to stay out of the way and kept herself to the rooms set aside for herself and Rutspud. Both rooms were fairly large and therefore, the addition of Felix Winkstein to Rutspud's room was not a great inconvenience.

Sister Anne was initially perturbed to hear that her two guests were keeping a prisoner in their rooms. However, when she heard that the prisoner in question was the creator of the loathsome PrayPal, she swiftly turned a blind eye (the one that wasn't already blinded) and told them that, as long as they kept the noise down, it was none of her business.

After a day and a night on confinement to Rutspud's room, most of which Felix spent prodding the bits of himself variously bruised and concussed by a flying bottle of champagne to check they still hurt, he was still in an uncooperative mood. He sat, sulking on Rutspud's bed (which Rutspud had never slept in because he neither slept nor approved of lying on anything so soft and squishy unless it was a damned soul's internal organs).

"You can't keep me here," he said, not for the first time and long after a certain small but wirily powerful demon had proved him wrong on that point. "I haven't done nothing wrong."

"You ran when we tried to talk to you," said Rutspud, from his seated position on the edge of the hand basin.

"I thought you were spooks."

"Ghosts?" said Joan.

"Spies," said Rutspud.

"Thought you might be GCHQ or MI5. But you're not. You're those 'agents of a higher power' who've been bothering me. Who are you? Anonymous?"

"No, I'm Joan and this is Rutspud," explained the saint.

Felix looked at Rutspud.

"Yeah, she's for real," sighed the demon, absent-mindedly picking up a toothbrush from the edge of the basin and twirling it between his fingers. "She was raised in an insular and

294

technologically retarded corner of the world. S'called France. You might have heard of it."

Joan didn't know which to be more offended by, Rutspud's words or the nod Felix gave as though that explained everything.

"We just want to talk to you about the PrayPal app," said Rutspud.

"You want the source code?" asked Felix. "You want to buy me out?" He clicked his fingers in sudden realisation. "You're from bloody Apple, aren't you?"

"What? No."

"Google? Facebook? Amazon?"

"No."

"You know there are other 'pray as you go' and appsolution packages out there. Go pester them."

"Yes," said Joan, "but yours *works*."

Felix fell silent and did a very good impression of a confused goldfish, a goldfish that had just realised how tiny a bowl it was currently swimming in.

"Works, eh?" he said, slowly and cautiously. "So, you'd be religious types, yes? And I thought you were just staying in a house of crackpot nuns as some sort of cover."

"You don't believe?" said Joan.

"What? In God? A load of Freudian nonsense about the great big bogeyman in the sky?"

"Bogeyman?" said Rutspud. "I mean that would be a God I could get behind. The Almighty Snotmaker." He stuck the toothbrush up his nose and gave it an experimental jiggle.

"So, what do you believe in?" said Joan.

Felix gave her a blank look. "I believe in this world, in science. I'm a humanist."

"He believes in humans," said Rutspud. "That's quite easy when they're always bloody there. It's like believing in rocks. Or pigeons."

"I believe people are the masters of their own destiny. Our achievements are our own. Our failings are our own." A grin slipped out on Felix's lips. "You people..."

"We people?" said Joan.

"Christians. Bible bashers. And the Muslims and the Jews and the Mormons and all of those people. You believe you need a God to tell you right from wrong?"

"Moral commands need a commander," said Joan automatically.

"And if there was no God we'd all just rape and murder each other? Is that the idea?"

Rutspud had extracted the toothbrush from his nose and was examining the bristles for the spoils of his nasal excavations. "I think that's what humans do anyway."

"PrayPal doesn't make people do bad things. It only offers the illusion of forgiveness. If people are starting to do bad things because they can now get absolution at the tap of button then they weren't very good people in the first place."

"He's got a point," said Rutspud.

"The church – dogmatic religion in all its forms – is outmoded and obsolete."

"I object to that," said Joan.

"The church teaches that we can choose to do wrong because we have free will. But science now tells us that free will is an illusion cooked up by the subconscious. No one is born evil. It's pretty much all nurture and no nature. You want to blame someone for doing something wrong, you have to blame the person's parents. And you can't blame them because they're just products of their environment too. And the rules religions cook up about what you can eat, what you can say, who you can fall in love with..."

"I think the faith has made great strides in accepting all people," said Joan. "God's love is eternal but the church is willing to steer the faithful in new directions as society develops."

"You're kidding me!" said Felix. "You're not steering the faithful. You're the bloody anchor dragging behind! And just because society manages to drag the anchor in a new direction does not mean you're steering anything. And the worst thing is, it's those bloody stick-in-the-muds who are telling us to follow those outdated moral rules that are spending the weekend at one of those sex parties at Floxton House, snorting every drug under the sun and shagging every orifice they can find. Hypocrites, the lot of them.

The church is full of hypocrites who cling to the past and are frightened of the future."

"The church is not frightened of the future," said Joan.

"You are. The church. Bible bashers across the globe. You're frightened of the future, of technology. Anything new comes along and it's all up in arms and 'will no one think of the children?' and worrying that people will only use the new technology to look at porn and have sex with random strangers."

"This *is* what most people use technology for," argued Rutspud.

"But it's what people would do anyway, with or without technology!" said Felix. "The modern world is better than the past. There was no 'Golden Age', no time when Britain was truly great. For every person who is worried about sexting, cyberbullying and identity theft, there's a hundred people who are alive because of improved sanitation, GM crops and free condoms."

Felix glowered at them both.

"Have you finished ranting?" asked Joan eventually.

Felix huffed. "You know what? Whatever your problem is with my app you can go fuck yourself because I've done nothing wrong."

Rutspud picked a fleck of snot from the edge of the toothbrush and flicked it away.

"What sex parties at Floxton House?" he asked.

CHAPTER FORTY-TWO

Clovenhoof's private suite of the Hooflandian presidential palace (formerly the upstairs function room of the Boldmere Oak public house) was abuzz with the affairs of state. High Lord Baronet Ben Kitchen and Minister-without-portfolio Nerys Thomas, assisted by her pet boyfriend Okra, were overseeing the installation of The Game which had been brought over board by board, stack by stack and counter by counter from its original home at four-hundred-and-something Chester Road. The High Lord Baronet consulted a series of photos on his phone and the Minister-without-portfolio arranged the pieces to millimetre accuracy so that there might be no accusations that anything at all was out of place.

In the farthest corner, President Clovenhoof's personal *a cappella* choir provided background music. They specialised in beatboxing and barbershop quartet music, a crossover genre that Clovenhoof thought was criminally underappreciated, and were performing their own interpretation *If I Were a Rich Man*.

Clovenhoof wasn't paying attention. He stood at the largest window of his presidential suite and surveyed his country.

"I need a balcony here," he said. "A president needs a balcony if he's to do some proper surveying."

"I'm sure one could be put in place by the morning," said Nerys. "Now, Okra has been talking to me about some excellent investment opportunities."

"Does he ever talk to anyone else?"

"Oh, oh, y-yes, quite," mumbled the boyfriend. "In so much that... I-I-I –"

"Okra was saying," said Nerys, steam-rolling over him, "that most people don't see ships full of toxic waste as an investment opportunity but as long as you're not the one carrying the can when it all finally leaks out then they can offer great returns..."

Balcony or not, Clovenhoof had adopted the proper pose for a tyrant surveying his country: feet placed slightly apart, hands together behind his back, crotch not thrust fully forward but presented boldly enough to suggest it was available if needed.

Outside, in the orange glow of late afternoon, his realm offered a rich and varied sight. The presidential yacht was now permanently moored in the centre of the moat. Of course it wasn't much of a moat now, being an incomplete horseshoe shape and also being filled with solid concrete. Ben had cleverly suggested that once they were certain it had set all the way down, they should simply excavate both sides of it and the Hooflandian moat would become the Hooflandian wall. In the meantime, the Boldmere Ponies were using the moat as their private skate park and practice ground. If the British Queen could have her soldiers in silly helmets poncing up and down Horse Guards Parade, so President Clovenhoof could have his trolley-based cavalry performing manoeuvres on the moat. Inside the ring of the moat, a lone figure moved across the ground. He appeared to be scuttling along, digging holes with his trowel and listening intently before moving on again. Around Festering Ken the remains of the family fun day still scattered the ground. A coffee stand lay in ruins, its monstrous coffee machine trampled and dented by a thousand feet until it now looked like an aircraft crash site. A bouncy castle, deflated, flapped forlornly in the breeze. A nun's wimple rolled across the ground like tumbleweed. Oddly (and Clovenhoof couldn't decide if this was deliciously perverse or just annoying) the only constructions that still remained undamaged from the fun day were Milo's *Croquembouches Biscuit* Christmas tree displays. Clovenhoof itched to run down there right now and kick them over.

"Has anyone seen Milo Finn-Frouer since the fun day?" he asked.

"He's locked himself in my kitchen and won't let anyone go in," said Lennox.

"He's gone crispy pancake crazy. He says he's not coming out until he's solved it 'once and for all,'" added Nerys. "I think we're ready to start play in a few minutes. But here's something to think about. Okra says that if you're interested in being part of the exciting work of toxic waste management and wish to have a meaningful impact on lives up and down Africa's shipwreck coast, he's got the paperwork right here. All you need to do is sign."

"Jeremy won't be signing anything until he's sorted out his tax position," said Narinda Shah, brushing past a presidential guard to enter the room.

"Narinda!" said Clovenhoof, unclasping his hands from behind his back to greet her. "Now, you must remind me because I do forget. Do you work for me now?"

"I don't," said the taxwoman.

"I thought I offered you the job of Hooflandian finance minister."

"You did and I said no."

"If there's a job on offer, Okra might be available," said Nerys, massaging Okra's compliant face affectionately, as though she was determined to mould him into a finance minister before Clovenhoof's eyes.

"Did I mention the incredible salary I was offering?" said Clovenhoof.

"Yes, and I didn't think it was credible," said Narinda.

"But you're here now."

"As I said, there's the matter of your personal and business tax to settle."

"But I've given you lots of money. Surely, we're square."

Narinda paused by The Game board and picked up a house piece to briefly inspect it, causing Ben and Nerys to go into joint squeaks of frustration.

"Tax is an on-going issue, Jeremy," she said. "Just because you're now super-rich, it doesn't mean you can forget about paying tax."

"I thought that was exactly what being super-rich meant. I've set up my little tax haven here and seceded from Great Britain. Hooflandia has very attractive tax rates to encourage the forward-thinking entrepreneur to take up residency here."

"Residency? Hooflandia consists of a pub, a field barely big enough to count as a field, a rubbish tip and a trench full of building waste that I can't decide is meant to be a moat or the foundations of a wall."

"It can be both," piped up Ben.

"Residency of Hooflandia doesn't have to be literal or actual. As you know, I invented something called virtual residency, as successfully demonstrated by several schoolchildren who were able to put a local address on the application form for St Michael's Secondary?"

Narinda briefly closed her eyes and shook her head.

"Let me come on to the reason for my visit," said Narinda.

"Ah, have you been appointed the British Ambassador to Hooflandia?"

"Hardly," said Narinda with the most fleeting of smiles. "I have come as a representative, chosen primarily because those so-called soldiers of yours - the ones with more gold frogging on their uniforms than a hotel doorman – it seems I'm one of the few people they're willing to let upstairs. I've come on behalf of various local council committees plus the police, highways authority and local business forums."

"I'm sure I paid off the cops and the council."

"And wiser, more honest individuals have stepped in. This Hooflandia stunt –"

"Our glorious declaration of independence, you mean."

"This stunt has caused widespread problems. Your building works have closed off a number of local roads, cut through mains water supplies, telecoms lines and is a health and safety nightmare for anyone walking within fifty feet of this place."

"Those sound very much like *British* problems. Now that we have broken free from the yoke of British bureaucracy, we can forge our own destiny."

"No one is taking this declaration of independence seriously," said Narinda. "The Home Office simply refuses to respond to the issue."

"I wrote directly to the secretary general of the United Nations as well."

"Who, I suspect, has more important matters to deal with."

"I don't know. I sort of hinted in my letter that Hooflandia might become one of those 'rogue nations' if he doesn't take us seriously."

"Rogue nation? You have no military forces!"

"We do!"

"No. What you have is bouncers with an identity crisis. You are unarmed."

"I've already arranged the purchase of Maldon Ferret's old ornamental cannons. Going to install them on the former presidential yacht out there."

"Former presidential yacht," said Narinda, too indifferent to make a question of it.

"It's a bit too stationary now to count as a yacht," Clovenhoof admitted, "so I'm designating it Hooflandia's first border fortress. Fort Floaty McBang-Bang."

"If you like," said Nerys, "Okra here could source some high-grade military equipment for you. There are certain embargoed African nations, even a number of former Soviet satellite states that could provide you with the kind of hardware –"

"You should not be buying," cut in Narinda. "Now, tomorrow morning, I have arranged a sit-down meeting between you and the various services, council workers and quangos that you need to appease."

"And if I throw enough dosh at them?" said Clovenhoof.

"If you listen and act to fulfil your responsibilities as a rational human being –"

"Bit of a stretch."

"– then you might just avoid jail time."

Clovenhoof tickled his chin and thought.

"So, this international delegation..."

"It's the council and the Boldmere business forum."

"This *political and trade* delegation wish to hold a summit with me tomorrow to discuss matters of mutual interest and Hooflandia's acceptance into the wider global community?"

Narinda pouted. "Well, in not so many crazy words, yes."

Clovenhoof nodded presidentially. "Nerys, what's my schedule looking like for the coming day?"

Nerys finished arranging a series of multi-coloured meeples on The Game board. "You were going to review the official designs for the Hooflandian stamps in the afternoon. I think the big debate was whether the licky side should taste like the picture side."

"There's no debate," said Clovenhoof firmly.

"No, the actual debate was what your face tastes like."

Clovenhoof presented a cheek to Narinda. "I told them I taste of victory, animal magnetism and just a hint of Imperial Leather. Have a lick. What do you think?"

"Is Jeremy free in the morning?" she said, ignoring the old devil completely.

"He's got a hangover lined up between eight a.m. and noon. Games night hangover, although that's not going to happen if we don't get started." Nerys gestured to the board.

The chairs were in place. The piles of cash were ready. Lennox – possibly the only man in history to work simultaneously as a barman and prime minister – was already pouring the games drinks.

"Then let's do this," said Clovenhoof. "Narinda, schedule that meeting for ten. I will be wearing sunglasses and might throw up from time to time, but I promise they will have my undivided attention. Poppy, pull up a pew, come see some financial gamesmanship in action. Guys." He clicked his fingers at his a cappella choir. "Give me something suitable for a high stakes game. Something rousing."

The little choir launched into some thumping bass harmonies with a beatbox 'dub-a-dub-a-tsssh' on top.

"And throw some swears in this time," said Clovenhoof, dropping into his gaming seat.

He swayed along.

"Eye of the fucking Tiger," he nodded approvingly. "Let's get this game started."

CHAPTER FORTY-THREE

Joan pulled Rutspud aside before Felix got to the Eddy-Cab car.

"I'm not happy about doing this," she whispered.

"It's okay. If Felix tries to run again," said Rutspud, "you break out some of the tin-plated whup ass and we'll restrain him."

"It's not that," she said. "Well, it's not just that. But mostly it's this... what is it we're doing?"

"We're going to Floxton House," said Felix, coming up behind them. "To the ancestral home of the vile Ferrets, where I'll show you what the great and the good get up to when they think no one's looking. And then we might do some light guerrilla hacking on the side."

He opened the rear door and climbed in.

"Yeah, that's what I'm not happy with," said Joan.

"He's just going to introduce us to a slice of his work," said Rutspud. "We show an interest, show this kid we care, and then talk him round to doing the right thing."

Joan wasn't convinced they should be letting this young man do anything at all until he had agreed to shut down the PrayPal but she said nothing as she got into the driving seat.

Clovenhoof had been good enough – well, indifferent enough to lend them Kylie 2. Kylie 1 was currently in a garage somewhere having a smashed axle replaced, several bodywork dents repaired and the computer interface thoroughly overhauled. The official Eddy-Cab mechanic had shed an actual tear when describing the 'brutal lobotomy' Rutspud had given one of their precious vehicles.

Joan gave Kylie 2 directions and the car set off through the evening traffic.

"This thing you want to do. This hacking," said Joan. "It sounds a bit illegal."

Felix, sitting in the back with laptop on his knee, nodded unashamedly.

"It is. But that doesn't make it wrong."

"Well, no, but..."

"Your issues with my work. Your mad as kipper's uncle issues with PrayPal are moral issues, not legal ones. Don't confuse morality with legality."

"I'm not," she said.

Felix gave her a blankly disbelieving stare in the rear-view mirror.

"New technology comes along and presents us with new ethical dilemmas, new moral situations and the knee-jerk conservative reactionaries – that's you, Joan, by the way – respond by trying to ban things."

"I don't!" said Joan.

"What if a self-driving car hits someone? What if Microsoft's AI twitterbot declares itself to be a neo-Nazi? That one's already happened by the way. What if your home automation smart speaker starts listening in on your every conversation and reports you to the police if you say something suspicious? The world is changing and we've got to be ready for it."

Traffic thinned and street lights became more spread out as the car passed through the outskirts of the town and into the countryside.

"Hacking is like a sharp knife," said Felix.

"Dangerous," said Joan.

"Useful," said Felix.

"I was going to go for 'fun'," said Rutspud.

"It's a tool," said Felix. "It can be used for good or bad. But it's not the tool that's ever to blame. The information revolution has levelled the playing field in so many ways and there are plenty of us who want to use the powers we've been granted for the greater good."

He tapped on his laptop. The display on the windscreen changed to a three-dimensional projection of the route ahead.

Joan frowned. "Did he just...?"

"Hack this car, yes," said Felix.

Joan's seatbelt unclicked and came loose by itself. Rutspud's would have done the same if he'd been wearing one.

"I could crash this car and ensure I was the only survivor if I wanted to," said Felix. It wasn't a threat; it was a casual observation. "That wouldn't be technology's fault if I did. It would be mine. But mummy Winkstein raised good boys and I'm not going to do that."

"Also, you'd find we're surprisingly hard to kill," said Rutspud.

The map on the screen shifted. The route through the village of Floxton Magor and onto the estate of Floxton House changed to one which took them round the estate and to a road that passed within a few hundred metres of the house.

"We don't need to go to the front door of their mansion to actually spy on them," said Felix. "We're not dressed for the occasion."

"I'd look dead good in a posh suit," said Rutspud.

"I think there will be more gimp suits than monkey suits at tonight's party."

"I'd look dead good in a gimp suit too," said Rutspud.

"Spare us the mental image, please," said Joan.

The car followed Felix's amended route, turning off before the village and down an unlit single-track lane, bordered on one side by a tall stone wall that marked the edge of the Ferret's considerable country estate. The car glided silently into a passing place beneath the wall and its lights turned out.

"Okay, let's see what we can make use of," said Felix.

A tap of the keyboard and the windscreen display changed to what Joan quickly perceived to be the downstairs plan for a large house drawn in dramatic reds and oranges.

"What are the flashing orange circles?" said Joan.

"Hackable devices," said Felix.

"There's a lot of them," said Rutspud.

"Aren't there just?" said Felix. "And if we do a surface sweep of phone IDs and fitness trackers we can..."

Many of the dots on the screen sprouted names.

Joan tapped one. "Anette Cleaver? Didn't we meet someone by that name? The woman at the church offices."

"Now, you know I mentioned home automation smart speakers?" said Felix.

"Sure," said Joan who didn't want to admit that half the words Felix said entered her ears as pure gobbledegook and were filtered out before they got to her brain.

"Everyone thinks smart speakers are so amazing," said Felix. "'*Alexis, play me some music*' and '*Cortina, tell me what the weather is*' and everyone is so dazzled by the tech they forget that, a, people have been able to play music and see what the weather is for years without needing a voice-activated house bot and, b, that putting a smart speaker in your house is an open invite to MI5, the CIA, the Kremlin and Fox News to all listen in on everything you're doing." He tapped on the laptop. "Or me."

The Eddy-Cab possessed a state of the art sound system which, to Joan's understanding, meant that you really felt like you were inside the music when it was playing from all around you. The noise that now came from the speakers was one that Joan really didn't want to be inside. Really, really didn't want to be inside.

There was a thumping dance track but that was the least offensive element of it. Above it was a moaning and groaning round, like a room full of people with stomach aches. Except that wasn't what it was.

"I've got over twenty phone and tablet cameras I can hack," said Felix. "Give me a moment and I'll bring up the visuals."

"No!" said Joan but it was too late. Joan thrust her hand over her eyes.

"Most of that bumping and grinding is coming from the movies their streaming in each room," said Felix.

"Yeah," said Rutspud. "Most of the party guests still have their clothes on."

Joan risked a peek. The map on the windscreen was overlaid with floating camera footage from various points in the house. Most of the guests did still have their clothes on but not enough of them for her liking.

Rutspud was a demon and not possessed of the same desires as humans. He found their love of fluffy animals frightening and disturbing. He found their desire to amass wealth in the form of paper rectangles and metal disks pointless and ridiculous. He found human nudity boring and their apparent obsession with getting each other naked and inserting things inside themselves and each other was dull in the extreme.

Even in death, humans were obsessed with sex. There were pits in Hell that positively writhed with rutting bodies, locked in a state of frustrated desire. How their empty and miserable fornications in Hell actually differed from their lives on earth was unclear but Rutspud was only a minor demon and it wasn't his place to ask. Some of the scenes played out in Floxton House and relayed to the windscreen of the Eddy-Cab were so reminiscent of certain pits of the Third Circle that Rutspud felt a sudden pang of homesickness and sighed.

Joan mistook that sigh for some other sentiment.

"The wickedness of humanity upsets you?" she asked, surprised. "I thought you'd be used to it."

"This video feed is going straight on the internet," said Felix. A little red record icon appeared in the corner of the screen.

"Does it have to?" said Joan.

"Don't you want to see these people exposed for what they are?"

Joan turned in her seat to face Felix. "I believe the centuries have mellowed me somewhat and I know the world is always changing. Even a few decades ago, if you'd asked me, I would have wanted these people punished."

"Okay, I don't know what you mean when you talk about being around for decades, let alone centuries, but –"

"I'm saying that I'm more of the opinion these days that what people get up to in their own homes is their own business."

"Really?" said Rutspud. "Progressive relative morality from the Maid of Orleans?"

"If two consenting adults want to show their love and desire for each other with simple and natural acts of lovemaking then – Oh, my God! What's she doing?"

"Which one?" said Rutspud.

"That one! That one! In the bathroom!"

Rutspud stood on the passenger seat to get a closer look.

"It looks like she's pissing on him."

"Why?! For the love of God, why?"

"I think it's called –"

"Couldn't she find a toilet? It's right there, next to her!"

"No, I think he wants her to –"

"I mean, that's got be unhygienic."

"I believe urine is almost entirely sterile."

Joan hid her face in her hand and took some deep breaths.

"You were saying..." smiled Rutspud.

Joan made a visible effort to compose herself. "I was saying that if two consenting adults want to show their... their feelings by... by..."

"Pissing on each other," offered Felix helpfully.

"Yes, by sharing some form of intimacy then... then... um, what are they doing now?"

Rutspud noted a quaver in Joan's voice. For a woman who had been around for several hundred years, Joan hadn't travelled much beyond the confines of her own small experiences and she was evidently easily shocked. Nonetheless, it took world-wise Rutspud a moment or two to work out what was going on in the peculiar charade being played out on the screen.

"Well, there's a cup and a little baggy of paper squares and – Ah," he said.

"Ah?" said Joan, tremulously.

"Yes, he's offering her Holy Communion."

"What?"

"Holy Communion. Mass. Eucharist. A Holy Communion of what looks like LSD wafers, washed down with a cup of fresh piss."

Joan's mouth opened but words failed to emerge.

"Two consenting adults," Rutspud reminded her.

Joan managed to produce a strangled squeak but no actual words.

"In the privacy of their own home," said Rutspud.

"Maldon Ferret's home actually," said Felix.

Joan closed her mouth as having it open clearly wasn't doing her any good.

"If it helps," said Felix. "That man isn't a practising priest. I don't know if that makes it better or worse. And that woman is on the Church of England's national strategy committee. You will be unsurprised to hear that they aren't married. Well, they are but not to each other."

Joan opened her mouth, gave an apoplectic squeak and closed it again.

"Now, shall we take a closer look at who everyone else is and what they're doing?" said Felix.

CHAPTER FORTY-FOUR

The Game had just become very interesting.

"My turn," said Clovenhoof.

A roll of nine took him around the corner of the board.

"St Chad's Cathedral. No one's bought that yet," said Nerys.

"Ooh, Catholic," said Clovenhoof. "I do like the Catholics."

"Really?" said Nerys archly.

"Sure. Their priests have much better bling and they believe their man in Rome knows what the Almighty's thinking, which is frankly hilarious.

Ben opened a file folder. "Let's remind ourselves of the new rules for the purchase of religious buildings after the St Philip's fiasco."

"Sure thing, Ben," said Clovenhoof with a roll of his eyes. He flung five hundred pounds to buy the space into the bank. "Now, can I turn it into houses?"

Ben read from the rules. "It's an automatically listed building. You can't knock it down."

"Nerys, you're the council dude," said Clovenhoof.

"Indeed, I am," she said, whipping on her official councillor's hat. "And I'm not going to un-list that building for you."

Clovenhoof peered at the square. "What kind of income does it generate?"

"Depends on which day of the week you land on it," said Ben. He began riffling through the pages of a much-thumbed desk diary.

"Stop" said Clovenhoof.

"Wednesday," read Ben.

"Balls," said Clovenhoof with feeling.

Okra Boddington, sitting next to Nerys, whispered in her ear.

"I can imagine," she smirked, patting his knee affectionately.

"What?" said Clovenhoof.

"As financial advisor to the Church, Okra knows how little money churches make mid-week."

"It's a negative multiplier," said Ben.

"How much do I get?" said Clovenhoof.

Ben set a stack of tiddlywinks and a shallow dish in front of Clovenhoof.

"It's based on how many tiddlers you can shoot into that dish before Nerys and I finish saying the Lord's Prayer backwards."

Clovenhoof reached for the tiddlywinks.

Ben nudged Nerys and they began the race, "Amen. ever and ever for... glory the and power the... is thine for..."

Clovenhoof winked his tiddlers for all his was worth. He was a superior winker and had had a near-eternity of practice. He had heard that too much winking could make you go blind (particularly if your aim was poor), but what could you do to occupy yourself when bored, apart from a spot of winking?

By the time Ben and Nerys had completed "heaven in art who, Father Our," Clovenhoof had amassed a tiny mountain of tiddlers in the dish.

"Booyakasha!" he declared and snapped his fingers. "Count 'em and weep, losers."

Ben did indeed count them and then, instead of weeping, announced, "Forty-one pounds, seventy-six."

"I beg your pudding?" said Clovenhoof, affronted. "I winked all them tiddlers!"

"You are a massive winker," agreed Nerys.

"Exactly!"

"And, on a wet Wednesday afternoon, that comes to just over forty quid," said Ben.

"Sounds about right," said Nerys as Okra whispered in her ear. "At least as a recognised religion, you get it tax free."

"Tax free, eh?" said Clovenhoof. "Is everything I do through my church tax free?"

"You are now a registered charity."

"It's my turn," said Nerys, reaching for the dice.

Clovenhoof snatched them away. "I'm thinking."

"Think on your own time, church boy."

Clovenhoof sat back, holding the dice out of Nerys's reach. "So, this cathedral of mine, it's – what? – a retail unit?"

"It's a church," said Ben.

"But it's in the selling business: the Almighty's good graces in exchange for cash."

"A very cynical interpretation," said Nerys.

"But it does sell those little Christmas cards and some locations have a coffee shop."

"Yes," agreed Ben cagily.

"So, I can add extra retail units," said Clovenhoof and searched among his playing pieces. "Let's see what I've got here..." He slapped a counter down.

"A massage parlour?" said Ben. "That's hardly... um, what kind of massage parlour were you thinking of?"

"I'm going to whip out the pews and replace them with coin-operated massage chairs," said Clovenhoof and put down another token.

"3-D cinema?" said Ben.

"We can do those national broadcast things, like what the cinemas do with the ballet and the opera. We get a superstar priest in and telecast it to all our churches."

"Are there superstar priests?" asked Nerys.

"Who was that one in *The Poseidon Adventure*? Is he available or did he get burned up at the end?"

"That was a film, not a documentary," said Ben.

"Not burned up then. Get him." Clovenhoof placed a tiny plastic loaf of bread on the counter too. "Art-is-anal bakery."

"It's pronounced 'artisanal'," said Nerys.

"However you pronounce it, it means bakery that's up its own arse," said Clovenhoof. "It can bake bread and cakes for my coffee shop."

Okra leaned forward to listen more closely.

"And my *piece de resistance*," said Clovenhoof, plonking a miniature pylon on the square. "Free Wi-Fi for everyone. All day. Every day."

"That will vastly increase the number of people coming through the doors," agreed Ben.

Okra took notes on his tablet.

"I-I-I say," he said. "D-do you have any more –"

"He wants to know if you have any other ideas for getting the church to make money," said Nerys. "You should mention your bishops calendar idea."

"I'm sure he's not interested in that," said Ben, disapprovingly.

"Go on. Okra could make something of it," said Nerys.

"Seriously, it's not worth your time," said Ben.

"Well, th-the thing is..." said Okra, "w-with revenues dropping like, er, well –"

"People are turning to Jeremy's app for instant absolution," said Nerys. "The march for solidarity resulted in dozens of nuns –"

"Actual, proper nuns," said Okra.

"Yes. Shush, dear. Nerys is talking. With all those nuns in police custody and scores more taking up NHS beds with their ridiculous injuries, there's a perfect shit-storm on social media. The church is out of money and goodwill and Okra is looking for a financial rescue package."

"I'm not sure –" Okra said but Nerys mushed his lips shut with her fingers.

"Go on, Jeremy. Tell him."

"So, you know that Calendar Girls thing?" Clovenhoof asked with one of his best grins. "The naked WI one?"

Okra nodded

"The one with their norks artfully concealed by floury bread rolls and the like," said Clovenhoof reliving the memory.

"Baps," said Nerys.

"Right. Their baps artfully concealed by floury bread rolls. Well, it did wonders for their public image and brought in a lot of moolah."

"So, the obvious thing for the church to do –" started Nerys.

"Bishops," said Clovenhoof. "Past and present. Let's get a few ex-Archbishops of Canterbury in there. A nude pose from each of them, one per month. And here's the thing, each of them is concealing their funky junk with a religious artefact or a symbol of the season. An Easter egg in springtime. A Christingle during advent – spicy! – or even a baby Jesus."

"You mean that the archbishop should hold a little baby Jesus over his...?" Ben gestured to his groin.

"I'm not saying it needs to be nestling right in there, like in the straw in the manger, although a completely pubic nativity scene could be very tastefully done."

"Tastefully," echoed Nerys.

"And whether your nudey bishops position the items to conceal their loaf and two fishes or whether we cover them later with peelable stickers so the more adventurous calendar buyers can have a peek... Well, that's entirely up to you."

They all sat in silence for a long moment.

Eventually, Okra whispered to Nerys.

"Yup. It's a viable idea, and all Jeremy's own work," Nerys said.

"Oh, yes," Clovenhoof said, enthusiastically.

"We certainly had nothing to do with it," said Ben.

Nerys grabbed Okra's phone from his pocket and made a call. "Get me Anette Cleaver for Okra Boddington. No, this takes priority. Who am I? The cheek!" She thrust the phone at her boyfriend. "Talk to them, honey. Tell them you've got a proposal that could improve the church's profile."

Okra scuttled into the corner, speaking in hushed tones, and returned very quickly with alarm in his eyes.

"Google what?" asked Nerys as Okra whispered urgently in her ear. "'Coked-up priest sex orgy?'"

Nerys tapped briefly, then held up her tablet so they could see.

The video appeared to be a live, split-screen feed of a very exciting party.

"It's old Ferret's place," said Ben. "Who'd have thought he'd host those kinds of parties?"

"All those plush furnishings," said Nerys. "They'll be scrubbing the lube out for weeks."

Okra stared at the screen, hand halfway to mouth in shock.

"Anyone there you recognise?" asked Clovenhoof innocently.

Okra nodded.

"What about the chap in the leather mask and ball gag?"

"All of them," he answered in faint horror.

"If that guy in the mask knows what's good for him, he'll keep it on and maintain some anonymity," said Nerys. As she spoke, little labels popped up next to all the people, identifying them for the benefit of the watching public.

"Ah," said Nerys, as Okra squeaked in her ear. "It's the minutes secretary of the Church marketing committee."

CHAPTER FORTY-FIVE

In the car parked round the back of the Ferret estate, Felix finished linking name tags to the devices of the party guests.

"Right, there's no escape now," he said.

"People could just throw away their phones and devices," said Rutspud, "and just walk away."

"Funny, but people never think of that," said Felix. "Let's see who we've got."

"I don't want to look," said Joan but actually unable to tear her eyes away.

"So, we've got the chairman of the archbishops' council and the chair of the pensions board in the hallway burying their faces in a mountain of Peruvian cocaine."

"It's nice to see the Church supporting the businesses of developing nations," said Rutspud.

"Then we've got a group in that room, playing... playing... what does that look like to you?"

"Pin the stiffy on the pope?" suggested Rutspud.

"Quite possibly so."

"What are those two doing?" said Joan, pointing at a couple in a secluded room as they pored over a book.

"Let me change the angle on that," said Felix and the camera view shifted. "What's that? The Illustrated Lives of the Saints."

"A spot of innocent reading?" said Rutspud doubtfully.

"Let's get sound from the nearest smart speaker," said Felix.

"Do her," said the one man on the screen. "And her. And her."

"I'd definitely do her," said the other. "How old was she when they killed her?"

"Nineteen," read the first.

"Young but legal," said the second. "That's how I like 'em. Pert and fresh, eh?"

"That's the party host, Maldon Ferret," said Felix.

"And that's *me* they're talking about!" said Joan. "That's me on the page! Filthy, filthy voyeurs! Oh, if I was there right now..."

"But you're not," said Rutspud. "You are spying on two men in private conversation."

"What's your point?" she snapped.

"None," smiled the demon. "Just muddying the moral waters. As you said, what people get up to in private is their own business."

"Even if the man currently giving a blow job to the chap in the gimp mask there has repeatedly spoken out against gay rights in church policy meetings?" asked Felix.

Joan growled with frustration. "This world is full of hypocrites. It's so confusing."

"Best not to think about it," said Felix. "Let me lighten the tone a little. *This* was what I'd been aching to try out. You see, that house is full of idiots who haven't set decent security settings on their web-enabled devices including... six plus five plus eight... *nineteen* Bluetooth-enabled butt plugs."

"Pardon?" said Joan.

"Bluetooth," said Felix. "It's a protocol by which devices can talk to each other within a relatively short range."

"I don't think that's the part of the phrase Joan was struggling with," interjected Rutspud. "Sheltered upbringing and all that."

"Ah, well, a butt plug..." Felix began.

"I don't need you to explain everything to me," said Joan. "A butt is a barrel and I guess a butt plug is that little cork you put in it to stop the liquid running out."

"If only it were," said Rutspud and gave her the briefest description.

"And these aren't used as some sort of preventative against incontinence?" she asked.

"Nope," said Rutspud. "Purely for recreational purposes."

"I remember there was a man put in the stocks in Reims for... interfering with himself with a carrot," she mused disapprovingly. "I remember thinking it seemed a waste of a good carrot."

"The world has since moved on from root vegetables," said Rutspud.

"These are vibrating butt plugs," said Felix.

"And why would anyone want them to have this Bluetooth?" asked Joan.

"Cos everything's better with Bluetooth," said Rutspud.

"And more fun," said Felix. He tapped his laptop and more than a dozen people across the visible screens gave little twitches, jumps or gasps. "Oh, would you look at that. I've somehow hacked into every single one of them."

"Really?" said Rutspud.

"Absolutely," said Felix and, at a finger tap, swathes of partygoers made involuntary jerks and moans.

"Sorry, I blinked," said Rutspud. "One more time, please."

Felix obliged. Rutspud tittered.

"This is funny, is it?" said Joan.

"Yes," said Rutspud. "It definitely is. The grunt of surprise that man there gave. And that woman, squeaking like a chipmunk." A thought occurred to him. "Mealcur, in the Seventh Circle, once conceived a musical instrument he called the scream-organ. It was basically a keyboard attached to a series of blades beneath a range of damned souls, each chosen for the precise tone of their scream."

"Way ahead of you," said Felix, fingers galloping on the keyboard. "Now, if I assign each plug to a different note, based on a sound sample... and then if I find a popular tune to feed through a transcribing program... and then we direct the cameras to cut to the relevant person as they're activated."

"What's he up to?" said Joan. "He's not going to hurt them, is he?"

"Not in any physical sense," grinned Rutspud.

Okra Boddington was panicking.

Clovenhoof could tell because his fear had burst through the bumbling politeness slash embarrassed stuttering slash domineering girlfriend barrier and he was actually using words.

These words were directed in a very loud whisper into his phone while the carnival of tasteless and hypocritical sex acts played endlessly on the big screen. Clovenhoof preferred it when he was the centre of attention but this was the best TV he'd watched in ages and a dose of outrage was the perfect accompaniment.

"Graham, this *is* a public relations disaster!" Okra hissed. "T-the feed is currently being watched by over ten thousand people and growing exponentially. Yes. I am aware that I am a lowly fund manager and PR is not my area but given that the Church's PR consultant is.. is..."

Nerys snatched the phone from Okra. "Is that the one?" she asked her boyfriend, pointing at the screen.

Okra nodded.

"Graham," said Nerys, "your PR dude is currently walking across a row of naked buttocks whilst wearing nothing but stilettos – Well, yes, a pair of stilettos, a rubber horse head and a – Christ, Graham! If you're watching it too, I don't need to describe it to you! No, Graham, I don't know how they decide who gets invited to these things. Yes, I'm sure you should take it as a personal snub. Now, take a cold shower and try to get hold of any of them on the phone. They need to know that the world is watching."

Nerys killed the call angrily. Okra's phone continued to chirp and buzz with alerts. Nerys calmly passed it back to him and took a long swig of drink.

"Now, I seem to recall," she said, "that it's my turn."

She held out her hand for Clovenhoof to give her the dice.

"You're able to continue playing while this is going on?" said Ben.

"I can multitask," said Nerys. "And I'm shocked that you'd imagine a live sex scandal featuring key church figures could actually be more important than The Game. You like this kind of stuff, do you?"

Ben gave her a look that was both stunned and sickened. "I am a man of simple tastes, Nerys. I'm going to have to wash my eyes with bleach just to erase some of the things I've seen." With a trembling hand, he picked up his cider and black and took a large swig. "I'd be grateful if we could actually turn that off."

"Not a chance, Ben," said Clovenhoof. "I'm loving every minute of this."

"You get off on this?" said Nerys.

"It's fucking hilarious," he said. "Middle-aged middle-class wankers acting like they're sex gods. Donkeys prancing about like stallions. They think they're sexual adventurers, plumbing the depths of human depravity. I tell you there's nothing on that screen I haven't seen in the Old Place a thousand times."

"Yet you're still enjoying it."

"Because they haven't got a clue that the whole world is watching. It's like when you walk in on someone singing to a hairbrush in the kitchen mirror." Ben took another hasty swig of cider. "By the way, I think *Hey, Big Spender* is a bold choice, Kitchen."

"Don't know what you're talking about," Ben mumbled into his pint.

"Yeah, you do. Oh, what's this?"

The image on the screen was no longer split screen but focusing on individual faces and rapidly cutting between them. The camera lingered on each only long enough to record a little moan or cry from each. Run together, the sounds were rhythmical, almost melodic.

"Is that meant to be a tune?" said Ben.

Clovenhoof turned up the sound.

"Unh."

"Urrrrr."

"Ooh."

"Ah."

"Mmmmm."

"Ahhhh."

"Ooh."

"Eek."

"Ooh."

"Nngg."

"Ooooh."

"Uh."

One of Clovenhoof's backing choir joined in with a soft and amused, "Oh come ye, oh, co-ome ye, to Be-e-thle-hem."

"Oh, my God, it is," grinned Lennox.

After the first verse, whoever or whatever was controlling these figures, had worked out how to get some chords going and, spread out across the house, the guests launched into a second verse of *O Come, All Ye Faithful* that was both harmonious and, in more ways than one, rousing.

Clovenhoof cackled deliriously.

"I think I might be sick," said Ben.

"I know, I know," grinned Felix. "It's hardly the season for Christmas songs but you have to admit that the lyrics are apt."

"Someone's coming," said Joan.

"My point exactly," said Felix.

She tutted. "No. Here."

She tapped the rear view mirror. Blue flashing lights were racing down the country lane. Rutspud turned in his seat to see them.

"The fuzz. They coming for us?"

"Doubt it," said Felix and then, to confirm this, a first and then a second police car sped past their parked Eddy-Cab. "I tagged Floxton House in the video upload. I should think the boys in blue are off to make a drugs bust. Right, any requests for the next tune?"

"Not everyone's keen to participate," said Rutspud, pointing.

"Yes," said Felix, "although you'll observe that it's quite tricky extracting a butt plug while it's buzzing to the max and your fingers are covered with KY jelly."

Joan watched a man on the screen as he spoke urgently on his mobile whilst simultaneously trying to disengage a buzzing toy from his backside.

"I think the penny's dropped," she said.

The man cried out to those around him but there were others too now who were getting calls or alerts on their phones. Some put their hands to their faces as though to cover their shame. Others ran about in search of cameras to cover up, an act that was clearly as ineffective as trying to swat a swarm of bees one by one.

Felix's laptop pinged.

"Ha!"

"What?" said Joan.

"Guess where there's a sudden surge in clicks on PrayPal?"

"They only want forgiveness because they think they've been caught in the act?"

"Of course," said Rutspud. "They're human."

Joan opened the car door and stepped out.

The cold night air was a bracing and welcome slap in the face. It did nothing to alleviate the sickness that had been broiling in her stomach but it cleared her thoughts, sweeping away the disgust, the ethical mess, the confusion if only for a few moments. She looked back at the car, at Rutspud and Felix Winkstein, faces in the dark illuminated only by the cold and unloving light of various screens. Joan didn't think herself a fool. She knew people were shallow and debased creatures but this... this wasn't part of her world.

She walked away, back the way they had come.

"Hey!" called Rutspud, leaning out of a car window. "Where are you going?"

"I can't do this," she said.

"That's the beauty," said Rutspud. "You're not doing anything. These people have done it to themselves."

She shook her head. "G'night, Rutspud. I'll see you back at the mission."

"But it's miles. You'll get lost."

She shrugged sadly.

"Already lost," she said and turned her back on him.

PART THREE –
THE FALL OF HOOFLANDIA

CHAPTER FORTY-SIX

Jeremy Clovenhoof, President for Life of the state of Hooflandia, rose from the silk cushions where he had fallen into an alcoholic stupor and walked naked to the balcony that had been erected in the night on the side of his presidential suite. The big TV screen was tuned to a news channel, the sound down low. Something terrible was happening somewhere – protests and riots – but that place was not here.

Clovenhoof scratched his balls and regarded the funfair wasteland that was Hooflandia.

"Here is my utopia," he said, feeling very pleased with himself.

Nerys entered the room. "Morning, Jeremy. Busy day today. You've got a ten o'clock with the Church Commissioners to discuss your suggestions for rehabilitating the church. You've got a midday with the builders to decide whether you want the moat-wall thing to be a moat or a wall. The antiquities chaps are coming round at one thirty to install the cannons on your yacht and we've taken a dozen calls from a woman called – Jesus Christ! Put some clothes on, man!" she yelled, having looked up for the first time.

"What?" said Clovenhoof, giving a bit of a wiggle because what was the point of having a penis if you couldn't take it out a spin now and then. "Are you not awed by my beautiful schlong?"

"One," said Nerys, "red really isn't a good colour for external genitalia. Two, we've all seen it before. You've posted pictures on lampposts saying, 'Have you seen this cock? Would you like to?' and, three, take it from a woman who's done extensive research, *that* is distinctly average."

"Ouch," said Clovenhoof, pretending to cover up Little Jeremy's ears. "It has feeling, you know."

"Now, stop scratching your balls –"

"I wouldn't have to do that if you'd hired me a Personal Ball-Scratcher."

"Would that be before or after I hire a..." She checked her list. "... Full-Time Flatterer, Crack-Wiper and Cold-Caller-Abuser?"

"And you said you could multi-task," he sneered. "Add Personal Person-Hirer to the list. And Official List-Maker."

"Come on," she said, clapping her hands. "Put on some clothes. Something understated and formal. The cars are waiting."

"Could you at least get Milo to rustle me up some breakfast," said Clovenhoof.

"I would, if we could get him out of the cupboard he's shut himself in. He's just rocking back and forwards muttering 'crispy golden breadcrumbs, crispy golden breadcrumbs' over and over." She stopped at the door as she went to leave. "Oh, and we've been getting a number of calls from an old biddy called Alice Calhoun. She wants to know when you're coming round again. I would have put her in the 'nutters and crackpots' blocked list but she seems to be very familiar with some of your personal habits..."

"Ah," said Clovenhoof as he trotted over to his walk-in wardrobe of smoking jackets. "How is Alice?"

"I wouldn't know," said Nerys.

Clovenhoof considered a black smoking jacket. It was made from space-tech fabric and practically sucked in light. It was lovely to wear but it was impossible to find the buttons.

"A president should have a wife," he said thoughtfully.

"I think she's in her seventies, Jeremy."

"Or a harem," he shrugged.

Joan stormed into the kitchen at the Mission of the Thrown Voice to find Rutspud and Felix sitting at the breakfast table, Felix merrily chomping at some yellow, buttered toast, both of them glued to their computer screens. Neither one gave her a word or nod of greeting.

She gave a vicious sideswipe with her sword. Flower heads from the vase of flowers on the table plopped to the floor like fat spiders.

"Oh, hi," said Rutspud, cheerily.

"Hi?" she said. She was wearing a furious grimace, but he seemed not to notice.

"I think we've reached a new low."

"You think?"

He prodded the bowl of cereal in front of him. "It's sawdust with added sugar and the odd dried grape. It is not, despite all appearances and taste, pet food for beavers who craved a sugar rush. It is – and you won't believe it – meant for human consumption."

"I don't care about the muesli," said Joan, seething.

"The name is stupid too," said Rutspud. He seemed to catch her expression for the first time. "Have you seen the news coverage for last night?" he asked.

"No, I haven't," said Joan coldly, "and do you know why?"

"Um, no," said Rutspud.

"Because I spent the night in a police station. The whole night. Locked in a cell and then questioned by a bunch of idiots."

Felix raised his head above his laptop screen. "You were arrested?"

"It brought back some very unhappy memories," said Joan.

"Wow," said Rutspud.

"What do you mean, 'wow'? It wasn't a fun thing to do."

"Did you get to ride in the police car?"

"Well yes," said Joan, "they picked me up just outside the Ferret estate. I shared a car with the couple that we saw in the bathroom." She grimaced with distaste. "His face was still damp, and I could smell what it was damp with."

Felix gave a small snort of laughter and Joan shot him a look. His head shot down behind the protection of his screen like a rabbit that had just seen the silhouette of an eagle cross the sun.

"And did they put the siren on?" asked Rutspud.

"Yes, they did," said Joan, but I really think you're focusing on the wrong –"

"And the lights as well?"

"Yes, but –"

"That is so cool!" said Rutspud.

"No, it's not cool!" yelled Joan. "It was very unpleasant. They assumed I was part of that horrible party and said that my armour was, and I quote, 'some sort of kinky cosplay for the dirty old buggers'. They even told me to knock off the fake French accent."

Surely that's not actually a crime?" said Rutspud.

"That's what I said, but they wanted to make sure that I didn't have drugs on me and they questioned me about what I had seen."

Felix swivelled his chair around, suddenly interested. "What did you tell them?"

"Obviously, I told them that I was simply going for a walk along the lane and I saw nothing," said Joan wearily. "Eventually they had to let me go."

"Well you need to catch up on all the fun," said Felix, turning back to his screen. "The 'net is buzzing, obviously. We have a backlash movement and a series of viral memes."

Joan looked at Rutspud for a translation.

"It's really big news," said Rutspud. "The church is becoming a laughing stock. The Vatican has been silent on the matter, which people are interpreting in different ways. Meanwhile, the world's computer users are commenting on the matter. A couple of memes are coming to the fore."

"Stop saying meme. It's not a word," said Joan.

"It is a word. It was coined by Dawkins to describe the spread of an idea. It's based on the word gene," said Felix.

"What's a Dawkins?" said Joan.

"He's a famous and hilariously angry atheist," said Rutspud.

"Right," said Felix, "and he coined the term to explain why religion is so popular. Obviously, there's no rational explanation."

Joan ignored the dig but was none the wiser. Felix had managed to explain in a way that was both baffling and insulting. No wonder Rutspud seemed to get on so well with him.

"If we show you what the sisters are up to, you'll soon understand," said Felix.

Joan looked round. None of the sisters or their talking hand puppets were in the kitchen. She had, in fact, seen none of them anywhere this morning.

Felix propped his laptop on his knees so that Joan could see the screen.

"You have a camera feed in this house?" asked Joan, shocked as she recognised this very kitchen.

"No. The sisters have uploaded it to the internet. Look."

Joan watched as Sister Anne stared grimly at the screen from a seat at the kitchen table with Tommy Chuckles at her side. Tommy bent down and picked up a piece of cardboard from the table. He lifted it up to the camera.

My love for God is a pure and wholesome love

He put that one down and picked up another.

I don't need a church that is run by corrupt perverts to love my God

Sister Anne shook her head in mute agreement. Tommy picked up another message.

#notmychurch

There followed another set of cards held up by Sister Valerie and Bubbles, ending with the same message.

"Do you see how people are distancing themselves from the Church?" said Felix. "*#notmychurch* is a meme, and lots of people are using it."

"I can't say I blame them," said Joan. "I would feel the same way. No, wait. I *do* feel the same way. But where are they going with these placards?"

Three sleek Eddy-Cabs pulled up outside the Birmingham cathedral diocesan offices in the centre of the city. There was a crowd of protestors on the pavement outside. Many waved placards. Some of them had hand puppets too. The Hooflandian soldiers (one 'centurion' and one 'Terminator') Clovenhoof had brought with him created a protective barrier as he battled his way to the door. Nerys, Ben, Narinda, Prime Minister Lennox and various other flunkeys had to fend for themselves.

As office security separated protestors from visitors and made sure only the right people got in, a man with a pastel suit and a perfect smile greeted them.

"Hello, Mr Clovenhoof! You are looking dapper, dear sir! And Freddy doesn't say that to everyone."

"Feeling good, Freddy," said Clovenhoof with a grin. "Love the welcoming committee."

Freddy gave the protestors outside a complex frown. "People are entitled to their opinions, aren't they, I suppose. And it's no good bottling things up inside."

"Better out than in," said Clovenhoof.

"Oh, you are a card, Mr Clovenhoof."

"Yes, I am. So, where's this meeting?"

Freddy gestured to the lifts. "The... remains of the Church Commissioners and the national strategy steering group are waiting for you on the fourth floor." He smiled brightly at everyone else, some of whom were still checking themselves to make sure they had got through the mob unscathed. "We weren't expecting such a large delegation – it's great being out with mates, though, isn't it? – so if I can ask you all to stay down here."

"Sending him off alone?" said Ben dubiously.

"I really think I ought to go too," said Nerys.

"Oh, he'll be fine, silly. Off you go, Jeremy. I will take good care of your friends. Freddy makes a double choco mocha that is simply to die for! Seriously. If I was taking a trip to Dignitas, it would be my last request: yummy scrummy choco-coffee and then bring on the pentobarbital. It is *that* good."

Clovenhoof stepped into the lift.

"Don't say anything stupid!" Nerys shouted after him.

"I'm just going to share my wisdom!" Clovenhoof shouted back. "What could possibly go wrong?"

Joan strode with a pace that Rutspud struggled to match.

He wanted to believe it was because she was still buzzing from a ride in a cop car like some gangland bad girl, but he sadly suspected it was because she was inexplicably angry about the whole thing.

"And what are we doing now?" he said, as they hurried along the Chester Road.

"Looking for Bishop Ken," she said.

"Because?"

"Because he deserves to know what members of his Church are doing. He is a good man."

"Are we taking him for breakfast?" he asked hopefully.

"That would be a very charitable thing for us to do," she said, her tone softening slightly.

"Something greasy and unwholesome?" suggested Rutspud.

She gave him a sideways look. "Demons don't need to eat," she said.

"No, but if you torment him with muesli, a demon might hanker for some of the good stuff."

Joan made a dubious noise. Rutspud pointed ahead.

"There he is, playing with holes again."

They approached Ken, who was scratching at the grass verge with his trowel and muttering darkly as a buried house brick impeded his progress.

"Morning, Bishop Ken," said Joan brightly.

"Bishop, am I?" said the man, scratching his filthy beard. "And what is a bishop, eh?"

"Bit early in the morning for philosophy," said Rutspud. "We wanted to take you for breakfast."

"Bishop," said the man, straightening up with an audible crack of his vertebrae. "From the Old English 'biscop' and that from the Greek 'episkopos'. One who sees from above, an overseer. And what should I be overseeing?"

"Bacon and eggs and a dirty great sausage?" suggested Rutspud.

The man's eyes positively gleamed. "Hot dang. Why didn't you say so before, eh?"

Twenty minutes later, at the Sutton Park pub, Ken and Rutspud were tucking into glistening mounds of fried food, while Joan looked mildly queasy. Rutspud couldn't be sure if that was caused by the food, or the re-telling of the appalling scandal that now beset the church.

Ken's frown deepened. "When I left my job, there was an excess of bean-counting and bureaucracy, but how did they get from there to butt plugs, and all of those other things that you mentioned?"

Joan shook her head. "I don't pretend to understand, Bishop Ken, but I think that your app might have had something to do with it."

"It's basic human behaviour," said Rutspud. "Certain people will behave one way in front of others and another way when they think that nobody's looking. Christians are just the same, but they think that God's watching, so they behave *more* of the time. What we've been seeing here is a cast-iron excuse for Christians to behave badly, knowing that they can square things with God. If their conscience is satisfied by the forgiveness that they get from PrayPal then they can sin as much as they like."

Ken paused in demolishing his fried eggs and looked troubled. "Then I am partly to blame for this," he said.

"No," said Rutspud. "Nobody here is bishop bashing." He watched Joan and Ken. Not a flicker of comprehension. "Bashing the bishop is not what we're about." Nope. "I've been a bishop basher in my time but it's not something I'm proud of." He looked from one to the other, both none-the-wiser. He chalked up a minor win for smut and innuendo. "Point is, bish, the people who commit these sins are committing them because they choose to do so."

"No, I must do something. I *will* do something," said Ken. "Although I'm not sure what. Not yet."

336

CHAPTER FORTY-SEVEN

A tall stick insect of a woman met Clovenhoof at the fourth-floor lifts, curtly introduced herself as Poppy Tollerman and led him through to a meeting room. The room was a disappointment. Clovenhoof had expected to find an audience chamber furnished with polished wood and gilt-covered furniture, perhaps even a throne or two, with Renaissance paintings (or the best knock offs Birmingham could source) along the walls. Instead, the dull walls were hung with photo prints of happy Christians doing good works in sunnier countries and the meeting table and chairs could have been bought from IKEA.

There were three men waiting for them.

"Okra Boddington you know," said Poppy, gesturing to Nerys's boyfriend-cum-slave. "This is Graham Duncan of the Church of England's national strategy committee."

"Ah, the one who was disappointed he didn't get invited to the party," said Clovenhoof. The round-faced man blushed deeply but shook his head.

"I am here as a representative of the Church's marketing committee and to speak for the Church Commissioners who are still in post," said Poppy. "And agreeing to chair this extraordinary meeting, we are grateful to have His Lordship Dominic Anyange, bishop of Coventry."

Bishop Dominic stood to politely gesture to Clovenhoof to sit. The white-haired man had a warmly open face, the kind given easy to laughs, though these seemed in short supply right. Clovenhoof sat at the head of the table, directly facing the bishop along its length.

"I am very glad you could join us today," said Bishop Dominic as Poppy took her own seat. "There are a great many Christians who would like to meet the man who created PrayPal." The tone of that last sentence was unmistakeable.

"Hey," grinned Clovenhoof, reaching for a carafe of drink that disappointingly turned out to be water. "I'm only one of the PrayPal guys. I didn't even write it. I'm just the one with the desire for fame, the ability to sell myself to the world, and the balls."

"The balls to... what?" said Graham.

"Just the balls," said Clovenhoof. "I hear your church attendance figures are plummeting, that the collection plates are coming back empty. You're losing ground to the Muslims, the Catholics and the Jedi every day. But you can't blame that entirely on us."

"No," agreed Bishop Dominic. Poppy passed down a spiral bound booklet of financial data. Clovenhoof didn't know what to make of it but he reckoned he could make a decent frisbee of the laminated cover.

"Our congregations are ageing, our church families shrinking rather than growing," said the bishop. "Young Okra Boddington spoke very... passionately about some of your ideas to reinvigorate the church."

"W-well, they were certainly remarkable," mumbled Okra. "That is to say, th-th-that we could at least –"

"We would be very interested in what you have to say," said Bishop Dominic. "We perhaps need some of your entrepreneurial spirit and insight."

"Okay," said Clovenhoof and leapt to his feet. "I'm going to need a flipchart."

"Certainly," said the bishop and Okra stood up to move one from the corner of the room into position.

"Cos if this meeting gets any duller, we're gonna have to break out for a game of pictionary or hangman." He grabbed a pen and drew four blanks, a slash and four more blanks in preparation. "Idea one!" he declared loudly. "Coffee and Wi-Fi."

"Many of our churches have pop-up coffee shops and we're looking at a national programme to get Wi-Fi."

"Not enough!" said Clovenhoof.

"Eh?" said Graham.

Clovenhoof wrote an 'A' on the hangman board.

"Good call, Graham. How many churches do you have?"

"In the UK, approximately twelve and a half thousand," said Poppy.

"How many Costa Coffee shops are there in the UK?"

"Um, I don't know."

"Three and a half thousand. I googled it. If you convert all your churches to coffee shops with decent Wi-Fi, you'll outnumber the competition four to one."

"And there's Starbucks too," Graham pointed out.

"No one cares about them because they're shit," said Clovenhoof. "You think people go to coffee shops because they like coffee? No one really likes coffee. They just think they ought to. It's like BBC Four or couscous or jazz. People want good Wi-Fi, soft seats and a place to sit out of the rain. And they'd pay for that. You need to make that transformation in all your churches."

Okra was concerned. "Al-although the expense of that, if we consider, that is, the financial impact –"

"We're looking at the closure of up to forty percent of those churches in the next financial year," said Graham, "so those costs will come right down."

"Closing churches, Graham?" snapped Clovenhoof. "Closing churches! Are you mad as well as sexually depraved? You don't sell when times are hard. If The Game has taught me anything it's that you hold onto everything you've got and push on through. Borrow, scrape and mortgage to the hilt but never give an inch."

"What's The Game?" said Poppy.

"Oh, it's the best. You should play it some time. It's the world in microcosm. You roll the dice and scoot around the board and you buy up properties and then charge other people if they land on them."

"Oh, sort of like Monopo –"

"No, Poppy," said Clovenhoof firmly. "It's not like any other game. If it was, I'm sure there'd be some sort of copyright infringement and someone could get sued. This is definitely different. Do not close any of your churches. Those ones you're thinking of closing, convert them first. I want a first-class coffee house in every backwoods and backward rural community in the country."

"Nonetheless," said Bishop Dominic with a gentle avuncular smile, "this would constitute an enormous outlay of money and we have little scope for acquiring new funds quickly."

"Very well," said Clovenhoof. "Idea two will cost you virtually nothing and make you millions. Do you know if churches can still offer sanctuary?"

"Why?" said Graham.

"Left-field guess," said Clovenhoof, writing a 'Y' on the flipchart and drawing the beginnings of a hangman. "Bold though. Churches could traditionally offer sanctuary to criminals wanted by the law."

"Abolished in the sixteen twenties," said Poppy.

"My legal team thinks they can create a workaround," lied Clovenhoof. "We offer traditional sanctuary to criminals and safe passage to the nearest port. I think that's how it worked."

Okra was intrigued. "I-I-I –"

"Much better guess," said Clovenhoof, putting an 'I' on the flipchart.

_ I _ _ / _ _ A _ _

"I can't see how that would make us any money," said Bishop Dominic.

"Because we're going to monetise it. You have men on the run all over the country. You can't take a walk across Wales or the Highlands of Scotland without bumping into one every ten minutes. How much would they pay for a one-month breather and a ticket out of Fortress Britain? We're talking tens of thousands of pounds."

"Apart from the immorality of it all," said Bishop Dominic, "it seems a ridiculous business model. Unbelievably ad hoc and so unlikely to be used."

"Fixed with decent advertising," said Clovenhoof. "A leaflet drop over every major prison in the UK with a map showing the location of your nearest church."

"No, no, too unpalatable," said the bishop.

"Idea three then. Best of both worlds. Relatively cheap. Definitely legal. You buy some old camera equipment and rig it up in the church and you let people know by word of mouth that a popular reality TV show is being filmed there."

"Y-y-you..." bumbled Okra.

Clovenhoof wrote a 'U' on the board and drew more of the hangman.

"Nope."

Poppy leaned forward. "You think a TV production company will be interested in producing a reality TV show –"

"A *sympathetic* television show," put in the bishop.

"Yes, a sympathetic reality TV show about one of our church communities?"

"God, no," laughed Clovenhoof. "Your Church is a shitty stick right now. No one will touch it, Poppy. I said you should tell the church members that there's a reality TV show being filmed there. The cameras are just to convince them of the lie. It will bring the flock pouring back with the promise and hope of TV stardom."

"Mmmm," said Poppy doubtfully.

Clovenhoof put an 'M' among the other incorrect guesses and finished off the hangman's scaffold.

"And on which of our churches do you propose to inflict this lie?" said Bishop Dominic.

"All of them, of course," said Clovenhoof. "Every single one of them."

Graham was shaking his head. "I just don't see it. I don't get it."

"Oh, come on. It's dead easy."

"No. No."

"Piss flaps."

"I beg your pardon?" said Bishop Dominic, his voice and eyebrows shooting up.

"Piss flaps," said Clovenhoof and filled in the final letters on the hangman. "And I thought I'd picked an easy one to start with." He tutted. "Well, I have got one more idea I'd like to share with you this morning."

"I sincerely hope it's better than the others," said the bishop.

Clovenhoof treated them to his widest and most devilish grin. "It is," he said. "And you will love it."

Joan and Rutspud left Bishop Ken in the pub, mopping up the egg and grease from both his and Rutspud's plates with a slice of bread and headed back for the mission society house where they might again hope to impress the importance of disabling or destroying the PrayPal app on Felix. Rutspud was wittering on about the apparent hilarity of the phrase 'bashing the bishop' but Joan wasn't listening.

Her attention was taken by the angry crowd gathered outside the brick-built church next to the pub. There were dozens of people shouting and battering at the door and waving dubious placards.

No butts! Keep sex toys out of church!

Sandals not Scandals!

Thou Shalt Not Covet Thy Neighbour's Ass!

As they stood and watched, the door gave way and the crowd surged inside the church with a triumphant bellowing. Moments later a huge wooden pew crashed through a nearby window and out into the car park, stained glass skittering across the pavement as the pew splintered.

"It's not even a Church of England church!" Joan exclaimed in exasperation. "It's even got the words 'Catholic' in big letters above the door!"

"You can't stop a mob with reasoned argument," said Rutspud. There was a series of thudding noises that they felt through the ground. "What in Hell's name…?"

"Step away," said Joan.

Another window smashed, but this time, an enormous piece of statuary came through the glass, and wedged in place, teetering heavily on the bottom of the window.

"It's Mary," said Joan. "Well, not in person, of course, nobody knows where she is."

"Well if that stone version of her comes down from there, she's going to make a hell of an impact," said Rutspud.

Joan was already running. She crashed through the door of the church and held her sword aloft.

"What do you all think you're doing?" she yelled.

There was a group who were using another pew to try and tip the Madonna statue out of the window, and another group who were hurling prayer books, kneelers and altar paraphernalia around in a general attempt to mess the place up.

It took a few moments for them all to hear Joan above the noise that they were making. Joan spotted Rutspud from the corner of her eye. He seemed to be looking for something in a dark corner, but Joan couldn't tell what, then a spotlight blazed into life, illuminating her from above. Light glinted off her broadsword and a small but discernible gasp went up from the crowd.

"You are upset and you feel let down. I can understand that," shouted Joan, "but this is not the way to make things better. You need to stop causing damage and endangering life. Good people don't do those things, and I think you are all good people."

Joan saw Rutspud cradling his head in his hands and shaking it gently, but the set of her jaw was firm. She had to believe in the innate goodness of people. Getting swept away with some sort of lynch mob mentality might explain what was going on here, but someone had to stop them.

"Will you join me now in stepping away from violence?" she asked the crowd. "Walk away from this and go home."

There was a long, long moment where nothing happened. Joan really couldn't gauge the mood of the crowd, but gradually there was something like a heartfelt sigh throughout the church and people dropped the things that that they'd picked up, instead of throwing them. As soon as they had changed their minds about the destructive rioting, there was an embarrassed and yet strangely polite scramble to get out. Everyone was silent apart from the occasional "no, after you". The church took less than two minutes to empty completely, leaving Joan and Rutspud alone.

Joan heard sirens approaching. Her eyes met Rutspud's and without speaking they both ran for the door and didn't stop until they were well away from the church. Joan looked at Rutspud who held something in his hand.

"What's that?" she asked.

He held out a rock, but when he turned it over Joan saw that it was the broken head of a gargoyle. Joan took it and held it alongside Rutspud's head, comparing the two. Rutspud struck a pose and attempted his best film star pout.

"Uncanny," she said.

CHAPTER FORTY-EIGHT

Bishop Dominic Anyange scratched his grey bonce and looked at Clovenhoof down the length of the meeting table.

"And when you say you want to 'buy us out', you mean...?"

Clovenhoof gave him a stupid look. "I mean buy you out. You invited me here today because Okra knows you're desperate. The Church is in dire straits. And I don't mean you're getting money for nothing. As a business enterprise, you were slowly going down the pan for ages and this – this!" He thrust his hands at the large window overlooking Pigeon Park and St Philip's Cathedral through which one could faintly hear a mob of angry Christians – "This is the nail in your coffin."

"That is a rash oversimplification and not at all true," said Bishop Dominic.

"W-well, in truth, Your Lordship," said Okra. "If... if w-we take a look at –"

"It is true?" said the bishop.

"Woolies. BHS. Carillion. You're just the latest big business about to go under," said Clovenhoof.

"And you're offering to inject some funds in?" said Graham.

"I'm not investing, Graham. I'm not giving you my money to spend. I want to buy you out."

"But we are not a company, Mr Clovenhoof," argued Poppy. "We do not have shareholders. Our properties are not held by individuals or a family firm or a trust. The Church of England is an entity unto itself."

"Piffle," said Clovenhoof. "If a new church is built, that money comes from somewhere. The debts you have are marked against something."

"The Church does own things it can sell," said Graham, "redundant churches, halls, residential properties, tracts of farmland..."

"Yes, I want those," said Clovenhoof. "And everything else."

"E-e-everything else?" said Okra.

"Your buildings will become mine. Your employees become mine. Your intellectual properties, your processes, your traditions and copyrights: they all become mine."

"But the Church of England sits at the heart of the worldwide Anglican church," said Poppy. "Damn it all! It is the Anglican Church. Its communion stretches across six continents. It's not just the ruddy Church of England."

"Fine," said Clovenhoof with a shrug. "Slice off the English bit – I'll have that – and let the rest of the world get on being Anglicans without you."

"There would be uproar," said Poppy. "They wouldn't stand for it."

"Well, you say that," said Dominic thoughtfully. "I can see some of the American Episcopalians and the African churches being quite keen for us to go our own way."

"We are sort of like the embarrassing liberal hippy father," nodded Graham.

"And what would your role be in the management of the Church?" asked Dominic.

"I'd be the CEO," said Clovenhoof. "The boss, the managing director, the chairman of the board."

"B-but that would make you the, well," said Okra, "in truth, your role –"

"You want to be the Archbishop of Canterbury?" said Dominic.

"Fuck, no," said Clovenhoof, disgusted. "I just want to own the thing. I don't want to join. No, I'll be appointing my own bishops."

"But that's the role of the monarch!" said Poppy.

"And is that for sale too?" asked Clovenhoof. "I'd look good in a crown."

Dominic laughed. It was a laugh like a rush of air from a fizzy pop bottle. He had to laugh or possibly explode.

"You have certainly been entertaining, Mr Clovenhoof, and I thank you for that. I suppose that you're either one of those wealthy eccentrics we hear so much about or you're rich enough to think that our time is worth wasting with a practical joke." He stood and there was a clear authoritative finality in his body language. "Thank you for coming."

Clovenhoof wasn't budging. Time to break out the numbers. Despite his constant pretence otherwise, he was a former angel and one of the things angels excelled at was numbers. They were among the few entities that could count up to infinity.

"On the plus side, you are one of the largest landowners in the United Kingdom –"

"Th-that is apart from, a-and not limited to –"

"Yes, the National Trust have trounced you on that score and done better with quality tea rooms. You have property. You have investments. Although these are all, sadly, legal and ethical investments. You also have a hardcore of committed members. Those are your pluses and worth hundreds of millions in the bank." He took a big theatrical sigh. "But then there's those minuses. Many of your churches stand empty and if you sell them they'll only be converted into second homes in the country for wealthy arseholes. Your personal stock is tumbling. Right now, no one wants your money. Your hardcore congregation is either dying of old age or currently waving angry placards. Your senior management has been decimated. Your leadership is gone. No cash, no credibility and no future."

He dipped into his ultra-black smoking jacket and after struggling for a moment to see where the pocket was, pulled out a cheque book.

"I will buy it all. I will take on your debts and scandals and build a new shining city on the hill – well, on the waste ground behind the Boldmere Oak."

Bishop Dominic's face wrestled with itself, trying to know what to say.

"But why?" it eventually said. "You don't strike me as a man of the faith."

"Man? No. Of the faith? Absolutely. I think the Almighty above would be very... interested," he grinned, "to see what I am doing right now. But as to why, let's just say I will enjoy utilising the tax-free status that a recognised religion will bring."

"Is that all?" said Poppy.

"Oh," he added, "and did I mention I would be paying enormously generous management bonuses to compensate you as part of the buy-out?"

Back in the society mission kitchen, Felix (who was evidently warming to the notion of being kept in genial custody) was keen to show Joan and Rutspud the latest developments.

"Guys, you have no idea how it's escalated," he said.

"Oh, I think perhaps we have a bit of an inkling," said Rutspud, as he carefully placed the gargoyle on the table.

Joan and Rutspud crowded around Felix's screen as he showed them footage of rioting in churches up and down the country.

"Rioting's a strange thing," observed Felix. "It's super contagious, like Ebola times ten."

Joan watched in dismay as mounted police clashed with protestors at York Minster. "Once the first few churches were shown on the news being smashed up, it spread like wildfire. This one is odd, though. It's not like the usual riots, where scumbags smash up JD Sports and steal trainers. Not much you can steal from churches."

Live footage showed a man running through the streets of York carrying a silver chalice in each hand.

"People surely don't believe an app can forgive them for all of these things," Joan said.

Felix turned to her. "I don't know what you think forgiveness is."

"It's the absolution of sin," she said.

He made an unconvinced noise. "You do know that some of us don't believe in sin. And when I say 'some of us', I do mean most people."

"How can you not believe in sin?" she said.

"Quite easily," said the programmer. "It's just some bollocks made up by religious types to make people feel bad about themselves and to keep order in our guilt-based society."

"So, you don't believe these people are doing anything wrong?"

"Wrong?" Felix blinked and pushed the hair away from his eyes. "There are things society doesn't approve of and there are things that are against the law. Right? Wrong? These are just words. Now, I'm perfectly able to forgive someone but that just means I put aside my anger."

"For a man who wrote a forgiveness app, you sure don't buy into the forgiveness business," said Rutspud.

Felix placed a finger on the image of the man in York with the stolen silver. "I forgive him." A police officer ran from off screen, tackled the man around the waist and dragged him to the ground. "He's still going to prison."

Joan wanted to say that she was in favour of forgiving everyone, that punishment in general, particularly the kind that was meted out by Hell was, by and large, pointless. And then she thought about the vile Claymore Ferret and his ilk who had caused so much upset and distress in the Celestial City.

"There does have to be justice," she said. "Now, if your app could provide forgiveness and the appropriate penance as well..."

"Penance?" said Felix. "As in – what? – a bunch of hail Marys?"

Joan grimaced. "I think hail Marys might not be sufficient for some of these people."

Felix tapped rapidly on his laptop and bewildering lines of gobbledegook scrolled past. It seemed to interest Rutspud greatly.

"Are you doing that?" asked Joan. "Are you making them pay?"

Felix nodded. "Yes, I think we can do that."

Joan looked at the gargoyle on the table. "Keep an eye on them for me," she said, patting it on the head as she left the room.

CHAPTER FORTY-NINE

A mere five days after sealing the deal to buy out the ailing Church of England, Clovenhoof was ready to show the world his vision.

He pulled aside the little curtain so that the journalists assembled in the presidential reception hall (the downstairs bar of the Boldmere Oak) could feast their eyes upon the scale model for the spiritual heart of his new empire. The model church stretched across a table that could have hosted a five-a-side tournament. Outside, builders clattered noisily as they assembled the materials to make it a living reality.

Clovenhoof's team of designers, engineers and feng-shui consultants had worked through coffee-fuelled days and drug-fuelled nights to create this model. When Clovenhoof had reviewed it this morning he'd tweaked it a little bit so that it would make the maximum impact. He'd jacked up the middle bit by inserting house bricks from underneath, and he'd given the side of the building some rakish dragon wings formed from rows of beer mats. The overall effect was of a slumbering dinosaur lying on a coloured box. Clovenhoof had insisted that traditional stained glass was too restrictive. He demanded that the architects work out something with lasers or somesuch so that he could change the designs and colours at will. He'd also decided that the traditional single spire just wasn't enough. He wanted six. Bells would be put in one of them, to satisfy the traditionalists. The second would contain a cinema. At least one of them would contain an exhibition space. He'd already pencilled in 'Smoking jackets through the ages'.

"Now, ladies and gentlemen, you've been invited here today to witness the launch of the Hooflandian Church. This will be the new seat of power for the Church of England, which I now own."

"Is this a stunt, Mr Clovenhoof? Surely you can't own the Church of England?" asked a blonde woman who pushed a microphone forward.

"I do own the Church of England," he said. "Call it a stunt if you like, but quite honestly, a stunt's only really a stunt if there's bodily functions involved. I can demonstrate once we're done here with a quick blast of *Oops I did it again*."

Another microphone shot forward, this one attached to an older man with a serious expression. "Was this your plan all along to get a stake in the legitimate religion business through your app business?"

"Um, might have been," said Clovenhoof, who couldn't honestly say he'd ever go in for 'plans' as such.

"Are you the Uber of the faith world?" called another.

"I've no idea what that means," he replied, "but you can put it in your papers. Now, let's get back to my amazing church, shall we? It will set the standard for changes that I'm putting in place in every local church, however small. Free Wi-Fi as standard, comfortable seating available in the premium areas. A coffee shop with all of the standard pointless variations on a cup of coffee, and a few new ones that I have invented myself. There will be samples of the Chocco Dongo available for those of you brave enough to try. We will have free screenings of all major sporting events and 'Fish and Chip Fridays' will be kicking things off as our first themed catering campaign. Questions?"

"Can worshippers expect any significant changes?"

"One of my advisors will be tasked with updating day to day operations, including services. We'll keep the parts that people like. Our work with focus groups suggests that Christmas carols should stay, for example, but we'll need to cut out the dullness. You can expect to see new-style weddings and christenings coming soon."

"Will you be appointing a new Archbishop?" said the blonde woman.

"Ah, very pleased that you asked," said Clovenhoof. "Step forward Nerys Thomas, who from this moment is the new Archbishop of Birmingham."

Nerys sashayed forward pouting and blowing kisses to the crowd. "Hello Birmingham!" she shouted, smiling widely and turning to each of the photographers in turn. "I want you to know that I'm thrilled to be your new archbishop, and I can't wait to get stuck in to the role."

"It's great to see a woman in the role. What issues interest you, Nerys?" shouted a voice from the back.

"The whole thing needs an overhaul," said Nerys. "Seriously, have you seen the clothes? I want to start with a uniform that works for me, as a woman."

"Right on, sister, smash the patriarchy!" came the voice from the back and an excited babble arose.

"As you can see," said Clovenhoof, "construction is underway already on my new church and it should be ready for you all to visit very soon. We're setting the pace of change for the Church of Hooflandia, and you need to keep up!"

Rutspud made two cups of tea and put one on the kitchen table by Felix's hand. The human had been working on modifying the app for several days and making few comments on what he was doing, apart from a little sub-vocal muttering about chunks of code. Rutspud was a tech-savvy demon, he understood computers, but watching Felix at work was like the greatest Victorian surgeon watching a geneticist unfold the human genome.

"What are you thinking?" said Rutspud, sipping his wonderfully scalding-hot drink. "You're making a modification, yeah?"

Felix nodded. "Barely any at all. It's just a question of what we do with the input data, where we store it, where we send it. We can literally turn the tables on all of these people and their secret sinning."

Rutspud saw a gap in understanding opening up. Not so much a gap, as a chasm that would surely create some difficult explaining later on. "You know, when Joan talked about fixing things, I think she meant that you should just turn it off."

"Yeah, yeah," said Felix with a dismissive flap of his hand. "Your friend is all about damage limitation." He turned to Rutspud with a broad smile. "Whereas you, I suspect, are all for making things more interesting. Am I right?"

Rutspud couldn't fault his assessment. "Well yes, that does sound like me." He shunted his chair forward to see better. "What is it that you can do to make it more interesting then?"

"There's a log of every sin that's been forgiven by the app, and which user committed each sin," said Felix. "It seems to me that it's time everyone was accountable for their actions. I'm setting a countdown clock for ten days from now, and when the time is up, I'm going to broadcast all of that data."

"You're planning to expose everyone's sins for the world to see?" Rutspud asked.

"Yup," said Felix. "Broadcast through the app, the app's social media pages and in a text file dump to news agency servers."

"Wow," said Rutspud.

Felix typed for a few moments and then hit the enter button with a flourish. "Done. A message is going out right now to all users to tell them what's going to happen."

Rutspud thought about the implications.

"PrayPal has just gone from being a super hip, best-selling app to being the most shitty and vindictive gossip on the planet."

"Yes, it has," said Felix with a cheesy grin on his face and picked up his cup of tea.

"And what's that going to do with your company stock value, huh?"

Felix shrugged. The cheesy grin wasn't going anywhere.

"You think I was ever in this for the money?"

Rutspud stared at him for a long second. He raised his mug and clinked it against the young programmer's.

"Here's to being poor but happy."

"I'm sorry, Okra," said Nerys, turning to admire herself in a full-length mirror while world-renowned designer Winnebago Kiss Kiss pinned her robes into a snugger more curvaceous fit. "I just don't have time for that kind of relationship. Archbishopping is a demanding gig and my church comes first. Now, if you want to see me, you can come to the opening service at the Church of Hooflandia."

She killed the call and sighed heavily.

"You know," said Ben from the games table where he was busy making notes and consulting his laptop, "for a man who barely speaks, that Okra sure opens up when you try to dump him."

"I'm just going to have to block his number." She looked down at the crouching designer. "When the robes of office are done, I want bikini, monokini, catsuit and thigh-length leather boots to co-ordinate."

Winnebago mumbled something muffled by the pins between her lips.

"That's right," said Nerys. "This archbishop is never going to be seen in the same outfit twice." The phone rang again. "If that's him, I'm going to hire a hitman."

"I'll do it for free if you ask nicely," said President Clovenhoof, slouching in his throne.

Nerys put the phone to her ear. "Call for you," she said to Clovenhoof and tossed him the phone.

"Hoof me!" he yelled into the receiver.

"Oh Jeremy," wailed the caller. "I need to level with you."

"Alice? Is that you?"

"I'm so sorry," said Alice Calhoun, "but when you didn't come round for so long I decided to find someone else to be my gigoloafer. I've been seeing other men, Jeremy." There was the sound of her blowing her nose while Clovenhoof pondered this. "If it's any consolation, none of them were a patch on you," she added.

"It's all right Alice. I should have made time for you. What made you call today?" asked Clovenhoof.

"Everyone's owning up to things," she said, sniffling, "since their secrets are coming out anyway. I heard everyone else being honest and I just couldn't live with myself anymore."

"Listen, I'll see you soon Alice," he said. "Farting on my own isn't as much fun anyway."

Clovenhoof ended the call, bounced to his hoofs and strode out to the balcony to admire the erection of his new church. It was amazing how quickly steel girders, pre-fab concrete slabs and a shitload of plasterboard could be raised up into a facsimile of a grand and ancient building.

"Confessions! People are making confessions," he said, savouring the words.

"Seven days until the sin list is made public," said Ben, looking up from his computer. "Twitter is on fire with it, people tweeting their guilty secrets in a pre-emptive strike before the broadcast of PrayPal's sins."

"Numerous hashtags are trending," said Nerys, "like #comingclean, #confession and #mybad. We're seeing press releases from every C-lister you've never heard of."

"And should we be doing something about that?" said Clovenhoof.

"We've got the PR team working to reinforce our message that this is the work of a rogue programmer. Winkstein has helped by vanishing into thin air," said Nerys.

"I mean, should we be taking advantage of this sudden guilt-a-thon?" said Clovenhoof. "Can we monetise confession?"

"I'm not sure how," said Nerys.

"You see the problem with this book," said Ben, looking up from the mass of notes on the table, "is that there are so many rules and edicts that I'm sure there must be something we could use but I don't know where to find it."

"What book?" said Clovenhoof.

Ben held up a weighty copy of the King James Bible.

"No, Ben," said Nerys, "we don't want to know what the Good Book says."

"We don't?"

"No, we want it to say what we want it to say."

"What? Do a rewrite?"

"What it needs to say," put in Clovenhoof, "is that Hooflandia is the centre of the bloody universe. That this church –" He pointed out the window at his magnificent burgeoning erection "– is the centre of the bloody universe."

"And I'm the rightful archbishop," added Nerys. "Like it was my destiny or something."

"Okay, okay," nodded Ben, jotting down some notes. "I mean this is music to my ears because the inconsistencies were driving me nuts. Get this. Here in Chronicles there are one point one million fighting men in Israel. Then here, in Samuel, there are only eight hundred thousand fighting men. At the same battle! Ridiculous!"

"Typos creep into books all the time," said Nerys.

"Not when it's meant to be the word of God! There's so much that needs fixing."

"Ooh," said Nerys, wagging a finger and nearly ripping her robes out of the dress designer's hands. "Can you put more female characters in the new version?"

"You want more women in the rewritten version of the Bible?"

"More speaking roles," said Nerys and the pin-lipped dress designer mumbled in wordless agreement.

"And it has to pass the Bechdel test," she added. "At least two named female characters who get to talk to each other about something other than men."

"The virgin Mary and Mary Magdalene," said Clovenhoof helpfully.

"Right. Beef up their parts. Maybe change one of their names so people don't get them mixed up. And they can't just be talking about Jesus. I want them going off and having their own adventures."

"Sort of a spin-off gospel?" said Ben.

"Right. Except it's not a spin-off. It's totally central. Doing their thing."

"There was a Gospel of Mary," said Clovenhoof.

"Are you going to go all *Da Vinci Code* on us now?" said Nerys.

"No, it's true. There's lots of books that didn't make it into the Bible. You think the Church Fathers didn't pick and choose what they wanted?"

"I'll look them up," said Ben, bending with enthusiasm to his new task.

"Sure thing, off you go," said Clovenhoof. "Now, back to me. What's the media saying about my wonderful new church, Nerys?"

"Well, the headlines are –"

"In a Yorkshire accent, Nerys, please."

Nerys gave him a look. "You'll need to find a different employee to humiliate like that, someone who's prepared to abandon all dignity."

"Did I mention that Hermès had been in touch?" asked Clovenhoof airily. "Something about someone of my status bypassing the waiting list for their new limited-edition handbag."

"By 'eck, tha's mebbe onta summat there, Jeremy," said Nerys, contorting her face to get the vowels out. "Let's 'ave a look at t'eadlines, shall we pet?"

"Is pet Yorkshire?" asked Ben. "Surely it's more Geordie."

Nerys had already gone red in the face as she concentrated on her mangled accent, and she turned to Ben in fury. "If you're such an expert, you do it!"

"But I don't want a Hermès handbag," said Ben primly, fixated on his work.

"It's fine Nerys, you can stop the accent. I want to be able to understand what you're saying," said Clovenhoof.

"Fine," huffed Nerys. "Well the PrayPal news is taking up a lot of space. Everyone's gearing up for a massive banquet of sordid tidbits. The tabloids are all bringing out an extended special edition with the top thousand celebrity sins listed."

"Cool," said Clovenhoof, "although someone's got to read through all of those broadcast sins. That's a lot of reading."

"So, there's quite a few pieces that talk about crunching the numbers. They go on a lot about Big Data and artificial intelligence and yadda yadda maths stuff, but the main thing is that they seem confident that they can dish the celebrity dirt in time for the morning edition. There will be a Sunday special analysis of who's done what as well."

"Think about how we can use this when we open the doors of our church," said Clovenhoof. "The big screens should have a scrolling feed with all the latest updates. A multimedia sermon should be a lot of fun."

CHAPTER FIFTY

Joan was stuffing the last of her belongings into her rucksack when Rutspud knocked on her door.

"Ready?"

She shouldered the pack. "I guess so. I need to say goodbye to Felix."

"He's already gone," said Rutspud. "But I suspect you'll see him again before I do."

"Really?"

"If there's any true justice in the cosmos."

She shook her head and sighed.

"Hey, why so glum?" he said.

"I'll be glad when I'm back in the Celestial City."

"Won't we all."

"I mean..." She wasn't sure what she meant and she didn't continue until they were on the landing and had locked up. "This journey has just made me feel soiled. The world was a crazy mess when we arrived but it's an even crazier mess now."

"We've corrected the sin imbalance. The wicked have been exposed for what they are. There's a renewed interest in faith all across this country. What's not to like?"

She clumped unhappily down the stairs.

"Yes, there's certainly a new air of piety but it's not..."

"Not what?"

Sister Anne and Tommy Chuckles were waiting in the hallway downstairs.

"Are you checking out now?" said Tommy with a cheery eye-roll.

Both Sister Anne and Tommy Chuckles were dressed in sack cloth. Well, Sister Anne was dressed in actual sack cloth. Tommy was wearing a brown pillow case with a hole cut out for his head. They both had ashes smeared on their foreheads.

"Yes," said Joan. "You both look very... penitent."

"It is a time of spiritual cleansing, child," said Tommy. "All must repent and renew their relationship with God. We must wipe the filth from our minds and from our streets."

"That's nice," said Rutspud.

"Sister Anne and the others are going to the Hooflandian church for devotional worship. You can join us if you wish." There was, for the first time ever, a sinister tone to Tommy's little voice, a suggestion that those who did not join might have their names written down at some point – written down and remembered.

"That is unbelievably kind," said Joan with a false smile plastered on her face, "but Rutspud and I must be moving on. We have a, um, higher calling."

"Or lower," said Rutspud and sidled past the holy sister. The puppet's gaze followed them to the door.

"God be with you," said Joan in farewell.

"Oh, he is," said Tommy Chuckles. "He is."

"See?" said Joan, when they were a safe distance down the road. "Part of me is very pleased that Sister Anne has found a fresh sense of piety but it's still a bit..."

"Creepy as fuck horror movie, Bible basher piety?" suggested Rutspud.

"In not so many vulgar words, yes. God's love is warm."

"Like the fires of Hell?"

"And although his love is fierce and challenging and sometimes frightening –"

"Like the fires of Hell."

"– it is open to all."

"Like the fires of Hell."

She tutted and gave an exasperated arm shake that rattled her armour. "Let's go home. What do we have to do? We just find a church, hook up into those spiritual desire lines your lot have hacked and get Belphegor to bring us back?"

"Exactly," said Rutspud. "We'll have you home before you know it."

362

Finding a church that was open was not as easy as planned. In the rioting of the previous days, some had been sacked so thoroughly that they were now boarded up, too dangerous to enter. Others were simply locked up, no longer in use, like the Roman Catholic church next to the Sutton Park pub. The statue of the Madonna still leaned precariously out of the window, looking up the road as though she might be calling the boy Jesus in for dinner.

Joan considered the distance from the ground to the broken window.

"Give me a leg up," said Joan.

Rutspud gave her a look and she compared their relative sizes.

"Fine," she said. "When you get inside, go round and unlock the door."

"And how am I expected to get – wooah! Woah! Put me down!" Joan tossed the smaller demon up. He latched onto the head of the Virgin Mary and wrapped his limbs around it in a most unseemly manner. He gave her a vicious glare. "Those gauntlets are cold, lady! Like your heart!"

He scrambled round and jogged down the length of the statue into the church. Ten seconds later there was click at the door and Joan was able to go in.

She looked at the mess and destruction that had remained untouched since they were last here.

"I would have thought some of the faithful would have returned, began the cleaning up process."

Rutspud had his phone out and was looking at it with concern. "This place has been abandoned."

"I can see that," said Joan.

"No, I mean it has been abandoned." He tapped his phone. "No signal. No spiritual desire lines."

"And what does that mean?"

He put the phone down. "I mean I cannot contact Hell from here. If Belphegor is going to take us back to the afterlife, we will need to find a place of worship where there is still faith."

"And most other places could be like this?" said Joan.

He nodded grimly. "There is of course one place that we know will be heaving with the faithful."

"The devil's own church," she said. "I had hoped to avoid that."

"Really?" said Rutspud. "I quite fancied having a shufti."

Clovenhoof walked out onto the stage of his new church and made sure he turned slowly so that the crowd and the cameras could feast their eyes upon the gold, longer length smoking jacket that he wore for his first official ceremony. Winnebago Kisskiss had promised to whip up something that combined the smoking jacket aesthetic with a startling new approach, and just a nod to church-like statesmanship. The gold jacket featured contrasting shoulder pads made from flattened-out bicycle tyres, which would be really handy if Clovenhoof wanted to train a pet eagle to land on his shoulder. As soon as the idea had occurred to him he'd asked Nerys to source an eagle trainer with a pair of birds available (on the basis that he had two shoulders).

The bicycle tyre motif was repeated on the elbows of the jacket, which Clovenhoof wasn't at all sure about, but Winnebago had assured him that 'geography teacher cool' was a hot new trend.

The stage was raised high above the electro-massage chairs, bean bags and sofas where the congregation sat. Clovenhoof had given the architects strict instructions that the feel of the place should be ten percent church, twenty percent theatre and seventy percent tripped out Woodstock-style rock festival. He had even suggested that free hallucinogenic drugs should be distributed to the punters, but suspected that Nerys had vetoed that.

The audience in the church was a mixed bag. There were family and friends of today's celebrants and a significant number of press photographers up in the galleries but there were also the hundreds of locals, hardcore Jesus freaks, general gawpers and happy-clappy hand wavers which filled the building to the extent that there was standing room only at the back and even some who had to stand outside and watch proceedings on the big screens, watching camera feeds that were also being live-streamed to other venues around the country.

Clovenhoof tapped his radio mic and gave the audience his best grin. Hell, he loved an audience.

"Ladies and gentlemen!" he cried. "Boys and girls! Brothers, sisters and Hoofanistas!" He paused for dramatic effect. "Welcome to my new church!"

The crowd roared and clapped and cheered.

"We got the best Wi-Fi in town! We got the best coffee in town! Sit down, take a load off, and kick back! Because this is your new church too!"

The cheered again. There were even a few 'Amen's. Clovenhoof waved his hands to quieten them down.

"It seems appropriate for our first ceremony to be a christening, so today we have not one, not two but three tiny tots who will be taking a dip for your entertainment!" There was a brief ripple of nervous laughter. "Let's introduce the stars of our show. First up we have Olivia Mole."

A woman stepped forward with a baby in her arms. The crowd clapped loudly and Olivia responded by wrinkling up her face and bawling.

"Smile for the camera," said Clovenhoof, pointing out the nearest lens. "Next up we have little Charlie Smith."

Another woman presented Charlie to the crowd.

"And last, but by no means least, please welcome Noah Bottom."

Noah's mother held him high above her head, and the crowd responded with louder applause. Clovenhoof was impressed to see that competitive parenting could start before the age of one.

"Now let's move on. We've optimised the ceremony, and I think you'll like what we've done. First, a brief blessing on each of these infants."

Clovenhoof turned to the row of babies and murmured the words to 'Baby Love' under his breath as he played a brief game of peekaboo with one hand over his face, while the other hand moved in a series of imperious gestures.

"Now, the formal bit. Archbishop Nerys!"

Nerys stood on a dancers podium and raised her diamante-encrusted shepherd's crook.

"Parents! Godparents!" she boomed. "Reject Satan! Protect the child! Raise it right with God's help! God's help may go down as well as up. Terms and conditions apply!"

"Now they must each be dipped in the font," said Clovenhoof. He nodded to Olivia's mother, who slipped off the tot's elaborate, frilly robe and handed her to Clovenhoof. Olivia started to wail loudly. "Don't worry, munchkin," said Clovenhoof. "This next bit's fun. Bring on the waterslide!"

CHAPTER FIFTY-ONE

Hooflandia was only a short walk away and yet, to Rutspud's eyes, it was truly like another country now. The fact that it had been erected in suburban England perhaps added to its abrupt foreignness. One moment, one was walking down an unremarkable high street of charity shops, curry houses and pawnbrokers and the next there was a high fence, a concrete barrier that still couldn't decide if it was a wall or a moat and the watchtowers and fortifications of the Hooflandian army. And beyond that, at its heart and now towering over President Clovenhoof's formal residence was the Hooflandian church, the seat of power of Archbishop Nerys.

Billboard-sized screens, visible even from the road, displayed images from the service currently taking place within although it took Rutspud a while to realise he was looking at a church service and not an advert for a water park.

"Do churches normally have flume slides in them?" asked Joan.

"Not the ones I've been in," he replied.

A constant stream of worshippers poured in and out of the entrance gates of Hooflandia and up to the military checkpoint further in. Rutspud and Joan slipped in among the faithful and made their way forward. As they approached the metal detectors and guards at the checkpoint, Rutspud found himself becoming increasingly nervous.

"They won't let us," he said.

"Course they will," said Joan.

He looked at the soldiers. They'd clearly taken some assertiveness training since the happy-go-lucky fighting on Clovenhoof's family fun day. They had also, Rutspud noted keenly, been given access to weapons. One was carrying a policeman's night stick. Another had a bandolier of throwing stars. A third carried a bulky paintball gun.

As he watched, one of the soldiers drew a visitor aside and started aggressively searching through his bags.

"They'll make you take off all your armour before you go through the metal detectors," he said.

"They won't."

"They will. They will stop us, search us and kick us out."

"They've never done that to us before."

"Well, I think Hooflandia has started to take itself a bit more seriously since then."

"We've got nothing to hide," said Joan.

"What? Apart from the oodles of Hell tech, the fragmentation grenades and the invisibility cloak."

An idea struck him and it appeared the same idea had struck Joan too.

"Grenades!" he said.

"Invisibility cloak!" she said at the same time.

He growled at her.

"Fine!" he snapped, bitterly.

They stepped out of line, put the bags on the ground and Rutspud searched through for the bags. He couldn't see the invisibility cloak (it was invisible) but he could feel the edge of it with his fingertips. However, the bag was so densely packed that he couldn't pull it out.

"It's all caught up with the grenades," he muttered. "I think we were perhaps over-equipped for this mission."

"I've just remembered," said Joan, "I didn't pack everything."

"What do you mean?"

"The money printing machine! I had to put it in a chest of drawers at the mission because it wouldn't stop. It's still there!"

"Well, that's just peachy!" said Rutspud. "Going to be a nice surprise for whoever opens that drawer! Grrrr!"

In frustration, he picked up the bag, upended it and shook out its contents onto the ground.

"To hell with it all!"

Joan quickly crouched to gather the scattered items. "Getting angry won't solve anything, Rutspud. Violence is rarely the answer."

Joan stacked the electronic items and the little odds and ends they had accumulated in their stay.

"Is the cloak still in the bag?" she asked.

"What?"

"The cloak. Is it still in the bag? It's not here."

"It's clearly on the ground somewhere," said Rutspud. "It's invisible, isn't it?"

"And the grenades?"

He dropped to the ground and helped her feel around for the cloak. "They're probably just wrapped up in the cloak."

He only started to panic when he had checked and re-checked the immediate area. They patted the ground and swiped at the dirt and swung their arms about to try to brush up against it.

"Excuse me, madam, sir," said a Hooflandian soldier in blue and gold, now standing over them. "Can I ask what you are doing?"

"Nothing," said Joan. "We're just..."

"Visitors are requested that any charismatic acts, speaking in tongues and general freaking out be carried out only in the cathedral itself."

"We're looking for an invisible cloak," said Rutspud.

"If sir could keep all metaphors and godly outbursts to himself until he is actually in the church, it would be greatly appreciated."

Rutspud was now moving in a wide circle, methodically searching the area but was now convinced he must have moved beyond any place the cloak and grenades might have reasonably fallen.

"Sir! Madam! I must insist!" said the soldier and put a hand on Joan's shoulder. It was possibly an unwise move.

Joan stood and threw back her elbow at the same time, catching the soldier under the chin and knocking him out cold.

"Enough of this!" she said, drawing her sword. "To the church, Rutspud!"

He scooped up what he could of the items on the ground and scurried after her. At the checkpoint, she bopped one soldier on the head with the hilt of her weapon, swung the sword warningly at another and sprinted through the metal detector. As alarms sounded and shouts went up and Joan took more than a couple of paintballs in the back, Rutspud dove and wove and tried to keep up.

"What was that about violence not being the answer?" he panted.

"Rarely," snarled Joan. "I said rarely."

They ran through the piazza before the church where the faithful milled, prayed, wept and took selfies. There were the shouts of soldiers some distance behind them but Rutspud could see that the guards on the great steps of the cathedral were becoming aware of the commotion brewing before them.

"Tell me you have a signal!" Joan shouted back at him.

Rutspud juggled tablet, absolution detector and phone and tried to read his screen.

"Yes!" he shouted. "Strong. And stronger inside."

"Good!"

Joan bounded up the steps, barging through the thickening crowd. She met a soldier with his truncheon already swinging for her. Rutspud thumbed for Belphegor's contact details.

Joan ducked a clumsy swing, sliced the end off the soldier's truncheon and booted him down the steps. Rutspud's phone chirruped as they ran on.

"Rutspud?" said Belphegor's crackling voice. "We thought you'd forgotten us and gone native."

"Not a chance, boss," said Rutspud. "We need a pick up."

"Is the mission done?"

A soldier slammed into Joan as they ran up the bustling nave. They tumbled over the coin-operated vibro-massage pews and Joan came up victorious.

"Mission is done to a crisp, boss," said Rutspud. "But we're kind of in a hurry to get out of here, so..."

There were the sounds of clicks and whirrs.

"Well, if the two of you could stand still for a second," said Belphegor.

"Not going to happen, sir."

"I've never transported two moving targets into one shunter before."

"To the altar!" Rutspud yelled to Joan.

The white marble altar was on top of a raised platform on stage. On that stage, previously smiling but presently confused couples were standing next to Jeremy Clovenhoof who, for reasons Rutspud had neither the time nor the inclination to fathom, was dandling an infant over a frothing water slide.

People were standing throughout the cathedral, straining to see. Paintball pellets clattered against Joan's armour. One clipped the tip of Rutspud's ear. That was going to sting later. He nearly tripped but caught up with the sprinting saint. The stage altar was mere yards ahead. Joan reached down and grabbed Rutspud's hand and dragged him with her as she vaulted onto the stage.

Belphegor's voice whistled on Rutspud's phone. "Please keep your arms and legs inside..."

Lights span across Rutspud's vision. If he had been human, he would have thought he was having a heart attack.

Clovenhoof threw Rutspud a lazy salute of farewell.

Together, Joan and Rutspud leapt for the altar.

There was a flash and an implosive inrush of anti-noise, almost the precise opposite of a bang and the saint and the demon vanished.

There were gasps and cries and various competing declarations that this was either a miracle or a sign of the devil.

"All part of the magic of entertainment," Clovenhoof assured them. "Now, it's Charlie's turn."

Clovenhoof plonked baby Charlie onto the chute where he slid promptly into the font pool below the stage to be caught by his father and wrapped in a towel. Charlie chortled loudly. The congregation 'aww'ed and all notions of mystically vanishing visitors from the afterlife were conveniently forgotten.

Baby Noah followed down the chute and by the time he was plucked out and held aloft, the crowd was on its feet, stamping and cheering.

"Thank you everybody," said Clovenhoof. He pointed to the large screens. "You can see that our specially placed cameras have captured this magical moment for the parents."

The pictures of the babies entering the water of the font appeared, side by side and the crowd reacted with a mixture of laughter and cooing at the adorable expressions of shock and glee.

The screen switched to a live Twitter feed and showed that #Hooflandia and #Christening were trending. Clovenhoof smiled, knowing he'd created a hit.

"And now we sing the hymn *God Gave Rock and Roll To You*. Archbishop Nerys!"

The opening notes of the Kiss hit pumped out of the massive speakers throughout the church. Atop her podium, Nerys wielded her bishop's crook like the coolest air guitar in history and led the congregation in a communal rock-out.

Clovenhoof displayed a few of his best dance moves, twerked at the freshly baptised tots and then moonwalked off stage. Vice Lord Baronet Ben Kitchen passed him a towel to mop his sweaty brow and Prime Minister Lennox cracked open a refreshing bottle of Lambrini.

"That seemed to go well," he said.

Clovenhoof nodded. "Apart from that weirdness halfway through. Flash, bang. I think I ad-libbed it well enough."

General Florence ran up.

"Sir," she said breathlessly. "We've had a security incident."

"Too right we did," said Clovenhoof.

Florence pulled an uncomfortable expression.

"*Another* security incident. We apprehended a man acting very suspiciously round the back of the church."

"Are our toilets that hard to find?"

"We believe he was trying to undermine the church."

Clovenhoof paused mid-swig. "How?"

Florence held up a mud-flecked trowel. "With this, sir."

Clovenhoof sighed. "Oh, Festering Ken. What are we to do with you?"

A hiss and slobber and the metal door to the shunting chamber swung open. Joan's ears popped at a sudden change in pressure and she stretched her jaw to try to alleviate the sensation.

Belphegor wheeled backwards to give them room to exit. Joan had to cling to the door frame for support and she stepped out into the Infernal Innovations laboratory.

"All limbs intact?" said Belphegor.

"Yes," said Rutspud, earnestly checking himself over. "And attached to the right bodies, which is something of a surprise."

The reinforced tank on the other side of the room rumbled.

"I believed it would work even if you didn't, Boris," said Belphegor.

Joan swung her pack onto an empty workbench (making sure it was clear of homicidal technology first). Rutspud dumped his gear next to it. Belphegor eagerly pored over it.

"Successful field tests?" said the plump inventor demon.

"Everything worked exactly as advertised," said Rutspud tactfully.

Belphegor rummaged through.

"The invisibility cloak? The grenades?"

"Lost on the field of combat," said Joan.

"Ah. And the currency printer?"

"Destroyed," said Rutspud quickly and gave Joan a look.

"Earth is such a violent place?" said Belphegor.

Joan gave that some thought. "Action-packed, certainly."

"We had a car chase with robot cars," said Rutspud. "Joan was nearly crushed by a church bell. I had to dress as a school boy. Joan started a war with some nuns. Oh, and there was a musical number involving Bluetooth butt plugs! Action-packed doesn't even begin to describe it!"

"Yes," said Belphegor and gestured casually to a bank of wall screens on which various uploaded web videos played. "We have been granted certain colourful insights into your adventures. I think we will need a detailed report."

"Of course, boss," said Rutspud.

"*And*," Belphegor continued heavily, "you might both want to think about which elements to embellish and which to draw a silent veil over. Our counterparts in the Celestial City are expecting us presently."

Joan gave him a sceptical look. "We're not in trouble, are we?"

She noticed the demon lord's eyes flick just for a moment to the giant metal tank.

"Who are we to know the minds of Heaven?" he said.

CHAPTER FIFTY-TWO

Clovenhoof sat at his presidential desk, an afternoon glass of Lambrini by his left hand, a covered silver platter by his right hand and the paperwork of office in front of him. The silver platter was supposed to have contained Milo Finn-Frouer's latest attempt to recreate a crispy pancake. What it had contained was a scrap of paper on which the words 'I am a pancake' had been scrawled in a mysterious substance which, on closer tasting, had turned out to be chocolate sauce. Clovenhoof suspected that Milo was a broken man and might have to be taken to the shop to be repaired.

Clovenhoof wasn't overly concerned. He was luxuriating in the success of his recent appearances before the faithful. On the giant view screens around the nation, a montage of highlights from services over the past week was playing on a loop.

Some unseen minion had been tasked with ironing the morning papers for him. It was a tip that Maldon Ferret had mentioned, and Clovenhoof loved it. He rapidly extended the instruction to include all of his post and any flat meals he ate (freshly ironed pizza leftovers from the night before was a taste sensation), and he was currently working his way through a pristine pile of paperwork.

"Do I want to go on the Graham Norton show?" he asked Ben.

"Find out who the other guests are," suggested Ben without looking up from his screen. "That might influence your decision."

"Good shout, Kitchen," said Clovenhoof. He pressed a button on the voice memo recorder. "Graham Norton show. I'll do it if there are hot women there."

Ben sighed. "That's not quite what I meant."

Clovenhoof shrugged. "How's the Bible re-write coming?"

"Not bad, not bad. We've researched and included Nerys's lineage back for the last one thousand years."

"Have you?" said the Archbishop, who was having her nails painted while her Yorkshire terrier was having his claws done to match.

"In the hope of lending your position some regal and religious credibility. We've set ourselves an achievement goal of getting back to St David. If we're really lucky, we might get to King Arthur or even Joseph of Arimathea."

"Wow. And I'm descended from them?"

"Um," said Ben. "Beyond a certain point, tracing your family tree is less of a science and more of a... a creative endeavour."

"And who is this Joseph of Arimathea?"

"Legend says he brought the infant Christ to England. Legend says."

"Yo, choir!" called Clovenhoof. "Give me some *Jerusalem*."

As the beatboxing barbershop singers launched into a powerful "And did those feet in ancient times, walk upon England's mountains green?", Clovenhoof added to it with funky cries of "Yes, he did!"

"I'm trying to work out a way of demonstrating that Joseph of Arimathea, instead of going to Glastonbury, actually came here to Hooflandia," said Ben.

"Oh, that's clever," said Nerys.

"I think we can actually do whatever we like with the narrative. The Bible has such an unreliable narrator, we could probably get away with anything. It's just such a mammoth undertaking."

"Well, what do you need?" said Clovenhoof. "The resources of a nation are at your disposal."

"Oh, it's okay really," said Ben. "It occurred to me that the original Christian Bible had many authors and so I took it as read that it would be okay for me to bring other helpers on board with the rewrite."

"Who did you invite?"

"The internet. I tweeted about re-writing the scriptures and we've had an absolutely massive response. Seriously, you could fill ten volumes with the suggestions we've had for the Dawkins Bible."

"The Dawkins Bible?"

"It picked up the name along the way. I think it sort of got hijacked by angry atheists who have serious Jesus issues and the name's sort of stuck. I quite like it," said Ben. "They have been very keen to point out some of the factual problems in the old Bible."

"Like what?" said Nerys.

Ben flicked through his notes. "What came through very strongly in one of the discussion threads was that there weren't enough dinosaurs in the Bible."

"Not enough dinosaurs?"

"No. Actually, there's none."

"Not true," said Clovenhoof. "Genesis one twenty-four."

Ben hurriedly searched through the King James Bible. "And God said, Let the earth bring forth... blah, blah... creeping things and beasts of the earth."

"There," said Clovenhoof. "Beasts of the earth."

"That just means animals."

"And dinosaurs aren't animals? Anyway, there's other references. There's behemoths and leviathans and dragons all over the place."

Ben was clearly unconvinced. "Okay, okay. But then there's other stuff. There's no mention of the Big Bang."

"Let there be light!" declared Clovenhoof grandly.

Ben grumbled and rummaged through his notes. "Okay, what about this one? In the Bible it makes reference to a cauldron or something that was ten cubits across and thirty cubits round."

"So?"

"Pi!"

"No thanks, I'm full," said Clovenhoof, which wasn't true because the word 'I am a pancake' whether written in chocolate sauce or not was hardly filling.

"If that verse is true then pi would equal three but we all know it's three point one four something something something."

Clovenhoof laughed. "Your people are getting their knickers in a twist over a decimal point. What kind of people are they?"

"Angry atheists," said Ben. "Speaking of which Richard Dawkins' publisher has already been in touch to tell us they will sue if we call it the Dawkins Bible."

"Tell them I look forward to it."

"I think the big question we need to address is what guidance this new Bible should be offering. What commandments should we give?"

"Better out than in?" suggested Clovenhoof.

"Equal pay for women?" put in Nerys.

"He who smelt it dealt it?"

"Please," said Ben. "Something a bit more serious."

Clovenhoof shrugged. "Then you are looking at the wrong mofo, Ben. People aren't going to pay attention to them anyway so just stick any old rules in it."

Clovenhoof saw Ben's eyes flick to the complicated landscapes and boards of The Game which still held pride of place on the table.

"Any rules?"

With demons to guide her, the journey from the flood-ruined lower levels of the Fortress of Nameless Dread to the gates of Hell was much quicker than her journey to get there. The queues of damned souls waiting to get into Hell were much longer now and snaked from the checkpoint booths, back through the concrete archway and beyond the great rock where Cerberus would normally be chained.

"I must make a note to collect my dog on the way back," said Belphegor.

The walk from Hell to Heaven was neither short nor long. Limbo was indefinable nothingness. To express anything in terms of time or distance was impossible. Nonetheless, approximately halfway between the inferno and paradise, they came to a hillock and a high-walled construction of marble and gold and diamante.

An angel stood on the hillock throwing disco shapes in a twinkly spotlight of his own creation.

"Eltiel!" called Joan and ran up to greet him.

The angel did a final super-tight spin and then gave Joan a kiss on each cheek.

"Well, look at you!" he declared. "Earth does not agree with you, does it?"

Joan considered the paintball stains on herself and her general state of poor appearance. "It wasn't a holiday, Eltiel," she said. She nodded towards the gated community for the Celestial City's less desirable residents. "How have they been?"

"It's been Hell," said the angel. "Cruel and unusual doesn't even begin to describe it."

Rutspud scampered down the hill to the gates.

"They're open!" he said. "We locked these gates. They could only be opened if one of the Celestial City's committee wanted to open them. That was the point, Eltiel! We were locking them in."

The angel strolled over. "Oh, but you didn't hear the noises they were making! They were so distressed, so unhappy. Anyone with a heart would have been touched by their plight. I relented. I opened the gate."

Rutspud spun around. "Where did they go? Did you take them back to the City. Are they wandering Limbo?"

Eltiel pointed through the gate.

"They're all still in there, demon. I opened the gate. I called to them. I went to speak to them. Not one of them was willing to leave."

Rutspud frowned.

Joan cautiously made her way through the gate. Rutspud was soon beside her.

"Careful," called Eltiel. "They're armed."

Joan wasn't sure what she had expected to find in there. What would happen if you gave people everything they had ever wanted? What would happen if you left the greedy and entitled in a wish-factory wonderland? Part of her had expected to find a ruin – palm trees in flames, furniture overturned, beauty spots a mess of wine bottles, party food and gore. Initially though it looked like very little had changed. Everything was still clean and tidy except...

"Where is everyone?" she said.

"Vanished?" said Rutspud. "Disappeared up their own arses?"

They came down to the edge of a swimming pool. This had definitely changed. There were towels over all of the sun loungers. Not only that, there were obstructing iron bars and padlocks and coils of barbed wire over all of the sun loungers and weird sensory devices on the top with rotating heads and red laser eyes. Strange though this was, it was not the weirdest aspect of the pool.

Joan crouched and rang her fingers through the pool water, except it wasn't.

"It's liquid gold," she said, feeling its weight and pressure against her fingertips. "Pleasantly warm, liquid gold. It would be very hard to swim in it."

Rutspud tapped one of the security-chained sun loungers. Amid great whirring, metal arms sporting multi-barrelled spinning guns sprang up and targeted Rutspud.

"Step away from the sun lounger. You have twenty seconds to comply."

"Oh, poop," said Rutspud, stepped back and in doing so nudged another lounger. Further automated weapons popped up.

"Back away from the sun lounger or I will open fire."

The first sun lounger swung its weaponry towards the second.

"Step away from the sun lounger. You have fifteen seconds to comply."

"Back away," retorted the second.

"We ought to move," said Joan.

Her leg knocked another sun lounger as they hurried away. It unfurled something that looked very much like a rocket launcher.

"Do not touch me or I will retaliate!" it declared.

The first two loungers swung their guns to the third lounger and then back to each other. For no visible reason, a fourth and a fifth lounger joined in.

"This is private property," one declared. "I have every right to defend myself."

"You have five seconds to comply."

"Back away!"

"Retaliate!"

Joan and Rutspud leapt over a short trellis wall into an open air restaurant and found shelter behind a carved stone urn just as the firefight began. It was brutal, loud and short. When the last bangs and pings had died down they looked over the now bullet-pocked urn. The smoke slowly cleared but it was impossible to say which of the shattered piles of plastic and metal had been the victor in the conflict. Scraps of beach towel floated briefly on the golden pool before disappearing below the surface.

"Do *you* have a reservation?" said voice behind them. It was a painfully posh voice, like it belonged to a person so uptight they spent every moment clenching every muscle in their body.

Joan turned. A ghostly waiter figure stood before them.

"What the hell?" said Rutspud.

"A shade," said Joan. "A mindless servant created by a wish."

"I asked, do *you* have a reservation, mademoiselle? Sir?"

Joan stood. The restaurant terrace was filled with tables laid out for an evening meal. There were candles stuck into wine bottles on every table. Their rosy glow created a pleasing warmth in the dusky light that hung over this particular area. Ghostly waiting staff moved back and forth with bottles of sparkling wine and baskets of fresh bread. There were no diners in the restaurant.

"Do we need a reservation?" she said.

"This is an *exclusive* restaurant," said the shade, "and residents have the *right* to determine who is *not* permitted entry." He waved his little leather-bound folder at them. "If *your* name is not down, you are not *allowed* in."

Joan could see the page inside the waiter's folder. It was entirely blank.

"No, no, it's fine," she said, pulling Rutspud away. "We were just leaving."

"As I thought," said the shade and went about its business.

"This place is creepy weird," said Rutspud. "And I live in Hell."

They crossed a headache-inducingly twee bridge across a pond through which koi carp the size of whales threshed against each other in their attempts to claim a breathable space in which to exist.

A voice called from above. "Hey! Boy!"

Joan and Rutspud looked up. There was no sign of the speaker among the barricaded windows of the surrounding mansions. A rifle barrel waggled at them between the golden slats of a shutter.

"Hey, boy! Come up here!"

"When he says 'boy'," said Rutspud, "do you think he's talking to you or me?"

"Either way, we should be offended," said Joan.

The two of them cautiously made their way round to the ground floor entrance of the mansion in question.

Rutspud rapped on the door. Joan made a conscious decision not to draw her sword and hoped she wouldn't regret it.

"Hang on!" said the man.

There was a long sequence of bolts being drawn and locks turned. There was a strange clinking clatter.

"Hang on," said the man again.

More clinking and clattering and the door inched open. A small landslide of sparkling gems tumbled through the gap and onto the doorstep.

"Don't mind the diamonds," said the man. "Just climb over, what."

Joan pushed herself through the gap and onto a layer of beautiful fine-cut diamonds that must have filled the room to a depth of two or three feet. Rutspud squeezed in after her. When the man let go of the door, the weight of gems forced it closed again.

"There," said the man.

It was Claymore Ferret. Lord Claymore Ferret. It would have been easy to say he looked terrible but that wouldn't have been true. He had the glow of eternal youth in his face, the teeth and hair of a pampered film star and the finest clothes Joan had ever seen outside of France. And yet there was a look in his eyes – not a tiredness around them; no, this was a man who eternally felt he had just had eight hours of quality sleep – but a look in his eyes, a pleading, desperate, quivering madness in the core of his soul.

"What do you make of this, eh?" he said, a hunting rifle over the crook of his arm. "Bloody disgrace, isn't it? Knew we couldn't trust you continental types to organise it."

"What appears to be the matter, Mr Ferret?" said Joan.

"That's Lord Ferret to you, girlie."

"Not to split hairs, Claymore," said Rutspud, "but your son, Maldon, is the current Lord Ferret, although I should imagine he'll be putting his peerage on eBay any day now to try and recoup some of his horrific debts."

"Christ," said Claymore and waded through the sea of jewels to reach a drinks cabinet. "What's the young pillock done now?"

"That would be hard to say," said Rutspud, "without using the words 'gambled it all away' and 'massive sex scandal.'"

Claymore made himself a large whiskey from a full decanter which stayed full even after he had poured a quarter of it into a glass.

"Boy's a blasted fool!" snarled Ferret Senior. "So, what are you going to do?"

"Nothing," said Joan. "Maldon Ferret makes his own mistakes and will have to pay for them like anyone else."

"I meant about this!" Claymore thrust his arms out at the jewel-filled house.

"You want us to get rid of the diamonds?" said Joan.

"No. Of course not. Do you have any idea how much each of these is worth?" He picked one up, the size of a tangerine. "Got to be millions, right? Never accuse Claymore Ferret of squandering his wealth, huh."

"It makes it sort of difficult to move around the house," said Rutspud who had managed to clamber on top of the diamond layer in a spread out and precarious crouch.

"You tell me where else I should put them!" demanded Claymore.

"You could put them in the cellar?"

"Do you think I'm an idiot?"

"Think? No. I assume you've used the cellar for something else."

"More diamonds!" said Claymore. "And the rubies and ten thousand *Mona Lisas* by Da Vinci."

"You have ten thousand copies of the *Mona Lisa*?" said Joan.

"Copies? Don't be a pleb. That's ten thousand originals, you daft bitch."

"The original? The one original? You have ten thousand cop- that is, ten thousand of them?"

383

"And I don't even bloody like the painting. Every time I go down there, the damned impertinent woman is looking at me. The cellar is full."

"Maybe wish for an extended cellar?" suggested Rutspud.

"For fuck's sake!" Claymore hefted his rifle. "I'm going to put some bullets in this thing if you don't start being useful!" Immediately, magically, there were a dozen rifle shells in his hand. "I wished for another cellar and when that was full, I wished for another. It goes down and down for... I can't remember. It's in triple figures. They're all full!"

"I see," said Joan. "And you wouldn't consider just getting rid of some of these riches."

"What? And let some nouveau riche bastard across the way come and steal them? No thank you. And Cynthia would never forgive me."

Joan looked around. "And is she about?"

Claymore gave a bark of laughter except there wasn't much laughter in it. On the balance of probability, it was just a bark really, with an added tinge of insanity. He led them slowly through the house, wading across diamond-filled rooms that resisted their progress like a vast and slightly-painful ball pool.

In the kitchen, he waved his hand at a table laden with food.

"Have some. Got some wagyu beef, finest sushi, black truffles, Beluga caviar, pate made from dodos' livers and the world's most expensive lobster."

"It looks lovely," said Rutspud without taking any.

Claymore shrugged indifferently. "I don't think I actually like seafood," he said, and yet tore aware a large chunk of soft lobster flesh and stuffed it in his mouth. He chewed it like he had been forced to eat his own hat.

They approached a closed door.

"You probably want to stand back," said Claymore. He stood to the side of the door and knocked gingerly.

A second later a hole the size of a football was blasted out of the door.

"You can't have it!" screeched Cynthia from the darkness within.

"Nobody's going to take it from you, you stupid cow!" Claymore shouted back at her.

"Take what?" asked Joan.

"I've got the crown jewels!" shouted Cynthia, sounding almost on the verge of tears. "All of them!"

"Oh, that's nice," said Joan generously.

"They're mine!"

"Okay."

"I look fucking beautiful!"

"Of course you do, my stupid darling!" shouted Claymore. "You don't need a crown to make you look beautiful."

There was the click of a shotgun being re-cocked and another shot which blew a second hole in the door.

"You're not having it!"

"I've got the people here!" said Claymore. "I'm going to get them to fix things!"

There was a sob from the darkened room.

"I'm not happy here," wailed Cynthia. "I don't like it."

Joan, who considered these to be among some of the worst human beings she had met this side of Hell itself, was nonetheless touched by their despair.

"You know, the angel Eltiel has unlocked the gates. You can leave if you want."

"We can?" said Claymore with a sudden and desperate tone of hope.

"Really?" sobbed Cynthia.

"Really," said Joan. "If you come now, we will guide you back to the Celestial City."

Rutspud gave her a look like she had lost her marbles but Joan ignored him.

"Come back to the Celestial City and just leave this all behind," she said.

"Hang on a second, sweet cheeks," said Claymore. "Do you mean leave all this behind as in... emotionally? Or do you mean –" He gestured widely. "– leave all this behind?"

"I don't think we can really carry much of it," said Joan. "But do you need to?"

385

Claymore started feeding bullets into his rifle. In the darkness, there was the click of Cynthia cocking her shotgun once more.

CHAPTER FIFTY-THREE

It was three days before the PrayPal list of sins was due to be made public and the news seemed to be full of nothing else. Clovenhoof hoped to steal some of that limelight with Hooflandia's first wedding.

The christenings had proved such an enormous success that he'd been performing back-to-back ceremonies and was in with a chance of setting a world record by sending fifty infants down the chute in half an hour. Adults were flocking to enjoy the same experience, so the engineers were working on a set of interchangeable chutes with varying thrill levels.

Nerys would preside over the wedding ceremony in her familiar role of Archbishop, but Clovenhoof would be wearing a new hat for the job.

"Time for our big entrance," said Clovenhoof as he put on his train driver's cap and hit the power.

The train chugged out of the 'Tunnel of Love' as artfully-placed palm fronds waved aside to reveal the spectacle to the audience. Clovenhoof could see himself on the big screen and he grinned with pride. He was driving the Love Train and he looked the business. The couples behind him all waved and blew kisses as the audience roared with approval. Someone had brought an air horn, but Clovenhoof didn't mind. His public adored him and only the sternest admonishment from Nerys, standing in what she called her 'bossy goddess' pose, would quieten the crowd so she could begin her performance. They had shortened the ceremony by replacing most of the words with confetti showers and 'kiss the bride' photo opportunities. Moments after the air horn ran out of gas, Nerys pronounced all six couples married.

As they walked back to their suite of offices, Nerys and Clovenhoof exchanged a high five.

"We killed it," said Nerys. "Did you hear them when the train came out? But don't think you can get away with upstaging me like that in the future."

"Upstage? Moi?"

"You're looking at the queen of upstaging and I've got something out back that will put your train to shame."

"Really?" he said, intrigued and was following her out when Florence walked over with two of her soldiers dragging a man between them. The man was bound and gagged.

"Prisoner for processing, sir!" Florence shouted at Clovenhoof. "Does Hooflandia have a law against the unauthorised carrying of weapons?"

Clovenhoof glanced at the soldiers, who were armed with a nerf gun and a Klingon bat'leth, and shrugged lightly. "What's he got?"

"House brick, sir," said Florence, holding up the evidence.

"Oh wow, check this out Nerys!" said Clovenhoof, taking the brick. "It's one of the special commemorative bricks that I made for crowdfunding sponsors for the cathedral!"

"Sir, it's just a brick that's been written on with a sharpie," said Florence.

"In my own fair hand," said Clovenhoof.

"I have been trying to tell these oafs that I am an investor," said the man, as Florence released the gag. "Will you please tell them to let me go now?"

Clovenhoof nodded to Florence who released his bonds.

"I hope you're pleased with your brick," said Clovenhoof. "Is there something else I can do for you?"

"I've come to claim my share of the privatised church," said the man, straightening. "You must be making a fortune and it's built using my money."

"But you've got your brick," said Clovenhoof.

"I gave you five hundred pounds!" said the man. "I'm owed more than a brick."

Clovenhoof smiled at him. "Sure. Now listen, I'm a reasonable man. Florence here will escort you out of Hooflandia with her capable army. On the way, I'd like you to select another brick from the builders' supplies. You can choose your favourite and take it with my compliments." He shook the man's hand and walked away. "A pleasure doing business with you."

With the man's indignant disagreement echoing in his ears, Clovenhoof followed Nerys out to the car park directly behind the Hooflandian church. There was a new vehicle parked there, taking up five car parking spaces.

Clovenhoof would have been hard-pressed to say for certain what it was meant to be. The chassis and body were those of a double decker bus, but the finish had some of the unmistakeable design hallmarks of Winnebago Kisskiss. The outside was entirely white, but the bumpers were covered in slightly kinky rubber spikes.

"What is it?" he said.

"My popemobile," said Nerys and climbed on board.

"Couple of problems with that," he said, following her on.

Nerys sat in the big cushioned driver's seat and started the engine.

"You're not a pope," Clovenhoof pointed out.

"Pff. Ben can sort that out with his new Bible. I'd make a good pope."

"And isn't a popemobile, by definition, a fairly small thing?"

"Says who? My popemobile, my rules."

The interior of the popemobile was carpeted throughout in a thick shagpile carpet. There were comfy recliners, television screens and a bar. Nerys swivelled her chair around from the gigantic driver's console.

"What's your opinion then?"

"It's vulgar and excessive. You couldn't ignore it if you tried. It's the absolute embodiment of you," said Clovenhoof.

"Why thank you," said Nerys with a saccharine smile. "Check this out."

She pressed a button above her head, and something like an ice cream van chimes could be heard, loudly playing *Jerusalem*.

"I'm planning a tour," she said. "I've had quite a lot of requests. Twenty branches of the Women's Institute have asked me along as a motivational speaker. Five others have informally requested that I be removed from office until I dress more appropriately."

Clovenhoof nodded. "Your family?"

"At least one of them, yeah. Anyway, I thought a tour would be fun. The bar converts into a little altar for emergency communions."

"Sweet! You could do with a driver for the bus, so you can spend more time, you know, officiating at the bar."

"Tina's doing an intensive course, so she can be my driver as well as wardrobe assistant," said Nerys.

"Well played Nerys. The old saying about keeping your friends close and your enemies closer is something you'd recommend then?"

"It all becomes workable when you set clear pay-related objectives," said Nerys. "Tina has an objective that my outfits must generate headlines on at least a weekly basis. Nobody could do a better job than someone who hates me as much as Tina does. She has some others as well to keep her from causing me actual harm, but so far it's working well."

Clovenhoof nodded in admiration. As always, Nerys seemed almost as if she'd been Hell-trained from birth, but then again, he'd met her mother.

Two demons and a saint continued towards the Celestial City, alone.

The angels standing at the gates to the Celestial City looked sceptically at the two demons, but one look from St Joan of Arc (even a St Joan of Arc who felt she had been dragged through a hedge backwards and who had been liberally painted with high velocity lime greens and pinks) made them comply and open up.

They variously walked and trundled over to the Heavenly Moral Records Centre. Joan hadn't expected a hero's welcome or a victory parade but had at least expected a delegation to meet them. Instead, they found the records centre looking exceptionally busy, and not in a good way.

In the impossibly huge hall, entire shelves of books were being systematically emptied. Records centre employees were being corralled at a set of tables and taken off one by one by stern-faced angels. In the centre of the hall, the Archangel Gabriel and St Thomas Aquinas conferred in grim whispers with various underlings while Mother Theresa checked off items on a scroll.

Thomas caught sight of the saint and two demons, tapped Gabriel's arm for attention and strode over.

"We need a word with you," he said.

"And hello to you too," said Joan. "What's going on here?"

"We are still trying to get to the bottom of that," said Gabriel. "But it's not good, not good at all. And I think you two can help us with our enquiries."

"Us?" said Rutspud.

"Where's St Hubertus?" said Belphegor.

"The *former* director of the Heavenly Moral Records Centre is in his office, doing what he does best."

Gabriel led the way downstairs into Hubertus's hi-tech office from which an awful and almost human wailing could be heard. The sound was coming from a corner of the office where the patron saint of hunters, accountants and more besides lounged in the company of his deer.

Hubertus sat at the cushioned end of a chaise longue with Hirsch the holy deer laid out with its head in his lap. A sticky mess of drinks bottles and shot glasses were laid across a nearby table and Hubertus swung his current glass around as he part-sung, part-sobbed his way through a sorrowful song.

"*Wie du weinst, wie du weinst, dass I wandere muss, wandere muss.*"

Joan walked over (with Thomas Aquinas following with suspicious closeness). She couldn't tell if the deer was awake, dead drunk or sleeping. She rarely had need to assess the inebriation levels of ruminants.

"What's happened?" she said.

"Friends!" declared Hubertus, seeing them for the first time, blinking through teary bloodshot eyes. "Friends! They've taken it from me."

"You did this to yourself," said Thomas.

"Taken it!" wailed the drunk saint. "The HMRC! My baby! They're auditing us. Us! The official records office of official office records. Us!" He reached out to Belphegor with sticky fingers. "Belphegor! They want to pin this on us!"

Belphegor, poker-faced, spun his chair to face Gabriel. "Perhaps you would care to explain what is happening here, Gabriel. Or what you think is happening here."

"Careful how you speak, demon," said the archangel. "You came as a guest last time. You might not be treated so kindly this time."

"Why?" said Rutspud. "What's happened?"

"Discrepancies," said St Thomas curtly. "Monstrous discrepancies."

"Look at this," said Gabriel and tapped one of the screens. It did nothing. He tapped it again. "Blasted thing. It was working earlier. I'm not much of a techno-geek." He tapped it again and then slapped it a few times. "Curse you! I'm the Archangel Gabriel and when I want things to work, they work! Don't make me get out my horn and show you who's boss."

Rutspud rolled his eyes. "The number of times I've heard that line," he muttered but it seemed to do the trick. The screen sprang into life.

"Now if we look here," said Gabriel, pointing to the graph. "This is the current level of sin in the cosmos. Twenty-seven mega-thingies per second."

"Megapeccados," slurred Hubertus.

Joan could see it had bounced right up from the figure it had been previously. "That's great!"

Thomas Aquinas fixed her with a steely gaze.

"Well, obviously not good," she said. "That's a lot of sinning. But it's a normal level of sinning."

Thomas's gaze did not waver.

"I'm not saying any sinning is 'normal,'" she continued, "but it's a level that's... expected. No one's using PrayPal anymore. Souls aren't being unjustly forgiven. Balance is restored."

"But it's not," said Gabriel. "Look! It doesn't add up!"

Joan approached the screen, Rutspud beside her.

"Here's the sin being generated..." she said.

"Take away those bits erased by forgiveness..." said Rutspud.

"Minus the cleansing effect of purgatory for those entitled to it..." she added.

Rutspud was muttering sums to himself. "And you're left with a ton of sin unaccounted for. Approximately thirteen megapeccados per second."

"Exactly!" said Gabriel. "Where has it gone?"

"Hell, one assumes," said Rutspud and looked to Belphegor for confirmation. The great purple demon gave him a tight-lipped look and said nothing. "Or not?" ventured Rutspud.

"But where did it go from there?" said Thomas. "The demon lord here said they couldn't allow it to slosh about Hell, clogging things up. The sin has to go somewhere."

"Ah!" said Rutspud. "But that's where Satan comes in, right? Right? All the sin goes to him."

"Be quiet, Rutspud," said Belphegor.

"But he just gathers it, doesn't he? All the sins of the world pour into him, don't they?"

"Be quiet!" barked Belphegor.

Rutspud immediately adopted the pose of a person who had clearly spoken about things he had no knowledge of and was going to shut up at once.

"But he's right!" said Joan. "That was what happened. Sin in Hell flew to Satan. And we've met him on earth and he's not a very nice man, not really."

Gabriel gave her a reproachful look. "Really, Joan? That man you met, Jeremy Clovenhoof. Would you say he's evil personified? We've been watching. Selling cheap funerals? Committing acts of petty fraud? Parading around on stage and pretending to be the lord of the manor? Are those the acts of evil personified?"

"I would say they're *fairly* evil," she countered weakly.

"When we first banished him to earth, he *was* evil. He was willing to commit vile abuses of power. He even founded a heavy metal band and through the power of his followers alone tried to punch a hole through creation and back to Hell. He was powerful and he was evil. But now? Be honest."

Joan thought honestly. "He's more of a disgusting and grumpy old man."

"A man," nodded Gabriel wisely. "Jeremy Clovenhoof has shed the sins of a thousand generations, burned them up. Sin no longer gathers round him. The only sins he generates are his own. And, yes, now he is nothing but a disgusting and contrary old man. A pathetic creature."

"And so," said Thomas, "we ask again. What happened to all the sin?"

Hubertus burst into tears. "We should never have lied to you! I am so sorry, my friends! How can I make it up to you?"

"Lied? What lies?" demanded Thomas.

Hubertus wiped his snotty nose with his red felt hat. "If we had told you the truth in the first place, this would have never happened!"

"We?"

"If we'd told you the truth," said Belphegor, the picture of self-control compared to the blubbering drunkard, "you would have done nothing."

"I knew it was *you!*" crowed Thomas. "You did it! Whatever it was! What was it you did?"

Belphegor wheeled over to the screen. Joan noted the archangel and Aquinas taking a step back. Her hand went unconsciously to the hilt of her sword.

"You removed Satan from Hell without a thought for the consequences," said Belphegor. "Hell is an ecosystem like any other. What's more, it's a closed ecosystem. You removed Satan from the equation and let gigapeccados of sin flow in. Yes, it clogs things up. It's a force. It is energy. What happens if you put more and more energy into a closed system?"

Gabriel and Thomas Aquinas looked blankly at each other. Joan was of no help either. None of them were exactly up to date on science-y matters.

"Boom?" suggested Rutspud.

"Boom indeed, Rutspud," said Belphegor. "A few years ago, Hell suffered a catastrophic over-heating event. What do you think caused that?"

Rutspud started to speak but held himself in check.

"Yes, yes," sighed Belphegor wearily, "we all know that you stole fuses from Hell's furnaces, Rutspud. But, seriously, do you think that in the vast history of Hell there wouldn't have been other such incidents if all it took to start them was the stupidity of a minor demon?"

"Stupidity is a strong word," said Rutspud.

"The sin energy in Hell has been in constant unbalance since you sent Mr Clovenhoof to earth," Belphegor said to Thomas and Gabriel, and Joan noted how he had gone from accused to accuser in only seconds. "And since the over-heating incident and subsequent flood," Belphegor continued, "I have implemented a solution that works just fine, thank you. Without your help. Because I knew help wouldn't be forthcoming! Not without the kind of strings Heaven attaches to everything."

"And where does Hubertus come into this?" asked Joan.

The drunken hunter saint didn't seem to hear her. He was now staring down into his open hat and looking both very repentant and nauseated. Joan hoped he could avoid throwing up while there was company in the room.

"Hubertus was necessary," said Belphegor. "He was needed to hide the numerical discrepancies. He did me the favour of keeping shtum and in return" – Belphegor did a little wheelchair pirouette, arms stretched out to the computer screens and augmented reality equipment – "we gave him all this lovely technology to play with."

"I knew this was Hell technology!" said Rutspud. "I said!"

"And what was the solution that you came up with, Belphegor?" said Joan.

Rutspud chuckled. She could see he himself had just realised. "You know, Joan. You've seen it. You've seen it all."

"Have I?"

"I think we had all better take a look, hadn't we?" said Gabriel firmly, trying to reassert his mastery of the situation.

"Very well," said Belphegor and led the way back up to the main hall.

At the top of the stairs, Joan called back. "Hubertus? Are you coming?"

There was a response. It didn't contain any words, but it was certainly vocal. And judging by the indignant bellowing of the awoken deer and the subsequent antler bashes and screams, Hubertus had missed his hat entirely.

CHAPTER FIFTY-FOUR

It was less than twenty-four hours until the PrayPal sin list was to be broadcast to the world and Clovenhoof was taking a tour of his kingdom. He'd inspected the crew and armaments of Fortress Floaty McBang-Bang. He watched the Boldmere Ponies go through their trolley-mounted parade drill. A portacabin Clovenhoof had not seen before had appeared near to Hooflandia's southern border wall and he went inside to investigate.

Ben sat as chair of a very busy and vocal meeting. Flipchart papers were pinned to the walls and post-it notes and scribbled comments abounded.

"What's all this then?" said Clovenhoof.

"Hi Jeremy," said Ben, "this is our Bible creation team. That's Leigh, Lindsay, Lara, Lola and Tim. Lindsay's managing the community of wiki editors working on the text. Lola and Lara are working on packaging and manufacture. The publishers think we can get print-on-demand copies ready overnight."

"Righto," said Clovenhoof.

"Righto?" said a petite woman who was holding a giant portfolio under her arm. "I don't think you realise how ground-breaking this is! We're talking about compressing an eighteen-month process into no time at all."

"Righto with knobs on," said Clovenhoof, "and you would be doing that because you think you can make a ton of money, is that correct?"

"Commercial considerations are a factor, yes," she sniffed.

"It's going to go down a storm," said Ben. "Seriously. There's so much wisdom in here. It's bang up to date with gems like The Parable of the Self-service Checkout, The Gospel according to Levi the Taxi Driver and a brand-new book of Rap Psalms. The rules of The Game form a whole new testament."

"You've got a new New Testament?" said Clovenhoof.

"We decided to call it the Third Testament to get round that," said Ben. "We've got a lot to cram in and not all of it makes sense. That's why Leigh has flown in from LA to act as story editor."

"Do we need a story editor?"

"Do you ever!" said an American woman. "This thing is a narrative nightmare. It's *Catwoman* all over again and Halle, let me tell you, barely recovered from that horror."

"Did she?" said Clovenhoof, who had no idea what she was talking about.

Leigh stabbed a marker pen at a sheet on the wall.

"First of all, we have no clear hero in this narrative. Who's it meant to be? God? Moses? If it's Jesus, then he doesn't turn up until the third act. No, we need some clarity on who we're meant to be rooting for."

"I see."

"And this Jesus character. Who is he? Is he a sort of Superman, last son of a dying planet? Is he more like Neo from *The Matrix*? That whole messianic thing has been done to death. What are we looking for? This is a story trying to be a thousand things at once." She turned to Ben. "Are you sure this wouldn't be better as a trilogy?"

"I'm not sure we have time to break it down."

"Trilogies sell well," said Leigh. "Look at *Star Wars*, the *Godfather*."

"*Big Momma's House*," said Clovenhoof.

"We could probably get a TV or film deal if it was a trilogy. I know Marcus at HBO. You could be sitting on the next *Game of Thrones*. Or we could even sell it to Disney if you worked towards building up a whole cinematic universe."

"I think some people might have issues with your idea of Jesus, Mohammed and Krishna teaming up to fight the bad guys," said Ben.

"And who is the bad guy? Really?" said Leigh. "Satan? He barely gets a mention. He doesn't even get a proper scene as the devil until the wilderness sections near the end. I just don't buy him as our main antagonist."

"You know, that's what I've always thought," said Clovenhoof.

"And he never really gets to flex his muscles. You've got an Old Testament that's just punishment and reward, punishment and reward, some very confusing talky bits with the Christ boy and then things just get worse and worse until it all ends in a big mish-mash and – uggh! – the tritest deus ex machina you could imagine. Do you know what deus ex machina means?"

"Well, I think..." began Ben.

"It's Latin for 'too lazy to think of a proper ending,'" said Leigh.

"I tell you, if I ever find myself reading a book which is just madness piled on ridiculous madness and the only way the writers can get themselves out of it is having some sort of implausible supernatural intervention, that book's going straight in the trash."

"Well, let's hope that doesn't happen with this book," said Clovenhoof.

"Hmmm," said Ben.

"What?" said Clovenhoof.

"Are we totally sold on it being an actual book?"

This nonsensical question suddenly sent the room into an uproar of loud argument.

"Surely, that's the one thing it definitely is," said Clovenhoof to Ben over the hubbub. "What is it going to be if it's not a book?"

"I was thinking it could be a non-linear, open-ended narrative space with room for expansion modules."

"What the hell does that mean?" said Clovenhoof but Ben's answer was lost in the shouting.

The contingent of demons, angels and saints made their way across Limbo to Hell. Joan was going to tell Rutspud to take a detour so they wouldn't have to pass that appalling den of tortures Claymore and company had built for themselves, but she realised she didn't have to. Rutspud had no desire to go back there either and took them on an elliptical course on which they saw nothing at all (except some distant shadows in the mist which might have been St Francis, a lion and a three-headed dog frolicking gleefully together).

As they passed through the enormous concrete arch that had replaced the original gates of Hell, Belphegor pointed out the sucking air pipes that dotted the inner surface.

"Damned souls undergo a thorough sin-scraping when they enter Hell," he said. "We try to capture every picapeccadillo."

Rutspud pointed toward the line of pipes running up from the arch and away.

"And what happens to that sin, hmmm? Hmmm?" said Thomas, trying to sound fierce and interrogative but failing to hide his basic curiosity.

"It's sent to the Infernal Innovations Centre," said Belphegor. "This way."

The rest of the party had to jog to keep up with Belphegor as his all-terrain wheelchair cut a speedy path over demons, damned and generally inconvenient geography on his way back to Infernal Innovations.

Beyond the furnaces and ironworks in the basement of the Fortress of Nameless Dread, they came to the entrance to the Infernal Innovations Programme. Belphegor indicated the pipes and the sin detector docking stations around the door.

"Any sin we pick up during our work and tests is safely gathered and piped away."

"But to where?" said Gabriel.

Onward they went, across the open plan office and through the swing doors to Belphegor's creativity hub. Thomas Aquinas gazed critically at the shunter capsule, the workbenches of schematics and the piles of prototype technology.

"What is this nonsense?" he said. "Some sort of workshop?"

Joan slapped his hand away as it strayed towards an interesting looking button. "You don't want to press that," she said. "Trust me."

"Well?" Gabriel said to Belphegor. "Where next? Or is the tour over?"

Belphegor went to the large metal tank that dominated one side of the room. He banged it with his fist. It rumbled violently.

"It's in here," he said.

Joan stared. "Boris?"

"Boris?" said Gabriel.

"But I thought you had a thing in there," said Joan.

"I do," said Belphegor. "Sin. All the sins of Hell."

"I meant something *alive*."

Belphegor gave a broad shrug. "What is life in Hell?"

"But you gave it a name?"

Gabriel approached the tank and, hesitantly at first, placed his hands against it and then an ear.

"What sins are floating around in here?" he mused.

"Almost any you can imagine," said Belphegor.

Gabriel stepped back and appraised it. "And these sins are dangerous?"

"As any form of energy source can be if it's not properly contained."

Gabriel tapped the tank as though confirming its solidity. The contents groaned and roared.

"And it is properly contained?" asked the archangel. "No leakage."

"None," Belphegor assured him. He pointed to a big red dial switch. "As long as the containment field remains switched on and that's connected directly to a dedicated furnace. It's failsafe and fool proof."

"Well," said Gabriel slowly and clearly prepared to backtrack if need be, "this seems to be an intelligent and prudent solution to the problem. I'm surprised you felt the need to hide it from us."

"I have perhaps been a little paranoid," demurred Belphegor. "If you have no issues with this system, we will gladly continue to use it."

Rutspud made a tiny cough and nudged Joan. His eyes were looking pointedly at a needle gauge on the side of the tank.

"And what will you do when it's full?" she asked.

"Pardon?" said Gabriel.

Joan stepped forward and away from Rutspud in case Belphegor's suspicions suddenly fell on him. "This system has been

401

running since the heating crisis," she said. "Two or three years have passed in the world above and yet..." She approached the gauge. "It looks like your tank is nearly full."

"We can build another," said Belphegor.

"Not much of a solution," she suggested.

"It would only be an interim until a more permanent storage solution can be perfected."

"And what kind of solution would that be?" said Thomas.

Belphegor grumbled bitterly. "This is not yet perfected but I suppose a small demonstration can be given. Rutspud, the triple-valve compressor unit please."

Rutspud picked up a bulky contraption of metal and glass and carried it over to Belphegor where the two of them attached it to an outlet valve at the base of the tank. Belphegor flicked a succession of switches, opened a valve and cranked a handle. The contraption groaned and hummed.

"Sin is a malleable substance," Belphegor explained, "and can be compressed to a thousandth of its original volume. In a solid state we can store up to eleven point one terapeccados in one cubic metre, a block that would have a sin decay half-life of approximately ten years."

"Words," said Thomas. "It's all just words. And not even that."

The device on the side of the tank gave a hiss and a pop and a cigar-shaped pellet of shimmering blackness dropped out. Belphegor caught it deftly. The attachment began to groan once more, working on another.

Belphegor held the pellet up, weighed it. "Several megapeccados there, perhaps."

St Thomas reached out to touch it but Belphegor drew back.

"Careful. This thing is pure sin. Demonkind are immune to it – we are unable to sin or be sinned upon – but if a human, dead or alive, were to touch it..." He shook his head. "Our method is, as I say, not yet perfected."

"So, it is dangerous?" said Gabriel.

"But can be stored in this form until it has exhausted itself and dissipated."

"Stored here?" said Joan.

"No," said Belphegor decisively. "I believe I have made it clear that our energy ecosystem is fragile and this lump of sin, even in this solid and physical form, is an unbalancing factor but I believe there are a number of deep caverns on earth where waste such as this could be easily stored and have minimal effect –"

"Earth?" blurted Thomas. "You would put that lump of evil on earth?"

"There are many abandoned mines – deep mines – which the humans will only fill in. This will be safe if placed at such depths. Or perhaps dropped into the deepest parts of the ocean."

Joan's grasp of the realities of the situation were slim but her mind couldn't help but wonder what monstrous terrors might be created when blocks of sin came into contact with the giant creatures of the deep.

"No, no, no," said Gabriel. "That will not do! That will not do!"

"It is not an ideal solution..." began Belphegor reasonably.

"Better Hell burn and destroy itself a million times over than let that happen!"

"Yes!" spat Belphegor, angrily. "*That's* the attitude I expect from the Celestial City! Let others suffer for your short-sightedness!"

The contraption on the side of the tank produced another hiss and pop and another pellet dropped out onto the floor.

"Turn it off!" yelled Gabriel. He ran forward, flicked off every switch, pulled down every lever and turned every knob he could reach from on to off.

"Not that –" called Belphegor but Joan could see it was too late.

A little red emergency light in the ceiling, more jaunty that alarming in this Hellish cavern, began to spin.

The tank and all the surrounding apparatus was now entirely silent and Joan suspected that wasn't a good thing.

"What happened?" said Gabriel.

Belphegor's huge raisin-like face was screwed up in such an expression of malevolent annoyance that Joan thought it might burst.

"You turned off the containment field," hissed Belphegor in a fierce whisper.

"What?"

He jabbed a finger at the red dial switch Gabriel had turned off. "The field that keeps it all contained."

"Oh, right," said the archangel, reached over and rotated it back to on. "There."

"That won't do any good! We now have to reconnect the dedicated furnace and that's in another part of the fortress!"

"Will that take long?"

"Who knows?" spat Belphegor. "Our only hope is that we can get it done before Boris realises that the prison gate is open and its free to leave."

"'It'? It's just stuff. Energy. It's not a living thing."

"I'm glad you know because I've never had to deal with a mountain of uncontained sin before!"

"You said it was fool proof!"

"Yeah? But I clearly didn't make it angel proof!"

Rutspud tugged on Joan's gauntlet. "Let's do this," he said and began to run for the door. "I know where the furnace is."

Halfway to the exit, the contents of the tank gave an abrupt roar, louder than any before.

"Not good," said Rutspud.

With an ear-piercing crunch, an outward dent appeared in the side of the tank.

"Too late!" shouted Belphegor. "Too late!"

He scooted away from the tank and, at the press of a button, a flamethrower and what look like some sort of automated scythe unfolded from the rear of his wheelchair. Another thump and another dent.

Thomas Aquinas leapt under a bench to hide. The Archangel Gabriel flailed about in panic.

"What do I do?"

"What did you do last time you faced an entity of vast and unspeakable evil?"

A third strike and the tank burst. A black fist bigger than a man punched through to freedom.

Trembling, Gabriel put his angelic horn to his lips and blew for all he was worth.

CHAPTER FIFTY-FIVE

"Quickly, come on, we might miss something!" yelled Nerys as they all settled into comfy chairs on her popemobile bus. They'd decided to combine a bus-warming celebration with an evening of drunken schadenfreude as they watched the live coverage of the PrayPal sins being published. The television schedules had been cleared, and there was a six-hour programme devoted to analysis and discussion of the sins revealed. Celebrity guest panellists had been chosen for their clashing personalities and caustic views, so there was the promise of character assassination, trash talk and generally appalling behaviour. Nerys was in her element.

Ben had constructed bingo sheets for them to use as they watched. He'd also created a calculation to feed the points they scored into The Game using the new currency they'd recently introduced called Social Moolah, with which they could buy and sell knowledge and influence. Nerys had a considerable stockpile, so Ben was keen to find ways that he might claw some back. Nerys looked set to make it a hard battle though, she had armed herself with a set of special bingo dabbing pens and she'd fastened her sheets onto a clipboard so that she could easily glance down and mark them. There were points to be scored for key phrases and also for celebrity names. Clovenhoof looked at his list and saw that he had Mary Berry and Tom Hanks. He didn't hold out much hope there, but he did at least have Prince Philip.

The deadline passed and the screen was filled with scrolling text, while a pointless BBC voiceover talked viewers through the fact that there was a lot of data and it would take the analysts several moments to find the first 'items of interest'.

Next came a room filled with desks. These were the analysts. Rows of them sat at computers typing earnestly and talking into headsets. There was a live studio audience, and the atmosphere was tense as the large overhead screen that would display the sins as they were live tweeted by the analysts remained blank and the announcer had to keep filling with breathless commentary about what people could see with their own eyes.

The first tweet went up on the board and Nerys squeaked with excitement.

Sybil Wainwright travelled without a valid train ticket

"Who's Sybil Wainwright?" asked Nerys. There was an embarrassed pause as the same question echoed throughout the television studio and perhaps the country. The voiceover man on the television took a few moments to deliver the news that she had a minor hit in the sixties with a novelty song about donkeys. "Come on!" yelled Nerys, "where's the people we've heard of?"

Moments later, the screen was filled with tweets, and it became challenging to follow them as they scrolled up.

"Ooh, Ed Sheeran!" shouted Nerys, dabbing at her bingo sheet.

"What did he do, I missed it?" asked Ben.

"Used the last of the toilet roll without replacing it," said Nerys shaking her head. "To be honest I think some of his songs constitute greater sins than that, anyway."

"I quite like his music," said Ben.

"Ha! Let's hope there's better stuff coming up."

"Hey look," said Ben. "Claymore Ferret pushed his butler down the stairs. Do you think he's related to Maldon Ferret?"

"His father," said Clovenhoof. "Dead now, which is how Maldon came to be lord. I see Claymore racked up quite a list before he went."

"Wow, he shot animals for fun," said Nerys, scowling as she reached into her ostrich-skin handbag to pat Twinkle's head. "I hope the bastard's rotting in Hell."

Rutspud and Joan did their best to help Belphegor fight a rear-guard action as the collected sin of billions of souls took its first steps to freedom. The thing that emerged from the tank walked on oily black tree trunk legs which supported a barrel-like torso and a fat, malignant tumour of a head. It crashed with a toddler's indifference through workbenches, maintenance cables and the general structures of the room.

Belphegor doused it in another sheet of fire from his flamethrower (which seemed to do little but dazzle the thing). Rutspud picked up a device that appeared to be mostly blades and needles, flicked the activation switch and flung it at the thing's face. Joan sliced at any hand that that swung within range of her blade.

"Why's it taken on a humanoid form, boss?" Rutspud shouted over the din of its rampaging progress through the room.

"Human sin!" Belphegor shouted back. "Boris is composed of human desires, human evils. It is nothing but human thoughts and feelings. It might even think it's human."

They were now in the relative shelter of the doorway to the Infernal Innovations office. Gabriel had fled before them, blabbering something about reinforcements.

"I'll lay down covering fire," said Belphegor, "and you two go back to prepare to barricade this entrance. This is the only exit from the room."

A fist swung at them. Joan sidestepped and brought her sword round and up, gouging the monster's arm. Boris reared back and roared. He had a voice with a depth and reverb that would have made Darth Vader reach for a copyright lawyer.

"Now!" said Belphegor.

He swung left and right, filling the room with flame. Rutspud and Joan dashed back through the to the office beyond.

"You, you and you!" yelled Joan to the damned who were simply standing and staring. "Desks, cupboards and wardrobes, against this door!"

With a strength born of adrenaline (and a regular weights and Pilates training regime), Joan hauled a filing cabinet into place and prepared to brace it against the door. She waited for Belphegor to get out first and get out he did, reversing at speed through the doors and not stopping until he collided with an unfortunate damned in a roll neck sweater.

"Ah, Steve. Glad to see you're making yourself useful," said Belphegor.

The door swung back and Joan shoved the filing cabinet against it.

"Heaven preserve us!" she whispered and heard the tremble in her own voice.

"Heaven is here," said Gabriel in a voice suddenly more confident and louder than before.

Joan looked round.

A phalanx of angel soldiers, armoured in gleaming gold and bearing standards, spears and swords came trooping into Infernal Innovations. Their glorious rank and file was disrupted by St Peter barging his way to the front.

The one-time rock of the Christian church, now disgraced saint and replacement overseer of Hell was followed by his pudgy PA, Emperor Nero.

"What is the meaning of this intrusion?" he demanded.

"Heaven can do as it wishes, Peter," said Gabriel sternly. "Remember your place."

"This *is* my place! It's Hell! The question is what are you doing here?"

"We are rectifying a gross negligence of duty by one of your chief subordinates," said Gabriel, pointing at Belphegor. "Hell has deceived us."

"I would have to add," said Joan, honestly, "that it was done with some collusion from our side."

Boris the sin-beast slammed against the double doors, shaking the barricade and sending furniture tumbling.

"What is that?" said Peter.

"It's Boris, my lord," said Rutspud.

"A demon?"

"A giant lump of sin, my lord."

"It's alive," said Joan. "It speaks."

"See what your underling has wrought!" said Gabriel angrily.

"It was under control until you let it go," countered Belphegor.

"That switch should have had a label on it!"

"It was big! It was red! It said 'do not touch'!"

Their argument was cut short by another bash at the door. Damned workers hurried to replace fallen bits of the barricade.

"It's contained for now," said Belphegor. "And no one is harmed."

"Yeah," said Rutspud slowly. "There's a couple of issues with that."

"Like what, demon?" said Peter.

"Um, first of all, the shunter is in there."

"The what?" said Gabriel.

Joan groaned. "The mechanism that took us to earth. If it figured out how to use it..."

"It won't, it can't," said Belphegor although he did not sound overly sure.

"And, secondly," said Rutspud, "and I can't over emphasise how secondary and insignificant this second issue is..."

"Yes?" said Gabriel.

"Has anyone seen Thomas Aquinas?"

CHAPTER FIFTY-SIX

Clovenhoof, Ben and Nerys had finished the bingo game. Nerys won by a landslide after Ben wasted valuable minutes looking up what frottaging was and Clovenhoof was banned from having a pen after defacing the tour bus.

The announcer had spent a considerable time crowing about the viewing figures for the programme, which was in its third hour. It had broken numerous records and nobody was walking away as the sins kept coming.

"Isn't it funny how the small sins are almost as interesting as the big sins," said Nerys.

"No they're better," said Ben. "They're more relatable."

Clovenhoof wondered about that. Could it be that being exposed as a minor sinner might be beneficial for some of these celebrities?

"Ooh, you got a mention Jeremy!" shouted Nerys.

There was a banner across the screen, asking *Where did the PrayPal app come from?*

"The three entrepreneurs are thought to have made millions from the app, and it's unclear what motivated them to reveal all of the personal data that it captured from their customers," said the presenter. The screen was filled with portraits of Clovenhoof, Felix and Bishop Ken. "We have attempted to locate them for comment, but two of them appear to be in hiding, and all attempts to contact Jeremy Clovenhoof have been rebuffed with marketing messages for his breakaway church and nation state of Hooflandia. On the one occasion that we managed to get a call through to his personal mobile phone, we listened to thirty minutes of him singing the hits of *Kiss* before terminating the call."

"I remember that evening," said Nerys. "I didn't realise you were on a call."

"Neither did I," said Clovenhoof with a shrug. "Surely, people can't think I'm up to anything. I'm as honest as the day is long –"

"In the Arctic winter perhaps," muttered Ben.

The TV presenter was interviewing some talking head, identified as 'Anette Cleaver, former Head of Communications, Birmingham Diocese.'

"Anette, you believe that Mr Clovenhoof has been less than honest about this leak of sin data."

"That's right, Huw," said the woman in the severe suit. "We have been fed a line about this leak being the responsibility of a rogue programmer. Felix Winkstein has been presented as a lone wolf, a Julian Assange type who was willing to sabotage his own fortune and livelihood for some puritanically moral purpose. This is entirely untrue. It is clear to anyone with a marketing diploma or two years' experience of dealing class A drugs that this is a blatant misuse of personal data and a deliberate tactic by the so-called Church of Hooflandia."

"That piss-gargling, stuck-up bitch," spat Archbishop Nerys. "Just because she got caught receiving holy communion from some knob's piss-pipe, she wants to drag us down too."

"What we see here," continued Anette, "is an aggressive takeover of a beloved institution. They undercut the valuable work of the Church with their tacky little app, flooding the market with free forgiveness, until such point as the Church was pushed to bankruptcy. And then – and this is the clever part, Huw – having got millions hooked on their faith brand, they pull the rug out from underneath them and force everyone to shift to their more expensive product, the Church of Hooflandia. Basically, it's the plot of the James Bond film *Live and Let Die* and Clovenhoof is our drug-pushing Dr Kananga."

"And for our younger viewers, Anette, *Live and Let Die* is...?"

"The one with the speedboats, Huw. The speedboats and the voodoo man."

"Thank you, Anette."

"Shit-biscuits," said Nerys.

"The annoying thing is that it's a really good conspiracy," said Clovenhoof. "If I'd thought of it, I'd have definitely done it."

"I'm starting to think you have," said Ben, suspiciously.

"It'll all blow over by morning," said Nerys, with more hope than conviction in her voice.

Joan stood before the doors to the barricaded laboratory and glanced back at the spearhead formation of angelic soldiers.

"Ready?" she said.

"*I* am the one leading this assault," said the Archangel Gabriel at her shoulder.

"Oh, do you want to go in front of me?"

"I meant I am in command."

"Just get on with it," said Rutspud, who was nearby but clearly not part of any attack formation. He knew his place. He was a lover not a fighter, and what he loved most of all was his limbs and vital organs. "By the sounds of it, Boris is getting increasingly violent."

"You're right," said Joan. "Thomas needs us."

"I was thinking more of the valuable equipment," said Rutspud.

Joan nodded to the damned souls and they quickly dismantled the barricade. She adjusted her grip on her sword and rolled her shoulders.

The second before Joan led the charge through the swing doors, Rutspud found himself thinking that if Boris had just pulled instead of pushed, he could have got through those doors any time he'd liked. There was probably something deeply philosophical in that, but the minor demon didn't have time to ponder what that might be.

Joan ran forward, sword raised high.

"By the power of all that is holy, I command you to stand down!" she shouted.

413

"Oh, yeah. That'll do it," muttered Rutspud and followed the charging soldiers at a safe distance.

The creativity hub was a ruin. Tables were overturned. Ducts and machinery were smashed. Chemicals, alchemicals and diabolicals fizzed, burned and screamed in little puddles on the floor.

Boris turned to face his attackers. He was still a giant, malformed humanoid but there was now a greater definition to his features. His nose was a proud slab of evil. His brow was a heavy ridge above empty eye sockets. His hands, no longer shapeless mitts, had sprouted fingers like distended German sausages.

"Stand down!" demanded Joan.

Boris lifted a giant hand and swatted her aside, but not before she'd briefly skewered a leg with her sword. Angels poured in around her, jabbing, slicing and making a general effort to look like they were doing the decent thing. Boris swung his hands back and forth like machetes, chopping at angels like dry stalks of grass. Belphegor zipped forward in his wheelchair and sprayed the creature with flamethrower fire, but to little effect.

"Remember!" he shouted. "That's concentrated sin! Keep a safe distance!"

Gabriel scoffed. "Yea, though I walk through the valley of the shadow of death, I will fear no evil!"

Boris kicked out and an angel went flying, a smear of black ichor across his face. The angel came down on his feet and wiped the goo away with the back of his hand. Rutspud saw the fiery frenzy now in the angel's eyes.

"I fucking hate being an angel!" he roared. "I hate harps! I hate hymns!" He lowered his spear towards Gabriel. "And I fucking hate you!"

The angel lunged at Gabriel and if Belphegor hadn't intervened, knocking him out cold with the flat of an auto-scythe, the Celestial City might have needed to advertise for a new archangel to blow their horns.

"Now," snarled the demon lord, "does anyone else want to quote trippy Psalms at me or shall we all listen to sound, scientific advice?"

414

"Y-yes," said Gabriel, stunned. "Everyone keep a good distance!"

Rutspud didn't need telling. If the lab were bigger, he would be keeping an even better distance. He had already scanned the room and was waiting for the right moment to act. If he could disable the shunter and if they could also seal all the pipes and vents leading from the room, then Boris would be trapped. They could leave Boris to rage and rampage in solitude until Doomsday.

For now, Boris stood directly between Rutspud and the shunter. There was no way through without risking an existence-squishing and promising-career-ending attack. Although, if Rutspud squeezed under that desk, maybe he could sneak by...

There was something under the desk. It was fat, wrapped in a monk's habit and making a most undignified sobbing noise.

"Oi, Tommy boy," hissed Rutspud.

Thomas Aquinas looked up from his hiding place. His face was blotchy with tears.

"Quit blubbering and get out of the way," hissed Rutspud.

"I wasn't blubbering," sniffled the saint. "I was praying."

"You've got tears in your eyes."

"Overcome with love for our Lord?" suggested Thomas but crawled out from under the desk anyway.

Across the way, several brave (stupid but brave) angels distracted Boris with their bronzed spears while Joan snuck up from behind. With a powerful overhead chop, she sliced off the creature's hand at the wrist. Any sense of victory was very short-lived because, even before striking the floor, the hand had shifted and remade itself and now an oily dwarf of solid sin stood beside its ogreish brother.

Little Boris reached out, snatched a spear from the grip of an astonished angel and used the blunt end to smash the angel's nose.

Boris laughed. This time, it was much more like a real laugh and, yes, Boris's features had found greater definition still, no longer a child's attempts to fashion a human but, at worst, a C-grade effort from an art college student.

"Is that all you have?" said Boris in a baritone voice that was at once mellifluous, malevolent and a shade Shakespearean. "Is that the best you can do?"

Rutspud helped Thomas Aquinas to his feet.

"I don't think this will end well," said the demon.

"Not well at all," agreed the saint, fearfully.

CHAPTER FIFTY-SEVEN

Morning dawned on Archbishop Nerys's popemobile and the Clovenhoof-bashing of the night had definitely not blown over. It had now turned into a televisual parade of pundits and pious celebrities taking it in turns to have a go at Clovenhoof, Archbishop Nerys and the whole beautiful Hooflandian nation. Not only that but people were clearly enjoying sticking the knife in.

"It's disgusting!" said Clovenhoof. "Laughing at other people's misfortunes!"

Nerys grunted. She was in that late-drunk stage where she felt compelled to just keep on drinking because the hangover that would surely come when she stopped would be worse than death itself. Ben had curled up under one of the cushioned seats and fallen into a fretful sleep. He twitched intermittently like a dog dreaming of chasing rabbits or, more likely, like a rabbit dreaming of being chased by dogs.

On the television, one by one, every villain and scumbag popped up to air their pointless and unfounded grievances about the church.

A man appeared, waving a brick with Clovenhoof's signature on it. "This is evidence that Mr Clovenhoof has entered into a formal contract with the sponsors and owes each of us a ten percent share in the Church's profits. Twenty of us have launched a class action lawsuit against Mr Clovenhoof and his company, demanding two hundred percent of the Church's profits to date and in perpetuity."

Narinda Shah, that one-time trusted tax advisor, was on the screen. "Although the HMRC does not comment on individual cases to the media, it is worth reminding all employers that they must meet their commitment to pay into their employees' National

Insurance, not to mention offering a workplace pension, paying business rates and any tax owed on company profits and capital gains."

"Et tu, Narinda?" said Clovenhoof bitterly, reached for a fresh bottle of Lambrini, shook eight bottles until he realised they were all empty and turned instead to an unopened bottle of that cider piss Ben enjoyed so much.

"Pardon?" said Narinda, in response to a question off-screen. "No, I first met Mr Clovenhoof to discuss the tax settlement for his cat cremation business. That's right. Cat."

The camera cut to another studio and another discussion already underway.

"- and you don't think Archbishop Nerys is a positive role model for women?" asked the presenter.

"Her clothing choices are only reinforcing the sexual objectification of women," said a freckled commentator. "Women are already the oppressed sex and these outfits she wears, which are nothing short of pornographic, are only harming the political cause of women everywhere."

"Wuz that bitch talking about?" slurred Nerys.

"Don't think she likes your go-go boots and crop top robes of office," said Clovenhoof.

"Do you not regard Archbishop Nerys as the very symbol of a powerful woman?" asked the presenter. "She is the head of a worldwide organisation and has the conviction to dress as she likes."

The commentator sneered. "She sits at the top of a patriarchal and misogynist church and dresses like some fetishist's private fantasy. She has all the glitz of power but she wears chains of gold."

"Chains of gold," murmured Nerys. "I could rock that look. Golden handcuffs. What do you reckon?"

Clovenhoof fumbled for the remote. Maybe there was some better news on the next channel.

"He told me he had cremated Mister Fuzzkin and gave me a tub of ashes," said an old dear to a roving reporter. "Next week, I heard he'd sold my pussy to an unlicensed taxidermist." She held up a stuffed animal with bulging eyes that pointed in wildly different directions. "I mean, it doesn't even look like him anymore!"

"Jeez," said Clovenhoof and flicked onward.

There was a familiar face on the next news channel.

"That's right," said Detective Inspector Gough of the West Midlands Police Fraud Office. "We are investigating rumours that this 'Jeremy Clovenhoof' is an alias and that the head of the Hooflandia Church is, in fact, one Mr William Calhoun. We are working on the hypothesis that Mr Calhoun faked his own death some years ago, for reasons as yet unknown in order to start a number of fraudulent businesses including child-farming, cat-napping and the founding of a bogus worldwide religion. It's basically the whole Scientology thing all over again."

There was a rap on the popemobile door. Clovenhoof turned off the television and threw the remote as far away as he could before stumbling to the door. It was Florence, the head of the Hooflandian army.

"Morning, sir," said Florence. "I've come to escort you inside."

Clovenhoof screwed his face up at the morning light and the lurid brightness of his general's uniform.

"It's not time for the morning service yet, is it? I didn't think we had the Christening Splash Fun Hour until ten."

"It's not that, sir, no."

"Oh, good. Because I wanted to talk to Lennox about sticking some more chairs in the 'splash zone' and charging extra for them. Get Milo to rustle us up some breakfast if you can. Or is he still locked in the kitchen? Is that what you came to tell me?"

"No, sir. It's the angry mob outside our borders."

"Whazzat?" called Nerys.

"We've got an angry mob outside," Clovenhoof called back to her.

"What? Another one? That's like the second this month?"

"I've drawn a graph," mumbled Ben, waking up. "We average six a year. I don't know how many angry mobs most people get."

"You know," said Nerys, stood on one foot to put on a shoe and fell over. "I think the average person doesn't get any angry mobs."

"Fuck off," said Clovenhoof.

"No. S'true."

"Anyway," continued Florence. "Apparently, your flock are of the opinion that you're some sort of con artist and chancer and I think you'd be safer inside the presidential home."

Clovenhoof sniffed loudly and blinked to clear the tiredness from his eyes.

"No. You know what. Fuck it. Invite them in." He stretched. "Nerys, Your Ladyshipness. Let's go meet our public. Ben. Is that new Bible hot to trot?"

"Just about," said Ben, sitting up.

"Good. Let's show them what we've got."

The angelic attack force had almost gained the tactical upper hand against Boris but the creation of Little Boris from the beast's severed hand added one element too many to the confusion and they were suddenly thrown into disarray. While Little Boris ran round, whacking anyone and anything with the wrong end of his confiscated spear, Big Boris extended more of his essence into forming a new hand and set about doing his assailants some serious damage.

"We can't kill it," Belphegor whispered tersely to Rutspud. "No more than you can kill an idea."

"Then what do we do?"

"Containment is the only option. The storage tank is ruptured but it's just a scaled-up version of the sin detection equipment. I might be able to jury-rig one of the detectors into a sort of vacuum cleaner."

"You're going to need a big bag on the end of it," said Rutspud.

"One problem at a time," said Belphegor and zoomed from the room.

The sight of Belphegor apparently fleeing was a momentary distraction to Boris, time enough for Joan to come in again and slice him open from groin to sternum. Boris roared. Oily black ichor-blood sprayed her from head to toe. She tumbled aside, her sword clattering to the floor. Rutspud scuttled forward to help her.

Joan spluttered and rubbed at the mess on her face, staggering woozily for a few long moments.

"Wuuurgh," she declared.

"Um. What?"

Joan growled, her head snapping up. "Waargh!" she added, for further clarity.

Rutspud backed away as Joan shook her fists and roared at the ceiling.

"I will destroy! Waaah! So much terrible food! Fried breakfasts and cremated steaks!" Joan howled, her face distorted in a grimace of extreme distaste.

"Are you all right?" Rutspud asked and wondered what made such idiotic things come out of his mouth. His body had got the message well ahead of his brain.

"Sunday carveries! Wuuurgh! Plates piled high with stinking overboiled vegetables and the dreaded roast beef. Merde, all of it! Waargh!"

"Okay, it's not going well here," said Rutspud. Joan had clearly been infected with a sin leakage and, as best as he could tell, she was set to avenge the crimes against food that she'd seen in England.

He tried slapping her across the face to snap her out of it. The only consequence of this was the gauntleted punch to the chops he received in reply.

"Ow!" he yelled. "Not going well at all!"

Boris roared with laughter.

"What hope do you stand against me? I am the evillest being in creation. I am every vile deed rolled into one. I am every toxic spill and every genocide. I am the credit crunch and Chernobyl – every dirty banker, every serial killer, every dictator, every sleazy politician. I'll sell your crippled grandmother to the highest bidder and eat your children for supper."

Rutspud, who had heard boastful shrieks of false bravado from a thousand damned souls, returned his attention to the sin-infected Joan of Arc.

But Gabriel rose to the bait. The archangel lunged at the creature, slashing at it with his flaming sword.

"We've fought worse than you before!" he grimaced.

Boris spat. "Worse? Impossible!"

"We defeated Satan!" Gabriel retorted.

Rutspud's mind leapt ahead. "Ah, no. Wait. Let's not go down that line..."

Boris swept an angel aside, flinging it headlong into a wall. Little Boris leapt on top of it, spear ready, just in case it hadn't yet given up the fight.

"And where is this Satan?" demanded Boris.

"Gabriel..." called Rutspud and tried to reach for the archangel only to find an angry French saint holding him firmly by the shoulder.

"We cast him down!" said Gabriel. "And then we cast him out!"

"Out?"

Boris looked round. Little Boris was already running for the shunter controls.

"There can only be one master of all evil," said Boris. "Only one Prince of Darkness."

"Well, that's just torn it," said Rutspud.

Boris turned, pulled open the door to the shunting chamber and poured his enormous frame into the pressurised tin can.

"Stop him!" Rutspud yelled.

"Let him run. Let him hide," replied Gabriel.

"He's not hiding, you idiot!"

With a grim fatalism, Rutspud saw it was far too late to do anything. Boris was in the shunter. The door was closing. Little Boris, symbiotic off-shoot off the sin-monster, punched control buttons and span wheels.

"He's going to earth!" said Rutspud.

CHAPTER FIFTY-EIGHT

The angry mob were cordially invited into Hooflandia and politely directed by soldiers to the church. The angry mob didn't really know what to do about that. Angry mobs generally expected, even wanted, to meet some sort of resistance. An angry mob being treated with generosity and assistance was as perplexed as a person trying to punch the wind. They stormed politely into the church. Some of them kicked chairs over and then righted them so they could sit while they waited. The boiling rage of a crowd who felt they had been lied to became a low simmer of muttering.

And then Clovenhoof, Nerys and Ben took the stage and the congregation abruptly remembered what they were angry about.

"Liars!"

"Charlatans!"

"Whore!"

Nerys squinted at the crowd. "That's bloody Okra Boddington," she seethed. "Some people just can't take being dumped."

Clovenhoof patted her arm to calm her and addressed the crowd. The cameras were on. Good. The world needed to see this and hear this.

"Ladies and gentlemen! Boys and girls! Brothers, sisters and Hoofanistas! How nice to see you all here!"

This was met with jeers, screams and several thrown objects.

"No, that was *my* brick," complained someone from the crowd.

"Archbishop Nerys, Vice Lord Baronet Kitchen and myself want to talk to you in response to some of the accusations we've heard in the past few hours."

"You stole our church from us!"

"You owe me money!"

"You made us look stupid!"

"You stuffed my pussy!"

"You dress like a prostitute!"

Nerys pushed in front of Clovenhoof.

"How we dress is one of the most powerful ways that we can express who we are!" said Nerys. "And I make no apology for who I am. Why would I? I'm brilliant. What puzzles me more is that there are people out there in twenty first century Britain who think it's acceptable to complain about the clothes that a woman chooses to wear. Seriously, that is not cool. I will be the person that I want to be, and I support everyone else being the person they want to be as well." Nerys lowered her voice and softly added, "Unless they want to be a cock, obviously."

"He's the cock!" shouted a sharp-eared individual in the front row, pointing at Clovenhoof.

"Why?" demanded Nerys. "What? Because he sold the world an app that promised confidential absolution from sins and then, when those sins were leaked, his church reaped the rewards of a suddenly shamefaced public?"

The sharp-eared individual thought for a second.

"Yes! That!"

"Let me tell you all," said Nerys, sweeping her bishop's crook round to take in everyone present, "I applaud his actions! It's time that we all took a long hard look at ourselves and spotted the rampant hypocrisy. Seriously, if you're only prepared to commit a sin if nobody ever finds out about it, then I don't want to know you. Either take the consequences on the chin or don't do it in the first place."

The crowd considered this and Clovenhoof took the opportunity to step forward once more.

"It's true!" he said.

"Yes," nodded Nerys.

"I am a cock!"

"Yes," nodded Ben emphatically.

"I did all those things you accused me of," he told the crowd. "I've done terrible and wicked things. I have made blood sausage from embalming leftovers, I formed a rock band to satisfy my overblown ego, I stole a baby for several weeks, I unleashed an elephant into a huge crowd and I spawned a hellish beast from my

424

toenail clippings." Clovenhoof took a big breath. "I did all those things. I confess. Publicly. To you."

"And you expect us to forgive you?" shouted a mocking voice.

"Fuck no!" shouted Clovenhoof and there was laughter throughout the crowd, partly nervous, partly shocked. "I don't want forgiveness! If I've done something wrong, you can't just make it go away with words!"

"No, you can't!" shouted someone.

"You can't pay money to a priest to have him wash your soul!"

"No, you can't!" shouted someone else.

"You can't be a cock and expect people to not mind you being a cock!"

"No, you can't!" chorused dozens of voices.

"If you do something wrong, you need to learn from it and make sure you don't do it again!"

"Yes!"

"And if you don't intend to learn from it then you need to own what you've done! Own it! Own up to it! Live with it!"

"Yes!"

"And maybe I needed some help and some guidance from time to time! Hell, I didn't even know how to look after a baby, but SCUM showed me what to do. Maybe I need friends who will accept me for the cock I am and show me how to be less of a cock!"

"Yes!"

"Maybe I need someone to teach me how to live!"

"Yes!"

"To tell me what to do!"

"Yes!" yelled the crowd.

"What must we do?" cried out a woman.

Clovenhoof flung out a hand to Ben and invited him to speak. Ben clearly wasn't expecting this and goggled in alarm.

"Come on," Clovenhoof urged him. "Tell them about the Dawkins Bible."

Ben wobbled. "I'm not ready. It's not..."

"This is the moment," said Clovenhoof. "Seriously, they're either going to rip us limb from limb or worship us as gods. And I'm not sure which way it's going to go."

Nerys pulled a face. "I'm still going with limb from limb."

Ben came forward nervously. He had a fat cardboard box tucked under his arm.

"Hi," he said to the crowd, almost inaudible. Clovenhoof slapped a mic piece on his ear. "Um, Hi!" said Ben and his voice rang to the rafters.

"What must we do?" cried out the same woman, either because she thought Ben might have forgotten the question or because she had found her one niche in life and was, as Clovenhoof had instructed, owning it.

"Er, well," said Ben, his voice filled with hesitation, "I was tasked with... well, my group was tasked with re-editing the holy books of... well, I suppose I suggested it because I was sorting through the rules and..."

"What have you got for us?" someone yelled out.

Ben swallowed hard. "I was just going to keep it as the Bible and then some people called it the Dawkins Bible and then when we were story editing we thought we were going to call it the Third Testament but really in the end..."

"What is it?!"

Ben shut up and held the cardboard box aloft. It was matt black. Across the front were written two words in a heavy no-nonsense font: The Game.

"Why's it called The Game?" asked a man.

"Er, because it is a game," said Ben.

"How will a game tell us what to do with our lives?"

"Yeah," said Clovenhoof. "They think you've lost your marbles, Kitchen, and I'm inclined to agree with them."

"No, not at all," said Ben. "It just came together. All the times we were playing The Game, trying to replicate the cut and thrust of the property market. And what's the Bible but a collection of rules and sayings and teachings which we're meant to interpret and use as the rules for living our own lives?"

"So, is it the Bible or not?" said Nerys.

"It's the Bible and The Game and all those tweets and comments and edits and..." He held up the boxed game to the congregation. "You've got to play it to understand it. The standard version is available to order now. It comes with playing pieces and a board and cards to tell you what to do."

"But what are the rules?" shouted a man.

Ben put down the box, removed the lid and took out the War & Peace-thick rule book. "There's a free open source version of the rules available on-line," he said, "but..." He licked his thumb and flicked to the first page. "Rule number one! No one is allowed to know all the rules of The Game!"

"True dat!" came a shout.

"Rule number two! No one is allowed to know if they're winning or not until The Game ends!"

"Sounds about right!"

"Rule number three! The Game ends when you are dead!"

There were nods in the crowd.

"Rule number four! The first player is the player who goes first! Start!"

Ben calmly put the rule book back in the box, sealed it up and handed it to the nearest member of the congregation.

"Your turn," he said.

There was a long silence and then the room erupted into cries of "I want one!" and "Tell me what to do!" There were cheers and there was applause and a fair few 'Hallelujah's.

Ben stepped back between Clovenhoof and Nerys. "To be honest, I thought I'd lost my marbles too. But what do you think?"

Clovenhoof watched the massed congregation, the chattering, smiling people of Sutton Coldfield and beyond. He watched them clamouring peaceably to touch The Game. He watched the phones appearing, people searching the internet to buy their own copies.

"It's the strangest thing..." he said.

"It's bloody Scientology all over again," said Nerys, equally amazed.

A figure at the front, tried awkwardly to climb onto the stage. Clovenhoof's natural instinct was to boot them off before they could get any purchase but then he saw who it was. He went forward and helped Festering Ken up.

"You'd find it easier to get up if you didn't carry that sodding trowel everywhere."

"And what would I use then to dig for devils in the earth, eh?" said the stinky old man.

"You don't have to dig to find devils round here," said Nerys with a pointed glare for Clovenhoof.

The former bishop of Birmingham was smiling. He looked round at the people and then patted Clovenhoof on the arm. He leaned in to whisper conspiratorially.

"Even if you don't want it, you bad lad, I forgive you." Before Clovenhoof could do anything to stop him, the man had placed his hand on Clovenhoof's forehead and mumbled a prayer.

Clovenhoof flinched. "Not sure that's a good idea."

"Eh?"

"Forgiving Satan. That sounds like an invitation to blow up creation. Or worse, me."

Ken chuckled. "Now, give us a quid."

Clovenhoof put a hand in his pocket to see what loose change he had in this magnificent outfit. As he did, the stage beneath them began to rumble and vibrate.

"Earthquake?" said Nerys.

"Shoddy building materials?" said Ben.

Clovenhoof touched his blessed head. "Ken? What have you done?"

The whole church began to shake and soon even the most religiously distracted realised that something was amiss. Many turned to the exits. Some had started running.

And then the stage ripped apart, the altar exploded and a giant, reeking mass of raw and uncontrolled sin burst from the ground.

Ken stared at his trowel.

In the Infernal Innovations creativity hub, Rutspud stared at the now empty shunting chamber. Little Boris turned away from the controls with a smug smile, and Rutspud knew that Big Boris had been unleashed on earth.

Rutspud wriggled out from the grip of the sin-infected Joan and lunged for the workbench.

"Hey, munchkin! What you gonna do now your daddy's gone?"

"Get rid of the damned roast beef!"

"Not you, Joan," said Rutspud.

Little Boris gave a quizzical grunt and moved towards Rutspud.

"I am evil personified," said Little Boris in a voice that was pitched somewhat higher than the original monster. To the extent that a sin monster might worry about its credibility (probably not at all, in Rutspud's estimation) it definitely had more gravitas when it kept its mouth shut.

"You're just an iddy biddy sin monster," said Rutspud, feeling around on the bench behind him. "Not as big and tough as your old man, no. Not by a long way." He held up the box that his groping hand had finally located. "No guts, no intelligence, no curiosity."

He tossed the box to Little Boris. The pint-sized monster looked at it with interest and pressed the shiny button.

"PERSONAL TORTURE SEQUENCE INITIATED. SCANNING..."

Joan's hands found Rutspud again. There was a wonderful crazed look in the Frenchwoman's eyes that Rutspud would have enjoyed more if it wasn't fixed on him.

"VICTIM HAS 0% FUNCTIONALITY IN NERVE FUNCTION. PAIN-BASED TORTURE DEEMED INEFFECTUAL FOR THIS VICTIM. INITIATING KNIFE FLAIL TO DISSECT AND RENDER VICTIM INOPERABLE."

"Ah, you hear that?" said Belphegor, rolling back into the lab. "Fascinating. We could learn from this, so be sure to observe carefully."

Rutspud was concentrating hard on not being crushed by the iron-clad fist of Joan of Arc, who had grabbed his head on both sides and was squeezing, while muttering all the time about the boiling of cabbages.

The rotors and cutting arms burst forth from the torture box and it buzzed briefly around Little Boris before starting work with its knives. Tiny chunks of sin splattered onto the floor as Boris lost an arm to the rapid cross-cutting effect of the device.

"Right, we must make sure that this doesn't spawn any more mini-monsters," said Belphegor and came forward with one of the liposuction pumps they were building for the Pit of Gluttons. "Give a hand, Rutspud!" he tutted.

"Need a little hand myself," grunted Rutspud.

The Archangel Gabriel stepped forward promptly and lifted Joan of Arc away from Rutspud. The demon staggered upright, checking that his head was in one piece and that he still had the right number of ears.

Belphegor was already vacuuming up the last squealing bits of Boris. The personal torture device, its job done, snapped its eviscerating arms back into their seamless sockets and fell still.

"Boris has gone to earth," Rutspud said.

"An unfortunate turn of events," agreed Belphegor.

"Unfortunate?" said Gabriel, struggling to hold the kicking and flailing Joan in his grip. "You wanted to dump it all there anyway."

"In proper storage!"

"Whatever," said Rutspud. "I suspect we might need to intervene." He waved Gabriel towards the shunter. "Help me get her inside."

"She is a bit... fighty," said the angel.

"She's my partner," said Rutspud. "She was never perfect, but I've got used to her." He opened the shunter door. "The rest of you angels going to tag along?" he asked.

The finest warriors the Celestial City had to offer looked a little unwilling.

"Fine," said Rutspud and helped Gabriel man-handle Joan into the shunter. "Come on then, Joan. Let's go sort out the roast beef, eh?"

CHAPTER FIFTY-NINE

Clovenhoof was transfixed by the sight before him. On the one hand it was a serious bummer that his gobsmackingly brilliant church had suffered so much damage. He was becoming used to the killjoy pessimism of builders, and he knew that gaping holes in the roof, wrecked walls and a giant chasm in the earth would probably take some fixing. On the other hand, it was a spectacle of destruction on an epic scale, and he always enjoyed those. A fascinating addition to this particular scene was the jet-black monster that had risen from the earth and climbed out of the dark pit. It scanned the fleeing crowds and sniffed the air, as if it was searching for something.

"What the fuck is that?" whispered Archbishop Nerys.

"Devils from the earth!" declared Festering Ken. He almost sounded pleased.

"Which one of you ridiculous specimens is Satan?" the monster demanded, in a voice so deep that it could have made a decent career recording movie trailers.

Clovenhoof pointed at Ben, but Nerys kicked him in the shins. He sighed and straightened his smoking jacket.

He stepped forward, spreading his arms wide. "I no longer go by that name," he said. "People here call me Jeremy Clovenhoof. Or, you know, Big Boy, depending on how well they know me."

The creature crashed across to take a closer look, stomping down its feet on furniture and shattering flooring tiles as it went. The congregation was fleeing to the emergency exits, even the ones that were just artfully painted onto the walls so that the building could pass the health and safety checks.

The creature was a very deep shade of black, Clovenhoof realised. It was even darker than his space-tech, light-sucking black smoking jacket. Whatever this thing was, he had already decided to have it skinned and made into a suit.

The black thing loomed over Clovenhoof, as high as a house, and then bent to sniff at him.

"Bwahaha!" The monster rocked back in mirth and pointed at Clovenhoof. "No sin at all. Most of these humans smell of more sin than you."

He waved a hand round at the remains of the congregation, including those less-than-bright specimens who were clawing at the painted-on exits with their fingernails.

"They told me that you were the ultimate adversary," gloated the creature.

"They?"

"I am wasting my time with you, old man."

Clovenhoof grinned. "I see you are still wet behind the ears, whatever you are. I mean that literally by the way. Did you know you're oozing?"

The monster frowned in puzzlement and put a hand to its ear.

"You foolish excuse for a special effect," said Clovenhoof. "I mean, seriously, what are you supposed to be?"

"Boris."

"What?"

"I am the accumulation of all the sins in Hell."

"Ooh, evil black sin-monster, so very scary." Clovenhoof used one of his favourite voices to mock the monster. He called this one *Derek Zoolander on helium*. "I have forgotten more about sin than you've seen in your lifetime, sonny."

"Why's he antagonising it?" whispered Ben. "Why's he doing that?"

"Why are we still standing here?" Nerys whispered back.

"Don't know about you but I'm rooted to the spot with utter terror."

"There is nothing you can tell me about evil," Clovenhoof said to the Boris-thing. "Nothing at all. I'm all for bringing along new talent in the industry, but you need to learn subtlety. I'm afraid you're just going to burn out with all this sabre-rattling nonsense. Now go back where you came from and think about what I've said. We'll talk again when you've grown up a bit."

Boris crouched at the edge of the stage to better regard Clovenhoof. "You have *indeed* forgotten what sin is, old man. When did you last commit an act of pure evil?"

"Eight a.m. this morning in the presidential toilet," said Nerys to no one in particular.

"When did you last squeeze the life from another living soul, just to revel in the majesty of sin?"

"Easy tiger," said Clovenhoof, "you're trying too hard. Makes you look like a trashy wannabee. Post-sin is what the cool cats are doing now. It's where you've been there, done that and quite honestly it's all just too much effort."

"I see that you have assimilated the human condition. You are full of pompous wind and petty emotions. You are enfeebled and I despise you."

"Do they know each other?" said Ben.

"It's complicated," said Nerys, "you see –" But she got no further as, with a roar, Boris reached past Clovenhoof and plucked her in its huge fist.

"Hey!" she screamed, halfway between indignation and fear. "That's unwanted touching!"

"Put her down!" yelled Clovenhoof. "There are better ways to show us all what a badass you are. You're in England now. Queue jumping would probably do it."

Boris sniffed again.

"You... care for these mortals?"

Clovenhoof stuck two fingers in his mouth and pretended to throw up.

"Oh, for the love of my big fat lady-pleaser! No!" he yelled. "Who writes your script? I'm not the earth's protector! I am not Superman! You are not the Joker!"

"The Joker is Batman," said Ben, who was apparently such a geek, even fear couldn't overcome his need to get the nerd-stuff right.

"Fine. Darth Vader."

"That's Star Wars."

"Well, whoever then!"

"Zod."

"What?"

433

"Zod. You're thinking of General Zod," said Ben.

"That's not even a proper name!"

"Off topic!" shouted Nerys, who was trying and failing to lever open Boris's hand with her episcopal hook-a-duck.

"You care," said Boris, "and that is your weakness."

"I don't care!" yelled Clovenhoof. "I don't give a flying butt-fuck about these pathetic humans." He turned and punched Ben.

Kitchen reeled in shock and pain, a hand to his jaw.

"See?" said Clovenhoof. "They mean nothing to me!"

He punched Ben again.

"Aagh! Stop it!"

Clovenhoof grabbed Ben by the collar to stop him falling down.

"What are you doing?" wailed the injured man.

Clovenhoof pulled him close. "Saving Nerys by showing him she's unimportant," he whispered.

"Oh?"

"Just play along."

"Okay."

Clovenhoof pulled his arm back for another punch. "Also, this is fun," he added.

There was a flash of brilliant white light.

Rutspud hardly registered the feeling of being pulled inside-out. They emerged onto the altar of the Hooflandian church. Or at least the remains of it.

There had been some changes to the interior of the church since they were last here. It looked like Clovenhoof had decided to redecorate in demolition chic. Rutspud didn't dwell on this for too long, as he had a high priority task to tackle first.

"I think I see some over-boiled vegetables. Over here Joan, come on."

Joan stumbled almost drunkenly at him, swiping at the smashed altar with her sword as she went past. Rutspud led her forward and then shoved her for all he was worth. She toppled onto the plastic Christening slide and down into the font where she landed with a hefty splash. She was under the water for a moment and then she emerged, gasping and dripping.

"Gagh!" she shouted, spitting holy water as she climbed out of the font.

Streamers of the black filth writhed angrily, like worms in a boiling pan.

Rutspud grinned. "You okay, Joan?"

"That was seriously unpleasant," she said.

"You want to get some payback?" he asked.

Let's take it down, Rutspud."

Rutspud grinned. "We're a team again."

She gave him a grateful look and led the charge. Rutspud (who would gladly tell anyone who asked that he was definitely not part of the charge but simply keeping the charge company) followed her along the trail of destruction that ran from the stage, through the church and out the front door.

Some distance away, Boris stood atop the rubble of the Hooflandia Log Flume and Waterboarding Centre. Soldiers scrambled into position along the moat/wall and atop the concrete-embedded presidential yacht, but Boris appeared too engaged in conversation with the tiny figure of Clovenhoof to notice them. It looked like an animated conversation.

"Ah, good, some help," said Nerys, who was tending to an injured Ben with the help of Bishop Ken. "Or maybe even someone who can tell us what the Hell is going on."

"What happened to him?" said Joan, looking at the livid bruising on Ben's face. "Boris?"

"Is that what it's called?" said Nerys. "No, Jeremy did this, but his plan worked."

She spread her hands like a magician's assistant to indicate herself as though that explained how and why Clovenhoof's plan worked.

"Uh hepped wi' uh pwan," mumbled the semi-delirious Ben through swollen lips.

"Boris is the result of a slight problem that Hell has created," explained Joan.

"Heaven and Hell," Rutspud corrected cheerfully.

"Rutspud has the technical details but it's basically an unstoppable sin monster."

"That's it, in a nutshell. Also, it wants some sort of showdown with Clovenhoof, as he's the, um, traditional poster boy for sin."

"Whatever," said Nerys. "He's managed to keep him busy for a few minutes. And now you're here, you can carry out your plan to get rid of him. Yeah?"

Rutspud looked at Joan and they both glanced up at Boris. They both nodded, but Rutspud knew that his all-too-expressive face had already betrayed his complete and utter lack of a plan.

Something – some things! – wriggled past Rutspud's feet. They were fast, snake-fast, but he caught a glimpse of them. Ribbons of sin, finally escaped from the font, raced through the scattered brickwork and smashed concrete in the direction of Boris.

Clovenhoof shouted up to Boris. "Hey, loser!"

"What?" bellowed the stupid sin creature.

"I don't like the way you're stomping all over my country."

"Oh, you do care about something then?"

Clovenhoof spat. "Care? No. It's just that I hadn't quite got round to paying my building and contents insurance and I hate to see money wasted."

Boris turned and kicked out casually, ripping the wall and roof off a concession stand, and sending brickwork and bottled drinks flying everywhere. This Boris thing acted like a petulant toddler, a quality Clovenhoof deeply admired in himself but couldn't stand in others.

"Stop playing with the scenery and face me," said Clovenhoof.

"You? You're an embarrassment. A shadow."

"I'm Jeremy ladies-drop-your-knickers Clovenhoof, the original sinner."

Boris crouched suddenly, causing an earth tremor. "You say original, but what you mean is *old*."

"Experienced."

"Past it! I have come to replace a failed lord of sin."

Clovenhoof stamped a hoof and bellowed back. "That's it! Fight me, fuckwit! I will rip off your head, reach down your stupid excuse for a windpipe and rip off your balls. No wait! You haven't got any, have you?"

"What?"

"How can you be the master of sin without balls?" Clovenhoof grabbed his crotch and thrust it forward. "Sin central, baby!"

"Maybe I'll take yours then," growled Boris and reached forward.

Boris came for his balls with thumb and forefinger. Even if each digit was the size of a man it was pretty degrading having someone attempting to pluck your dangling fruits with just their fingertips.

"Okay, okay," said Clovenhoof. "That's probably enough now."

"Enough?"

"Enough stalling," said Clovenhoof.

"Stalling? To what end?"

"This." He raised his hand and yelled to the crew aboard Fort Floaty McBang-Bang. "FIRE!"

The yacht's cannons, so recently transferred from Maldon Ferret's back terrace, spat fire and smoke and an indeterminate number of cannon balls. Whether it would turn out to be an effective attack or just a distraction was uncertain, but it was certainly at least a distraction. As Boris turned, Clovenhoof picked up a brick from the rubble and, mildly amused to see it had his signature on it, ran forward to club this invader into oblivion.

He stood on the slope of the monster's foot and whacked his brick into its shin. It made no discernible impact, physically or emotionally. Clovenhoof bashed again and again and then threw the brick away and just went at it with teeth and fingernails.

CHAPTER SIXTY

Joan and Rutspud hurried forward. The assault from the cannons seemed to be having as little effect on Boris as the paintballs and hurled throwing stars of the Hooflandian soldiers.

"What are we doing?" hissed Rutspud.

"Looking for an opportunity," hissed Joan in reply.

"Opportunity to do what? It's unkillable."

Joan tripped on the uneven ground and looked to see what it was. Strangely, there was nothing. She crouched down and patted the earth.

"What?" asked Rutspud.

"I think an opportunity just showed up," said Joan.

"Huh?"

Her hand brushed against soft imp skin. "Here! I've got it." She held the bundle in her hands, even though she couldn't see what was inside.

"The invisibility cloak?" said Rutspud.

She felt around, found an edge, and opened the cloak on the ground. Inside were six fragmentation grenades on a fabric bandolier.

"And we need this for our plan, yeah?" said Rutspud.

"There's a difference between need and want," she said. "And, yes, I have a plan."

"Great. What is it? And does it involve me having to get personally involved in fighting this thing?"

"You don't need to fight it," she said.

"Good."

"I just want you to antagonise it."

Rutspud gave her a look.

"Just keep it occupied and don't let it escape."

Rutspud continued to give her a look.

"You know," she tried, "there's something noble about laying down one's life for a good cause."

"That's lovely if you have a life to lay down," grumbled Rutspud.

There was a splintering crunch. On the moat/wall, Clovenhoof's presidential yacht was scattered to the four winds by a backhanded swing from Boris. Wood, life rings and cannon rained down across a wide area as crew members and artillerymen leapt for their lives and ducked for cover.

Clovenhoof did not feel well.

This was partly because he had just seen his beloved Fort Floaty McBang-Bang smashed apart like a Lego model. It was also partly because he was clinging to Boris's leg for dear life as Boris tried to shake him off. But it was mostly because he had a mouth full of oozing, sickly sin monster and it didn't taste good. Clovenhoof knew the taste of sin. He had savoured the richness of personal betrayal, the fine gravy that was cold-blooded murder, the piquant tang of selfish moral deviance. This, this creature had all the flavour of an adulterous tryst in a rain-lashed caravan park.

"Aw, crap, I do not feel good," he murmured.

Sin sat heavy in his stomach. Except it wasn't exactly sitting. It felt like it was throwing a party. It had opened up a drinks bar, hired in a bouncy castle and was breaking out the loudest punk records it could find. Tendrils of sin struck out from his core, worming their way through every vein, bone and passageway of his body.

"Not good."

A vigorous kick at a moment of vulnerability and Clovenhoof went flying. He came down hard and nearly puked up his internal organs.

"Are you done already?" laughed Boris high above. "Have you bitten off more than you can chew?"

Clovenhoof groaned. "I'm going to get you a better speech-writer, mate. I'm going to kill you and then get you a better speech-writer." He thought about it. "I'm going to kill you, take some indigestion medicine, lie down and die for a bit and then... fuck the speech-writer. That'll do."

Boris raised a foot to stomp Clovenhoof into oblivion. A pink paintball exploded on his dark brow.

"Oi!" shouted a demon from atop the moat/wall. Clovenhoof woozily recognised it as that cheeky little chap, Rutspud.

"I will deal with you next," growled Boris.

"Deal with us now," replied Rutspud and the heads of the valiant Boldmere Ponies display team popped over the top of the wall and the boys let loose with weapons dropped by the retreating Hooflandian army.

Joan found Nerys, Bishop Ken and a limping Ben working their way through the ruins, looking for any injured individuals among the rubble. Most people had wisely run far and run fast and so far they had only managed to find a solitary man who was weeping because, apparently, he had lost his special brick. Joan wasn't sure if this was modern slang for something or not.

Joan grabbed Bishop Ken's hand.

"You're still a bishop, yes?" she said.

Bishop Ken tugged at his beard. "Ah, ah. I wouldn't know. They might have found someone else in the interim and..."

"I'm a bishop," said Nerys.

Joan looked at her skimpy outfit and diamante encrusted crook and then back to Ken.

"Are you still a *priest*?" she asked.

"Forever and always," said Bishop Ken.

"Good," said Joan. She held up her bandolier of grenades.

"Weapons have no effect on it," said Nerys.

"Holy water might," said Joan. "That thing is sin, pure and simple."

"Nothing about today is simple," mumbled Ben.

"Sin is destroyed by absolution," said Joan, "the touch of the divine."

"You want to napalm it with holy water," said Nerys.

"Holy water?" said Bishop Ken and turned around as though a handy font might suddenly spring into view.

Nerys bent down and picked up one of the many bottles of fizzy drink that scattered the area. "Can we bless this?"

"Yes, we can," said Joan.

"I just don't think any of this makes any sense anymore," said Ben. "Maybe I have concussion." He gazed upward at the hazy morning sun. "Or maybe I'm just dying. Are those angels?"

Joan looked to the sky and the host of winged silhouettes. "Yes, they are."

Boris swept his arms across the top of the moat/wall, grabbing at his assailants. But the boys in their converted shopping trolleys were too nimble and swift. Pairs of runners kept the trolleys moving at speed while gunners front and rear let loose with paintballs, nerf pellets and good old-fashioned catapult shot.

Rutspud naturally kept clear of the actual action and scampered along the top of the wall, shouting warnings and trying to keep some sense of strategy. This wasn't helped by the boys yelling random cool-sounding phrases at each other.

"Gamma formation! Gamma formation!"

"Bogey at four fifteen!"

"Rogue Five! I'm going in!"

By accident more than design, a wild swipe of Boris's arm caught the underside of PJ McTigue's trolley, capsized it and sent him and Jefri Rehemtulla rolling across the concrete. Rutspud ran forward. Jefri managed to leap aboard Spartacus Wilson's craft before Rutspud even got close but he was able to assist PJ in getting to the dubious cover offered by a smashed chunk of Clovenhoof's yacht.

PJ hissed and stared at the bloody graze on his knee.

"It stings, man! It really stings!"

Rutspud poked it.

"Don't touch it!" said the boy and sucked his teeth at the pain. "Do you think they'll have to amputate?"

"Hard to say," said Rutspud.

Over the edge of the wall, Rutspud could see Clovenhoof lying on the ground. The old devil clutched his belly as though he had been stabbed in the gut. Stranger, Clovenhoof's flesh seemed to be rippling, bulging, as though he was about to burst with the offspring of some terrible parasitic insect.

"What the Hell...?"

The pain hadn't left Clovenhoof's stomach but it had changed in tone and quality. It was, he realised, the ache of muscles that hadn't been used in ages. It was the creak and pull of a body finding its old strengths again. Had he so easily forgotten what this had felt like?

Sin. Hell had always been overflowing with the stuff and it had always found its way to him. It was the cocaine on his cornflakes. It was the four heaped teaspoons of sugar in his tea. Sin. He had indeed forgotten what it was like to be filled with the stuff. Somewhere along the line, it had simply seeped away from him, used up in dribs and drabs until he had become – what? A mere imp of mischief? A blathering fool? Nothing but a grumpy and dirty old man rotting in English suburbia?

He rose to his feet effortlessly. New strength coursed through him.

Boris's attention was still elsewhere. Good.

Clovenhoof ran forward, grabbed at the monster's leg where he had bitten it before and ripped off a chunk of sin flesh. Boris gasped and looked down. Clovenhoof rammed the black meat in his gob and barely chewed it before he swallowed.

"What are you doing, little man?" spat Boris. "Won't you just lay down and die?"

"Little man?" Clovenhoof flexed and grew, drawing in mass and muscle from the sin energy. "Little man?! I'M FUCKING SATAN, SUNSHINE!"

"And now Jeremy's grown into a giant as well," said Ben, in the light conversational manner of someone describing what they assumed must be a dream.

Gabriel touched down lightly next to Joan. Even fully extended, you could hardly see the mends that had been made to his shotgun-ravaged wings. If one looked closely one could see a glint of sparkly thread and just one or two concealing sequins but the tailor-angel had truly worked a wonder on them.

"Update, Joan," he said.

"Right," she said and took a deep breath. "This here is Hooflandia, an illegal breakaway state created by Jeremy Clovenhoof. Boris came up through the church which is that mostly demolished building over there. The locals have tried to engage them with artillery fire from a now-destroyed battleship. Rutspud is currently directing a gang of local youths in shopping trolleys to hold Boris in place with distracting attacks. Conventional weapons appear to have little impact. I believe that Clovenhoof has now become infected with some of the sin and has also grown to monstrous proportions, perhaps regaining some of the powers he previously held as Satan. Holy water and its powers of absolution clearly help disperse the sin. Rutspud used it to cleanse me of Boris's filth. I'm working on a plan to disperse Boris for good with a combination of fragmentation grenades and bottles of water, well, caffeinated cola drink, blessed by Bishop Kenneth Iscansus here."

Bishop Ken gave Gabriel a jaunty wave, like a man who was used to greeting archangels every day.

"I'm a bishop too," said Nerys.

Joan ignored her.

"I'm Ben," said Ben.

"Good," said Gabriel. "That all makes sense."

"It really doesn't," said Ben. "I think I'm having a psychotic episode."

"Oh, by my balls, this feels good!" laughed Clovenhoof and planted a solid punch on Boris's face, temporarily squashing his proud nose into putty.

"A proper fight at last!" roared Boris and swung back at him. Clovenhoof didn't even duck. Each blow was a sudden and powerful affirmation of who he was, of who he had once been. He was four storeys high and happier than he'd been since he discovered a bottle of barbecue lighter fluid and set fire to all the wheelie bins in a half mile radius.

"I was once the Great Dragon, you know!" he bellowed. "I rebelled against the Almighty. A third of Heaven's forces were at my back, prepared to follow me to the Throne!"

"You lost!" sneered Boris.

"I nearly won though!"

Energy crackled and pumped through Clovenhoof's limbs. Every scrape and every gouge transferred more of Boris's evil power to him.

"I used to be someone!" he yelled.

"No more!" replied Boris.

Bronze spears rained down on them from above. A flock of angels circled them at height, weaving as close as they dared whilst still staying beyond the considerable reach of the two titans.

"Those gits were the ones who stopped me!" cried Clovenhoof and tried to swat angels from the sky.

CHAPTER SIXTY-ONE

As Clovenhoof diverted his attention to the angels above, Boris took advantage of the moment, plunged its hand into the top of the moat/wall not twenty yards from Rutspud and yanked free the embedded keel of Fort Floaty McBang-Bang.

"Get down!" cried Rutspud, shielding young PJ with his body as concrete debris rained about.

Boris swung the keel at Clovenhoof like a club. Clovenhoof was clearly too buzzed with his own potency to give it much attention. This was undoubtedly a mistake. Potent or not, a metal keel to the face was enough to send his brains spinning and put a dent in one of his horns.

"Gah! You bastard!" spat Clovenhoof, stumbling away.

Rutspud saw a lump of black sin-spit hit the ground. It immediately galvanised itself into a mobile lump and oozed towards Boris. Whatever pseudo-scientific force held the sin beast together, his attraction was greater than that of Satan. However much Satan had regained his powers, Boris still sat at the bottom of the gravity well towards which all foul deeds ran.

Clovenhoof's stagger only came to a stop beside the presidential palace, the much extended and built-upon Boldmere Oak. He shook his head to clear it and then looked around for a weapon with which to fight back.

"Ah-hah!" he declared loudly, spotting one.

"Don't you dare!" yelled Nerys. "That's my popemobile!"

The titanic Clovenhoof picked up the bus by its rear end and swung it with more force than accuracy. It crunched into Boris's shoulder and sheared in two. The front end went sailing into the moat/wall with enough power to make utter scrap of it all.

"But you're not the pope," said Joan.

"No," said the woman, her face screwed up in an incandescent and entirely un-papal snarl. "I'm a bloody archbishop!" Nerys slapped Bishop Ken on the shoulder. "If absolution can blast this thing apart, I reckon we can take it apart right now."

"What are we going to do?" said Ken, confused.

"We're going to forgive it, Ken," said Nerys.

"Oh, right."

"Forgive it to death. Come on!"

Joan arranged the bandolier of grenades and blessed cola bottles across her shoulder and prepared to wrap the invisibility cloak around her.

Ben still sat, dazed, on the ground beside.

"Are you going to be okay?" she said.

He waved her concern away nonchalantly. "Pfff. I'm totally fine. Oh, look, here comes a man riding on a deer."

He wasn't wrong. St Hubertus had entered the already busy field of combat riding Hirsch in the manner of a drunkard who didn't trust his steed to steer him straight.

"What in Heaven's name are you doing here?" said Joan.

"Fighting the good fight, baby!" he slurred. "Righting wrongs. Bringing the party to the people."

"You are inebriated."

St Hubertus raised a green bottle of spirits. "Just a little Dutch courage." He peered at the bottle. "German courage." He frowned. "North European courage of some description."

He then slowly and gracefully fell off his deer and onto the ground next to Ben.

Joan shook her head.

"Ben, look after him."

"Sure," said Ben, took the bottle from Hubertus's unresisting hand and, after giving the label a cursory glance, took a swig.

Joan looked to the deer. The glowing cross between its antlers reflected as a fierce and entirely un-deer-like intelligence in its eyes.

"You willing to help me bring this monster to heel?"

Hirsch bowed solemnly and turned slightly to offer her its back. Joan swung herself up, gathered the grenades closely and tried to arrange the invisibility cloak over herself and her mount.

"This might just work."

Hirsch bleated. Joan didn't understand deer. It was possibly just as well.

Clovenhoof used the tail-end of the bus as a knuckleduster with which to pound Boris's face until there was no bus left with which to pound.

"I had myself a nice little country here once, you know!" he panted, exhausted. "A palace, a church, a nudist beach and an adventure playground for the little kiddywinks. Fun for all the family. Now, look what you've done!"

Boris fumbled and dropped the keel and, taking anything it could, gathered up a fistful of masonry to smash over Clovenhoof's face.

"I'll tear it down!" Boris panted, equally exhausted. "Burn it all to a cinder! The Almighty made a mistake in giving this world to the humans! It needs remaking! In my image!"

"That was my plan!" screamed Clovenhoof. "You can't nick my plan!"

"Stealing's a speciality of mine!"

Clovenhoof felt a new sensation. It had been a day for new sensations. This one didn't hurt but it felt weird and unpleasant. It reminded him, if anything, of the evening he'd spent with a powerful vacuum cleaner, a catering-size tub of margarine and no clothes on. Like that evening, he suspected this sensation might start pleasurably enough but might end with pain, shock and a trip to the hospital. Something was tugging at his insides, the very core of his being and it was tugging in... *that* direction.

Two dots stood in the ruined heart of Hooflandia, both with hands held high. One was a white-haired beardy-weirdy. The other was swinging her crook around like it was some magical rod of power.

"No..." said Boris a look of equal discomfort and surprise on its face.

"They're praying," said Clovenhoof.

"Forgiving us..."

"Sucking out our..."

Alarmed, Clovenhoof clutched at himself, at the air around him, as though he could drag the power-giving sin back in but it was no use. Boris was faring no better, his physical body unspooling in streamers of sin, a cloud of unholy matter unfolding around him.

"What's going on down there?" asked PJ.

"Nothing good," said Rutspud. "They're trying to cast the sin out of Boris. But he's all sin. There's nothing for the sin to be cast out of. It's all just going to..."

He stood, put two fingers in his mouth and whistled loudly. He jumped up and down and waved his hands but no one was paying attention. The boys of the Boldmere Ponies display team crept forward to watch.

"I've got to stop them before they do something really stupid," said Rutspud.

"What's that?" said Spartacus, pointing.

A galloping deer with an armour-plated saint on its back had just winked into visibility as Joan threw off the cloak.

"Something really stupid," said Rutspud.

He could see her raising herself up on Hirsch's back, swing a bandolier round her head several times. He could see the grenades and something else. Bottles? Rutspud understood.

"Really, really stupid. Time to duck and cover again, boys!"

Clovenhoof could feel himself shrinking, becoming diminished again. As Boris flailed about with his own personal problems, something flew up and wrapped itself around Boris's neck. The sin monster raised a hand to touch it. The initial explosion blasted Boris's head clean off and then, as the other grenades detonated, all became fire and steam and a cloud of vaporised sin.

Clovenhoof dropped to the ground with a thump, reduced to his regular, human size.

The base of the moat/wall was wreathed in smoke and rapidly dying fire.

There was no sign of Boris.

Clovenhoof patted himself down to check three things: that he wasn't on fire, that nothing was broken and that the departing sin hadn't taken more than its fair share in his trouser department.

"Easy come, easy go," he shrugged.

Across the hazy landscape, he saw the ruins of his beautiful church. There was virtually no sign of his vanished flock.

"They would have worshipped us like gods," he sighed.

"Then we've averted two disasters today," said Joan, approaching carefully over the rubble, a deer with a glowing cross between its antlers following closely behind.

"Did you do that?" said Clovenhoof, pointing at the spot where Boris had just stood.

"Might have done," said Joan and then tutted as she discovered a dent in her armour. "Come with me. I think there's some explaining to be done."

She helped Clovenhoof up and the three of them made towards the knot of people in front of the presidential residence.

Clovenhoof looked at the deer and nudged Joan. "Hey, you'll like this one. What do you call a deer with no eyes?"

Joan looked at him. "There's a deer with no eyes?"

"No. It's a joke."

She shook her head disapprovingly. "That's not very funny. Poor thing. Where was this deer?"

"Forget it," said Clovenhoof. He nodded to the deer. "Nice hooves, mate."

It was an eclectic bunch waiting for them outside the Boldmere Oak. Florence was mustering those elements of the Hooflandian army that were still present and mobile, all the while waving away the fuss that her uncle, Prime Minister Lennox, was making over her. Nerys was busily recounting her part in the beast's downfall to Ben, Festering Ken and a comatose saint in hunting garb. The Archangel Gabriel was deep in a collective moan-fest with any angels who would listen.

"I'll never hear the end of this from the Miracle Authorisation Team," he whined. "We've not had a large scale event like this since the *Milagre do Sol* event in Portugal. If there's television footage, I might as well hand in my horn."

"No one will want that horn after you've touched it," said Clovenhoof.

"Regard, here comes the architect of all our woes," said the angel.

"Me? I'm just a humble demagogue, trying to pull a religious scam with some light tax avoidance on the side. I want to know who I send the bill for repairs to. I expect you angels to fix this whole thing up as good as new."

"We could just retcon the whole thing," said an angel with more than the usual amount of glitz on his robes.

"And what does that mean, Eltiel?" said Gabriel.

"Rewind. Reset. Localised of course but give this town the full Bobby-Ewing-in-the-shower treatment."

"I have no idea what you're on about."

"Some of us could definitely do with a therapeutic mindwipe," said Nerys making unsubtle head jerks towards the utterly perplexed Ben.

The rear door of the Boldmere Oak flew open and a grubby and bedraggled chef staggered out.

"Great news, boss!" said Milo Finn-Frouer.

"I heard," said Clovenhoof. "The angels are going to fix things up and the Guy Upstairs is going to foot the bill."

"We agreed no such thing," said Gabriel.

"I have it," said Milo, holding out a wide plate on which sat a dozen crescents of steaming, golden deliciousness.

"My crispy pancakes?" said Clovenhoof.

"Yes, boss."

"As good as they used to be?"

"Cooked to the original recipe, boss, using ingredients that are no longer commercially available."

The chef was in tears as he spoke, bubbles of emotional spittle forming on his lips.

"They smell good," said Ben.

"Good?" Milo's voice was a whisper of choked passion. "May I never smell another thing again. May I cut off my fingers to stop me creating such sublime food ever again."

Clovenhoof looked down and did a quick finger count to make sure none of Milo's digits had made it into the finished product.

"I guess I'd best try them then," he said.

"Please, boss. Please." Milo dropped to his knees, head bowed, and held the plate aloft. "Say you love them or I will die."

Clovenhoof wiggled his fingers and debated which of the seriously tasty looking parcels he should try first.

"No!" came a distant cry.

"No?" said Clovenhoof.

He looked round. Rutspud was running and tumbling across the ground towards them, a trail of Boldmere Ponies (all now apparently pony-less) trailing in his wake.

"What's wrong with him?" said Gabriel.

"He's heard there's crispy pancakes on offer," said Clovenhoof. "That chap has a taste for the finer things in life."

"He's shouting something," said Nerys.

"Sounds like 'Morris,'" said Ben. "Does anyone know a Morris?"

"Has it got something to do with all this black stuff?" said Festering Ken, pointing at the rivulets of sin pouring down the hill towards then.

"Boris," said Joan, drawing her sword.

"But I killed it!" said Nerys.

453

"Dispersed it, not killed it."

"I don't think I'm up for a second bout," said Clovenhoof.

"Get the humans inside," said Gabriel.

"Devils and crispy pancakes first!" said Clovenhoof, took Milo's offering and darted inside.

He ran through the presidential reception hall and up the stairs to the presidential suite, clutching his pancakes tightly. Oh, these smelled right. They smelled perfect. As spinach was to Popeye, as Scooby Snacks to Scooby Doo, surely these were the real source of his earthly power...

Maybe just one nibble would give him the industrially-processed, cheesy and hammy energy he needed to fight that blob of sin once more...

"Yes."

In fact, running off to restore his strength so he could leap back into the fray wasn't the act of cowardice it might appear to be...

"Exactly."

Just one bite...

He slid into his throne and picked up the nearest pancake. Thrilling, piquant aroma of yumminess!

A huge hand came down and dashed the presidential balcony to pieces.

"Just a minute!" he called.

Cracks appeared in the corners of the room and the entire wall was pulled away with the ease of child ripping open a birthday present.

"No!" yelled Clovenhoof. "I'm having a private moment here."

Boris waded into the collapsing building, his torso ploughing through the floor between ground and upper storey.

"We're not finished, little man," grinned the sin thing.

"Final meal for the condemned man?" suggested Clovenhoof.

Boris's brow furrowed cruelly, and he struck down with his hand. Clovenhoof whisked away his plate as titanic fingertips cut through the games table sending boards and playing pieces flying.

"What the Hell?" snapped Clovenhoof. "I was winning The Game!"

"There's only one winner here," leered Boris. "Evil always triumphs."

"Screw you!" Clovenhoof pouted. "I'm the devil. I'm the king of gamblers. I can't be beaten!"

Boris laughed. "I'm every underhand move, every shady deal. I am the fixing of odds, the playing of markets. I am every trick in the book rolled into one body. I can beat you at any game!"

"Any game?" said Clovenhoof.

"Name it."

"And the loser?"

"Pulverised," smiled Boris. "Pummelled into oblivion."

Clovenhoof bit the end off his crispy pancake.

PART FOUR –
MEMORIES OF HOOFLANDIA

CHAPTER SIXTY-TWO

Four-hundred-and-something Chester Road.
Boldmere.
Sutton Coldfield.
The house was built something like a hundred years ago, back in a time when people were shorter but ceilings were inexplicably higher. In recent years, it had been the home of a man, a woman and a devil. The man and the devil lived in the first-floor flats. The woman lived on the second floor with her pet dog, Twinkle. The ground floor, however, had more recently become home to a fourth resident.

Jeremy Clovenhoof, Nerys Thomas and Ben Kitchen stood outside the door to flat 1b. Each of them unlocked and removed their padlocks and, with a bit of jostling for first place, the three of them entered the flat.

"Games night!" said Clovenhoof in greetings to the room.

"I've been waiting," said Boris sulkily.

"The rules state that following agreed breaks, The Game can only continue at times convenient to all players," said Clovenhoof. "That's right isn't it?"

"It is," agreed Ben.

A table stood in the centre of the room. And the table had a board game at its centre. Other game boards sprouted off on every side.

In the history rewriting and reality bending that Heaven had undertaken to tidy up the horrid mess of the 'Hooflandia Incident', nearly everything of the past few months had been undone and replaced with a more pedestrian series of events. Clovenhoof had argued that to just press a massive reset button on the event was lazy thinking and insulting to everyone involved, that it meant that those many people who had rightly received their just punishments and rewards were going to go unpunished and unrewarded, that no one would have had the chance to learn from this exciting episode. But Gabriel didn't care and had insisted that he wasn't going to depart this plane without erasing everything he considered to be 'moronically implausible'. That, apparently, applied to a great many things, not limited to Hooflandia, its church and army, the PrayPal app and Clovenhoof's billions.

Clovenhoof didn't really miss the money. He was never motivated by wealth, only by what it could achieve, and he'd generally found that the same things could be achieved through belligerence, bravado and a loose attitude towards rules.

Two of the few things to survive the reality-edit were Nerys (who threatened to rip Gabriel's wings off if he so much as glanced at her memories) and The Game. The black cardboard box of committee-developed, computer-refined, Bible-encompassing gaming fun they now played with was currently the only version in existence. Ben was keen to develop it further and perhaps start a crowdfunder campaign to get it put into full production, but he was even more keen to do a full play-test first, so the world would have to wait for a few years yet.

"Initiating start-up routine," intoned Nerys.

As she began to count the pieces, Ben got up to prepare their games night drinks. "Lambrini for Jeremy, Chardonnay for Nerys and Boris...?"

"Just a small sherry for me," said the sin creature.

"Small sherry for Boris, of course."

Ben placed the drinks in front of each of the players and sat down with his own cider and black. He leaned over to Nerys.

"Remind me," he said, as he said so often these days, "Boris is...?"

"An old acquaintance of Jeremy's," said Nerys. "From the old days."

"Right. Right. And we lock him in here when we leave because...?"

"He likes it that way," said Nerys. "All he wants to do is play The Game."

"Right. Right."

"He just wants to win, really."

"It's nice to have ambition, I suppose." Ben opened the rules book. "Rule number one: no one is allowed to know all the rules of The Game. Rule number two: no one is allowed to know if they're winning or not until The Game ends. Rule number three: The Game ends when you are dead."

He passed the dice to Clovenhoof. "Shall we begin?"

CHAPTER SIXTY-THREE

Anette Cleaver collapsed in her front hallway, hands pressed together in humble apology.

"Please, spirits! Please, forgive me!"

"Well, that will be between you and your husband, lady!" said Joan hotly. "If I was him –"

"Which you're not," Rutspud added helpfully.

"I wouldn't let you back in the house, let alone the marital bed! How can you even kiss him after you've used you mouth to –"

"Stand in for a men's urinal," said Rutspud, again helpfully.

"In an absolute mockery of the most holy of all Christian sacraments!"

"I'll change! I'll change!" wailed the Head of Communications for the Birmingham Diocese.

"And if I hear you've gone to another of Maldon Ferret's sordid sex parties –"

"But I haven't! I haven't!"

"Yes, true, but you might have –"

"In a deleted alternate reality in which your scandal indirectly led to the Church of England being sold to Satan," said Rutspud.

The tearful woman sniffed and gave them a quizzical look.

"Just be good!" snapped Joan, waving her sword around in a generally threatening manner. "Or else!"

"There will be a pit in my place with your name on it," said Rutspud.

Joan continued to fume. Rutspud coughed politely and then surreptitiously dragged Joan out by the back of her chainmail shirt. He slammed the front door behind them.

"And breathe," said Rutspud. "Deep, relaxing breaths."

Joan breathed. But if there were relaxing breaths to be had, she couldn't find them.

"I had to ride in a police car with that woman and her..."

"Wet-playmate?" suggested Rutspud. He woke his tablet. "We're done."

"Done?" said Joan.

"The list. We've delivered thirty-four dire warnings from the afterlife. Church leaders, captains of industry. It's the least we could do considering they've all been given a second chance to screw their lives up. Ha! That moment when I showed Maldon Ferret a vision of the Pit of Big Cats with Assault Rifles!"

"You built that for his father, not him."

Rutspud shrugged "Needs must when the devil drives. Pint?"

Joan let go of a ragged sigh and the last of her anger. "A pint would be nice."

They walked the streets of Sutton Coldfield in the deepening twilight.

"I've never understood that phrase," said Rutspud. "Needs must..."

"Does the devil even drive?" said Joan.

"No. Can't. His hoofs are too tiny to operate the pedals."

"Huh."

The Boldmere Oak was back to its original form. Or, rather, it had never been anything else. Joan bought a pint of beer and a white wine spritzer and they settled into a cosy corner booth. Rutspud sipped his spritzer with evident pleasure but he was tactful enough to not mention how much it tasted like fizzy urine.

"We make quite a team," she said.

"Indeed, we do," said Rutspud.

"But..."

"It will be good to get back home," he said, firmly. "I've had enough of earth for now."

"Amen to that," she replied and chinked her pint against his smaller glass.

A sharp wind sprung up, as though an unexpected hurricane had rolled into town and decided to pop in for a drink.

"Someone shut the door," said Rutspud, a half smile on his face as he turned to look round. The pub door *was* shut.

The sudden gale was very localised, focused just on this room. No, Joan realised, it was focussed just on this booth. No, not even that. It was centred entirely around Rutspud.

"Is this Hell's doing?" she said.

The tornado tightened around Rutspud, dashing his spritzer loudly against the wall as the air blurred, obscuring him from view.

Joan reached forward to grab him, but the funnel of blasting air batted her hands back.

"Rutspud!"

"Satan, help me!" he shouted.

She could no longer see him at all.

"God, even!" his fading voice cried. "I'm not picky..."

There was a clap of in-rushing air and in the blink of an eye, the wind vanished.

Joan stared.

Rutspud had vanished too.

TO BE CONTINUED...

The Authors

Heide Goody and Iain Grant are married, but not to each other. Heide lives in North Warwickshire with her husband and children. Iain lives in south Birmingham with his wife and children.

CPSIA information can be obtained
at www.ICGtesting.com
Printed in the USA
FSHW020651030119
54804FS